THE DANCE OF THE SERPENTS

Oscar de Muriel was born in Mexico City, where he began writing stories aged seven, and later came to the UK to complete a PhD in Chemistry. Whilst working as a translator and playing the violin, the idea for a spooky whodunnit series came to him and Nine-Nails McGray was born. Oscar has now written six Frey & McGray titles and splits his time between the North West of England and Mexico City. *The Dance of the Serpents* is the sixth book in the Frey & McGray series.

Also by Oscar de Muriel

Strings of Murder
A Fever of the Blood
A Mask of Shadows
Loch of the Dead
The Darker Arts

THE DANCE OF THE SERPENTS

OSCAR DE MURIEL

ORION

An Orion paperback

First published in Great Britain in 2020
by Orion Fiction,
This paperback edition published in 2021
by Orion Fiction,
an imprint of The Orion Publishing Group Ltd.,
Carmelite House, 50 Victoria Embankment
London EC4Y 0DZ

An Hachette UK company

3 5 7 9 10 8 6 4

A CIP catalogue record for this book
is available from the British Library.

ISBN (Paperback) 978 1 4091 8767 7

Printed and bound in Great Britain
by Clays Ltd, Elcograf S.p.A.

www.orionbooks.co.uk

The sixth one is in memory of dear Aunt Hilda

Author's Note

Though mostly fiction, crucial elements of this book are an extrapolation of well-documented historical facts.

All the 'Diary' entries, for instance, are quoted verbatim from a real-life primary source. Its author shall be revealed in due course.

An indistinct and phantom band,
They wheeled their ring-dance hand in hand,
With gestures wild and dread;
The Seer, who watched them ride the storm,
Saw through their faint and shadowy form
The lightning's flash more red;
And still their ghastly roundelay
Was of the coming battle-fray
And of the destined dead.

Sir Walter Scott
'The Dance of Death'

1818

23 August, 11.45 p.m.

The little girl clung to the crone's long skirts, even though the woman scared her as much as the surrounding darkness.

They stood in the middle of the leafy road, the cold breeze making the candle quiver. Held firmly by the old hag, who protected it from the wind with her bony hand, that flame was the only light available. Beyond its range, merely a few yards ahead, the entire world was a solid mass of blackness.

'Not long now, child,' the woman said, surely feeling the girl's tremors. 'Keep still. And don't drop that or I'll have you.'

Her yellowy, veiny eyes pointed at the small basket on the girl's arm. The child grasped it more tightly, letting out a fearful moan. Inside, the bottles clanked.

The girl looked ahead, straight into the shadows, until she heard a faint sound. She shuddered.

'Is it them?' the woman demanded, and the girl nodded. The time had come.

Very slowly, the sound became louder and clearer. Hooves. Even the crone, whose ears were old and beaten, could hear them now. Her thin lips stretched into a crooked grin, revealing an uneven set of brown teeth.

A lonely torch glowed in the distance, and as soon as they saw it appear, the crone's smile faded. Instead, she pulled her most miserable face and raised her arms.

'*Stop!*' she wailed with a rasp, the sound of misery itself. '*Stop! For God's mercy!*'

A tall, sturdy stagecoach, lustrous and as black as the night, halted in front of them. The muscled horses, whose breath formed steaming clouds in the night air, seemed exhausted.

The lean, red-faced driver had pulled the reins with all his might, looking at the crone with disconcerted eyes. He opened his mouth, but did not manage to speak before a male voice cried from within the carriage.

'What the hell?'

'A lady on the road, sir,' said the driver.

'A what? *Blast! Move on!*'

'*Please! For God's mercy!*' the crone insisted, dropping on her knees and raising her trembling hands. Her candle fell to the ground and the flame died. '*Help me. I have a child!*'

Her wails echoed across the lonely woods, and the girl was shaking from head to toe, the dim light of the carriage's torch glinting in her eyes. She was about to shed tears of fear.

The driver's lip quivered. 'If I may, sir,' he said, 'you should have a look.'

They heard a groan, followed by a very reluctant, 'If I must . . .'

Only then did the driver alight, just as they saw a new light inside the stagecoach. The door opened and a young man jumped onto the ground, carrying a little oil lamp.

He was not especially tall, and had the smooth, plump cheeks of the well-to-do gentry. His clothes, a double-breasted tailcoat of fine green velvet, and a snow-white shirt and cravat, also spoke of wealth. His eyes, though bleary, were of the palest blue; clearly the man had been in a deep slumber before the unexpected stop.

He cast light on the crone and the girl, scrutinizing them with haughty looks.

'Is this your granddaughter?' he demanded.

'Aye, sir.'

'What are you doing here?'

'*We was robbed, sir!*' the crone babbled. 'They took the cart, they took our wine, my son, our—'

'Slow down, slow down!' the gentleman said. 'Douglas, give them some water.'

The driver went back to his seat, fetched a waterskin and passed it to the crone. She gave it to the girl, who looked confused, but after the old woman gave her a discreet pinch, drank a few drops. The crone then took long swigs, coughing and spitting, and then poured some water into her hand and rinsed her soiled face. She handed the skin back.

'Now,' said the gentleman, 'tell us what happened.'

The old woman forced in deep breaths, a hand clutching at her chest.

'We was – we was on our way to Canterbury with my son. He works for a wine merchant and tomorrow's market day. My girl got tired so we moved to the back, to get some sleep in between them barrels. We was fast asleep when we heard shouting. My son stopped the cart and we heard these horrid men . . .'

She shuddered violently, and the girl could not suppress a yelp.

'They beat my son till they got tired,' the crone went on, pulling the frightened child towards her and locking her in a tight embrace. 'The things we heard! The –' she gulped, stroking the girl's golden hair anxiously – 'there was nothing we could do. We just hid and kept quiet.'

Her eyes flickered from side to side, as if madness began to creep inside her.

'Then we heard something drop. My son's body, I think. The cart moved on . . . And we . . .'

The gentleman frowned, and the oil lamp began to shake in his stumpy fingers.

'Did you two stay in the cart?'

The crone's face wrinkled further in an unsettling grimace. She brought a hand to her mouth and spoke on, her voice muffled.

'*There was nothing we could do!*'

The driver offered more water, but the woman was too stricken to take it.

'How did you get off?' the gentleman asked.

The crone again had to breathe deeply. 'Whoever got the cart had to stop for a piss. Somewhere around here. I took my chances; grabbed my li'l girl and jumped off and hid in them bushes. We've been here for hours, sirs. For hours.'

The gentleman's lip had softened just a little. Enough for his driver to speak up.

'If I may, sir – we're not far from the inn. We could take them. Someone there can take care of them, surely.'

'*Yes, yes, please!*' the crone begged, still on her knees. She stretched an arm, trying to pull at the folds of the gentleman's coat.

He took a quick step back. 'Very well, very well! But you shall travel with Douglas.'

He turned on his heels and went back to the stagecoach, as the driver helped the crone stand up.

'Thank you, sirs. *Thank you!*'

Just as the gentleman was about to jump back into his seat, the crone stretched a pleading hand.

'Uhm, sir?'

'What now?' he snapped.

'Please, take my girl inside. She won't be a nuisance, I swear.'

The gentleman snorted.

'*Please*,' the crone insisted. 'She heard things no child should know of. And look at her, the poor thing's so cold.'

The gentleman only saw half the girl's face, the rest hidden behind the crone's skirt.

'We don't even know if her father—' The old woman covered her mouth and looked away, letting out faint sobs.

The gentleman snorted again, opened the door and pointed in.

'Quick,' he said curtly to the girl. The crone patted her on the back.

'Go on, Marigold. Be good to the kind sir. Don't upset him.'

The girl hesitated, until the crone gave her a hard push. In the dim light, neither the driver nor the gentleman noticed.

Marigold rushed to the door, the basket swaying in her arm. She jumped up the steps and settled quickly on the cushioned seat. She'd never sat on red velvet; against it, her faded dress looked like filthy kitchen rags.

The gentleman followed and set the oil lamp into a sconce. They heard the crone struggling to get up onto the front seat, and soon enough the stagecoach rode on.

Sitting perfectly still, with the basket on her lap as the crone had instructed, Marigold stared at the gentleman with her wide green eyes.

He was in his mid-twenties, but he carried a deep frown already. His hands were as smooth and unblemished as his face, and his rounded cheeks spoke of a healthy, if slightly overfed man.

On the other hand, he seemed quite uneasy in front of the child, drumming his fingers, shifting on his seat and not knowing where to fix his eyes.

For a few awkward minutes he exchanged looks with the silent girl, until the stagecoach hit a bump. The bottles in the basket clanked, catching the gentleman's eye. Had that not happened, had the stagecoach not run quite so fast, had the bottles not touched each other, the world might have become an entirely different place.

'What are you carrying in there?' the man asked.

The girl cleared her throat. 'Wine, sir.'

'Wine?'

Marigold looked down, so nervous that the crone's instructions muddled in her head.

'It's . . .' she began, feeling how her fingers went deathly cold. Her very life depended on how she delivered the next few phrases. 'It's the wine my dad gave . . . for tasting at the market. It's all I could pull from the cart.'

The gentleman rolled his eyes and then pretended to look out the window, even if the night remained as dark as before.

Marigold trembled. She could see her only chance fading away.

'Would you like some, sir?' she forced herself to say.

The man sneered. 'I don't drink cheap liquor, girl.'

Another quiver. Marigold pulled out one of the bottles.

'It's good wine, sir. For the gentry. My dad's boss brings it from some place called France.'

That caught some interest, just as the crone had said, but not enough. Marigold felt as if she was treading on a rope, keeping her balance by pure luck, yet about to fall irredeemably into a deep void.

She pushed the bottle a little closer to the man, the gap between them suddenly looking like an abyss. She could hear the crone's shrieks already. *All you had to do was make him drink!*

'Try it,' she uttered out of sheer fear, clutching the bottle so hard she thought it might burst between her fingers. And then, as if by miracle, she recalled the crone's words and recited them to perfection. 'It's all we have to thank you for your kindness.'

The man stared at her. Marigold thought her fear had ruined everything, but the crone was crafty. She knew the child would be scared to death; she knew how pleading she'd sound, how her eyes would be about to burst into tears. No one with an ounce of heart would refuse her offerings.

With a swift move, the gentleman snatched the bottle and pulled the cork. He brought the bottle to his nose and sniffed the wine.

Marigold waited in silence, staring at every movement and shift in the man's face.

There was no smile. No hint of any appreciation.

The girl wrung her hands. She could not stand it anymore. She wanted to scream. She wanted to—

And then the gentleman drank.

It was not a shy swig, but a long, deep glug, the man raising the bottle and throwing his head back. He gulped several times, keeping the bottle stuck to his lips.

It was done.

Marigold smiled, the exhilaration of her first triumph like sparks all across her body. She would not be flayed that night. Maybe never again.

And as he gulped down the best of French wine, Sir Augustus sealed his fate forever.

DIARY – 1822

The death of Strowan.
Effect upon my Eyes.

In the month of December 1822 I travelled from Ramsgate to the Highlands of Scotland for the purpose of passing some days with a Relation for whom I had the affection of a Son. On my arrival I found him dead. I attended his funeral: there being many persons present I struggled violently not to weep, I was however unable to prevent myself from so doing. Shortly after the funeral I was obliged to have my letters read to me, and their answers written for me as my eyes were so afflicted that when fixed upon minute objects indistinctness of vision was the consequence. Until I attempted to read, or to cut my pen, I was not aware of my eyes being in the least impaired. Soon after, I went to Ireland, and without anything having been done to my eyes, they completely recovered their strength and distinctness of vision . . .

1889

3 December

Windsor, close to midnight

Caroline Ardglass leaned over the witchcraft book, slightly disgusted by the crude illustrations and struggling to decipher the handwriting without a candle.

Her eyes were itchy with tiredness, her back sore, and her bones ached in the damp, draughty loft, but she ignored the discomforts. This was not a Christmas holiday. This was a hunt.

She envied the magpie, with its beak stuck under its wing and sleeping placidly in the little brass cage. The black and white plumage, fluffed up, seemed to keep the bird sufficiently warm. Caroline, despite the thick blanket around her shoulders, could not say the same.

The loft was ghastly, smelly, and the noises from the adjacent public house were anything but pleasant. However, she'd paid dearly for the space, atop a shabby three-storey house.

She looked up, through the narrow window in front of the worm-eaten desk, at the view that had cost her so much.

Outside, the gentle fields were covered in snow, silvery under the crescent moon. The sky was clear and the trees along the Royal Mews were bare, so young Caroline had an ideal view of the castle's east wing. The Queen's private apartments.

She'd seen the windows light up one by one, picturing the servants as they did their evening round. Only one or two rooms in that brooding wing were usually lit, but it was different tonight. At least a dozen windows glowed with candlelight, signalling that Queen Victoria had arrived.

Caroline lifted the small yet powerful binoculars that lay next to her book – the ones that Lady Anne, her grandmother, used to take to the opera to spy on her business rivals.

Patiently, Caroline perused window after window. She could only just make out the frames, and in some cases the curve of thick curtains. Her window was too distant to identify faces, but that was not what she was after. She moved the binoculars east, to the bulky tower at the south-east corner of the ward – the narcissistically named Victoria Tower.

If those weird sisters had told the truth, it was *there* that—

The wooden floor creaked then. Caroline startled, looked backwards and lifted the lenses, ready to throw them at the—

'There, there, child!' cried Bertha. 'It's just me!'

Her short, plump nana stood there in the darkness. Only one side of her wrinkled face could be seen, and the silver tea set she carried caught but a faint glimmer from the moon.

'Good Lord,' said Caroline, a hand on her chest. 'You scared me!'

The magpie was flapping its wings in the cage. It gave Caroline what looked like a disapproving gaze, before turning its head and resuming its sleep.

'I thought you might want tea, my child.' The woman placed the tray on the table and closed the book with a thump. 'Rest for a minute. You're a bundle o' nerves these days.'

Bertha did not wait for approval. She proceeded to make the tea, while Caroline lounged on her chair. Still, she kept her eyes on the castle.

'How much longer do we have to stay in this flea-ridden dump?' Bertha remonstrated as she passed her a cup.

Caroline sipped the tea and did not bother to answer. She'd told Bertha many times.

'If you at least had a fire . . .'

'*We cannot have a fire, Bertha,*' Caroline hissed, turning to face the woman, and at once regretted her curtness. Bertha had looked after her ever since she could remember. She had followed her in this mad pursuit, even after Caroline offered her an eye-watering amount of money to retire. Nobody else in the world loved her as much as this ageing maid. Her late father had, of course, but then again, he was the very reason they were at Windsor, hiding in a dilapidated loft.

Caroline forced a deep breath.

'We cannot be seen,' she said in a more composed tone. 'This is the highest point on this godforsaken street. Even the one candle lit all night, every night, would be suspicious.'

Bertha understood. The dark, cunning eyes of Miss Ardglass told her all. The task had been appointed, and the young woman could not – and would not – stop.

But still, the child Bertha had once rocked to sleep in her arms, the little girl she'd seen grow up . . . Watching her consume herself like this was heartbreaking.

'I wish you didn't have to do this,' Bertha whispered. She could not face Caroline's eyes anymore. 'I wish you—'

She went silent, her glinting eyes now fixed on the window.

'What is it?' Caroline said.

'Look!'

There was a new light on Victoria Tower – Caroline had been staring at the building for so long she noticed at once. It did not come from a window; it rather looked like a flickering spark at the very top.

She groped for the binoculars, which Bertha found and handed to her. The magnified image made Caroline's eyes spring wide open.

It was a clear ball of fire on the roof, its flames curling and rising like pleading arms. And right then, with a sudden burst, the fire turned the brightest green. The witches' sign.

Caroline gasped, dropping the lenses. Even without them she could see the emerald shade. Both women watched in awe for a moment, their breathing the only sound, until Caroline came back to her senses.

'It is time, Bertha,' she said. 'Prepare the mag—'

But hers were not the only watchful eyes. The bird was already perched up, looking about with agitation. Suddenly it flapped its wings, hitting the cage bars in a fit of panic.

Caroline looked at it, her lip trembling.

'What . . . what frightened it?'

She heard heavy footsteps on the stairs, the unmistakable tread of towering Jed.

The broad-shouldered man, whose weathered face Caroline had feared in her childhood, stormed into the loft. He had to crouch under the angled ceiling, and wiped perspiration from his forehead as he spluttered.

'Miss, they're coming for you!'

Bertha gasped, covering her mouth with quivering hands.

Caroline crossed the loft in two strides, to press her hands against the glass of the opposite dormer window.

Her heart stopped.

Two carriages approached, pulled by muscled percherons as dark as the night. The drivers carried torches, the flames billowing as they darted ahead. The glowing yellow suddenly turned into a flash of intense blue.

Caroline jumped backwards as if struck by electricity.

'*We have to go!*' she cried, running instinctively to the old cabinet. She grabbed her father's leather bag and began throwing books, tools and wallets inside.

'Quick, quick!' Jed grunted as he checked his gun had bullets. 'Remember what happens when they corner their prey!'

'Leave that!' cried Caroline when Bertha brought a bundle of clothes. 'Just the books and the money.'

They heard the neighing of horses on the street, followed by yelling from the pub.

A wave of chilling thoughts invaded Caroline's mind – people flayed, burned alive, their tongues cut out, given poisons that made them contort until their spines cracked . . .

'We have to go *now!*' Jed hissed, grabbing Caroline by the arm.

She let him pull her to the door, the bag still open and Bertha still shoving in the binoculars and a pouch of coin. The woman raised a pointing hand.

'The bird!'

Caroline ran back and grasped the cage, the magpie cawing and flapping its wings as they made a frantic run for the stairs.

The narrow steps cracked loudly under their feet, as if about to give way, and Caroline pictured herself plummeting to the ground. The thought made her trip, but Jed managed to pull her back. Right then they heard the first gunshot.

'Lord!' Bertha gasped.

They reached the ground floor and instead of darkness found the dim glow of a candle. The owner of the house, in his nightclothes, held it as his entire body trembled.

'*What have you brought upon us?*' he bellowed. With his dishevelled grey hair and his terrified eyes, he looked like a spectre himself.

The racket on the street became louder then, and there was a second shot.

Caroline pulled a gold ring from her finger and pressed it onto the man's hand.

'For your troubles.'

They made haste to the back door. Jed kicked it open and the slam made the horses snort.

The icy breeze hit them like a fist, swirling in the darkened backyard. Three derelict battlements, all that was left of the castle's most ancient walls, cast their shadows on their brougham carriage and the two horses. Jed now always kept them harnessed and ready.

He ran to the door and opened it for Caroline. She threw in the hefty leather bag and then placed the cage with more care, but then she heard several noises at once: a thud on the snow, Bertha whimpering, and just as Caroline looked back, the loud cracking of wood.

Bertha had tripped and fallen on her knees, and while Caroline and Jed pulled her upwards, the cracking noises intensified. They heard shouting inside the house; the witches and their thugs had broken in.

'*Leave me, child!*' Bertha cried, being almost dragged to the carriage.

'Don't be a goose,' Caroline growled, though struggling to push the old woman onto her seat.

The shouting grew louder and they heard the throttled voice of the landlord.

Jed forgot all delicacy and pushed them inside. He then closed the door and hopped into the driver's seat. The creaking of the carriage coincided with that of the back door, which opened just as Jed threw the first whip at the horses.

'*Killing time!*' a nasty female voice howled, the sound sending prickles of fear throughout Caroline's body. She looked through the back window and saw half a dozen brutes, two of them carrying blazing torches. They brought the landlord, who writhed desperately as they dragged him to the yard. A cloaked woman came behind them, draped in jet black, her hood trimmed with golden embroidery.

As the carriage began to move, Caroline saw that the tall men threw the landlord to the ground. The man fell on his knees, howling. The cloaked woman seized him by the hair, pulled his head up and in one swift movement slit the man's throat. The blood sprayed all over his white nightgown, an almost perfect fan of scarlet liquid lit by the torches, and Caroline could not repress a terrified yelp.

She crouched in the back seat, the carriage rocking violently as Jed turned it towards the gate. Through the frosted window she caught a chilling glimpse of those men running towards her, scratching and battering the carriage door. They were so close that for a moment Caroline even saw their yellowy teeth and their faces contorted with rage.

The carriage turned swiftly, but Caroline still saw the men lifting guns. She ducked at once, pulling Bertha down, and at that precise moment a rain of bullets began.

The carriage finally stopped turning and Caroline guessed they were now darting out of the yard, towards the road. She heard the shouting of drunken men – they were riding past the pub – and then just the racket of the wheels and the stomping of hooves. The gunshots could still be heard, but ever fainter.

Caroline crouched for a moment, hearing Bertha's frantic breathing and feeling her heart thumping in her chest. The shots became sparser, and only then did Caroline dare rise.

The brougham had a front window, through which she could see Jed's back and the galloping horses. But the glass was splattered.

'God, they hit Jed,' Caroline cried. She let go of Bertha and jumped to the front seat. She grasped the window's handle and was about to pull it down, but then there was another shot, instantly followed by a massive splash of red on the glass.

Caroline and Bertha hollered, unable to take their eyes from Jed's broad torso, which fell sideways against the driver's seat, smearing his own blood on the window.

Caroline shed tears of panic, the world around her a whirling blur. She saw the horses gallop on, now zigzagging along the road – saw Jed's moth-eaten overcoat, now stained in crimson – saw his face, flailing about with his eyes still open – she heard Bertha's unintelligible babble . . .

And the shooting continued behind them.

The carriage bounced on a pothole, sending Caroline into the air. She banged her head against the ceiling, and the blow brought her back to her senses.

No one would help. No one would come and save them. She'd have to do it herself.

Caroline pulled down the windowpane, smearing her hands with Jed's still-warm blood. She tried to pull herself onto the driver's seat, but Jed's body was blocking the way, leaving next to no space for her to move.

The wind went past her at full speed, bringing the shouting of the witches' men. She saw the horses run erratically and felt how the carriage slowed down. She had no time to be squeamish.

She pushed, growled and panted, moving Jed's heavy body out of the way. Hands, dress and face covered in blood, she squeezed over the dead man's torso, shuddering.

With one final pull she fell forwards, face and hands squashed against the driver's footboard. Clumsily, Caroline curled around, found the reins as she groped, and seized them before stumbling upwards.

Jed's body lay across the seat. Caroline pulled him by the shoulders, trying to prop him up, panting under his weight.

The man's glazed eyes were an inch from hers, and Caroline felt sorrow and revulsion in equal measure.

Then came another shot, so close that Caroline's ears hurt. She looked up and saw the head of a horse in pursuit emerge from the side of the carriage.

She let out a shriek as a man's savage face appeared, his gun at the ready, pointing directly at her forehead.

Without thinking, without time to doubt, Caroline let out an animalistic snarl, pushing Jed's body with all her might and letting it fall in the direction of the rider.

It was a ghastly sight; Jed's blood-dripping body hitting the thug, diverting his aim, and then falling further, right in front of the percheron's legs. The animal stomped and tripped over the corpse; Caroline heard bones being crushed, and then the horse fell on its flank and she saw them no more.

'*Sorry-sorry,*' she moaned on and on. She sat on the driver's seat and could finally take a good grip at the reins. Caroline steered the horses back to the centre of the road and whipped them mercilessly, hearing more gunshots behind her.

She crouched. That was all she could do, not even daring to look back. All her attention, all her senses, were on the horses and the road.

Suddenly, perhaps a long while after it happened, Caroline realized the shooting had ended. Her heart, on the other hand, still beat faster than ever. She did not slow down until the horses began to stumble against each other, exhausted, and then she let them trot on for several miles.

They passed through the dense Windsor Forest, the branches of the trees arching over the road like menacing claws. Then the woodland gave way to a wide meadow, entirely covered in white.

Caroline halted then, preferring the open field, where she could see if her enemies approached. She jumped off the carriage, nearly dropping on her knees, and took a few clumsy steps to the edge of the road. There she bent forwards and let out a violent spurt of vomit.

She coughed and gagged for a moment, the horses' heavy breathing the only other sound, and only then did she feel how the cold air crept through her thin clothes. She'd not even had time to put on a coat.

And still, she was thankful.

Caroline forced deep breaths, straightened her back and looked ahead. *One problem at a time*, she told herself, as she now did whenever she felt overwhelmed. They'd need to find shelter; that should be her immediate concern.

She walked to the horses and patted their heads. The larger of the two, a splendid jet-black Carthusian, stomped its hooves.

'There, there,' Caroline said, resting her forehead against the horse's neck. 'I'm exhausted too, but we need to move on.'

She headed back to the seat, but then she heard a familiar whimper.

'Bertha . . .' she mumbled, running to the passenger's door. The entire carriage was dotted with bullet holes.

Caroline opened the door and jumped in. She found Bertha still seated, very straight, her face slightly bent down. One would have thought she was in the middle of a peaceful trip, were it not for her hands folded tightly on her stomach. All drenched in red.

'*Bertha!*' Caroline yelled, rushing to hug the little woman.

She tried to pull up her hands and examine the wound, but Bertha clenched firmly. Even in the shadows, Caroline saw the dark stain all over the woman's skirts.

'Why didn't you scream?' Caroline sobbed, her eyes shedding uncontrollable tears. How long Bertha must have been bleeding! And yet, the woman managed to lift her face and smile through the pain. 'I would've stopped!'

Bertha barely whispered. 'I was doomed from the very start . . .'

Caroline wept like a child; rage, guilt and despair clutching at her like invisible claws. How silly of her even to comfort the horses before checking on her beloved nana.

'We'll find a doctor,' she said. 'We'll find a doctor and then—'

Bertha shook her head, looking at Caroline with pleading eyes. 'I want you here with me, child. Not out there – when . . . when it happens.'

Caroline cradled the woman's face in her hands. She didn't even have water to give her.

'*I'm so sorry!*' Her voice came out as a high-pitched sob. 'I should have never brought you—'

A painful gulp took hold of her throat and she could say no more.

'I was where I was needed,' Bertha mumbled, her voice growing fainter. She let out a sigh, her face suddenly relaxing. Her entire body must be going numb.

'There's plenty I need to tell you, my child,' she said, resting her head on Caroline's shoulder, as if she were a young girl again. 'And so little time . . .'

I

13 December

Edinburgh

The sky was a smudge of grey and white, the evening wind slowly dragging the thick clouds eastwards.

It was an odd sight, for the last rays of sunlight, filtering through a gap in the sky I could not see from my window, bounced on the buildings across the street. Their façades, solid blocks of Scottish granite, glowed in golden hues, bright amidst the darkness below and the dullness above.

There, perched proudly atop the Georgian townhouse right in front of mine, and facing me almost defiantly, stood a rather large raven.

The black bird had sat there for days; it had been there in the morning when I'd gone out, it was there again in the evening when I came back, and it was still there when the streetlights came on at night. I could not help thinking that the blasted creature was watching my every move.

'Tea, Master Frey?'

That was not really a question, for Layton, my very stiff valet, was already extending me the cup and saucer, which I took distractedly.

'What did my uncle do when he wanted to get rid of birds?' I asked him, before indulging in the scent of my favourite Darjeeling blend.

Layton frowned a little, lifting his thin, aquiline nose as if sniffing for memories.

'He used to shoot them, sir.'

I allowed myself a sly smile, picturing late Uncle Maurice discharging his gunshot whenever a pigeon dared empty its bowels on the marble effigies of his estate.

'Is that foul thing still there?' Layton asked, gazing out the window.

'Indeed, so shooting it is not an option. I do not want to hit the bust of Pallas.'

Layton regarded me with incomprehension for a second, before coming back to practicalities. 'I can talk to the McKees in the morning, sir. They might be able to oust the—'

'No,' I said. 'They will think me odd.'

They already did, I suspected as I sipped my tea. Most people in Edinburgh did.

Defender of murderous mediums, performer of dark-magic tricks before the gallows, footman to Scotland's most deranged and infamous detective inspector. Such was my reputation these days. And I had no choice but to stay put in that grey town, watching winter settle in, none of my superiors at the CID minding too much whether I showed up at work or not. Even Nine-Nails McGray had become lethargic over the past three weeks, exhausted after the case of Madame Katerina, his gypsy clairvoyant.

We both felt as if we were wearing invisible shackles, unable to leave Edinburgh, at the mercy of an invisible will.

At least I found comfort in my little study, with its snug leather armchairs, warming hearth and crammed with my favourite comforts – books, whisky, blankets, tobacco, and Layton to bring me trays of food before I even realized I felt hungry. There I could ignore the neighbours, the newspapers, and even the constant correspondence from my London relatives. Indeed, how much I loved whiling my evenings away, relaxing in that cosy room.

I wish I'd basked a little more in those civilized comforts, for hell itself would break loose even before I had finished that cup of tea.

I was savouring the brew when the sounds of mad neighing and trampling hooves came from both sides of the street. I thought it was the echoes playing the trick, but I was wrong. Not one but two carriages appeared, one from each end of the road and rolling frantically towards each other. Just as I thought they would collide, the drivers reined back the imposing horses, both coaches stopping right before my doorstep.

Two gigantic, broad-shouldered men jumped down from each carriage. They rushed ahead and banged their fists on the door.

At once I left my cup on a nearby table, but miscalculated and the china crashed on the carpet. I made my way downstairs, tying my smoking jacket a tad more tightly. Layton had moved like the wind, and was already at the door when I reached the entrance hall. I would have told him to keep the door shut, but it was too late. He had barely unlocked it when the men pushed it forwards, cleanly ripping the chain off the wall.

Layton tripped backwards and nearly fell onto his back, as the sturdy men stormed inside. They were all dressed in fine suits and jackets, one of them biting what smelled like a rather expensive Cuban. Their faces, nevertheless, were rough and calculating. And they stank of sweat.

'Ian Frey?' the frontman barked. He had a southern English accent.

'*Inspector* Ian Frey,' I corrected.

All four men showed sardonic grins.

'You're to come with us – inspector.'

I raised my chin. 'And who the bloody hell are you?'

The four men chuckled, the man with the cigar taking it from his lips, only to spit on my landlady's carpet.

The frontman's voice became even deeper. '*Friends.*'

The word hung in the air like a foul stench, and I saw no reason to resist. I knew perfectly well what was happening. The summons I'd feared for the past months was finally here. I should be glad it had taken so long and I'd had a few weeks' rest.

'May I at least dress?' I asked, and at once Layton ran to the cloakroom.

'No,' replied the frontman, who wore a ridiculous black moustache curled at the tips.

I took a deep breath, and then a first step ahead. Right then Layton reached me and threw a heavy overcoat on my shoulders. I secretly thanked him, for the wind out there was ice-cold.

Like a prisoner sentenced to the gaols, the men flanked my path and led me to the coach to my left. I could see many curious faces peering from the surrounding windows; once more, I was living up to my quickly acquired reputation.

The frontman went into the carriage first, to block my way in case I attempted to escape through the other side. Then they pushed me to follow him, and a second man stepped in behind me. As soon as he shut the small door, we were moving.

Behind the carriage, I heard the raven letting out a mocking caw.

2

The carriages separated just around the corner. Mine took several unexpected turns, most of them illogical, in a clear effort to lose anyone who might be following. After a while, just as an insistent sleet began to shower the city, I realized we were drifting south-east.

We rode through the dingy, narrow side streets of the Old Town, some of which I had never seen. The carriage racketed on the pebbled roads, splashing on puddles as the world grew darker all around us. The windows of the towering dwellings were already lit up, casting their amber glows on the wet, eroded walls.

It was not late, but with the wintry weather and early sunset, the streets were nearly deserted, yet not enough for our carriage to seem an unusual presence. These men had chosen the perfect time for their chore.

We took a turn around a medieval-looking tenement block, and before us I saw emerge the solid, black silhouette of Salisbury Crags – rather fitting, considering whom I was about to meet. We turned left, going further east, and within seconds our destination became evident.

The pointy towers of Holyrood Palace came to view, like daggers pointing to the sky. They were visible only because of the glow from their own windows, and I had to squint to make out the wrought-iron fences, the outlines of the desolate forecourt and the majestic stone fountain at the centre, its water-spitting lions now dormant.

We rode into the court from its south end, rather than the usual entrance from the busier High Street. I was expecting the carriage to turn right, to the palace itself, but instead it took me left, to an archway only a little less impressive than the one of the residence. The small battlement led to a long courtyard surrounded by the Queen's stables.

The carriage halted near the north-east corner, in front of an open gate. The only light in view came from there.

Before those men could shove me around I stepped out, to the merciless sleet and the smell of horse manure. Even the royal stables could not do away with that odour.

'There,' the moustachioed man told me, even if I was already heading to the only open gate. I walked briskly, the sleet hitting me on the back of the neck, and saw the stable's floor covered with a uniform layer of fresh straw. Just as I crossed the threshold we heard another carriage come from behind, and that one did not sound peaceful.

Its horses were agitated, stomping their hooves on the flagstones, their breath like gusts of steam as the sweaty driver pulled the reins manically.

There was rumbling and shouting inside the coach, which jerked as if a beast inside it jumped from side to side.

'Oh,' I said with rapid understanding. 'You fetched Nine-Nails too.'

Someone kicked the carriage door open, and almost instantly a man was propelled outwards, landing on the wet floor on all fours.

A second man managed to put a foot on the ground, pulling with all his might, until a long leg, with unmistakable tartan trousers, kicked him right in the stomach. The man fell backwards, landing on top of his colleague, who'd just begun to stand up.

The two men who'd brought me ran to their aid, while the many horses around began a restless neighing. As the men reached the carriage and joined the skirmish, I was tempted to step away quietly and get lost in the safety of the night, but then a third and fourth carriage arrived, blocking the only way out.

I let out a resigned sigh, crossed my arms and stared at the scene.

Another four men alighted and darted towards the rocking coach. Two opened the back door and the other two went to the one facing me. The coach shook mightily and I heard punches land, the wheels and axles creak, men screech, and then the half-throttled voice of Detective Adolphus 'Nine-Nails' McGray.

'Och – youse . . . *Twats!*'

I then saw two men step down, each one carrying a restless, tartan-clad leg, followed by McGray's mismatched plaid waistcoat. He writhed like an angry salmon in a net, while another three men struggled to restrain his torso. Even though his hands were manacled, he still managed to throw indiscriminate blows. One hit a man right on the nose, his blood splattering all around.

'Always manacle across the back,' I said with my most unflappable English voice. 'Never the front. You idiots.'

The moustachioed frontman – I shall call him *Boss*, for I never heard his name – approached Nine-Nails with dedicated strides, unsheathed a gun and pointed it directly at his forehead.

'It's over, *laddie*. I was told to shoot to kill if needed.'

It took Nine-Nails a moment to settle down, his rage more powerful than the sight of a canon a few inches from his brow.

He still jerked and snorted, but at least allowed the men to put him on the ground and lead him in my direction. His head stood well above everyone else's, his shoulders wide. I noticed he was not wearing his usual moth-eaten coat, and pictured the men breaking into his house and dragging him out of his messy library. His dark hair stuck to his face, dripping sleet and sweat, and his unkempt stubble was smeared with mud and blood – the other men's, that is, not his own.

Just as the captors were letting out their first breath of relief, McGray lifted his hands and in a swift, precise blow, broke the nose of the man to his right (if I had a shilling for each bone I have seen him break in the relatively short time I have worked for the Scottish police . . .).

The man fell backwards, wailing, only to be replaced immediately by one of his fellows.

'Do that *one more time* –' Boss howled, pressing the gun against McGray's temple.

They led us inside the stable, lit by a single hanging lamp. There were two lines of horses, all twitching and snorting in their compartments. The two bleeding men rushed clumsily and kicked a pair of soiled wooden boxes towards us.

'Sit down, *sirs*,' said Boss, and his men immediately pushed us down.

McGray spat blood on the straw, wiped his mouth with the manacles and cast me the most recriminating stare.

'Look at ye all prim 'n' pretty! Am sure ye offered them tea and biscuits and a foot rub.'

I felt a draught, so I lifted up my coat's furry collar.

'They did not give me time,' I said, and turned to Boss. 'Can we help you in any way, gentlemen?'

'You can shut your mouth,' he scorned, and then made a sign to one of the broken noses, who limped away as fast as he could.

We waited in silence, the only noise the occasional neighing or snuffle of a horse, until we heard a gruff male voice in the distance.

A moment later, a familiar figure stepped into the stables; plump and not too tall, wrapped in a black overcoat and followed by a young assistant, who struggled to carry a stack of files while balancing a black umbrella over his master.

I had a good idea of why we'd been brought here, but I was still shocked when I saw that face emerge from the darkness.

Lord Salisbury. Prime Minister.

He looked exactly as I remembered him, with his wiry, bushy beard, his bald scalp and his downy, almost non-existent eyebrows. The bags under his eyes had grown more swollen, but his small eyes themselves still held the most piercing stare – that which I'd seen inches from my own, just over a year ago, in London, in what now seemed like a distant dream from another life.

He was puffing at a short cigar as he stared at us with only a hint of satisfaction. A moment later his booming voice filled the building.

'Will you lazy halfwits get me a seat?' At once one of the men brought him a carved chair from the shadows.

The Prime Minister sat with a grunt, handed his cane to the scrawny young assistant, and glared at us without even blinking. After a while I was going to greet him, but Nine-Nails spoke first.

'Are ye gonna talk or ye just brought us here to stare at yer ballsack face? Who the fuck are ye, anyway?'

I sighed and covered my brow. 'I should make the introductions. Sir, this is Adolphus McGray. McGray, this is Robert Gascoyne-Cecil, third Marquis of Salisbury – and Prime Minister of the United Kingdom.'

Lord Salisbury made a sort of smile, baring his teeth while still biting his cigar.

McGray did look slightly abashed, if only for an instant, before whispering at me. 'He does look like a bawbag.'

'McGray!'

'*He does!*'

'Oh do shut up,' the Prime Minister snapped, and as if the order were implied, Boss rapped the back of McGray's head. 'You two must know why we are all here.'

Of course we did.

Though McGray had struggled for a while to create his preposterous police subdivision – the *Commission for the Elucidation of Unsolved Cases Presumably Related to the Odd and Ghostly*, devoted entirely to his ridiculous interest in the supernatural – the department had only been approved to serve as a convenient smokescreen, so that the Prime Minister could investigate a very thorny case in Scotland without public scrutiny. Allegedly, Lord Salisbury had kept our subdivision open (and McGray and me posted in Edinburgh) 'in case' he needed such cover again. Nine-Nails and I knew better; we knew that the man had had a very specific problem in mind from the very start.

McGray chuckled, surely thinking the same. 'Are the witches givin' ye trouble again?'

'Not only them,' said the Prime Minister, spitting out what little was left of his cigar, which died out on the damp straw. He lighted up a new one and puffed at it a couple of times before delivering the crucial blow. 'Her Majesty the Queen wants you dead. Both of you.'

3

I have received bold, ghastly, tragic and implausible sort of news before. This, however, struck a nerve I did not even know existed. I heard the words, I understood them, but they still felt like something told in a different language. The same happened to Nine-Nails, and we sat there, dumbstruck and open-mouthed, for a good while.

When we did manage to speak, '*Fuck!*' and '*You must be joking!*' came out of our mouths at the same time.

McGray leaned back, covering his face with both hands, and I felt my chest go deathly cold.

'The Lancashire affair . . .' I mumbled. 'The Queen surely—'

'Her Majesty,' Lord Salisbury interjected, 'wishes to . . . *talk* to the late Prince Consort and her two dead children. She claims to have done so every Christmas Eve since her husband died. She resorted to witches for the task, and you two happen to have killed her two most trusted crones.'

I nodded in McGray's direction. '*He*. He killed them. He killed them both within minutes.'

Nine-Nails made to punch me and I barely dodged the blow. 'What? Ye'd be *dead* if I had nae, ye ungrateful sod!'

'Before you go on arguing like a ripe old married couple,' Lord Salisbury said, with a voice that quietened even the horses,

'I need you to tell me precisely what happened in Lancashire.' He raised a hand and the scared assistant handed him a thick file. 'My contacts managed to put together the main facts, but I want to know the fine detail. Tell me absolutely everything.'

McGray chuckled. 'Don't ask this dandy to give ye details. He'll be telling ye how many sodding scones he had for breakfast each day.'

Lord Salisbury stared at him with pure, undistilled wrath, his left eye twitching.

'It all started on last New Year's Day,' I said promptly. 'We were summoned to the local lunatics asylum, where a nurse agonized.'

'Agonized?' the PM echoed.

'Indeed. She had been poisoned by the very patient she'd been looking after. To our utter shock, that patient—'

McGray cleared his throat so violently I thought he'd regurgitate. I remembered the darker details of the case, some of which compromised his own connections. I should volunteer nothing but the bare essentials.

'To our utter shock,' I continued, 'that patient had in fact been driven insane by this band of so-called witches. The nurse we saw die – Greenwood was her name – turned out to be a witch herself, and had been administering careful doses of narcotics to keep the man out of his wits. She was aided by another young woman – you might call her a *novice* witch – called Oakley. We followed the tracks of the patient—'

'What was the patient's name?' Lord Salisbury asked, his assistant readying a pen to write it down.

I felt a trickle of sweat, the name *Joel Ardglass* sounding loud in my head; his connection to one of McGray's dearest friends and foes . . . The involvement of his daughter Caroline . . . I could not lie. I could not—

'We never kent,' McGray jumped in.

'You never what?' snapped the PM.

'Och, sorry. We never *knew*. He was from an almighty inbred family of upper-class twats. Like ye. His relatives dumped him there in secret.'

That much was true, and then came the lie.

'Even the asylum's superintendent didnae ken the real name.'

'They nicknamed him Lord Bampot,' I rushed to say, for the PM was beginning to show a quizzical brow. 'As I was saying, we followed his trail and managed to track him all the way to Lancaster.'

'Where you found a hub of the band of witches,' said Lord Salisbury, leafing through his file. 'And a storehouse full of – what shall we call them?'

'Witchcraft items,' McGray said without shame. 'Potion ingredients, poisons, drugs, amulets; the lot.'

'The storehouse was found empty a few weeks later,' I added, and the PM stared at his file, his lips tensing up.

'I know,' he said. 'I had to allow that.'

'*Ye what?*' Nine-Nails cried, his voice like a whip. The PM did not move a muscle.

'Continue,' he told me.

I cleared my throat, 'Lord Bampot killed a man imprisoned in Lancaster Castle, who was a former servant to the – shall we call them anything else, other than—?' I received impatient looks both from Nine-Nails and the PM, and could only roll my eyes. 'Very well. The surviving *witches* fled further south in Lancashire, to Pendle Hill, where they had their main lair. We came into a . . . confrontation. Lord –' I very nearly let out *Ardglass* – 'Lord Bampot was murdered, and it was then that Inspector McGray killed the two lead witches – the ones in question, I assume – so that we could escape.'

'Did you act alone?' the PM asked.

I felt a pang on my chest, the name of Caroline Ardglass coming to mind once more. Again, I decided I'd stick to the essentials.

'We were aided by two other witches. Miss Oakley herself, who wanted out from the coven, and also an old crone whose tongue had been cut out by her weird sisters – a form of discipline amongst their ranks. We only know that the woman responded to the name of – Nettle.'

Lord Salisbury now showed a deep frown. 'And all this happened in Lancashire?'

'Why d'ye think we call it *the Lancashire affair*?' McGray mocked, but the PM simply gave him a scornful little smile.

'I understand that *you*, inspector, had a personal connection to this incident.' And those few words were enough to put McGray on edge. 'Lancashire is really far from your home and jurisdiction, yet you chased this man and these witches all the way there.' Nonchalantly, the PM turned the pages. 'I see that your own sister was also an inmate at Edinburgh's asylum.'

McGray straightened his back. I imagined him as a hound being taunted with a stick. His sister was the very reason he had instigated the creation of our subdivision, her tragedy still a sore point.

Lord Salisbury pulled out a long document I recognized at once – an inquest transcript. It must be from the inquiries held after the deaths of McGray's parents.

'According to this, your younger sister, Christian name Amy, nicknamed Pansy, lost her wits six years ago, claiming she'd been *possessed* by Satan, and murdered her – *your* – mother and father . . . It says here, *mother killed with fire poker, father stabbed with kitchen cleaver* . . .' McGray shuddered visibly, angered and disturbed in equal measures. 'And it also says here that she was responsible for *that*.'

He eyed McGray's right hand, still manacled. The butchered stump of his ring finger – the wound that had inspired his infamous nickname – was all too noticeable.

'Furthermore,' the PM went on, visibly pleased, 'my contacts tell me that her condition worsened steadily after these Lancashire events, and we know for a fact that a few months later she had to be relocated to another institution.'

McGray tensed his jaw, baring just the tips of his teeth. The gesture made him look far more disquieting than one of his open outbursts.

'Was it something she saw?' the PM asked. 'Or heard?'

McGray looked far too angered to reply, so I spoke for him. 'That is correct, my lord. The room of Inspector McGray's sister was adjacent to the one where the nurse was murdered. She must have heard everything.'

'*Must?* Are you not sure? Was she not questioned?'

I answered as composedly as I could. 'Miss McGray has not spoken in six years, my lord.'

That, again, could be classed as a lie. In a blood-curdling episode, Pansy – thus nicknamed because her long, dark eyelashes made her look like those flowers – had scribbled the name of the head of the coven. Ironically, that turned out to be the name of another bloom: *Miss Marigold.*

However, she had never spoken or written ever again. Mentioning that small fact would only put her in the eye of the PM and his enforcers, who might not hesitate to torture her if they thought they might wring any information out of her. I trembled at the thought of the poor creature, crouching in the corner of a dark room as these thugs interrogated her.

'Even if we had questioned the girl,' I added, 'given her condition, her statement would have been less than reliable.'

From the corner of my eye I saw that McGray's face was all gratitude. The PM, however, would not let the matter go so easily.

'Where is this – Miss McGray, now?' he asked.

'None o' yer fucking business!' McGray snapped, and the PM burst in rage.

'*Answer me*, you truculent nine-fingered brute! I am trying to keep you alive. Both of you!'

McGray, nonetheless, kept silent, and I saw the perfect chance to take the attention elsewhere. I lifted my chin and spoke with my most suspicious tone.

'What do you want from us, sir?'

Lord Salisbury nearly snapped his neck when he turned to me. 'What?'

'You have just said that Queen Victoria wants us dead.'

'Indeed. And I know her majesty very well. She is a capricious, vindictive, bitter old hag who never forgets. And you two have meddled with one of her dearest, most intimate affairs. She shan't rest until she sees – what she considers justice.'

'Yet,' I murmured, 'here you are, warning us. Were you not told to find us and be rid of us?'

Lord Salisbury squinted with suspicion. 'Indeed.'

'So you *are* disobeying direct orders from Her Majesty. You will excuse my frankness, sir, but I doubt you are doing so simply out of the goodness of your heart. No competent politician has ever done such a great favour without a hefty price.'

The man's beard seemed to stand on end, his indignation painting his bald scalp bright red.

'What makes you presume I shall not let her have you both killed?'

We stared defiantly at each other; a silent duel of wills. Only a year ago I would have prostrated myself before that man, ready to take orders without question. So many things had changed.

'What do you want?' I reiterated.

Lord Salisbury ruffled his beard with a frustrated hand.

'Marigold and Redfern . . .' he said, naming the two lead witches with unexpected familiarity. 'You killed the queens, but you left the drones alive.

'You left them scattered and leaderless. When they were a hive, the queens contained them; they schemed and thought long term; they would only come to me occasionally and for *very* special favours. Now there is a horde of ruthless whores, aware of all the dirty linen of the ruling classes. All of them ready to wield that power at the first chance!'

His voice had risen steadily, until his last words were a frantic growl. He had to take a deep breath and a few smokes to regain composure.

I also had to do my best to conceal my enjoyment.

'They have been blackmailing you,' I said, quite clearly not as a question. Lord Salisbury said nothing, but neither did he meet my eye. 'We know they helped your son conceive after years of a barren marriage,' I added, again with plain certainty. Even the rough guards went uneasy. The PM looked surprised, but not overtly so. He allowed himself a bitter smile.

'Augmenting people's fecundity appears to be one of their particular talents.' He sighed. 'Yes. Those crones have been extorting me and my son since late January. That is why I had to let them vacate their warehouse . . . amongst other things. I thought they'd go away, but they keep coming to us demanding more and more.'

'With all due respect,' I said after a short silence, 'what is the real extent of their knowledge of you?'

The PM inhaled in a throaty gasp. 'What?'

'They helped your son conceive,' I said quickly. 'That does not seem enough to hold such a grip on someone half your rank. What could they possibly—?'

'*That doesn't concern you!*' the PM barked, and I flinched at the outburst.

The echo of his voice lingered, everyone grave and silent; again, even the horses. The first sound was a faint chuckle. McGray was doing his best to contain himself, but failed miserably.

'Do you find any of this funny?' the PM hissed.

McGray smirked. 'A band o' country lasses holding the Prime Minister by the balls . . . Ye must be hating it so much!'

The PM chewed his lip as if intent on making it bleed, then nodded, and Boss once again hit McGray at the back of his head. His chuckle did not diminish, though.

'So you want us to find the witches for you,' I concluded.

Lord Salisbury brought a trembling hand to his cigar, shuddering with anger.

'Yes.'

I arched a brow, drawing the situation in my mind. 'Do you want to silence them?'

Salisbury's gaze darkened, his eyes squinting like those of a preying wolf.

'Yes,' he said. 'In whichever way is needed.'

His tone made me shudder. The man saw it and snorted. 'My men can do it if you tell them where to shoot. They are not as fastidious as you.'

As he said so he cast a quick look at Boss, who let out an eerie chuckle.

I was going to protest, but McGray blurted out. 'Wait-wait-wait. There's something I don't quite get. How, just how, is finding those blasted witches so ye can shoot them in the head going to help *us*?' What's in it for us?'

A very mild sentence from him, but Lord Salisbury spoke in an irate stammer.

'Whah— what's in – what's in it for—? *Your pathetic little lives, you stupid Scotch!*'

McGray wrinkled his nose as if smelling something foul. 'How? If yer German bitch wants us dead, I cannae see how bringin' ye a few crones for slaughter will save us from—'

Boss punched him on the side of the head. He must be mighty strong, for even the hard Nine-Nails was momentarily stunned. Lord Salisbury seized the moment to speak on.

'I plan to bring her majesty the one witch to perform the séance. That is, after my men get rid of the other *weird sisters*.' I was going to interject, but preferred not to after seeing that McGray still shook his battered head. The PM, however, saw my quizzical brow. 'I know how the queen's mind works. If I bring her a replacement, a witch who can help her commune with her beloved Albert, she'll be prancing again like a heifer in spring. I'll be able to ask anything from her after that.'

I nodded. It was well known that the PM did not have a majority in Parliament, and that Queen Victoria was still happy to exert her power to *persuade* representatives to vote for whichever policies she favoured – to 'tame the excesses of democracy', as she called them.

It was a cunning plan – the PM would be ridding himself from the witches' grasp and gaining yet more political power. All in one move.

Still, my most cynical self came to the fore. 'Sir, if the goal is simply to humour her, why do you not bring her a random quack who can throw a convincing enough spectacle? I am sure my colleague here would be able to arrange that.'

Lord Salisbury shook his head. 'Impossible. Those crones are good at their craft. They convinced her majesty that they, and only they, are capable of communing with the prince; that any other who might claim so would be a charlatan. Also, along the years, they became aware of certain . . .' the man shuddered, 'intimate details. The queen will surely ask the sort of questions that only the late prince could answer, to make sure she is not being fooled.'

I quivered too. Such 'details' would surely abound. It was no secret that in the early days of their marriage, Victoria and Albert would have spent days on end locked in the royal bedchambers.

'So,' said McGray, 'ye want all the witches silenced, but at the same time ye expect us very carefully to extract one o' them from the coven, and then take her to fuckin' Windsor Castle so that Queen Vicky can talk to her dead boyfriend?'

The PM nodded. 'Her Majesty is currently at Osborne House on the Isle of Wight. The rest of your summary is perfectly accurate.'

Nine-Nails showed a sarcastic smile. 'What if we refuse?'

Boss made to punch him again, but Lord Salisbury raised a hand.

'Stop that! I need what little brains he still has!' and then he mimicked McGray's smile and tone. 'If you *refuse*, young man, pray tell me and I will take you both to her majesty right now. I'll be commended for my swift action, and then I'll keep on dealing with the blasted witches with the . . . extremely *meagre* resources the leader of a nation tends to have at hand.'

Nine-Nails began to say something, but Lord Salisbury nodded at Boss, who covered McGray's mouth with a hand and pushed the gun against his temple with the other. The man let out a soft, hissing laughter.

'And I want to make something very clear, inspectors,' said the PM as McGray struggled, his eyes alternating between the two of us. 'I am only coming to you because I believe your previous experience in these affairs might yield quicker results, and because you must be better equipped to select the right witch. As you already know, that is the only reason I have allowed your pathetic little subdivision to remain open for this long, and that is the only reason I am allowing you to stay alive, but don't assume I won't strike if I have to.

'Betray me and you are dead. Attempt to take a ferry to the Continent and you are dead. Give me but a hint that you intend to make this matter public, and you are dead.' He eyed Boss and the others. 'I will have men watching you closely. If you struggle, they shall aid you in whichever way they can. But keep in mind they are *not* your friends. They may also scuttle away if your actions put you in a position that might compromise me, her majesty or the government in any way. I have authorized them to silence you if needed.'

There were a couple of cruel chuckles from the men.

Lord Salisbury made another nod at Boss, who finally released McGray. The man searched in his breast pocket and tossed me a large wallet packed with sterling.

'That should cover any expenses for the endeavour,' said Lord Salisbury. 'My men will now take you to whichever quarters you deem fit to begin the task.'

And without further ado, he called for his walking cane and stood up.

I clasped the outlandish amount of money as I watched the PM and most of his men walk away.

'How long do we have?' I asked.

'Not long,' Lord Salisbury snapped over his shoulder. 'Her majesty has not missed a single Christmas Eve with her late husband. And she is a creature of habit.'

4

We asked Boss and the remaining driver to take us back to McGray's house. If we were to begin work immediately, the best books on witchcraft were there.

Fortunately the sweaty, moustachioed Boss did not sit with us, but with the driver at the front, and as soon as the carriage moved across deserted streets, I dropped my bravado. I buried my face in my hands and began stammering like a child.

'Queen – Queen Victo— Queen Victoria wants us dead . . . Oh, dear Lord, *Queen Victoria wants us dead!*'

McGray was still rubbing his head where Boss had hit him. 'Och, settle down, Frey. She cannae just do that. We've laws now. This is nae *Alice in* soddin' *Wonderland.*'

'I wish it were. At least I could ask the bloody Cheshire cat to paint me a door to bloody Timbuktu!'

'Och, calm down! Don't make me slap ye. We need to weigh out our chances. How much d'ye have there?'

He signalled the fat wallet on my lap. I forced a deep breath, opened it and did a quick count. 'I'd say – just over two thousand pounds.'

'Shite!'

He snatched the money and spent the rest of the journey counting, while I moaned on to deaf ears. In no time we made it to the sumptuous New Town, its wide roads and its Georgian terraces. The carriage turned into the wide circus that was Moray Place, its central garden now covered in snow that shone under the yellow streetlights. When the carriage halted in front of McGray's large townhouse – which I secretly envied – I was only too glad to jump off that blasted coach.

All the house's windows were lit up, and as soon as I alighted the main door opened. I recognized the plump though ashen face of Joan, my former housekeeper (snatched from me by McGray's butler, I shall never tire to say), stepping down the slippery front steps.

'Sirs, are you all right?' she cried with her thick Lancashire accent. In her haste she nearly fell forwards. 'Did they take you as well, Mr Frey? Where did—?'

'We'll tell ye all inside,' McGray interjected, pushing her back in, for Boss had also alighted and followed us closely. Nine-Nails turned to face him. 'Where the hell d'ye think yer going? Yer nae coming in here, ye twat!'

Boss's mouth twisted in a cruel smile. He took his time to answer. 'Remember we'll be watching you. Don't try anything that might upset me, or—' he pulled out his gun just enough for us to see it. 'Well, I'd hate having to shoot that old sack of bones you have for a butler, or that fat Lancashire—'

'*Piss off!*' and Nine-Nails shut the door so hard it nearly fell off its hinges.

I looked around in astonishment. The entrance hall, usually kept pristine by Joan, was a wreck – broken furniture, shattered vases, the wallpaper ripped off . . .

Poor George, McGray's ageing butler (and the object of Joan's affections), sat miserably on the staircase, a thick steak pressed against his left eye.

Even Larry, the servant boy we'd rescued from chimney-sweeping, had taken a blow to his lip, now engorged with blood. He regarded my untouched coat, silk smoking jacket and elegant slippers with shock.

'How come they didn't beat you, master?'

I looked at them with befuddlement. 'I just . . . I did not resist.'

McGray snorted. 'I hope ye never end up in prison.'

'But what happened, master?' George asked, being tenderly nursed by Joan.

'They came to give us an – assignment,' McGray growled, and then shoved the wallet into his breast pocket, for Larry was leering at it. 'The less we tell youse, the better.' He pointed at Joan. 'I'm nae joking, hen! Don't try to fish any gossip out of us, unless ye want them to come 'n' give auld George an even worse thrashing!'

'Didn't even cross my mind, master,' she mumbled, her chest swollen proudly like a pigeon's.

'Aye, right,' McGray mocked. 'George, ye all right? Need a doctor?'

'Och, neh. Am as hard as— *Ouch!*'

'I'll fetch one if he needs,' said Joan, who'd just poked the man's face a little too firmly.

'Alrighty,' McGray replied. 'Come on, Percy, we have work to do now.'

I was so tense I did not even react at the mention of my abhorred middle name. Instead I turned to the boy. 'Larry, as soon as it is reasonable, go to my lodgings and tell my valet I am all right. And that I will need him to bring me a fresh change of clothes.'

'Aye, master.'

'And Joan, could you please fix us some sort of meal? Cold meats, bread, fruit, that sort of thing. We might not sleep at all tonight.'

'Right away, Master Frey.'

I then followed McGray into his library. The place looked as if recently ravaged, but unlike the entrance hall, this was its usual state, with leaning towers of books, the collection of odd artefacts and the many half-empty glasses and tumblers. These were McGray's domains, and the servants were only allowed in to bring coal, clear out cutlery and clean only the worst spillages.

As soon as he stepped in, McGray was nearly knocked backwards by his two dogs; Tucker, his playful golden retriever, and Mackenzie, a gigantic black mastiff with an odious tendency to drool.

'Calm down, calm down, I'm all right!'

While McGray consoled the hairy beasts, I went straight to the decanter and helped myself to a generous measure of whisky.

Suddenly I felt lightheaded, my fingers numb around the tumbler, my feet hovering rather than touching the carpet. And no, it was not the whisky; it rather felt like the sort of shock and disbelief one experiences after a blow to the face.

'I knew this case might come back to haunt us,' I said. 'But not quite like this. The PM and the queen – the *queen* herself involved . . .' I breathed out. 'Gosh, I miss the good old days when we only had disembowelled violinists to deal with!'

After ordering the dogs out of the room – too boisterous to let us work – McGray lounged on one of the two ragged sofas by the huge fireplace. I passed him a drink and sat in front of him.

'Where do we start?' I asked, massaging my forehead and feeling utterly overwhelmed. 'What day is today?'

'The thirteenth. Well, fourteenth in an hour.'

'Damn! We only have eleven days to save our necks, if we trust Salisbury's word.'

'Ten. He said Christmas Eve.'

I banged my tumbler on the low table between us. 'How can we possibly trace a network of crafty women who could be anywhere in the British Isles in only ten days?' I pressed my temples, and when I looked up I found Nine-Nails in deep thought. 'What is it?'

'Nae . . . nae everywhere.'

As he said so he jumped up and began rummaging through his piles of books and loose sheets. I'd always been astonished by the ease with which he found specific pieces of paper amidst that sea of debris, and tonight he would not disappoint. He pulled out a yellowy, crumpled sheet, folded many times on itself, and extended it on the table. It was a faded map of Great Britain, but there were several markings in red ink dotted throughout.

'That wee witch Nettle showed us a map o' hers, remember? When we couldnae find our way.'

'How could I forget?' I said, thinking of the poor old witch. Silenced, mutilated and exiled by her sisterhood, she'd been forced to live in the Lancashire wilderness for years. She had found us in our moment of greatest need, and her directions had been only one of many aids. I wondered where she might be these days.

'These are most of the spots I remembered in that map,' McGray said. 'Where the witches had posts. I retraced it from memory as soon as we came back, just in case.'

'McGray . . .' I panted, pressing my hands on the map with sudden joy. 'For once, this is . . . *brilliant*!'

'Brilliant? When ye saw me doing it ye said it was another idiotic waste o' time.'

'One in a million had to turn out useful! How accurate would you say this is?'

'Very. I have a good memory for maps.'

I ran my fingers over the marks. There was a wide pentagram drawn on Pendle Hill, and then smaller circles on Edinburgh, York and several smaller towns all across Lancashire and Cumbria.

'I doubt they would have gone back to their previous outposts,' I said, 'especially if some of them have angered the Prime Minister. But this is a very good start.'

'We also ken a good deal o' their history.'

'*You*. You know a good deal. Quite frankly, I only remember what I told Salisbury. Would you mind refreshing my memory? For once I have a motive to pay full attention to your stories.'

Nine-Nails did not need much encouragement. This was his favourite topic, even above single malt and horses.

'They began their history around Lancaster, at the time of the witch hunts of James I.' He tapped the town on the map; one of the spots circled in red. 'They'd been working in isolation for centuries. Most o' them were midwives, village healers and the sort. When the king began burning and hanging them, they were forced to come together for protection. Most o' them were Catholic too, well used to hiding their imagery and their practices, so this new persecution wasnae too different for them.'

'But they were not all good sisters, were they?'

'Course nae. There are bad apples on every tree. Many o' those women were honest healers, but others wouldnae hesitate to charge dearly for a curse or a love filter – which *do* work, don't ye pull that face!'

'Or a discreet poison?'

McGray sighed and had a swig of whisky. 'Aye. Sometimes they handed out "amulets" which were just creative venoms that killed slowly, or they "cursed" people, only to take care o' them later on with more mundane methods. It was then that they got their bad reputation, all o' them tainted by the actions of a few.'

'Unfortunately,' I added, 'it seems to me that "those few" were the ones who prevailed.'

McGray grimaced. 'Yer kind of right. Those were the things that folk remembered – the placenta potions, the sacrificed babies and the cat entrails to tell the future. The witches surely heard people telling those tales, most o' them exaggerated, and I think they even encouraged them.'

I raised my eyebrows. 'In order to keep nosey people at bay?'

'Aye. It was also at around this time that they created their grimoire.'

I nodded. 'Of course. That secret code only they understand.'

'*Eye o' newt and toe o' frog, wool o' bat and tongue o' dog . . .*'

'Do *not* butcher Shakespeare with that accent of yours, I beg you.'

'*Butcher!* That's from the bloody Scottish Play, ye damn – Och, never mind. Those weird recipes were code names for other ingredients. But *never*, in more than two hundred years, have they put that code in writing.' He signalled the vast collection of old witchcraft books and pamphlets piled around him. 'I've searched 'n' searched, but never found a codex.'

'And they also chose the most disgusting codenames,' I added. 'Parts of dead human bodies, livers of Jews . . . Was all that part of their act?'

'Indeedy, and it also worked to make the curses stick to people's minds. They made it very public when they cursed someone 'n' the hex seemed to work.'

Like the Ardglass curse, I thought, but did not mention it yet. That name was like bile to Nine-Nails, and I needed him focussed.

'So when did the witches become the very sophisticated network of contraband and blackmail we found in January?'

McGray frowned and stood up, to rummage through his books one more time. 'Fairly recently. They *were* powerful and well connected amongst them from the very start, but they still remained a very small group; very secretive and with a very select list o' clients.'

He leafed through a few books, some of them crumbling apart and held together with strings.

'I cannae tell exactly when the shift happened, but it must have been some fifty years ago.'

'That recently?'

'Aye. That's quite short considering how ancient some o' their rituals are.'

'What do you think triggered it?'

McGray shrugged. 'Maybe they blackmailed the right sod. Maybe a very ambitious witch took over and was inspired by the scale o' the new cotton factories.'

'Marigold . . .' I mumbled, thinking of that horrendous woman, whose bulging eyes still haunted me at night. Thankfully she was now dead. 'If the dates you estimate are correct, it would have been either her or her predecessor who widened the coven's range.'

'Indeedy. But they still kept the inner circle small. Only the more senior witches were told the full extent o' their secrets. I think the younger ones honestly believed they were performing magic all the time.'

'So you *do* admit that—'

He interrupted me. 'How many witches would ye say ye saw at Pendle Hill? How many o' their servants?'

I closed my eyes. Those had been terrifying moments; a frantic blur in my head even as they occurred. I remembered their torches, alight with blue flames – coloured fires were their most effective means of communication across long distances. As I recalled the greens and blues, other torches, more sinister, came to mind.

'Hard to say,' I whispered, shaking my head. 'Thirty? Forty?'

'Aye, me too. And at least twice as many male thugs, all brainless muscle.'

I sighed, feeling another wave of despair. 'Not many, but still a hefty number to strike . . . How many would you say died that night?'

McGray looked sideways, unwilling to answer. Still, the disturbing truth was floating in the air.

'Just a handful,' I had to say. 'And other than Redfern and Marigold, the two arch-witches, I think nearly all the casualties were their easily replaceable thugs.'

McGray sighed, leaning back on his wide sofa. I waited for a moment, partly to let him process things, and also because I feared his reaction to my next suggestion. It was time to mention the Ardglass family.

'There is someone,' I said as tactfully as possible, 'in this very city, who might be able to help us. Someone whose lineage was – *cursed* by these alleged witches centuries ago.'

McGray caught my tone. He looked up, smiling wryly.

'Lady Glass?'

'Anne Ardglass, indeed. Was it – thirteen generations that the witches cursed? Is she not the eleventh? Lord Joel the twelfth?'

Nine-Nails laughed. 'I don't care. I'm nae talking to that auld bitch!'

'I'd never ask you to do so. That would be like setting two famished gamecocks on each other. I can go, unnerving as the meeting shall be.'

'Pff! Good luck. She hates yer guts too!'

'Perhaps, but not with the ravaging fury she reserves for you and your kin.'

McGray shook his head. 'She'll never help us. It wouldnae surprise me if she turned out to be a sodding witch herself. The hag just lives on and on and on. That cannae be natural.'

I mused for a while, swirling my tumbler as I stared at McGray's collection of deformed animals preserved in formaldehyde. If he called someone unnatural . . .

'I think she *will* help us,' I said, and then frowned. 'In fact, the more I think about it, the more convinced I am.'

Before I could probe further, there was a shy knock at the door and Joan came in with a large tray. Cheeses, bread, a jug of claret, two bowls of a hearty beef stew and a small pile of her famous fruit scones. I nearly whimpered at the memory of her delicious suppers and breakfasts.

She took her time displaying the food and pouring the claret, visibly expecting to catch some gossip. Her alert eyes reminded me that she was amongst the most efficient spreaders of news in the country; sometimes faster than telegrams.

'Joan,' I said, rather casually, 'what have you heard of Lady Anne lately?'

She gave me a confused looked. 'Your drunken landlady, sir?'

'Indeed.'

'Oh, not much,' she said with visible annoyance. 'She hasn't conned anyone for a while, which is always the talk around her. Though she did kick out some tenants from one of her houses on George Street recently. A very refined family, they seemed, but it turned out they owed her fourteen months' worth of rent. She made a right fuss, she did, tipping off all her business contacts.'

'That can only mean she is in reasonable health,' I said.

'I think so, sir. I hear her bill at the wine merchant's as high as ever.'

'What do you know –' I bit my lip, knowing the unpleasant implications of my next question – 'about her granddaughter?'

Joan showed a saucy smile.

'Joan, it is not that I—'

'It's all right, sir. You've been on your own for a while, and men just don't know how to be alone. Last thing I heard, she's still abroad, but nobody knows where; not even the servants. People are starting to whisper she went away to get rid of . . .' she went on whispering, 'some trouble, if you take my meaning.'

'Do you believe that?' I asked with sudden belligerence, which only widened Joan's smile.

'Guess the worst and you'll guess right, like my old gran used to say.' And then she winked at me with a motherly look. 'I'd stay clear of that gal, if I were you, master. Plenty more fish in the sea.'

'I do *not*—'

But by then Joan was gone. Thankfully, McGray had not paid too much attention; he was already juggling with food, his old books, spotting places on the map and reaching for a pencil to take notes.

'I will visit Lady Anne in the morning,' I concluded.

'Just don't take long. We've got very little time, and we need to go through all the information we already have.' He looked up. 'Ye wrote one o' yer theatrical reports on the Lancashire case, right?'

'Theatri—? Yes, I did. It will be in our files at the office.'

'Very well, I'll have a look tomorrow while ye visit that crusty mummy.'

We ate in silence, both of us savouring the claret and the warm, nourishing food. We might not say it out loud, but we knew we were about to plunge into very murky waters. The privilege of supping at home, next to a fire and at relative ease, might simply never happen again.

'Do you need any help with that?' I asked when I was finished, pointing at the daunting mountain of old texts.

'Nah, it'll take me longer to tell ye where everything is.'

'Will you not—?'

'Ye ken I don't sleep,' he interjected. 'Even less after this.'

I nodded and left the room, to find that Joan had already prepared one of the guest rooms for me. Thankfully I was still in my nightclothes, so I only had to take off my smoking jacket and jump into bed.

Despite the exhaustion, I had strange, yet unsurprising dreams.

Bubbling cauldrons, cawing ravens . . . and green fires.

DIARY – 1827

Dr Spangenberg sent me to Driburg, a Watering place where I drank Steel-water, bathed in it, and douched my Eyes with it: my Eyes again recovered. The causes of my affliction continued, but their effects were somewhat mitigated by time . . .

5

The next day the temperature plummeted, freezing the sleet from the previous night into a solid scab all across the city. One of the first victims was Layton, who fell face first against McGray's front door as he brought me several changes of clothes.

'Ye all right?' Joan yelped as she helped him up. The poor man had saved my freshly pressed shirts at the expense of his nose.

'Please, have that wound checked,' I told him, joining them at the entrance hall.

'Yes, Master Frey,' was his stoic reply. 'Will you need me to fetch anything else? Your cigars? Your coffee?'

'He'll be well tended for,' Joan said, quarrelsome.

'In fact,' I raised my voice before we had another north-versus-south conflict, 'I do need you to prepare me at least a couple of travel cases and have them ready in the cloakroom. I may need to depart unexpectedly.'

Layton bowed, as if trying to show Joan the ways of the proper servant. 'I shall provide everything the master might need.'

Joan wrinkled her nose, brushing off imaginary dust from my folded clothes.

'These collars aren't starched properly.'

Layton gasped. 'How – *dare* you!'

'Thank you, Layton, that will be all,' and I promptly closed the door.

I dressed as fast as I could and jumped on the first cab Larry managed to stop. Even at the sluggish pace forced by the frozen roads, we made it to the Ardglass residence within minutes.

Firmly set on the corner between Duke and Queen Street, the façade was as imposing as ever: grey, solid granite under an equally dreary sky, with an offensively large number of windows, and front steps and columns clearly designed to intimidate visitors.

Their arrogant butler was indignant when I said I did not have an appointment (in normal circumstances I would have sent a note ahead, but I did not want to give the woman a chance to avoid me). The butler only allowed me in when I showed my CID credentials and threatened to bring a team of constables if he made me wait another minute.

He led me through the empty corridors, our steps echoing under the high vaulted ceilings. The mansion's interior was almost as cold as the outside – even if not owned by someone as miserly as Lady Anne, it would have been next to impossible to keep all that air warm.

'Wait here,' said the butler as we arrived at Lady Anne's personal parlour. He stepped in and closed the door behind him.

I waited in silence, rubbing my gloved hands for warmth. Those frosty rooms were a fitting prelude to my meeting. I knew I was there to discuss the darkest secrets of that family.

A throaty shout came from the room and I heard the clatter of books and glass thrown around.

'Here we go,' I muttered as the door opened.

The butler, a shade paler now, made way for me without a word.

I realized that I was walking into the same chamber where Lady Anne and I had held our very first (and sad) meeting. How simple life had seemed back then, when she was merely trying to force me into marrying her granddaughter.

The place was surprisingly well lit, its window open onto a misty view of Queen Street. The walls were lined with shelves, all crammed with ledgers and inventories, and behind a wide desk, entirely covered with notes and paperwork, sat the infamous Lady Glass.

I supressed a gasp. The slender septuagenarian had never been a pretty sight, but now her cheeks were sunken and her wrinkles deepened, so that her eyes, pale blue and veiny, looked like bulging marbles set in sockets too wide for them. She was clad in mourning black, her brittle white hair plaited around one of her trademark headdresses: a pair of black stuffed birds, set in between matching feathers that stuck out like a small crown (quite discreet, compared to the two-feet-wide hats she normally wore to town).

In her dark attire she looked like an ashen undead, and I fancied the cut-glass decanter next to her, full of claret, as a vessel of fresh blood. Her lips, already stained with the drink, were no surprise even at that early hour – people called her 'Lady Glass' with good reason.

She stared at me cunningly for a moment, saying nothing until she leisurely poured herself some drink.

'You look dreadful, Mr Frey. Sleeplessness?'

'Good day to you too, Lady Anne,' I said, sitting down without waiting to be offered.

She took a long swig (breakfast, perhaps), her keen, reproving eyes always on me.

'I am so glad you spurned my granddaughter's hand. It would have been most shameful to have you in the family.'

'So much for subtlety,' I said in a sigh. 'Do you also believe I performed witchcraft in public?'

'I know you have leapt from scandal to scandal ever since we met, and that last night you were dragged out of my property in the middle of the night by a pack of mysterious men with dubious intentions.'

'How – how did you—?'

'News travels fast, and I keep myself well informed.' She pointed at a three-day-old copy of the *London Times* that lay amidst her paperwork. 'Only a few days ago, the girl who, I understand, used to be your fiancée published the date of her marriage. To your own brother, I believe?'

Even if I felt an initial wave of anger, it was refreshing to be reminded of the fact by someone other than my stepmother.

'Silly me,' Lady Anne mocked. 'Of course you knew already. Surely your brother – Laurence, is he not? – has sent you a formal invitation already.'

I struggled to keep a neutral face. I'd recently received a telegram from Elgie, my youngest brother, telling me that Laurence had indeed planned on sending me an invitation. Elgie had fished it out of the mail bag to save me the grievance.

'Is Miss Ardglass in good health?' I asked, unable to repress a small retaliation. I was sure Caroline would not have spoken to her grandmother in months (because of matters I shall discuss presently), and the dreadful quarrel must still be a raw wound for Lady Glass.

As I expected, she poured herself some more claret before she could answer.

'She is twenty-six, Mr Frey. *Twenty-six!* Next year people will start calling her a spinster. Another two years and she'll be a lost cause. She'll be lucky if she can secure a paltry gold-digger with a half-decent reputation.'

'God forbid she does not marry at all,' I said with sarcasm.

'If she doesn't marry and produce a boy, my son's title will be lost forever. The Ardglass and the Ambrose dynasties snuffed in the wind just like that.' She snapped her fingers and then glared at me. 'And now that I know better, I even prefer that fate to seeing my Caroline married to the likes of *you*.'

I cleared my throat. 'Enough of pleasantries, ma'am. I am here to discuss urgent matters.'

'Of course you are. You only bring disgrace into this house.'

I almost enjoyed delivering my next phrase. 'This is an issue – not entirely unrelated to your son.'

How ominous a face can turn. As soon as Lady Anne heard that, all mockery abandoned her eyes. Instead, an unsettling rage began to burn in them.

Her son, the late Lord Joel Ardglass – whose name I had not dared pronounce in front of the Prime Minister – had been at the core of the Lancashire affair.

Lady Anne, as any old prudish upper-class matriarch, had feared what people might say if her son's madness became public – it would have ruined her granddaughter's prospects, for instance. So the crafty Lady Glass had feigned his death, only to lock him up in secret at Edinburgh's lunatic asylum. Lord Joel remained there for seven years, until that fateful night when he murdered the young witch who'd been passing as his nurse. That investigation had sent McGray and me into a frantic chase, for, as I have said, Lord Joel went on murdering indiscriminately as he made his way to Lancashire.

All those facts seemed to flash across Lady Anne's eyes. That woman's history was like a pit of sludge that dated back to the seventeenth century, when her ancestors, moved by nothing other than greed, had led the Lancashire witch hunts to please

King James I. It was then that the witches initially 'cursed' her lineage. She ground her teeth, which, in her slimmer face, looked larger and fiercer.

'*Don't mention my son!*' she rustled. 'He died in 1882. And *that* is the truth.'

'Indeed,' I said, acting out the lie. Even Lady Anne's most trusted servants ignored the full extent of Lord Joel's tragedy. 'However –' I took a deep breath, moved to the edge of my seat, and whispered – 'those women . . . the ones who' – I spoke even lower – 'turned him mad in the first place . . .'

Lady Anne opened her eyes wide, fear shining through her face as she let out whirring exhalations.

'The witches . . .' she whispered. 'Are they back?'

I gave her my most honest look, and nodded.

Very, very slowly, she leaned back, clenching her glass with her knotty fingers, struggling to take in the news.

Just when I thought the glass would implode in her hands, she jumped to her feet, pushing back her chair with a strident noise. She rose to her full height, her spine perfectly straight notwithstanding her years, and she stumbled to the window.

I rose too, thinking she'd fall, but then she reached the pane, pressed a long hand against it and scratched it with her fingernails. I almost felt the sound grating my teeth.

'*Will they never die?*' she let out in a hiss.

I gave her a moment. I knew it was my imagination, but on the other side of the window the sky appeared to have gone darker. Lady Anne turned to me then, her wrath giving way to sudden panic.

'Are they after Caroline? Have they found her?'

So even this ghastly woman had a heart.

'No, ma'am. Not that I know.'

She breathed out, her jaw a little less tense, but only momentarily. She had a good slurp of wine, which returned her to her senses. When she looked back at me there was a chilling spark in her eyes.

'Then . . . They came for you! They came for you and that damned Nine-Nails.'

'Not quite—'

'And now you need my help.'

'They have not come after us,' I repeated, raising my voice.

'Then why are you here? You know how much I loathe you and the grimy McGrays.'

I ground my teeth, knowing I could not fool that woman. She read my eyes and saw the enormity of the situation.

'Certain people,' I began, 'highly seated people, want the witches dead.'

'*Highly seated!* Who?'

'I cannot divulge those names.'

'I have a good imagination.'

'Then fantasize away, ma'am.'

The woman sighed, realizing I would say no more. Her twisted smile, however, told me she had a good idea as to who might be pulling the strings.

'What do you want from me?'

'Information, Lady Anne. Absolutely anything you might know about the coven.'

'Why would I know anything about them?'

'Oh, do *not* think me an idiot, ma'am! You knew of their existence long before your son's – misfortune. You knew about the alleged curse they set on your dynasty. You tried to destroy them yourself, did you not? You seized that ancient property, Cobden Hall, from them.'

'That belonged to my ancestors! I was only taking back what—'

'I said, do not think me an idiot! Your very own grand-daughter told us the truth. She also found it suspicious that

64

you went through so much trouble to acquire such a decaying manor, hundreds of miles from your claws.'

'*Mr F—!*'

'You own the best property in Edinburgh and everyone knows how crafty you are at seizing assets. You even attempted to snatch inspector McGray's townhouse at one point.'

Lady Anne smirked. 'You don't know the half of that.'

'You found out that the witches used that Lancashire manor as their headquarters, so you found the way to take it. And then they struck you back with a vengeance. I know that is the reason your son became their victim.'

'*Shut up!*' she howled, her eyes flickering. The witches had indeed inflicted a merciless revenge; Lady Anne's only heir turned insane, ultimately to become a murderous fiend, and her granddaughter now estranged from her, forced into exile for her own safety. I wondered if she even knew Caroline's exact whereabouts.

To my surprise, Lady Anne smiled. 'And now they might strike you and your beloved Nine-Nails,' she mocked. 'But if you confront them and fail, and they find out I assisted you . . .' She chuckled. 'Why would I ever put myself at risk – at a greater risk – to aid vermin like you?'

I stood up to face her more closely.

'We might rid you of them for good. I doubt you ever had a better chance. And I can tell how thirsty for revenge you are.'

Lady Anne gulped.

'I know how they . . . *cursed* you,' I went on. 'Thirteen generations fated to grim lives or untimely endings, am I correct? And for the past three centuries these witches have made sure that their prophecies come to fruition.'

I saw the spark of unmitigated hate in her pupils, and I fed it further.

'Caroline is the thirteenth, is she not? The last in the chain.'

She moved her lips, as if to say something, but not a sound came out.

'The witches may still prevail and drive your bloodline to extinction,' I pressed. 'But you can fight them. You can give us the ammunition.'

Lady Anne did not move. She simply stared at me, not even blinking. For a moment I thought I had convinced her, but then she looked down, to her decanter, now half empty.

She poured herself yet more drink and turned her back to me, staring out the window as she took short, anxious sips.

We stood thus for a good while, the sounds of the increasingly busy road muffled through the window.

And then, just when I thought I'd leave empty-handed, Lady Glass spoke.

'I'll do anything to see them dead.'

6

At once I made my way to the CID headquarters, tipping the driver to take me there as fast as he could. I felt relieved when I saw the towering tenements of the Royal Mile emerge in front of us.

I hardly even noticed that someone at the higher storeys poured the contents of their chamber pot onto the street, and the mess splashed on top of my (thankfully) roofed cab.

The driver, half drenched in filth, halted just in front of the arches of the City Chambers, cursing his luck. I alighted, almost exhilarated by my recent success, but then I felt something.

It was a sort of prickle at the back of my neck, quite faint, but enough to make me look back.

Across the street I saw a tall, thickset man, with half his face covered by the brim of a faded bowler hat. Arms crossed, he was leaning against the stones of Mercat Cross. The man brought a hand to his hat and nodded at me, to make sure I knew he was watching me. Simultaneously, a large raven, perched atop the monument's main pedestal, cawed loudly and took to the air.

I shook my head and rushed in. Immediately I was intercepted by Constable McNair, his ginger hair a tad more dishevelled than usual.

'Inspector Frey,' he said, 'Superintendent Trevelyan is waiting for ye.'

'Waiting for me?'

'Aye. Nine-Na— Inspector McGray's with him already.'

I sighed deeply and went to the upper level. The door to Trevelyan's office was indeed open, his young clerk posted there to send away unwanted visitors. As soon as he saw me he let me pass.

I first saw the milky silhouette of Edinburgh's Castle, perfectly centred behind the room's enormous window. The white sky cast its dim light into the office, so that McGray and the superintendent looked like sharp, dark outlines.

'Do be seated,' said Trevelyan, walking from behind his neat desk. He nodded at the clerk, who closed the door at once.

I sat next to McGray and Trevelyan settled down on the edge of his desk, his arms crossed and evaluating us with his auburn eyes.

Appointed only very recently, Trevelyan had already proven to be a worthy head of the police forces (much more so than his treacherous predecessor). He also carried himself with enviable equanimity, impervious to all the stress of his post. No wonder his hair still remained the exact same shade of brown as his eyes.

'So you two have been summoned at last,' he said.

Neither McGray nor I knew what to answer. Trevelyan nodded with understanding.

'I received a note, handwritten by the Prime Minister himself. He commands me to provide whatever you might need and – he underlined this – to ask no questions.' He paused, expecting us to say something. We remained silent, so he continued. 'Does that fit in with whatever he has told you?'

McGray looked away, leaving the talking to me.

'I am glad he made provisions for us,' I said, and nothing more.

The one wrinkle in Trevelyan's face – a long fold on his brow – deepened.

'I take it this is the crucial assignment he has been saving for you.'

'Indeedy,' said McGray, but with a tone that somehow made me think of a slamming door.

Again, Trevelyan nodded. 'As much as I hate being kept in the dark, I shall help you in any way I can. I simply need to know how urgent this matter really is, so that I can act accordingly.'

McGray smiled. 'As urgent as a bucket o' water when yer crotch is drenched in oil and on fire.'

'How evocative.' Trevelyan stole the words from my mouth. He breathed in. 'And speaking of blazing unmentionables . . .' He went back to his usual chair, sat down and interlaced his fingers. I did not like the face he was pulling. 'I suppose you know what is most likely to happen after you sort out this . . . mysterious affair.'

'*If* we manage,' I said with gloom, but McGray's face looked far more concerned.

'D'ye mean . . .?'

'The Prime Minister has not said so, but I cannot see he will want to keep your subdivision alive after this. Especially if this matter, whatever it is, must be kept secret.'

There was a moment of silence.

I'd had no time to think beyond the case, but now that I did, I could only agree with Trevelyan. Once the witches had been dealt with, Lord Salisbury would want to wipe out all the evidence. McGray's – *our* little subdivision would be the first official trail to erase.

'You'll understand I cannot justify more expenditure on the Odd and Ghostly,' Trevelyan added, and raised a finger as soon as McGray opened his mouth. 'And I shall *not* take bribery like the previous superintendent.'

McGray placed both hands on the desk, his missing finger more noticeable than ever. 'D'ye mean that after this ye'll kick us out?'

Trevelyan raised an appeasing hand. 'I shall give you a grace period, so that you can finalize any pending cases.' I thought I'd better not mention that at the moment we did not have any open cases at all. 'But then, yes, I will have to close you down.'

McGray sat back, utterly dejected.

I too felt a small pang of sadness (*very* small, of course), and Trevelyan noticed.

'Having said that,' he continued, looking at us with earnest eyes, 'you two are very valuable elements, and I would hate to lose you. If you were willing, I could find a place for you in some other—'

'We will see,' McGray snapped, standing up with a jump. 'Let's focus on today's shite before piling more on ourselves. I need ye to get us information about Lady Glass.'

'Lady Anne—?'

'Aye. All the documents ye can. And remember what I said about the burning crotch.'

And he exited the office in huge strides, slamming the door behind him.

I looked at Trevelyan with slight embarrassment. He simply sat back and said two short words, packed with meaning.

'*Good luck.*'

7

I left Trevelyan's office at once and chased McGray as he stormed down the stairs. He was heading to the dilapidated basement we had for an office.

'Why do you need him to investigate Lady Anne? Did you find anything I—?'

'Och, nae! I just needed a good punch line to get out o' there. He effectively just sacked us! I wasnae going to leave that damned office looking all meek 'n' lily-livered. Like *ye*.'

As he said that, we stepped into the office – that old underground cellar at some point had been part of the now-buried Mary King's Close. I looked at the clutter, the flaking walls, the precarious towers of books, gory amulets, magic fossils, embalmed beetles, dried fish . . . and the jars with specimens so ghastly even McGray would not keep them at home. Their murky formaldehyde was lit by streams of dull light that came in through the barred windows.

I allowed myself a sigh. This might well be my last assignment working from that damp little hole, and as much as I'd hated it from the very start, I felt a pang of nostalgia.

It was evident that McGray had been there since the small hours, and quite busy. He'd nailed a new, larger map to the wall, re-marking the witches' hubs and pinning notes to all of them. He had also collected his best books on witchcraft, herbalists, witch hunts and related gibberish, as well as all the files from the Lancashire affair.

'So what did she say?' McGray asked.

'Lady Anne?'

'Nae, yer bloody stepmother.'

I sat on my hard chair and lounged back, grinning – no wonder McGray called my ways theatrical.

'She will help us.'

'*What?*'

'Apparently, she hates the witches more than she hates us. And she knows they are very likely to go after her grand-daughter. Once I made her angry enough, she volunteered all manner of interesting facts.'

'Such as?'

'First of all, can you remind me of the content and purpose of a witch's bottle?'

McGray frowned. 'What? Why?'

'Humour me.'

'It's a protection charm. Blood of the household's head, piss, bent nails and special herbs; all into a bottle that ye hide somewhere in yer house. It keeps intruders and evil spirits away.'

I smiled. 'Originally, back in medieval times, yes. Now they are just another code. Witches did not always know each other. If they found one of those ghastly bottles in a prospective victim's house, they'd know that it was the dwelling of a colleague's client and leave them alone. That is how those charms seemed to work. And that is the same purpose of the red onions and sugar under the bed. That is why Lady Anne had at least one bottle placed in each and all of her properties.'

I shuddered. Somewhere in my own house there'd be a hidden bottle, full of blood and urine. I'd rather not think whose.

McGray pointed angrily at me. 'They do work! Why d'ye think they've been used for hundreds of—?'

'On more important matters,' I interrupted, 'Lady Anne does not know where Miss Ardglass is. The girl has only addressed her grandmother on two occasions since January. The first time from Seville.'

'*Seville!*'

'A city in Spain.'

'I know that, ye prick! I didnae expect her to hide that far away.'

'Far away indeed. And the second time she wrote, she was somewhere in Bavaria.'

McGray looked up, mumbling. 'Bavaria . . .'

'A region in Ger—'

'Shut it, Percy.'

He went to his desk, opened my report on the Lancashire affair and passed a few pages.

'Ye wrote here that Lord Joel spent quite some time there. Before he married Caroline's mother.'

'Did I? I mean, did he?'

'Aye. Ye also wrote that Lady Glass, his bitch mother, didnae let him marry the lassie he wanted. That's what we first thought had turned him mad. Before we found the witches.' He tossed me the file. 'Says here, from yer very own bloody hand. Oh, and after Caroline was born and her mother died, Joel took her to Bavaria. They spent plenty o' time there, before he lost his mind, o' course. I wonder if the lassie went back for some reason.'

I frowned. 'McGray, do not try to come up with obscure explanations. If Miss Ardglass knows the region, it is only natural she chose that place to hide.'

McGray simply let out an unconvinced *tut-tut*.

I closed the file and threw it back onto McGray's desk.

'At least she is abroad,' I said, 'which should keep her out of the witches' way for the time being.'

'Good. That's one neck we don't have to worry about at the moment.'

'But the most important thing Lady Anne said,' I added, 'was that she still has connections in Lancashire.'

McGray opened his eyes wide. 'Really? Who? Where?'

'Some dubious characters in Lancaster, to begin with. The very people who helped her seize Cobden Hall. And those connections have eyes and ears around Pendle Hill.'

Nine-Nails, for once, was dumbfounded.

'Have they been watching Cobden Hall?' he mumbled.

'Indeed. Lady Anne remains the legal owner of the manor, even if she did nothing with it when she heard the witches had abandoned it.'

'Fearing they might come after her and Caroline?'

'Precisely. And that is the same reason she decided not to chase them. If she will help us now it is only because she has never had a better chance to be rid of them for good. Remember that Caroline is the thirteenth generation – the last one in the witches' curse. Lady Anne must fear the coven will hunt her down.'

'Did ye tell her Queen Vicky was involved?'

'No, but it is clear she has her suspicions.'

McGray suddenly looked like a hungry hound. 'And her contacts can tell us where those bitches fled?'

'Perhaps. Lady Anne told me she has consciously avoided asking such questions for her own safety. But yes, that is our best trail right now.'

McGray remained silent, looking at me with distracted eyes. He stepped back and sat on his desk. His absent gesture looked strikingly similar to that of his mad sister.

'What is it?' I asked.

He shook his head, unexpectedly vexed.

'I'm goin' to hate it so fucking much if I end up owing my life to that mother-f—'

'Do not rush. Even Lady Anne admits this might lead us nowhere. We can only wait and see.'

'For how long?'

'It will take her a couple of days to gather the information. She does not like to contact them by post or telegram, for obvious reasons.'

'Very well. But we cannae just sit 'n' wait, can we?'

'That would not be advisable, especially with a prime minister and a wrathful Queen after our blood.'

'Speaking o' the bawbag face,' said McGray, 'what d'ye think the witches have on him?'

'For a politician? Phft! The possibilities are endless – corruption, mistresses, uncomfortable offspring . . . And I am sure it is not just information they hold. Those women must have hard evidence; documents, statements . . . God knows what else. Salisbury would not go through all this trouble and expense otherwise. Why are you asking?'

McGray stroked his stubble. 'It wouldnae be the worst idea to try and find out. Ye ken, like an insurance policy.'

'Indeed it would not, but how do you propose we do that? It is not likely to be something laying on Salisbury's bedside table. And we have a coven of witches to find first.'

'Madame Katerina could help us.'

Thankfully I was not drinking, else I would have sprayed a six-foot radius.

'Katerina!' I squealed. 'I bring you a solid, verifiable line of investigation, and you suggest we chase a gypsy trickster who—'

'Och, why do I even bother talking to ye?'

An argument ensued, which partly made me under-stand the 'old married couple' type of jokes at the City Chambers. We only stopped when Constable McNair cleared his throat, perhaps after witnessing our quarrel for a good while.

'Good yer here, laddie,' McGray told him. He went to his desk and picked a small stack of addressed envelopes. 'Here. See that these are sent right now. But don't use our mailbox. Tell one o' the clerks or the cleaners to take them to the post office.'

'What are those?' I asked.

'I'm writing to all my contacts in the black market, asking them for random books and witchcraft items. Things that only witches can source. That'll give us a good idea of which regions they're still supplying.'

'Good thinking,' I said. Then we noticed McNair's face, pallid and confused. It could not be because of the mention of witches, as the young officer was used to all this.

'What is it, laddie?' McGray asked him.

'Someone left this at the front courtyard,' he said, handing us a crumpled piece of brown paper.

'A note?' I asked standing to have a better look.

'Aye,' said young McNair. The folded paper read, in eerily childish handwriting: *For Inspector Nine-Nails.*

'Who brought it?' I asked.

'Don't know, sirs. It . . . it was tied to a black cat.'

McGray frowned. 'A black— where is it?'

'It ran away as soon as we untied the note,' and McNair showed us three deep scratches on his hand.

McGray shook his head, unfolded the piece of paper, and I read over his shoulder.

Dear Nine-Nails and Mr Frey,

Meet me at the glasshouse on the north-western edge of the Royal Botanical Gardens.

Alone and immediately. I shall wait for you all day if I must.

Tell no one. Fear for Pansy.

8

We said nothing as the shabby cab took us north. Thin snow-flakes had just begun to flutter over the city, but from the frosty air I knew they'd persist for a good while.

McGray looked ahead the entire time. He only moved when we were nearly there, to check that the cylinder of his gun was fully loaded. I followed his example.

The cab halted at the gardens' gates. We waited for the driver to go before making our way in, having to take careful steps on the frozen stone paths.

The gardens were as immaculate as one can expect in winter, the lawns under a growing blanket of snow, the winding foot-paths demarcated with perfectly trimmed yew. I had visited its imposing glasshouse the previous March, when I realized the pathetic Scottish spring would offer no solace. It had been a desperate attempt at finding some warmth and the illusion of mild outdoors, but the glasshouse exceeded my expectations, both by its splendour and by the heavenly warmth provided by a very sophisticated heating system – state-of-the-art hot water piping, which before then I'd only seen at some libraries in Oxford.

Today, the glasshouse looked unchanged: its tall, wide windows, as well as its glass domes, glowed with the scant sun in glares that made me squint.

As soon as we walked in, a blast of humid heat met us, bringing the musky, intoxicating scent that instantly transported me to tropical landscapes; a mixture of moss, earth and dewy flowers. If someone could bottle up that smell I'd be the world's happiest man. Sadly, I had no opportunity to bask in it, for my eyes and ears were instantly searching for the mysterious messenger.

Amidst the banana trees, the ferns and the birds of paradise, the only sound was the trickling of a little fountain, all the city noises kept out by the thick glass.

'*Oi!*' McGray yelled to the air, startling me, and his voice echoed as if we were inside a church. 'Here we are!'

We waited for a moment. My eyes flickered around, as if expecting to see a preying tiger in that exotic jungle.

Then the ruffle of clothes broke the silence, barely audible. I even thought it had been my imagination, but then McGray thrust himself forwards. I ran after him, but amidst the bushes and the narrow paths I soon lost him.

I followed the stomping sound of his strides, flinging broad leaves and branches out of my way. I heard the loud thud of his boots, halting, and then his booming voice.

'*What the hell?*'

I ran faster, following his voice. A three-feet-wide leaf obscured my view, and as I tore it away I found McGray. He was staring at a thin, lonely figure, clad head to toe in black.

'*You?*' I exclaimed involuntarily, as my eyes met those of Doctor Thomas Clouston.

The superintendent of Edinburgh's lunatic asylum, with his dark bushy beard and perfectly smooth scalp, awaited in silence.

Just like Lady Anne, the man seemed to become thinner each time I met him, his cheeks now sunken, and his perfectly groomed beard had finally begun to turn grey – quite an achievement at forty-nine, especially considering the man's constant tribulations.

My astonishment very quickly turned into comprehension, for very few men had been as embroiled in the witches' case as him – not even McGray and myself, I daresay.

Almost eight years ago, Dr Clouston had been forced to treat Lord Joel at his asylum in utmost secret. Set on keeping her son's madness private, Lady Anne had coerced him to circumvent the strict Lunacy Acts in the Scottish law. The poor doctor had always told us he'd only acted out of compassion, seeing that Lord Joel would have otherwise ended up in some dire bedlam, treated by dubious quacks; I, however, had my doubts. No sensible man – and he clearly was one – would have agreed to such a damning deal, and he clearly regretted the consequences. Not only had he had witches infiltrated in his institution for seven years, passing as nurses looking after Joel Ardglass; he was also forever bound to secrecy – after his borderline illegal actions, Lady Anne had all the weapons to destroy his career.

Indeed, I could not help suspecting he'd acted with some ulterior motive. McGray, on the other hand, could never think ill of the doctor. After all, he could not thank enough the devotion and care Clouston had shown to his sister for more than six years.

I could not wait to hear what the man had to tell us, but I'd be disappointed. Contrary to all my expectations, the doctor was casting us an impatient look.

'Well?' he demanded.

'Well, what?' said McGray.

The doctor sighed. 'I knew it was you, Adolphus, but why the act? You can summon me with a common note.'

McGray squinted. 'What?'

'Your black cat wreaked havoc in the asylum's gardens. The inmates tried to catch it and we had to send them all back inside. There were a few fits of rage and an injured orderly.'

'We didnae send a—'

'We *received* a summons,' I interrupted. 'Also tied to a black cat.'

McGray pulled the note out of his pocket as I said so. Clouston's eyes opened wider. He too produced a note and held it close to ours. The same brown paper.

'What does yers say?' McGray asked.

Clouston unfolded it and handed it to me. It was almost an exact copy:

Good Doctor,

Meet me at the glasshouse on the north-western edge of the Royal Botanical Gardens.

Alone and immediately. I shall wait for you all day if I must.

Tell no one. News re. Pansy.

'I wasn't sure what you meant,' said the doctor. 'Whether you *wanted* news on your sister, or you *had* news.'

'We were confused too,' McGray answered, and I showed him our note. 'Couldnae tell if ye – well, the bugger who sent this – was worried for Pansy or threatening us.'

'So we were all summoned,' I mumbled, folding the papers as I pondered. 'And the notes were delivered – by cats.'

We exchanged looks of mutual understanding. We all knew that the witches used ravens instead of homing pigeons and, somehow, cats as their omnipresent eyes. McGray affirmed those animals were enchanted, while I thought the so-called witches simply excelled at training even the most obstinate of pets. That was why that blasted raven, always perched across the road from my window, had unnerved me so much.

Suddenly my pulse quickened. 'This must be a trap . . .'

McGray unsheathed his gun. I did the same and we described slow circles around the doctor, scrutinizing the lush greenery. We heard nothing other than our own soft steps.

'A trap?' Clouston asked, drained of all colour. 'Are you hunting witches again? Are they a menace to—?' The doctor gulped, unable to finish the question.

'It has nothing to do with ye and Lord Joel,' McGray rushed to say, though looking as worried as if half the coven had already pounced upon us. 'Did ye see anything odd before we got here?'

'No,' Clouston said, carefully placing himself between McGray and me, for protection. 'The glasshouse and all the gardens around were deserted when I arrived.'

'They still were when we came in,' I added. 'Today's weather is not the best for strolling around the park.'

'Look after the doctor,' said McGray, becoming lost in the fronds. I watched out as we heard him shake branches and stir ferns. The heat began to creep through my clothes, drops of perspiration appearing on my temples. I had to undo my tie, and just as I did so, we heard McGray again.

'*Here!*'

I followed his voice, the doctor right behind me, and we found Nine-Nails nearby the glasshouse's northernmost corner, squatting before a patch of fresh flowers. The blooms were bright yellow, white and purple – pansies. There, nestled in the delicate petals, sat another small piece of brown paper.

McGray stretched his hand to pick it up, though he did so with some hesitation, as if fearing something might happen if he touched it. He spoke before doing so.

'Both messages mention Pansy . . .' he turned to Clouston. 'Has anything happened to my sister?'

Clouston shook his head. 'Nothing, as far as I know. I've only received routine updates from the—'

'*Shhh!*' McGray snapped. 'Someone might be listening!'

Very few people knew that Pansy was being treated in the Orkney Islands, where Dr Clouston originally hailed from, and it was imperative that it remained a secret. McGray, after all, *was* responsible for the deaths of Redfern and Marigold, and he feared the surviving witches might retaliate. If they did so, Pansy would be their first target.

'I've only been told she is doing well,' the doctor went on. 'That is, there has been no change . . .' he cleared his throat, 'for better or for worse.'

'That medicine I sent ye last summer . . .' McGray began.

Clouston gulped. 'The miraculous waters? Of . . . of course they did nothing.'

McGray was going to press on the matter but I interjected. 'Oh, please, let's look at that blasted note, for goodness' sake!'

And as I said so I picked up the paper and unfolded it swiftly. The same hand; a completely different message:

The Marigolds are heading to Pansy. Take her to safety before it is too late.

I cannot tell for how long we stood there, dumbstruck, staring at those words. It might have been full minutes.

McGray was of course the first one to speak.

'We have to go to her! *Now!*'

He was already stepping to the exit, but I managed to stand in his way.

'Wait, *wait*! We have no idea who sent this. It might be a trap – bait so that you lead the witches straight to your sister.'

Clouston covered his mouth. 'My clinic . . . Will my patients be in danger?'

Neither of us could answer.

'What else would ye do?' McGray asked me. 'Just ignore this? Ye ken what those damn witches can do for revenge!'

'That is precisely why we should not rush!' I raised all three notes. 'First we should try to find out where these came from. In whose interest would—?' I gasped then, and turned to face the doctor. 'Did *you* place this note here?'

Clouston's face went from white to red. 'How dare you suggest that?'

'You do have a history of misdemeanours,' I said bluntly. 'And you were here before us.'

'Stop spitting shite, Frey!' Nine-Nails cried. 'Why would the doctor do this?'

'There is plenty about him I do not fully understand,' I retorted. 'But right now—'

'Och, shut it! Think! Let's assume yer right and the – *Marigolds* did set a trap and want me to lead them to Pansy. What does that tell ye?'

I knew where he was going but did not want to admit it.

'It means they do not know where she is,' Clouston answered for me.

'In which case,' McGray added, 'we could get there without being seen and make sure she's fine.'

I rubbed my face. 'How precisely do you intend to do that? You know perfectly well those women might have eyes everywhere. Their ravens and cats . . .'

'Their enchant—'

'*Do not tell me they are enchanted again!*'

McGray growled and made a fist. It took all his effort not to punch me. 'But yer royal highness does agree we must avoid all cats and ravens.'

84

'Yes, I do. They are precisely—'

'Very well. The quickest way to Pansy is by sea.'

I laughed. 'You on a ship? With your seasickness? You will have vomited your spleen out before we even leave the Firth of Forth.'

McGray held his fist an inch from my chin. '*Let me finish or I swear—!*'

I put my palms in the air and said no more.

'The quickest way is by sea,' he resumed, lowering his voice. 'If we leave at night we could navigate far from the coast, nae lights. It'll be easy to shake off anyone trying to follow.'

I simply tensed my lips.

'Ye cannae deny it will work,' McGray insisted.

Indeed I could not. A lonely ship in the middle of the foggy, wintry ocean, far enough from the coast, would be untraceable even by those women's ubiquitous ravens.

I sighed. 'All right. Let us assume I agree and we go. It will take us –' I preferred not to mention specifics out loud. 'It will take us a considerable length of time to get there and back; time we cannot waste at the moment, with Queen Victoria after our blood and all that.'

'The queen after *what*?' Clouston echoed.

'Tell ye later,' McGray said, before looking back at me. There was a renewed spark in his eyes. 'Now that I think about it . . . going to Pansy wouldnae be a complete waste o' time.'

'Pray explain.'

He snatched the last note from my hand and pointed at the name.

'Marigold,' he said. 'The name o' the head witch. It was Pansy who first told us about her. Don't ye remember?'

'How could I forget?' I said.

'And d'ye remember how she came to know that name?'

85

'Again – how could I forget?' I repeated, only with much more bitterness. Lord Joel had been Pansy's neighbour at the asylum, both of them having adjacent rooms at the wing reserved for the wealthier patients. Apparently, the son of Lady Anne enjoyed reading to Pansy, which seemed to soothe them both, so their interaction – always supervised – had been encouraged. They'd only ever been left alone once, very briefly, and that turned out to be on the very night Lord Joel murdered the witch that passed as his nurse and fled the asylum. That was also the one and only time that someone had heard Pansy talk. To Joel Ardglass.

'What if she heard something else?' McGray said, knowing perfectly what I was thinking. 'What if that Ardglass sod told her much more than just a name? Pansy could really help us!'

Clouston and I exchanged wary looks. We were well used to that ring of desperation in McGray's voice.

'I have two objections to that,' I said, as politely as I could. 'First, have you forgotten what happened the last time you visited Pansy?'

Though not said as a reproach, it unavoidably sounded so, and Nine-Nails looked down. During said visit Pansy had managed to escape from her carers and make it all the way to the nearby beach. Had she not been found promptly, she could have drowned.

Clouston and I had reason to believe it was McGray's own presence that had worsened Pansy's condition – her brother would be a constant reminder of her past . . . of her crimes.

'My second objection,' I continued, while McGray still looked down, 'sadly, is your sister's condition.'

'*Och, Frey!*'

'You saw what this case did to her. This case was the very reason Doctor Clouston had to send her away. Even if she

86

were able to speak,' McGray winced, 'do you honestly want to go there and torment her with more questioning?'

He looked at me with eerie intensity. 'Maybe – *ye* could do it.'

My mouth opened in a perfect 'O'. 'Could do what?'

'Ye could question her.'

I looked away. 'Oh, dear Lord!'

'That's something we've never tried,' Nine-Nails insisted. 'I should've let ye question her back then, instead o' pressing her myself. I've thought o' that many times in the past months.'

I realized I needed reinforcements. 'Dr Clouston will not allow it,' I said, appealing to the man. 'Tell him, doctor.'

I was expecting an instant reply, the good doctor always quick to dismiss McGray's more brain-addled schemes. To my dismay, the man remained thoughtful.

When he turned to me he had a very odd expression. I cannot possibly describe it; I can only tell that there was some deep conflict brewing in him.

'It might not be . . . the worst idea . . .'

My jaw dropped. '*Not the worst!* Are you mad as well?'

The seriousness he now showed scared me. 'Adolphus is right. Amy has only expressed herself on two occasions that we know of. One was in front of Lord Joel . . .'

I covered my brow, suspecting where the doctor was going.

'And the second instance was in front of *you*, Inspector Frey. I witnessed that myself.'

They looked at me as if all of a sudden I'd become the Holy Grail.

'Are you suggesting Miss McGray responds better . . . to strangers?'

'Exactly,' said Clouston. 'We – and by that I mean both Adolphus, myself and all the staff at the asylum – perhaps bring too much stress upon the girl.' He saw McGray's frown. 'Despite our best intentions, of course.'

'The brother she mutilated,' I muttered. 'And her . . . *captors*.'

I bit my lip, about to admit that the theory made sense.

McGray crossed his arms. 'Don't think this doesnae scare *me*, Percy; leaving my wee sister alone with a dirty Englishman . . .'

'*Alone?*' I cried, my face flushing.

'And it must be that way,' said Clouston. 'It is crucial she doesn't know we are there.'

'We?' I echoed.

'Of course, Inspector. Did you expect me to let you carry out this little experiment without me? If you are to go, I shall come along.'

I sighed, all weariness. 'McGray, time has never been so precious. We should not even be discussing this. We must go back to the office and—'

'And what?' McGray jumped in. 'Wait? It will take a couple o' days for my contacts to get back to me, and Lady Glass also told ye she'll need time to get us more information.' Clouston perked up at that, quite anxious. 'Nothing on ye, doctor, don't worry. But Percy here is right; time's precious right now. If ye want to come along, I need ye ready tonight.'

'*Tonight?*' Clouston and I protested in unison.

'Aye,' said McGray. He put the note in my hand and turned on his heels at once. 'So I need to arrange our transport right away. In the meantime go home and pack up yer tiaras, Frey.'

He strode away before I could answer. Clouston saw my fury and placed an appeasing hand on my shoulder.

'His idea,' he whispered at my ear, 'does make some sense, Inspector. All things considered.'

I only snorted. 'Sense! How can you say that? How can you be so willing to carry out this ridiculous plan?'

Clouston simply looked down. His face, for some reason, was ridden with guilt.

DIARY – 1827

*17 October. [. . .] At Florence I began to suffer from a confusion
of sight [. . .] Each eye had its separate vision [. . .] I was
twice blooded from the temples by leeches – purges were
administered; One Vomit, and twice I lost blood from the arm
[. . .]*

*Now a new disease began to shew itself: every day I found
gradually my strength leaving me [. . .] A torpor of numbness
and lack of sensation became apparent about the end of the
Back-bone and the Perinaeum [. . .]*

*At length about the 4th of December my strength of legs had
quite left me, and twice in one day I fell down upon the floor
[. . .] I was obliged to remain on the floor until my Servant
came in and picked me up.*

9

Since money was no impediment, McGray hired a private steamer to take us directly from Leith Harbour to the Orkney Islands.

I headed home to pick up my luggage – Layton had my cases ready – and I then met Nine-Nails at Moray Place for a hearty meal. Doctor Clouston was the last man to arrive. Following McGray's advice, he joined us after the sun had set, which also gave him time to arrange things at the asylum before his departure. After a last dram for courage, we set off into the frosty night.

The snow had continued to fall throughout the day, soft but steady, so the streets were now completely covered in white. The roads around Leith Harbour, trodden incessantly by carts and coaches, were a slippery mass of dark slush.

'Here,' said McGray, pointing at the pier to our right, just as the driver halted.

Under the dim glow of the streetlights I saw the outline of a small, yet very clean, paddle steamer, the hull recently painted in dark green. Its tall funnel was already spurting smoke, the noise of the engine was rhythmic and steady, and warm light came from within the small portholes.

I was about to commend McGray (difficult as it is for me), but then I saw three men cross the boarding ramp. One of them was a short, plump man with a mat of grey hair; the skin on his face was more weather-beaten than an old boot, so he must be our captain. The other two, towering and broad-shouldered, I recognized at once, even with their hats and long overcoats.

We stepped off the carriage and met the trio while the driver unloaded our luggage. The snow fluttered all around us, carried by the salty breeze, and the steamer swayed gently on the mild waters. A most unfitting background to our tense gathering.

'Where do you think you're going?' Boss's familiar voice demanded. Between his bowler hat and lifted collar, I could only see his eyes and brow, and the curled tips of his moustache.

'None o' yer fuckin' business,' Nine-Nails burst out.

Boss's colleague took a threatening step forward. The middle-aged captain raised a hand, his thick, bristly moustache covered in frost.

'Haud yer wheesht!' he said in a dialect even thicker than McGray's. 'Am sure the lads can explain themselves.'

'This is part of our investigation,' I said before Nine-Nails spat more bile.

'You were told to inform us of all such movements,' Boss said. 'Not slide in the middle of the night like pathetic scuttling rats. We—' He pulled a gun from his breast pocket and pointed at the cab driver. '*You! Get out!*'

The chap lost all colour. He had been pretending to wipe dust from our cases.

McGray put some money in his hand. 'Quickly, if ye ken what's good for ye.'

The man had the good sense to oblige, and within seconds he'd taken the cab away. Boss lowered the gun, but did not put it away.

'I'll repeat my question. Where are you going? Captain Jones here tells me you simply told him to stock as much coal as he could.'

Again I spoke first, with a very well-calculated note of defiance. 'We cannot divulge that here, for obvious reasons. Come along if you must, but we will not tell you our destination until this steamer is out of reach.'

In fact, we counted on them coming. We still ignored who had sent the messages and why. It was very likely we were still heading into a trap, in which case having Salisbury's men around could only be to our advantage.

Boss remained silent for a while, brooding, but he did so only to assert his authority. In the end he stepped aside. 'I'll let you board. But don't think we won't be watching you.'

Captain Jones whistled and a young cabin boy rushed to pick up our cases. Boss and his man – whom I shall call Bob – waited for us to board before they followed suit.

'*Fuck*—' McGray growled as soon as he set foot on the polished deck. Was it my imagination or had his face turned green within a blink? Boss and Bob exchanged rough laughs.

Clouston held him by the arm. 'Come on, I'll give you something for the sickness.'

I followed the captain into the galley. As I went down the steps, I thought I heard the caw of a raven somewhere in the distance.

I told Captain Jones to navigate east until the lights of the coast could be seen no more, and then to come to me for further instructions. Until then I would not be able to reveal our final destination. Boss was not too happy about it, and he told me so in the most brazen language.

Disinclined to spend much time in the company of Salisbury's men, I went to my private cabin, which turned out to be far nicer than I expected. Polished wood, brass fittings, a little writing desk, and a narrow yet very comfortable bed made it a blissful little haven. It was a real shame I should occupy it under such distressing circumstances.

My suitcase was already on the bed. I saw that Layton had packed a nightshirt, two changes of clothes, a shaving kit and my favourite cologne, along with a little sachet of lemon verbena to keep everything fresh. When I unfolded the nightshirt I found a hunter flask full of single malt. The man knew me so well.

I lay on the bed for the next hour, even if I did not manage to sleep, until Captain Jones knocked at my door awaiting instructions. Boss came right behind him.

Even then, late at night and miles away from the coast, I could not bring myself to speak our destination. Paranoia was getting the better of me. I produced my little notebook and scribbled 'Kirkwall, Orkneys'.

'Right away,' said Captain Jones. He went away but Boss stayed put, casting me a mocking stare as he lit a thin cigarette.

'Did you not hear me?' I snapped. 'You can go away now.'

He got lost in the shadowy corridor, but only after an infuriating sneer.

I went to bed and did my best to sleep, but any rest felt like a waste of what little precious time we had left. This entire trip might lead us nowhere except to a more certain death. Very soon I pictured myself laying face up across a guillotine, seeing how the blade descended very slowly, closer and closer to my tender neck with every tick of the clock.

The thought gave me a pang of fear and I jumped up. I knew I could not possibly sleep after that, so I thought I'd make use of the free time. I grabbed the hunter flask, my notebook and the three crumpled messages, and went to the comfortable galley. Thankfully, neither Boss nor Bob were around.

I sat at the narrow table and poured myself a drink in one of the flask's little matching cups. After a well-deserved swig, I extended the notes on the table and examined them closely.

They were all scraps of brown wrapping paper, torn hastily from a main sheet. I rotated them until I noticed that the upper edge of one matched exactly the left-hand edge of the other. I tried the third one too, until I found a border that also matched the puzzle. So all three had been taken from the same piece of paper, at almost exactly the same time. I flipped them to examine both sides. They were all faded on the reverse; it clearly had been a used sheet, part of an actual wrapping, perhaps even sent through common post. Could the messages have originally travelled on the inside of a wrapped parcel? If that were the case, they could have originated from much further afield. From a witches' lair, perhaps?

I took the notes, stood up and brought them closer to the lamp on the wall. Some manufacturers still put watermarks in their wrapping papers. I held the sheets but an inch from the sconce, scrutinizing every spot, crease and fibre. I became more aware of the ship's endless sway, and for an instant understood the source of McGray's discomforts.

At that moment I saw – or thought I saw – a pattern emerge. An arched line, right on the edge of Clouston's note. It reminded me of a postal stamp, but it was terribly faint. It was as if only a shadow of ink had managed to seep through an overlaying sheet, on which the actual stamp had—

'Inspector!'

I jumped, banged my head against the low ceiling and let out a growl. When I turned, still seeing stars, I found the slim figure of Doctor Clouston staring at me from the door.

'Oh, inspector, do excuse me! Did I startle you?'

I rubbed my head as I sat down. 'An unnecessary question . . .'

'Indeed,' he said with a nervous smile. 'I do apologize. I could not bring myself to sleep. I can leave if you need privacy.'

There was a note of embarrassment in his voice, and I remembered my accusations at the glasshouse. I put the notes back in my breast pocket and decided it would be best to make amends.

'It is all right, doctor. Please, have a seat.' Clouston did so, even if still a little nervous. 'How is the – *laddie*?' I asked.

'Fast asleep,' he said, putting a small bottle of laudanum on the table. 'Would you like some? A very small dose is harmless and would do wonders for your nerves.'

I had witnessed the effects of laudanum addiction, and swore I would *never* depend on such substances to keep my poise. I turned back to my whisky.

'This is all the medicine I need,' I said, raising my little cup. 'Would you care to join me?'

Clouston ruffled his beard. 'I am not in the habit anymore . . . but the situation merits some indulgence . . .'

'I'd say,' and I passed him another cup, full to the brim. When we toasted I noticed a slight tremor in his hand. He drank half the cup in one gulp. 'Are you all right, doctor?'

He sighed, visibly tired. 'I am – worried.'

'About Miss McGray?'

He did not answer immediately, but stared at the little cup and how the lamp's light bounced on the silver.

'One tries not to become too involved with patients . . .' he whispered. 'But . . .'

'You would not be human if such things did not affect you sometimes,' I said, recalling how some of my most recent cases still gave me nightmares. 'I know that you were a close family friend even before the McGrays' – misfortune.'

'Indeed,' he said with another sigh, finished his drink and coyly pushed the cup forward for me to refill.

'How did you meet them?' I asked him as I poured. 'It may be presumptuous on my part, but you do not strike me as the sort of acquaintance the late Mr McGray would have entertained.'

'You are absolutely right. He owned farming land and distilleries; I have always been a scholar. We met by chance.'

'Did you?'

'I treated a man . . . somewhat connected to him. A gentleman from New Town, who was also a benefactor of the asylum – in exchange for my discreet services. He held a grand gathering at his townhouse. It was there I met the late James McGray.'

'McGray's father at a social gathering?'

Clouston laughed bitterly. 'The first and last he ever attended in New Town. The man was – what you might call *coarse*.'

'Like father like son?'

Clouston shook his head. 'Adolphus was somewhat tamed by his mother's good manners.'

'Gosh!'

'But he was a good man. Ruthless in business, irascible, not one to mince his words, yes; but his will was unbreakable, he was loyal to his friends and devoted to his family.'

Just like Nine-Nails, I thought. When I looked back at Clouston, the poor doctor had gone sombre. He reached for the flask himself and poured another measure.

'He did not deserve that death,' he mumbled, 'or the scorn he received.' He took another swig. 'Miss McGray was their best hope of ever joining good society. She had such a sweet temper and genuinely seemed to enjoy all the things appreciated by fine ladies: singing, dancing, drawing, horse riding . . . And – well, you have seen her. She is still a delightful thing to behold.'

The manner in which he said it made me blush. The whisky seemed to be going swiftly to his head.

'More than once I heard men at the New Club whispering how pretty she was, and ladies commenting how lucky the family would be if she secured a respectable husband.'

His eyes glowed momentarily, lost in his memories, but then he looked at his drink and his face went grave again.

'Alas, that shall never be.'

Those words lingered in the air, along with the continuous racket of the engine and the occasional splash of waves.

Clouston blinked then and, as if something had stirred him, jumped to his feet.

'Look at me,' he said with a nervous smile, 'I am only derailing you. You clearly have work to do.'

Before I could say anything the man was gone, as if suddenly ashamed of everything he'd just told me.

I stared at the swaying door, thinking I should have enquired more. The good doctor seemed to be full of secrets.

Despite all the worries and questions, I was so exhausted I fell asleep as soon as my face touched the hard pillow. My dreams, however, were dreadful; I kept seeing the ugly Queen of Hearts from *Alice in Wonderland*, as grotesque as I had pictured her when I'd read the book as a child. She had her hand on the guillotine as I lay under the shiny blade.

Thankfully I was awoken by the charge of ever stronger waves. My pocket watch read five past five in the morning, so I saw no point in trying to sleep again. I washed my face, got dressed and went to the galley. Captain Jones was already there, smoking a cigarette and heating a large pot of coffee. He looked incredibly fresh for a man who'd sailed throughout the night.

'Good morning, sir,' he said brightly, modulating his thick accent. 'We'll be docking at Kirkwall in a few minutes, ye'll be pleased to hear.'

'Indeed. Nothing untoward during the journey?'

'Onto-whah?'

'Odd. Suspicious.'

'Ah! Och, neh. Naething but a black sheet was the sky. Coffee?' he offered, though already placing a pewter mug on the table. I took a sip to appear polite, though it turned out to be one of the strongest, most delicious brews I'd ever tasted.

'We were lucky,' said Jones. 'The sea was really gentle for this time o' year.'

'My colleague will disagree.'

'Aye, the poor lad. I have nae seen a case so bleedin' bad in years!'

'Could you please repeat that, several times, when he awakes?'

The captain let out a frank cackle. I almost told him my joke had not been quite that funny, but then the boy who'd carried our luggage stormed in. His face, hands and clothes were now caked with soot, surely from spending the night feeding the engine.

'Cap'n! Ye better come see this! Quick!'

Boss came behind him.

'You too, inspector,' he said. For the first time, the man looked concerned.

I took a long sip of the excellent coffee and trotted behind them. I had to grasp the stairs' handrail, for the waters had grown choppy. The sea air hit me on the face, icy and salty, under the dark and thick clouds. The sun had not risen yet, so I felt as if trapped in a cavernous tunnel.

'There!' the boy shouted. He and two other sailors were pointing at the prow. Boss and Bob ran in that direction and I followed as quickly as I could. The deck was wet and the entire ship swayed with more and more violence. As I ran, a forceful lurch hit the ship, almost turning it on its side and sending me skidding to the gunwale. The bar hit me in the stomach, half my torso sticking out of the steamer, the foamy waves but inches from my face.

I clasped my hands on the gunwale as the ship swayed back, and then we heard Bob's panicked shout.

'*Jesus!*'

I looked up, and at once my heart jumped.

We were half a mile from the shore, the lights of Kirkwall's houses dotted along the bay like little stars. But one stood out, glowing brighter and higher than the rest, perhaps atop the cathedral's belfry. And bright green.

A wave of nasty memories surged into my head. I'd seen that shade of green before. And I had also felt its blazing heat, burning through my clothes and seeping into my skin. Coloured and fuelled with a foul mixture of oils, saps and metal shavings, it was the sign that the witches used to summon their sisters; their call for aid . . . or for slaughter.

I staggered towards the prow, sliding my hands on the gunwale, as if the emerald glow had cast a spell on me. The steamer continued to sail speedily in that direction, aiming directly to the light, and for a dizzying moment I felt as if we were falling into it.

I was still staring at it, panting, when I heard McGray's voice behind me.

'*What the fuck's happe—*'

He went silent. I looked back and saw him approach, Captain Jones holding him firmly, walking with the balance of a seasoned sailor. I could only make out McGray's face when they reached me. I'd never seen him so pale.

'Shit . . .' he whispered, the green light reflected in his eyes. 'They followed us?'

'No,' I said. 'They were here first. God knows for how long.'

10

We disembarked a few minutes later, which gave us just enough time to get our overcoats and guns. The engine boys brought three bullseye lanterns to the deck; McGray, Boss and I grabbed them and then rushed down the boarding ramp. There, all along the pier, fishermen, sailors and early risers were pointing at the burning belfry, their scared screams filling the icy air.

McGray bumped against me, still queasy.

'We'll check on Pansy,' he muttered swiftly, and then eyed the cathedral. 'Ye go see that fire. If the witches are still there, stop them!' And before I could ask how on earth I was supposed to do that, he ran to a nearby cart, followed closely by Doctor Clouston. Boss nodded at Bob, who ran after them at once. McGray very quickly *persuaded* the confused driver to take them to Clouston's clinic, and I saw them dart away amidst the fluttering snow.

'What in the name o' the Lord?' Captain Jones said behind me, staring at the green flames.

'Do you know the way there?' I asked him.

'St Magnus Cathedral, aye, but—'

'We'll follow you,' I snapped, pushing the short man forwards.

'Wait! I cannae just go like –' one of the boys brought him a loaded derringer – 'right, now we can.'

We left the harbour and ran across a narrow street all covered in deep snow. Jones soon turned to the right, taking us into what must be the town's high street. We passed shops and public houses, all shut except for a bakery, where two stout women stood with their snow shovels. They'd stopped their work, casting terrified looks in the direction of the cathedral, not visible from there.

'*It's on fire!*' a young girl cried, running back to join them. They gasped when we ran past them and they saw our guns.

The street opened up into a long esplanade, the town hall buildings unmistakable to our right, and to our left the darkened graveyard that surrounded the temple. Everything there, façades, tombstones and snow were lit by the emerald glow.

We looked at the tower as we ran on. The flames still billowed at the top but they were clearly waning. We crossed the graveyard, where people of all ages had already gathered, some bringing buckets and others filling them with snow.

When they saw us, armed and running frantically, they instinctively moved aside, and we made our way under the elaborate archway, into the desolate cathedral.

The long nave, if possible, felt colder than the outside. I slowed down, looking in every direction, my gun at the ready. Boss and Jones did the same. A couple of men, carrying empty buckets, were running back from the belfry, but they froze as soon as they saw us.

'*Get out*,' Boss barked at them, gun in hand, his eyes bloodshot, and the men scurried away without question.

Feeling my quickened breath and heartbeat, I pointed my lantern left and right. The Gothic columns rose to the vaulted ceiling, projecting impenetrable shadows behind them. The only other lights came from a few candlesticks at the altar, and also the green glow that filtered through the stained-glass windows. Every patch of blackness could be a hiding place.

I shed light on the right-hand side of the nave. Boss, needing no instruction, did the same to the left, and we made our slow way down the aisle. Captain Jones followed closely, looking nervously all around. He did not seem too confident walking on land.

We walked half the nave, the sound of our steps bouncing across the empty space. And then, along with the echoes, I thought I heard faint breathing. I looked at Boss and Captain Jones. Their chests went up and down, but not at the same pace as the sound.

I stopped, my movement intentionally abrupt, and the two men looked at me.

Quiet, I mouthed at them, and we all listened.

I heard the distant sounds from the street, muffled prattle and screams; I felt my heartbeat, pounding in my ears, and a bead of sweat rolled down my temple.

Then I heard it again, as faint as before, yet clearer in the deeper silence; a sharp exhalation, perhaps from someone who'd tried to hold their breath.

And yet, in the reverberating nave, I could not tell where it came from.

I moved my light beam from column to column. My heart jumped when I saw a woman on her knees, praying, next to an hourglass and an unnerving skull.

Just a tomb, I told myself, staring at the eerie monument carved on the wall. The skull's empty eye sockets seemed to stare back in mockery.

Then something moved.

It was but a glimpse, a quick shadow, flashing next to the skull and rushing into hiding—

'*Stop!*' Boss roared, thrusting himself towards the side aisle, behind the line of pillars. I chased him and so did Captain Jones. Our lights bounced manically on the pink granite, the shadows swinging like dark blankets in the wind. Boss saw something and focussed his light.

'*Stop!*' he repeated, and amidst the eroded stones I recognized the figure ahead. No mere shadows; those were real shrouds, blacker than the night and rippling like flames as they ran away.

We were gaining ground swiftly, and then, right in front of me, Boss dashed sideways, his body flying towards the centre of the nave as if hit and dragged by a potent wave. His lantern rolled and crashed on the flagstones, and I could only see the towering shadow that had struck him.

I shed light and caught a glimpse of a gigantic man who stood with his back against the wall. He'd emerged like a gargoyle, as pale as bones and grinning like a devil, so close to me I even saw the cracks on his teeth, and the mass of thorny tattoos all over his hairless scalp.

I did not get time to scream; the man grabbed me by the neck and lifted me clean from the floor. I gagged and kicked about, dropping my lantern and bringing my gun to the man's stomach. His thick hand clasped my wrist and pulled my arm until I felt my joints would snap. For a ghastly moment I thought he was going to rip me apart like a rag doll.

Then came a gunshot. The man howled in pain, his blood splattered on my face, and then he tossed me aside like a discarded fish. I hit someone before rolling on the floor; Captain Jones, I could tell from his growl. The cathedral was now as dark as a cave and I could only hear the frantic stomping of God knew how many feet.

I groped about and found my gun soon enough. My lantern had smashed but the wick still glowed like a dying ember. I picked it up and jumped to my feet, the old captain limping behind me, holding his derringer.

I tried to light my way, but all I could see was Boss's outline running like the wind towards the altar. As we went after him we heard the rattle of metal.

'To the crypts!' Boss shouted over his shoulder, and then he too became lost in the darkness.

My pathetic light only let me see a couple of yards ahead. After a moment I saw the glint of brass bars; a slim grille gate, ajar, and behind it impenetrable darkness.

I could barely see the stone steps, eroded after centuries of use, and descended as quickly as the light allowed me. Captain Jones breathed noisily right behind me. I had to shush him when we made it to the underground vault.

There was nothing but deathly silence there, the stagnated air reeking of damp. I raised the lantern, its light seemingly brighter in that solid blackness.

Before us there were two lines of raised tombs with poor carvings of sleeping characters, their hands pressed together in prayer. I looked to my left and right – that giant would not strike from the side again. There was nobody. I looked ahead again, but even Boss had vanished.

I took a step forward, as carefully as if walking on eggshells, my eyes wide open. I could almost feel their presence, hidden behind the tombs, crawling in the shadows and readying themselves to strike. What an eerie standstill that was, surrounded by dusty graves.

Very slowly, every muscle in my body tense, I bent down. I placed the lantern on the dusty flagstones, and turned it on its side. With a well-calculated push, I sent it rolling towards the centre of the crypt. In the complete hush, the racket of the lamp seemed deafening.

The outlines of the tombs appeared clearer as the light passed beside them, their shapes coming and going with the glow. The lantern passed the first row of graves and nothing; the second—

A savage roar filled the crypt and I saw the towering stranger rise from his hiding place like a black bear. He hurled himself not at me but from right to left, his huge hands set like claws. At once I pointed down, to his thick legs, lit brightly from below, and I shot.

The bullet only grazed him. The man still darted ahead, as if untouched, and a wild skirmish ensued. I saw fists and legs kicking and punching about, Boss cursing and the giant roaring. I ran in their direction to help, but then the second shadow rose from behind the next row of tombs, running into the deeper darkness. I followed the shroud, blindly after a few steps. I stretched my arm, groped about and seized the cloak, but then I felt an unyielding pull on my leg and I plummeted forwards.

I barely managed to put my hands ahead, dropping my gun and blocking my fall, but my cheekbone still hit the flagstones and slid on as if on sandpaper. I saw stars and was only half aware of what happened next.

A dim light came from behind and I had a blurry view of the black shroud, also lying on the floor right before me. I must have brought it down with me, but just as I thought so, the thick hands of the giant grabbed me by the shoulders. He only lifted me an inch and then someone hit him right on the head. The man dropped sideways, moaning. Then the light grew brighter and I saw the shining buckle of Boss's boot, kicking the giant's ribs without mercy. His wild growls as he struck made me shudder. He finished by stomping on the man's thigh, right on his bleeding wound. He shrieked in pain and Boss strode ahead.

'You almost let him kill me!' he shouted at my ear, not stopping.

I did not get to say, 'Better you than me,' before I saw the shroud stir and crawl away.

With one swift movement Boss seized the cloaked figure, his frame blocking my already starry view. I then heard a high-pitched cry; a woman shrieking like a harpy.

Captain Jones approached. He was the one holding the lantern. In his other hand he held his ridiculously small derringer, pointing directly at the giant's face.

I saw that the hooded woman still crawled frantically, until Boss pushed her rump with his boot and she fell flat on the damp floor. I was about to say that such display was not necessary, but Boss shouted in a blood-curdling shrill.

'*There!* I got you a damn witch!'

As he said so he pulled back her black hood.

I snatched the lantern, stumbled up and brought the light closer.

I could not suppress a gasp. I saw locks of wavy brown hair, a slender, pale neck and then, when she turned to face me, the dark, cunning eyes of Caroline Ardglass.

II

'*You!*' we roared in perfect synchronicity.

I rushed to her and helped her stand, seeing her face almost as grazed as mine. I produced my handkerchief and offered it as though we stood in Kensington Gardens and she'd just sneezed.

Boss was dumbfounded.

'Do you know her?' he shrilled.

Once standing, Caroline pulled herself away from me, snatched the handkerchief with utmost ingratitude and spat blood like a pedlar. 'I thought you were the witches' men!'

Her piercing stare reminded me why I disliked her so much.

'We thought *you* were – oh, what does it matter? What the devil are you doing here?'

'Were you seen?' she barked.

'What?'

'*Were you seen*,' she urged, 'when you barged in?'

'By everyone,' said Boss, still casting her an ominous stare.

Caroline brought a hand to her forehead and moaned. 'Oh, you stupid men! They know Miss McGray is here. They've known for a while.'

'The witches?' I asked.

'No, your stepmother.'

'*Why does everyone keep—?*'

'I set the fire to lure the witches and their men here, away from the clinic, and give us time before you arrived. I was not expecting you to be here quite so soon.'

'Expecting us—!' I cried. 'Was it you who sent the notes?'

'Yes, but there's no time to explain. Not now that you've made your grand entrance. They'll know it was all a trick. We have to get to the clinic as quickly as we can.'

'McGray is on his way there,' I grumbled.

'They'll need help,' she said.

'We can call the local constables,' I said, but Boss growled at me.

'We must leave no trace.'

'*No trace!* Have you not noticed the bloody ball of green—?'

'There's a way out,' Caroline interrupted, snatching the lantern.

'What? Through the crypts?' said Boss.

'No, through the weave of your socks.'

Boss raised a hand to slap her. Much to my frustration, I had to hold his wrist.

'And help my man,' Caroline commanded, nodding at the giant. 'Are you all right, Harris?'

The man did not speak, but simply grunted something that sounded vaguely affirmative. I went to him to help him stand, and only then did I give him a proper look.

'Harris' was a roughened, weather-beaten man, a good twelve inches taller than me and with biceps thicker than my thighs. His head was cleanly shaven and mercilessly tattooed, and the back of his scalp was indented, as if long ago someone had cut off a chunk of bone and brain.

'Can you walk?' I asked him, looking at his grazed leg. The injury on his arm did not look that bad. He said nothing, produced a frayed rag (perhaps a handkerchief to him) and carelessly tied a tourniquet around his injured leg.

'Can you understand me at all?' I asked again, but he snarled from the back of his throat. I understood a split second before Caroline explained.

'The old witches cut his tongue out years ago.' She looked at him with a most respectful gesture. 'He was sent to look after me.'

The giant smiled almost bashfully at her, and then Caroline turned on her feet, walking briskly into the depths of the crypt.

I looked aghast as we followed her. 'He was sent? By whom? And – do you mean to say you and this man travelled all the way here without a chaperone?'

Even Captain Jones laughed at my question.

'Can this woman be trusted?' Boss asked in a low voice. He was still pointing his gun at her.

'I am not sure anymore. But under the current circumstan—'

'*Quick!*' she yelped, and we had no choice but to follow Caroline's light along the winding tunnel.

'Is this some passage the witches used to smuggle potions?' I asked.

She shrugged. 'Boys for one of the old clergymen, I believe they said.'

I was only glad they could not see me blush in the dark. If only Lady Glass could see her now . . .

There was a sudden draught, telling us we were near the way out.

Caroline climbed a flight of eroded steps that led to a wide, angular exit, with the exact dimensions of a Tudor roaring fire. Thicker clumps of snow were falling all around.

We must not be far from the cathedral, for I could see a faint glimmer of green in the sky above our heads. We were at the base of a wide, roofless chamber, its ruined walls ascending some thirty feet. The stones were centuries old, and I recognized the lines of hollows where thick beams that supported the upper floors would have been propped.

'What is this?' I asked. 'An old castle?'

'Earl's Palace,' Caroline said, keeping the brisk pace. 'The history lesson will have to wait.'

She led us to a Gothic threshold, its door long gone, and we stepped into a darkened orchard. Through the bare branches I saw fragments of the belfry, just a hundred yards or so away. Still burning.

Boss gave me a push, and then I noticed the battered carriage that waited for us, right next to the ruined walls, the better to hide under their shadows. The muscly horse, waiting with enviable calm, could barely be seen, its coat pitch-black.

We ran there, our feet plunging into the snow. The giant Harris, who had in fact walked with barely a limp, opened the door for Caroline and then crawled up to the driver's seat.

'I better go check on the steamer,' said Captain Jones, his hands shaking as spasmodically as his voice.

Boss regarded him with blatant mistrust.

'We do need him to sail us back,' I said. 'And it looks like we will probably have to go in a mighty rush.'

Boss nodded, then grabbed the captain by the collar and snatched his minute weapon. 'Don't even think of leaving without us! Do you hear me, stupid little imp?'

Boss did not wait for a reply. Instead he pushed me into the carriage and then jumped after me. He'd barely shut the door when the horse set off at a staggering speed.

I peered through the window, watching how the green blaze atop the belfry faded in the distance.

Within minutes we were out of the town, the carriage jerking frantically on the bumpy road, the snow falling thicker as we advanced.

'This is useless now,' said Caroline, throwing the sorry lantern through the window. She leaned down and pulled another one from underneath the seat.

'How many witches and thugs can we expect?' Boss asked her.

'Not too many, I hope. They couldn't have known any of us would be here.'

'And you do not need too many men to break into a clinic for elderly patients,' I said, if only to calm myself down.

'They only had two women taking *care* of my father,' said Caroline, oozing bitterness.

'If we don't know the numbers,' said Boss, 'surprise might be our only advantage. Can we get close without being seen?'

'In the Orkneys?' I mocked. 'This is barren grassland. And Clouston's clinic is a seafront building.' I pointed at the darkened landscape outside. The snow was so bright that, despite the hour and the thick clouds, it perfectly delineated the smooth terrain to our right. To our left, the sea looked like a pitch-black pool. 'It will be like two galleons approaching each other.'

Boss exhaled in frustration. 'Then we have no choice but to launch our assault as quickly as possible. Can we go any faster?'

I could not see it happen; we were already going at a frantic speed.

'Yes,' said Caroline. 'We have a good horse.' And she stuck half her body through the window. 'Harris! As quick as you can.'

'On my signal!' added Boss, doing the same on the other window.

We heard strident neighing, the racket of wheels and a man's desperate wails. Forgetting all good manners I shoved Caroline aside and peered through the window.

'That's McGray's cart,' I spluttered, seeing the rickety wagon riding back, towards us. As it passed us I caught a glimpse of the terrified driver whipping his pitiful horse. Clearly, he had dropped McGray and Bob and then fled as soon as he could. What might they have found?

'Is that where we're going?' Boss asked, and Caroline and I rushed to his window.

A lonely cluster of lights glowed amidst the snowed plain. I had to squint to make out the details. It was a wide three-storey building, and all the windows were lit.

'Yes, that's the clinic,' said Caroline, and Boss passed her Jones's derringer.

'If you're a good shot, use it.'

Then the wind brought the sound of screaming voices, male and female.

'*Quicker!*' Boss hissed, and after a single whip the carriage darted like a bullet.

'Barging blindly into a potentially gory skirmish,' I grumbled, shaking my head and producing my gun. 'Better than dreaming of guillotines over my neck . . .'

12

The building grew wider and brighter, and the screaming came with more clarity. I even thought I heard McGray growling in pain.

I wanted to look, but Boss was blocking the window, his gun pointing outwards.

'Stop! *Now!*'

We heard the horse neigh, the carriage slowed down abruptly, and Caroline and I were thrown forwards.

Boss shot twice – at someone or as warning fire, I could not tell. The carriage was still rolling swiftly when he kicked the door open and jumped to the ground.

I stumbled to the door, the carriage bouncing on the snow, and saw several black outlines cut against the glow from the clinic's windows.

'Stay here if you can,' I told Caroline – knowing she'd ignore me – and hopped off.

I ran after Boss, whose frame was the only one I recognized. He shot once, the detonation glowing in the darkness, and I saw a towering shadow fall to the ground.

I shouted, '*Do you even know—?*'

But I could say no more. What I can only describe as a flying ball of fire came straight to me and I had to drop on my chest, the voices and blows now deafening.

'*What the—*'

Another bolt of flames flew at me. I had to recoil and roll on my back, only to feel a searing heat on my shoulder. The snow – *the snow* – was on fire. And so was my right sleeve.

I patted it with my left hand, just as a cackling figure ran my way; a thin, cloaked woman, holding a green-glass bottle that spurt fire from its neck. Behind her I saw McGray's unmistakable overcoat, flashing left and right in a frenzied fight. I barely caught a glimpse, for the woman threw the burning bottle at me and I had to roll on the snow once more.

The bolt exploded inches from my face, blinding me for an instant as I felt droplets of burning oil splatter on my cheek. Instinctively, I plunged half my face in the deep snow, shooting blindly as I grumbled in pain.

I jumped on my feet, still feeling the burn on my skin, and dodged the spots of flames on the snow around me.

The cloaked witch ran to my left, fleeing into the thicker darkness. I could not follow, for to my right McGray was being strangled by a gigantic thug. Without time to think, I pointed at the escaping witch – to where her legs would have been – and shot. Right then I heard McGray gag in pain and I could not even see if I'd hit her. I turned and ran to him, panting.

A few yards beyond, closer to the building, Boss and two orderlies were savagely fighting two beastly men, posted around a second cloaked woman, taller and stouter than the other, with golden embroidery on the trim of her hood.

Again I had just a fleeting sight, for McGray and his bully were enmeshed in a fierce brawl. I tried to aim, but they were rolling on the snow like a ball of yarn. I caught glimpses of a thick, hairy arm, clasping McGray's neck like a boa constrictor, and legs kicking indiscriminate blows.

'*Kill 'im!*' McGray gagged when he saw me. I shot at the ground and the man mechanically looked around, motionless for a split second, only just enough for me to aim at him and shoot.

The bullet hit him in the shoulder. He hollered and gave McGray a mighty kick, sending him face down into the snow, and then staggered towards me.

I shot again but he managed to dodge the bullet and, as if trained alongside Harris, grabbed my wrist with unyielding strength. I dropped the gun but he did not release me; instead he squeezed harder until I heard and felt my bones crack, *truly* crack, sending stabs of pain all along my arm.

I howled, seeing his other enormous hand rise towards my face. I pictured him cracking my skull like he'd done my wrist, but then the man dropped me and I fell on my side. A second later, amidst the crying and shooting, I heard a dull thump on the ground; inches from my aching body, the man's lifeless eyes were wide open. I nearly forgot the pain in my wrist when I saw the small, almost dainty bullet hole in the middle of his forehead.

Behind me came the thumping steps of Harris. I saw the man run past me, frantically pulling the derringer's trigger, perhaps given to him by Caroline, but it had run out of bullets.

McGray was already running to join the main fight, which, to my eyes, was but a frantic succession of blurry shadows. The two remaining thugs defending the tall, cloaked woman, clearly attempting to flee; McGray running to help the thinner orderly, who'd been taking a good beating; another orderly on the snow, dragging himself back to the clinic; the last thug was fighting Boss, who'd lost his gun somehow.

The witch with the golden embroidery saw Harris approach and let out an eerie, high-pitched howl. She then pulled something from within her cloak and threw it at the nearest orderly.

The poor man shrieked in pain; a throttled, agonizing sound I will never forget, and he fell down. I smelled sulphur, the ghastly stench of burning flesh, and heard an unsettling sizzle in the air.

Clumsily I jumped on my feet and ran to them, not knowing what I might do.

The woman raised her hand again, and this time I was close enough to recognize an amber glass vial.

McGray was already covering his face with his forearm, but then the sound of a booming shot filled the air, deeper and louder than all others. I looked at the clinic's gate and, outlined against the inner lights, saw the figure of a plump nurse. She was holding a heavy rifle, shooting at anyone she did not recognize.

I dropped to the ground, for in her eyes I was yet another intruder. So did Boss and McGray, as one of the brutes grabbed the cloaked woman by the waist and carried her away as if she were a beer barrel.

The nurse kept shooting with a deplorable aim, the two men and the witch getting further and further away. Boss, his chest still on the snow, raised both palms.

'I'm here to help! I'm here to—!'

'*He's here to help!*' McGray roared, just as the nurse pointed the rifle at Boss. He crawled up, stumbled along in the snow and retrieved his gun.

I looked at the snowy field, suddenly fearing for Caroline, who had remained in the carriage.

I saw her standing there, paralyzed and grasping the door, her skin so pale it seemed to glow in the dark. Her face, distorted with cold, inexplicable fear, stared at the witch's golden hood.

To my relief, the witch and her two thugs were not going for Caroline. They were now running east, and within a second they were barely discernible in the darkness.

Boss and the nurse kept emptying their weapons in their direction, their eyes equally wild, until they ran out of bullets and all that could be heard were the sea breeze and the waves breaking on the nearby beach.

13

Never had a deep breath felt so glorious, even with that excruciating pain in my wrist.

'Are you injured?' someone asked behind my back. It was Caroline, her eyes fixed on my dangling hand. She still looked ghastly pale, shaking from head to toe, her pupils flashing about, as if out of control.

For some reason, I blushed at once.

'I – I think that man needs you more,' I blurted out, nodding at the orderly who lay in the snow. I could still see smoke oozing from his skin.

Clouston emerged from the building then, and he and Caroline rushed to help the poor man stand. I could only see a side of his neck, all the skin gone and the red, blistered muscle palpitating.

'Mrs Jennings,' Clouston cried, 'the bicarbonate, *quick!*'

Immediately Nurse Jennings rested the rifle on the threshold and ran inside.

Even as he helped the injured orderly, Clouston had a head to nod at Nine-Nails.

'Your sister is fine, but I had to sedate her. You'd better help Mr Frey.'

McGray stood still for a moment, his lips slightly parted, until he let out a long, laboured exhalation. He leaned forwards, resting his hands on his knees as he caught his breath. I had never seen him so relieved. I thought that if I did not talk to him soon, he might burst into tears.

'You heard the doctor,' I said, feigning some sarcasm. 'I need your help.'

Nine-Nails straightened up, and in a blink was back to his hardened self.

'Och, aye. They scratched yer bonnie face?'

'*That damn devil just broke my*—! Oh, never mind. And we need someone to take care of that witches' minion that . . .'

I looked back, but Boss and Bob were already pulling away the dead man's body towards the shadows. As they did so, I saw Boss check his breast pocket with unexpected anxiety, as if fearing he'd lost something. He looked up and saw I was watching him. Immediately he bared his teeth, and his eyes seemed to glow under the lights from the clinic. Overall, he made me think of a hyena dragging carrion to feast in the dark – and I shivered.

McGray patted me on the shoulder, which made me jump, and whispered a sincere, yet very rushed, 'Thanks, youse arrived at the right time.'

'Had they just attacked?' I asked, holding my arm and wincing with the pain. 'We saw your cart rush away.'

'Aye. We got here very soon and asked the orderlies to watch out. If we had nae been here—' McGray shook his head, saying no more, and I saw goosebumps on the back of his neck. 'Come, I'll take ye to a nurse.'

'Thanks,' I said, and then looked at the snow around us, disturbed and splattered with blood and black tar. 'And we'd better sort out this mess too. The local police are most likely to come and ask questions.'

The constables did come to investigate, and we thought it wiser to let the Scot talk to the Scots (also, Nine-Nails was the least injured of the party).

He told the Kirkwall police that we were CID, but had travelled there simply to visit his sister, that we did not have the slightest idea as to the causes and nature of the green fires, and that our conspicuous intervention at the cathedral had been out of 'professional instinct' and a 'genuine concern for the safety of the town'. How he managed to keep a straight face as he told all those flagrant lies, I do not know.

When the chief constable asked him why he'd brought three armed men to a 'family visit', and demanded to know how we'd managed to leave the cathedral without being seen, Nine-Nails replied with sterling. They were about to ask more questions, but as soon as McGray produced some more money, they were gone.

I heard the conversation with my ear pressed against a nearby door. The rest of us had had to hide, for we were in a terrible state: Harris had been shot in the arm and leg (by – well, Boss and me), while I, on top of the unsightly graze on my cheekbone, had a broken wrist. And though McGray had been shot in the shoulder, it had been just a graze he managed to conceal.

Still, our wounds were nothing compared to Arthur's, the poor orderly who'd had acid thrown on the side of his neck. I could only be thankful that we were at a clinic, so the man was treated right away.

Nurse Jennings spent the best part of an hour flushing the acid with ice-cold water, the poor man numbed with laudanum and whisky. They could not even apply unguents or soothing oils for a while; all they could do was to douse the suppurations while rehydrating him with a constant feed of water and beef tea. Even if they could avoid infection, Arthur would have to live with the scar for the rest of his life.

As soon as my own wrist was splinted, I went to see how the man was faring. I found McGray brooding by the foot of the man's bed while a young nurse cleaned the wound. Arthur was sleeping deeply, though frowning, and he was not the only one. McGray's face was ridden with guilt. Here he was, in front of yet another person whose life had been ruined by that blasted coven.

'Damned, ruthless pack of bitches!' he murmured, knowing it was me without even turning.

'This was not your doing,' I said softly, though struggling to keep a straight face before that blistered neck. 'He will know.'

McGray shook his head and snorted. He understood that; however, guilt is anything but a rational feeling.

'Come to us if there's anything at all we can do,' he told the nurse, and stepped out.

I thought he might need some time on his own, so I went to the main dining room, attracted by the smell of breakfast treats.

The room's windows overlooked the road and the sandy beach ahead. The sea was choppy and murky grey, the sky a mass of billowing clouds with only a thin strip of white light along the horizon.

Caroline was already there, seeing how Mrs Jennings and her girls displayed large teapots and mountains of toast, eggs and bacon. They all looked at Caroline with some resentment, and the girl, for once, seemed ill at ease.

'This . . . this is a fine place, ma'am,' she said.

'Of course it is,' the head nurse replied curtly. 'We've damn good staff.'

There was a moment of awkward silence.

'Thank you for the clothes,' Caroline mumbled, and only then did I pay attention to them.

She wore a pale-blue dress, with white lace trimmings and subtle flowers embroidered on the cuffs; much more delicate than the sober, dark attires I knew she preferred.

'It was lucky Miss McGray and I are about the same size,' she added with a coy smile, for Nurse Jennings had not bothered to reply.

Nor would she. The woman simply left the room and urged her girls to follow her.

I knew the reason of their poor manners: here was the young single lady who'd arrived in the small hours, after having travelled – *alone!* – with several men.

And if they looked at Caroline with contempt, I could only imagine the scorn she'd receive were she ever to return to Edinburgh, where people already speculated as to the reasons of her long journeys. She understood this well enough, and seeing her thus dejected, wearing a borrowed dress and with her lip still sore, I felt terribly sorry for her.

'Ignore her, Miss Ardglass,' I said, pouring her some tea. 'A beautiful young woman will always be the cause of—' But as soon as I realized what had come out of my mouth I felt my cheeks heat up. 'I mean . . . of course Nurse Jennings would think that you are beauti— well, not that *I* do not share the opinion of . . . ermmm . . . How do you take your tea?'

She looked equally uncomfortable, surely remembering how her grandmother had effectively thrown her at me to marry.

'Just a splash of milk, please.'

'And I agree with you,' I added swiftly, unable to sit there in tense silence, 'this is a very nice clinic. Doctor Clouston set it up to look after the islands' elderly. He hails from here, so this is his contribution to the place. He also defrays all the costs from his own pocket.'

'That is very generous of him. I am surprised nobody in Edinburgh knows about this place. The good doctor seems to be full of secrets.'

I almost spilled my tea, for Caroline had voiced the very thoughts I'd entertained just a day earlier.

'Aren't we all?' she whispered on, and then sipped her tea, her gaze lost in the dull landscape. I was about to ask what she'd meant, but then McGray barged in.

'Och, nice! I'm bloody starving!'

He sat next to Caroline and began helping himself to all the food at hand. She looked at him with unexpected amusement.

'How d'ye doing, lassie?'

She sighed. 'Well enough, Mr McGray. Thank you.'

McGray ate a full fried egg in one mouthful, looking at Caroline with a strange expression. He even finished chewing before he spoke.

'I'm so sorry about yer nannie.'

Caroline looked up at once. 'How did you—?'

McGray nodded, his eyes all understanding, a warm glow in them.

'I ken auld Bertha adored ye, and she's nae with ye. That can only . . . I'm sorry, that can only mean one thing.'

Caroline had to put her cup and saucer down, her eyes welling tears.

Until then I had not even thought of the woman who'd looked after her since childhood. I did not even remember her name. I felt so silly, yet all I managed to do was produce a handkerchief and hand it to her.

Caroline covered her eyes at once and cried for a moment. It was not a loud display, but a measured, tired flow of tears, somehow much more desolate than desperate weeping.

She wiped her tears with equal poise, and then her features hardened again.

'She was here,' she mumbled. Her voice was somewhat muffled by the handkerchief, but there was also a dark, menacing note we did not fail to spot.

I frowned. 'She? Who?'

Caroline pressed the handkerchief on her face, her hand shaking with wrath.

'The woman who did it,' she hissed. 'The one who came after me when my poor Bertha—'

She could not repress a sob, and yet no more tears came out. Her frown had fixed in a bitter, sinister expression.

Somehow, no more words were needed. At once I pictured the tall cloaked woman she'd stared at from the carriage; the one with the gold-trimmed hood.

I was going to ask further, but Boss and Bob walked in right then and Caroline jumped in her seat. One quick look was enough to let us know she did not want to discuss her tribulations in front of those men. I would not have wanted to either.

Like McGray, they went straight to the food, but the way they devoured, almost with anxiety, tearing the meat with their bare hands, made me far more upset.

Again, Boss noticed I was watching him (he seemed to have a talent for spotting that). And he also saw Caroline still wiping her reddened eyes.

'Has she told you what the hell she was doing here?' he snapped.

'Would you care to measure your—?'

'*Shut yer fucking ill-gab!*' McGray roared over me. 'Don't ye see the lassie's upset?'

Boss chuckled. 'Do I have to remind you who wants you dead?'

'Och, aye!' cried Nine-Nails, his voice an octave higher with sarcasm. 'Cause yer toilet brush tash is such a fuckin' distraction we'd forgotten about the fat coo! *Thanks* – erhh . . . what's yer sodding name anyway?'

'What do you need my name for?'

'So that if I need ye, I don't have to go – *Hey ye, the twat with the tash!*'

'You can call me Boss,' he said – the nickname was not my brainchild.

'*Ha!* In yer fucking dreams. Am calling ye Piff.'

Boss frowned. 'Is that even a word?'

'Dunno. It's what comes to mind when I see yer twat's tash.'

I sighed with impatience. 'Enough of pleasantries. What did you do with the body?'

'Threw him in the sea,' Boss said with chilling nonchalance.

'Just like that?' McGray asked.

'Of course not,' Boss answered. 'We searched his pockets first,' and he nodded at his colleague. 'Show them what we found.'

'Please, call that one Bob,' I told McGray, before we had another argument. The man emptied his baggy pockets. There were a few coins, a packet of cheap tobacco, a pouch with bullets . . . and a little green glass vial.

McGray snatched it at once, looking at it against the light. I rose and went to him for a closer look. The vial was corked and sealed with wax, but there were no tags or markings, only a murky liquid and dark sediments.

'I would not open that here,' I said. 'Not before we inspect it thoroughly.'

McGray, for once, agreed, and shoved the vial in his pocket. He'd have his chance to use it, but not for a while.

'There was some money as well,' Boss said. 'We gave that to the clinic.'

'No guns?' I asked.

'I ken he had one,' said McGray, nodding at his bandaged shoulder. 'But we disarmed the stupid sod soon enough.'

I frowned. 'Only one gun? That seems a tad . . . sloppy for them.'

'They must have thought it would be an easy job,' Caroline said.

'Their *easy* onslaught,' McGray sighed bitterly, 'left almost all of us injured and one poor man maimed for life . . . I don't want to be around when the bloody adders throw their best at us.'

'Which takes us back to my question,' said Boss, staring at Caroline, this time with a disturbing hint of lasciviousness. 'What the hell were you doing here?'

She tilted her head backwards as if the question had been a slap. I too was curious to hear her story, but I did not want the PM's barbarians to question her as if she were a criminal. Fortunately, I did not have to intervene this time.

'I'm afraid that will have to wait,' said Clouston right then, walking briskly into the room. 'There is one more pressing matter we need to attend to.' He stared at McGray and me, his eyes all gloom. 'In fact, the very matter that brought us here. Miss McGray.'

Nine-Nails jumped to his feet, hitting the table and knocking over jugs and cups.

'And you cannot see her!' Doctor Clouston snapped. 'That would defeat the purpose.'

McGray's face went bright red. He clenched his teeth as he grabbed the back of the nearest chair, seemingly ready to throw it in the air.

'*I will not have you wreck this place!*' Doctor Clouston roared, pointing at McGray with a trembling index finger. His booming voice startled us all. I did not know him capable of such display. The doctor himself, once he took a deep breath, seemed astonished.

He rearranged his jacket. 'You can destroy my office, but this clinic is all these people have. And I already have a good orderly who has been scarred for life.'

McGray bit his lip, his blue eyes glowing with wrath, his chest heaving like bellows. We all stared at him, motionless, expecting him to lose control at any moment. Then there was a slow movement.

Though brief and delicate, it was as noticeable as a match struck in absolute darkness – Caroline's hand, moving coyly to reach McGray's forearm. He turned his face to her, almost startled. I feared he'd burst then; slap her or worse. Instead there was a shade of . . . I think it was shame, and he let go of the chair. Once more, he forced deep breaths.

'Is Pansy all right?' he asked in the end, his voice still full of anger.

'Yes,' Clouston said, quite firmly. 'As I told you before. I went straight to her when we arrived. You saw me.'

'She must have woken up,' McGray said.

'Indeed, and she *was* quite distressed. Understandably.'

I spoke before McGray. 'Does she know we are here? That – her brother is here?'

Clouston squinted. 'I . . . I hope not.'

'*Ye hope?*' McGray cried.

'You are not precisely quiet,' I said.

McGray raised a hand as if to strangle me, but again he managed to contain himself.

'Sadly, Inspector Frey is right,' said Clouston. 'When I went to her I didn't mention the presence of any of you, but the truth is—'

He stopped quite suddenly, as if about to choke. For an instant I thought he might burst into tears, and I recalled his heart-felt speech on the ship. He must really care for the poor girl.

'The truth is . . .' He shut his eyes, and gulped. 'I am not certain how *aware* she is of her surroundings. Again, all I can tell is that she is very distressed. I gave her some medication, but only a very small dose. I don't think more laudanum will help, if what you need is to get some sort of . . . declaration from her.'

The very mention of that scheme made us all tense. Bob and Boss, oblivious to Pansy's situation, were the only ones at ease, helping themselves to food.

I frowned. 'Do you think we should still try to question her? Even after this attack? In the best of cases she'll crouch in a corner rocking backwards and—'

'And in the worst?' Caroline interjected, somewhat sickened at my unfeeling expression.

Clouston sighed, looking down. McGray's lower lip trembled, his eyes asking the same question.

'Indeed, doctor,' I said, 'what is the worst that can happen if I press that poor creature? She has heard gunshots.'

'Could she go murderous again?' Boss asked from his side of the table, a slight snigger on his face. McGray hurled himself in his direction, and this time Caroline had to stand up. She and Clouston seized him by the arms and managed to control him.

'I was referring to the trauma that questioning her might cause,' I said, and then remembered I was supposed to question her alone. Doctor Clouston must have read my anxiety.

'She's not had a violent episode in years,' he assured me. Just as he said so, Nurse Jennings stepped in with accusing eyes. I wondered if she'd been listening at the door all along.

'The last time she was upset,' she said, 'was when her brother showed up against the doctor's instructions.'

'*Mrs Jennings, please!*' Clouston snapped, even if we all knew the woman was right. He looked at me then. 'I am certain you'll be safe, inspector.'

I buried my face in my hands. 'Oh, good Lord . . .'

'We will be outside,' Clouston added, 'just in the corridor, should you need – *aid*.'

His voice dropped low at that last word. I did not like it at all.

The corridor to Miss McGray's room was wide and airy, with a view of the snowy plains to the south. Still, each step was a torment, with Clouston to my right and Nurse Jennings to my left, like two gaolers leading me to the gibbet. We had asked McGray to wait downstairs, fearing his nerves might betray him and he'd storm into his sister's room at the first hint of an unpleasant sound.

As if to break the tension, Clouston took my forearm and examined my splint.

'Miss Young did a good job,' he said. 'You shall be completely recovered in no time.'

'How long is *no time*?'

'Assuming it is just the radius and your carpus is fine – five to six weeks.'

'Oh damn!'

Some help I would be. I could not shoot, I could not write . . . I could not even ride a horse without trouble. I'd soon be thanking that, though.

We reached Pansy's room. Clouston stretched his hand to the doorknob, but Nurse Jennings grabbed it first. She nearly dropped the breakfast tray she precariously balanced on her other hand.

'I'll go in first,' she said. 'Make sure she is decent.'

'Make sure she takes her medicine,' said Clouston, eyeing the amber jar next to the teapot.

Nurse Jennings replied with a perfunctory humph, opened the door only enough to get through and then shut it with a slam.

Clouston and I remained behind, staring at our feet in the most unnerving silence. I looked up and down the deserted corridor. This was my chance to talk.

'Now that McGray is not listening,' I said in a low voice, 'you can tell me what you really think might happen.'

He spoke after a moment, though in a barely discernible whisper.

'Knowing her case . . . I'd say it is most likely she will not react to your presence and remain as silent as ever.'

'Indeed,' I said. 'What is the alternative?'

The good doctor raised his chin, his eyes buoyant.

'If she does react . . .' he said, every word considered, 'I do not know what to expect.'

His tone sent a chill down my spine. I instantly remembered the gory details quoted by the PM – mother killed with a fire poker, father stabbed with a kitchen cleaver.

There was no time to say more, for Nurse Jennings opened the door and stared at me with her exasperating little eyes.

'I'll let you in now,' she said, raising her index finger. 'But don't you dare upset the lass or I'll—'

'Oh, do move aside!' I snapped, walking round her. The woman was going to remonstrate, her eyes irate, but I slammed the door shut at once and put the latch on.

I instantly regretted my haste.

14

There I stood, alone in the middle of the wide room, my mind suddenly struck.

I do not know if it was my imagination, or a draught was coming through some unseen crevice in the walls, but a faint sound swirled around me. It reminded me of the murmur one hears from a seashell, only deeper, like a never-ending sigh. And despite the fire crackling in the small hearth, it made me feel very cold.

And there, just a few steps ahead of me, sat Miss Amy McGray, Pansy, the source of all of McGray's disgrace.

How very similar she looked to the first time I'd met her, seated by a window, a little table before her, and wrapped in a light, white dress.

I gulped, suddenly realizing I'd been holding my breath, every muscle in my body tense. I made to take a step, but for an instant my legs did not respond. Never, not even at my moments of greatest peril, had I experienced such paralysis. That must be what a lion tamer feels the first time he stands face to face with his beasts, no meshes or bars in between.

I forced a deep breath, and the room's scent of lavender and chamomile took the edge off my anxiety. My foot finally moved, though I cannot describe the effort that it took.

As I walked round the cushioned armchair, I had a better view of the girl.

There was the same alabaster skin, the same soft jaw, the pointy nose and the thin lips, like those painted on china dolls. Her dark hair looked freshly braided, and her neck, long and slender, was as straight as ever.

Her eyes, however, told a very different story.

They were wide like McGray's, but framed by long lashes, and very dark brown, almost black. She always seemed to stare hard, her pupils fixed on some invisible point in the distance – but not today. I saw that they trembled, as if she could not quite focus them on whichever ghost she was seeking to look at. And fine wrinkles had appeared around them, the skin puffy and darkened. Those were not the shadows caused by a sleepless early morning, but the result of months under constant strain.

I would not tell McGray, but it did seem like her condition was worsening. I was used to seeing her like an empty vessel; now she looked more like a bundle of nerves, precariously held together with pins. Until then, I had never thought that she might live in an eternal, silent torture.

'Good mor—' I cleared my throat, 'good morning, Miss McGray.'

As I expected, she did not answer or even look at me. However, she did seem to know I was there. My words unsettled her further, the tendons on her neck suddenly popping out.

I looked for a place to sit. In her room in Edinburgh there was a second armchair by her little table. Not here. Nobody visited here.

There was a wooden chair against the wall, a basket of haberdashery and unfinished embroidery on top. All the bobbins had the name 'Jennings' scribbled on them. I put the basket on the floor, so I could sit. As I did so, a bundle of needles and a pair of sharp scissors caught a gleam of sunlight. Who left such things within a mad girl's reach?

I brought the chair closer to the table and sat down. Only then did I notice that her hands, clenched on her lap, did not cease to tremble. For the hundredth time, I felt a terrible sorrow for her – she would turn twenty-two in early May, but she'd lived in asylums since she was a child of fifteen. Almost seven years of precious youth spent like this. How many more to come?

I took a deep breath as I looked out the window. Pansy had a privileged view of the front road, the sandy beach and the sea beyond.

'You should be out there,' I said, the words slipping out before I could contain them. 'You should be playing in the snow. Picking your dresses for the coming Christmas balls . . . Telling your brother to stop belching at public functions . . .'

Oddly, I smiled, even if I felt that tears could well have pooled in my eyes.

'Not here,' I mumbled. 'You should not be locked in here – staring at nothing, hearing nothing . . . seeing no one.'

She moved her head a smidgen, turning her face slightly away from me. Her hands seemed to tremble a little more, or it could simply be that I was looking more intently.

Again I swallowed painfully. 'I am sorry you had to listen to . . . all that racket.'

I looked out. The marks of our fight were still visible on the snow. Pansy would have needed but to draw her curtains to see everything that had happened. The poor orderly getting his neck burnt with acid.

'There is something . . . rather unpleasant going on,' I said. 'As you can imagine.'

Could she? I thought. Could she imagine at all? The very question made me shiver.

'I hope you will not mind,' I said, reaching for the pot and pouring myself some tea in her cup. The brew was hot and strong, but barely enough to give me courage.

'We are in danger,' I blurted out, unable to put it in soft words. 'Your brother and I. There are people who want to see us . . .' I took a deep, hissing breath. Suddenly I felt the full weight of the situation. The queen herself and the highest-ranking man of her government; both of them going out of their way, sparing no expense simply to—'

I trembled.

'There are people who want to see us dead.'

Pansy drew in a throttled breath too, and then the seashell sound seemed louder, as if the room were at the edge of a vast void.

'It is so unfair that I come to you,' I said. 'It is so unfair that I ask *you*, of all people, to go through all this again . . .'

She exhaled, her breath the echo of another seashell.

'It is the witches,' I went on. 'Or rather . . . that band of shrewd snakes who call themselves witches. We need to find them.'

Pansy breathed in, lifting her chin, her eyes now fixed on the horizon.

'Lord Joel talked to you, did he not? Before he fled.'

Her chest began to heave.

'You *do* remember him,' I said, unable to contain a note of excitement. 'I know he was your neighbour at the Edinburgh asylum. I was told he read you stories.'

The heave grew more intense. I knew I was going too far too quickly, but I could not help myself.

'He told you the name of the arch-witch. Marigold.' I attempted a smile. 'You wrote it in my note pad! Do you remember? I still have it.'

She looked away from me, but it was not with the usual absence. It was a swift, deliberate movement.

'Did he tell you anything else? Where the witches might go? Where—?'

Then she moved.

Startling me, she grasped the edge of the table with both hands, digging her nails into the polished wood.

How reckless I was. I knew I should stop. I could see the frenzy in her eyes. I could see her heaving chest. And still, I spoke on.

'So Lord Joel *did* tell you something! Did he say where he planned to go after he got rid of the arch-witches? Did he tell you where they might head after he—?'

I could not finish.

Pansy drew a hoarse breath, and then let out the most piercing, most troubled shriek I'd ever heard, coming from the depths of her stomach. I thought it even made the window-pane quiver.

I heard someone pounding the door, and the voices of Clouston and Jennings. I crossed the room in a stride.

'*Stop that!*' I hissed, my face pressed against the door. 'We're fine!'

Right then Pansy's shriek faded. I turned on my heels and the sight sent a prickling all over my spine.

She'd flung herself onto the carpet, to the knitting basket, and she rummaged through it as she growled like a wild cat.

I took a step to her. '*Miss McGray*—'

She arched her back, the gleaming scissors in her hand. She was panting, each exhalation an eerie, throaty hiss, and her dark eyes glowed as if on fire.

I gasped and lifted my palms, forgetting my broken wrist, which sent stabs of pain up my arm.

'Miss – Miss McGray, *please*, put that down.'

My words only upset her further. Her panting became an agitated snort, as she crawled on the floor towards the bed. Again she made me think of a wild cat.

I tried to step closer but she wielded the scissors like a knife. The image of McGray's ghastly stump – where his ring finger had once been – rushed to my mind.

Slowly, like a sinuous snake, Pansy crawled onto the bed, her unblinking eyes fixed on me, her pupils, as well as the sharp scissors, aimed at my chest. She curled up, almost turning her back at me, but remained at an angle where she could keep her gaze on me.

Her breathing grew quicker and louder, as she gradually brought the scissors to herself. By now her hand trembled feverishly. I thought of going back to open the door, but I did not want to take my eyes from her.

'Miss McGray,' I whispered, moving gingerly in her direction, 'I beg you . . .'

She made a stab in the air when she saw me approach, and I had to take a step back.

'Miss McGray, *please* . . .'

She kept aiming at me, the light trembling in her teary, deranged eyes.

Then she moved so quickly her limbs seemed blurred. She turned her back fully to me, drew back the scissors and began jerking her arms in spasmodic blows.

Was she was stabbing at her own legs?

I hurled myself towards her.

'*Stop!*' I howled, just as she turned, her body a shapeless bundle of white cloth. I caught a flashing glimpse of her pale legs, as she lifted them to kick me at my broken wrist with unexpected precision. I shrieked, the pain so excruciating I fell backwards.

Clouston and Jennings were now hammering the door, screaming desperately. As I curled on the floor, clasping my broken wrist, the snip-snip of the scissors filled my ears – quick, sharp and revolting.

I crawled forwards, struggling for air. I heard Pansy's animalistic grunts, the shouting and the battering at the door, and the horrid sound of the blades working at full speed. The gory images that filled my head as I grasped the bed's quilt . . .

Then the door opened with a bang, lock and hinges darting in the air. Nine-Nails stormed in, crossed the room in two strides and pushed me aside.

I fell on my back again as the room filled with people. Nurse Jennings, Clouston, an orderly and another nurse.

Caroline came in too, covering her mouth and looking terribly pale. She never took her horrified eyes from the bed, even when she came to me, knelt down by my side and helped me sit up.

I too looked at the bed, but McGray's broad frame obscured my view. I only saw his back, as he locked his arms around his sister in a tight embrace. Of her I could only see the dark locks of wavy hair cascading over her brother's shoulder.

'Why d'ye do that?' he moaned, his body jerking in between sobs.

Nurse Jennings was the only one who dared approach, for even Doctor Clouston looked shocked out of his wits.

'She's fine,' she said, placing a reassuring hand on McGray's shoulder. Her voice came out with an unexpected motherly tone. 'She just cut her dress. Look.'

Clouston and Caroline rushed there, and they both let out sighs of relief. I did too.

'Why d'ye do that, ye silly?' McGray moaned again, rocking backwards and forwards. At that moment he too looked slightly insane.

Caroline, after taking in a few deep breaths, also rested a hand on his shoulder. 'She needs to change into a new dress,' she whispered. 'Come, let Mrs Jennings take care of that.'

McGray sobbed a couple of times and squeezed Pansy a little tighter, but let her go much sooner than I expected.

Mrs Jennings and the nurse tended to Pansy, the girl now her usual self. Her arms and hands were lax like rags, and as they steered her away, the scissors slid onto the carpet, along with a torn piece of material.

I only saw her eyes very briefly, again wide open, unreadable and staring into nothing.

'I'll get you into that nice pink gown, miss,' Nurse Jennings said soothingly into Pansy's ear. 'It's fresh from the laundry.'

Clouston helped me stand up. I winced, my wrist still throbbing, and we all watched the poor girl leave the room with dreamy steps.

Nine-Nails covered his brow, his knees still on the bed, and he hunched miserably as if someone had suddenly loaded his shoulders with an unimaginable weight. I felt glad that Caroline was there, for her hand on his shoulder appeared to be the only thing that kept him from falling apart. Whether he found her comforting, or simply felt embarrassed to make an even more dramatic display in front of her, I could not tell.

We all remained in silence for a long while, nobody sure what to do next. I was expecting everyone to pounce at me and blame me for the episode. Thankfully, nobody did.

Outside, the clouds had followed their course uninterrupted, until they let through a ray of slightly brighter sunlight. The first items that caught it were the scissors and the piece of cloth on the floor. Clouston rushed to pick up the former.

'Mrs Jennings likes to come here and do her needlework with Amy,' he said, visibly embarrassed. 'She gets the best light in this room and – well, the company is good for the girl.'

'She must never leave such things here,' I snapped. 'The fact that Miss McGray had not touched them before did not mean that—'

I stopped talking then, my eyes drawn to the floor.

'I shall tell her so,' said Clouston. 'I am sure she will . . . erm . . . Inspector, what are you doing?'

I had squatted down and was going through the white fabric strewn on the carpet. There was a long chunk of Pansy's skirts, but also another piece, much smaller; perhaps just a little wider than a shilling.

'What's that?' Caroline asked, and McGray uncovered his eyes.

I lifted the little piece of cloth and stood up to examine it under better light. It was a round piece, with five uneven lobes. Though gashed and frayed at points, it had been cut out with evident care.

Caroline frowned. 'Is that a . . . a clover?'

McGray stood up and came closer, his eyes still reddened. He stared at the piece as I held it on the palm of my hand, and after a moment he gulped.

'It looks like a wee flower.'

15

I placed the unshapely bloom on the table, and Nine-Nails, Clouston and Caroline stared at it in silence.

Caroline instantly showed a quizzical brow. 'The witches like to name themselves after plants or flowers. Marigold, Redfern, Oakley . . .'

'Nettle,' McGray mumbled.

'Could this represent the name of another witch?' Clouston asked.

'Perhaps,' I said, and then looked at McGray. 'Was she well versed in flower names?'

He nodded. 'Aye, she kent her dahlias from her daisies. I'm nae help in that field.'

We all looked at Caroline, but she snorted. 'Why do you expect *me* to know more about flowers? I'd say our best choice at present is Mr Frey.'

She was probably right, but I was not going to admit it. I simply reached for the cut-out.

Clumsily – for I was using my left hand – I rotated the piece, looking carefully at each 'petal'. There were five of them, all of slightly different shape and size, forming a very imperfect circle. I could not tell if those disproportions were deliberate or just the result of Pansy's unsteady hand. And the cut-out had no 'stem' or any other feature that might offer more clues.

'This could be anything,' I concluded. 'I could spend days looking at it and still get it completely wrong.'

'Days are precisely what we don't have,' McGray said gloomily.

'But it *has* to mean something,' Caroline said with unexpected insistence. 'That has to be the reason they attacked this clinic.'

I frowned, piecing the facts together. 'Indeed. They know Pansy was heard conversing with Lord Ardglass. They must fear she knows something about them. Something crucial.'

'Crucial enough to want her dead,' McGray mumbled. 'Where they'd been hiding – or maybe something they think is even worse. Which means . . .'

There was a moment of tense silence, broken only by a very worried Clouston.

'Do you think – they might attack again?'

McGray looked as guilty as if he'd attacked the clinic himself. He could only nod.

'When?' Clouston said, his mouth dry.

I had to speak for Nine-Nails. 'Very soon, I'd expect. Maybe as soon as the sun goes down.'

Clouston let out a short breath, bringing a hand to his forehead.

Caroline turned to McGray. 'Your sister cannot stay here.'

'And my other patients and my staff?' Clouston demanded. 'Should I remove everyone?'

McGray stroked his stubble. 'Am so sorry, doctor. Aye.'

'These people have nowhere else to go!' Clouston cried.

'It does not have to be for long,' said Caroline. 'It is Miss McGray they are after. Most likely because of that.' She nodded at the cloth flower. 'If we take her away, noticeably enough for the witches to know, I doubt they will take the trouble to keep guard on this place for long.'

'They did that with your late father,' I said.

'Aye,' McGray added. 'But they were well organized back then.' He looked at Caroline. 'The bit that worries me, lassie, is this *noticeably enough* part.'

Caroline nodded. 'I am not suggesting we parade your sister across Kirkwall with a torch and a banner. We can leave at night, after the clinic has been vacated. That will make the departure obvious enough.'

'But—'

'Two carriages,' she interjected. 'Two parties. One boards one steamer, one boards another, and then we go on different routes.'

Nine-Nails was raising an eyebrow. 'Yer so good at this ye scare me.'

'I have been in hiding for the past ten months, Mr McGray. And before that, I spent years sneaking into the asylum to visit my father.' She said all that with a clear note of pride.

'That would work ideally for me,' said Clouston, forcing himself to come to terms with all this. 'I think we can accommodate a good number of patients in the town, but not all. If we go separate ways I could take the remaining ones, and the poor boy Arthur, to a colleague's hospital in—'

'Don't tell us,' said McGray. 'Do what the lass said, and take Pansy with youse. She'll be safer that way. We will take the other ship and continue our . . .' he laughed bitterly, 'witch hunt.'

The plan laid out, the rest of the day was a busy blur. Doctor Clouston sent at least a dozen messages to the local parish, to the clinic's suppliers and to relatives of his staff, beseeching them to look after some of his patients. Meanwhile, residents, nurses and orderlies packed their valuables and essentials. Then, from noon until the early evening, there was a constant exodus on the main road, hired carriages taking people away, only to come back for more. Caroline offered her battered cart and her towering servant for the task, and McGray spent most of his time helping patients on and off.

I too offered to help, but McGray's reply was, 'If yer sodding useless with both hands . . .'

Instead of arguing I decided to have a much deserved bath and shave, if only to soothe my shattered nerves. It turned out to be a terrible decision, for I'd never yielded a shaving blade with my left hand; also, I could not keep my eyes from the white cloth flower, attempting – with no success at all – to see if I could read something in its shapes.

By the time I was done with my calamitous grooming, the sun was already setting – I could not believe how much shorter the days were this far north – and the clinic was almost deserted.

I walked through the silent corridors, pieces of paper and string and packing straw dotted all over the floor. All the fires had been extinguished, so the air was as cold as the outside. I was glad I'd brought my thickest overcoat.

Doctor Clouston was waiting at the entrance hall, lit only by the dim light of an oil lamp. The man looked at the airy chamber with nostalgia.

'You shall be back very soon,' I told him. 'You and all your patients.'

He nodded, but then struggled to swallow and the poor man had to look away, his eyes misting up. I felt so terribly guilty. This little clinic might be the crowning jewel of his career, his ultimate contribution to his hometown; and now, in a single day, we had forced everybody out.

After a moment a second light came from the staircase. It was Mrs Jennings.

'Miss McGray is ready, sir.'

Caroline came beside her, wrapped in a dark red cloak, the hood resting on her shoulders.

'Is Harris not back yet?' I asked.

'He is,' said Caroline, pointing at the window, through which we could see the silhouette of her black horse. 'We only have to wait for Mr McGray to come back from the harbour, if we are to leave at the same time.'

I nodded, and no more words were said. We simply waited, our nerves palpable, with nothing to do but watch how the evening grew ever darker. How I despise such moments; too early to move on, yet too late to do anything of use.

After a while I reached for the hunter flask, still in my breast pocket, and offered it to Doctor Clouston. He did not bother to use the silver cups, but swigged directly from the flask, and I followed suit. Right then we saw the hired carriage appear in the distance.

'I'll fetch Miss McGray,' said Nurse Jennings, climbing the stairs.

Clouston opened the door himself, a chilly draught whistling through the hall, and McGray appeared soon enough.

'All yer patients are safe on their ship,' he said, and then snatched the flask from my hand and had a long drink. 'I paid the crew more than enough to take youse wherever ye say. Don't let the rascal squeeze more money out o' ye.'

Clouston nodded. 'Thank you, Adolphus. Can you . . . can you do me a favour?'

''Course, doctor.'

Clouston pulled out a hefty envelope. It must have contained a letter at least a dozen sheets long. 'Please see that this reaches Miss Smith and Doctor Harland. These are my instructions, given . . . my unexpected absence.'

McGray received the envelope with no hesitation. 'Consider it done. It's the least I can do for youse.'

'Where are the PM's men?' I asked.

'Piff's waiting in the carriage. The other sod is with Captain Jones, just to make sure he doesnae leave without—'

He said no more. Pansy was coming down the stairs now on the arm of Mrs Jennings. Like Caroline, Pansy was wrapped in a long cloak, hers a very dark grey. Her hood was already pulled up, concealing the upper half of her face. Amidst the dim light and the dark fabric, her pale chin looked like that of a walking corpse.

Nine-Nails went straight to her and even raised both arms to embrace her, but then the nurse's cold stare stopped him.

'Can I?' he mumbled.

Mrs Jennings squinted, casting him a suspicious stare. 'Aye, but quickly. You don't want to smother her.'

With a tenderness unimaginable in a man his size, he cradled the girl's face in his hands (I wondered if she felt the empty space where his severed finger would have been), and then stooped to kiss her gently on the forehead. I wanted to look at her reaction, but at that moment McGray was the only one close enough to see her face.

'I'll see ye soon,' he whispered. It looked as though he intended to say more, but then Nurse Jennings pulled the girl towards the exit.

Caroline stood next to her for a moment, as she pulled up her own hood. The two young ladies were of very similar height and complexion, which only worked to our advantage. I remembered that once, from a distance, even McGray had taken one for the other.

Doctor Clouston lit two small oil lamps. He gave one to me.

'Mr Frey,' he said, rather earnestly, 'it has been a pleasure.'

I even felt a shiver. 'I – I say the same, doctor.'

He then went to McGray and very discreetly passed him a little bottle, which I knew contained laudanum.

'For the journey,' he whispered. McGray saw the label and then looked at the doctor, his eyes unexpectedly misty. 'Good luck, Adolphus.'

I nearly let out 'Oh, nobody is going to die!' but thought better. This was not the time to tempt fate.

McGray offered an arm to Caroline, while Clouston did the same for Pansy. And then, in a slow, grim procession, we all walked into the darkness.

16

The two carriages rode side by side, the racket of hooves and wheels the only sounds in the oppressive air.

We shared our carriage with Boss, but the man only made us more anxious, watching out the window, breathing noisily and keeping his finger on the trigger of his gun. Throughout the ride, McGray watched his sister's carriage, barely blinking, and Caroline cast wary looks to the left and right windows.

Despite the tension, we made it to the harbour without incident. Clouston's carriage, with Pansy and Nurse Jennings, stopped before ours, for their steamer was the first one along the pier.

I saw McGray straining his eyes, hoping to catch one last glimpse of his sister, but the night was far too dark.

We rode on, almost to the very end of the pier, where Captain Jones was already waiting for us, one of his deck boys holding a bright lantern. Bob, his gun sheathed but quite visible, stood next to them.

'We'll have two additional passengers on the way back,' said McGray as soon as he alighted. 'The wee lass and that large lad.'

Harris, struggling to climb down with his injured leg, only grunted.

'Three,' Caroline corrected.

Captain Jones melted as soon as he saw her, rushing to kiss her hand, but McGray did not give him time to pay her any compliments.

'Three?' he repeated.

'Yes,' said Caroline. 'I can't leave this horse.'

Bob laughed mockingly between his teeth.

'I – I don't think we have the space, lassie,' said the captain, but Harris was already untying the harness. 'Am sorry, but—'

'It's a Carthusian,' she insisted, taking off her glove to pat the horse's neck. 'A pure Spanish horse. He's worth a small fortune.'

'We need to go now,' Boss pressed. 'The hell with the horse.'

She appealed to McGray. 'Tell them he must come.'

Nine-Nails, a horse enthusiast since his childhood, looked at the animal with obvious conflict. As if to show off, the horse shook his elegant, muscly neck, so dark we could only see the shimmery outline of his mane.

'Lass, I ken what ye mean. It's a lovely beast, but—'

Caroline took a tiny step towards him.

'I was going to give him to you.'

Never have I seen so many faces turn in the same direction as if perfectly choreographed. Also, never had I felt such a sudden burst of inexplicable fire in my stomach.

McGray's jaw had dropped. 'Ye what?' he asked, in a squeal most unusual in him.

Caroline lowered her face, looking at McGray from the corner of her eye. She'd blushed deeply, noticeable even in the dim light, and her voice was suddenly soft and shy.

'I didn't – I didn't want to tell you like this but . . . I know my father killed your last horse, and he made you go through an unbearable ordeal. It is only fair.'

I nearly shouted, 'He made *me* go through an unbearable ordeal too!' My nose, for instance, was still slightly bent. I had to shove my hands into my pockets and dig my nails into my leg to contain my outburst.

McGray, still open-mouthed, kept looking alternatively at Caroline and the horse, his eyes glowing with disbelief.

'I got him in Seville,' Caroline mumbled. 'Six years old. Very poised and tempered as you can see.'

McGray was so impressed he barely noticed when Harris put the tether in his hand.

'How are ye, laddie?' he said, patting the horse's thick neck with pure glee. Suddenly his eyes glistened like a child's at Christmas, and very, very briefly, he looked his real age – that is, one year younger than me. 'Yer a good laddie! What's his name?'

'Onyx.'

'Och, why d'youse give those snooty shitty names to horses? Am calling 'im Inky.'

'Oh, dear Lord!' Caroline and I grumbled, with identical tones and grimaces.

'If you call him Inky, you cannot have him,' Caroline said.

'*Och nae!* Ye cannae take him back now. I'll fight ye for—'

'Are you done now?' I asked loudly. 'We have places to go.'

McGray simply laughed. 'Are ye sulking 'cause ye didnae get a pressie?' I could not think of an answer, but fortunately McGray turned to Captain Jones and barked at him. 'Are ye deaf? Make room for my horse! And if ye don't find it, we can throw *ye* overboard.'

A new horse and laudanum were just the balm McGray needed. He locked himself in his cabin and we heard nothing from him (other than his mighty snoring) until we docked at our final destination.

Onyx – for I refuse to call him *Inky* – was accommodated below deck. Harris would look after him, and the engine boys were only too happy to assist him. The horse exuded enviable serenity, like he'd done the previous night as we fought the pair of witches.

Boss took charge of the ship – there was nothing we could do about it – and we sailed north. Though the night was downcast, the waning moon shone brightly through the clouds, and the air itself was unusually clear, making it impossible to hide our position. After cursing the good weather, we had to go north for several hours, to make sure no one in the isles knew whether we turned east or west.

Needing some fresh air, I wrapped myself in my overcoat and went to the deck. I stood by the prow, breathing in the cold, salty air, and watching how our ship broke the waves. Despite the Arctic cold, the scene could not have been more peaceful or the landscape more beautiful. Perhaps it was the threat of impending death that made me look at things with renewed pleasure.

Clouston's steamer, which had set off a while before us – no equine conundrums there – could still be seen in the distance, quite a few miles ahead. I wondered where he might be taking Pansy. Would they even remain in Scotland? I knew the doctor had colleagues in the north and south of England.

Just when I thought how much safer they'd be without us knowing, the little light of their ship became lost in the distance, beyond the horizon. I felt somewhat unsettled when that happened.

I blinked a few times, hoping to see them again, but then I thought I heard the caw of a raven.

I looked in every direction, but found only the greys and blacks of the vast sea. The northernmost isle, Hollandstoun, was but a black line on the horizon, its lighthouse beam coming and going at slow intervals, as if floating in mid-air. It must be my nerves making me hear things, I told myself;

no raven, no matter how well-trained, would venture so far into the sea.

After a few minutes the cold became unbearable, so I headed back to the galley.

As I did so, I spotted a small golden spark floating on the other side of the steamer.

It was the lit end of a cigarette. At first I thought it was McGray, but then remembered that I'd just heard him snoring mightily in his cabin. I drew closer and very soon realized it was Boss.

Leaning on the gunwale, he was holding a small piece of paper, staring intently at it. The wind made it flick, and I recognized the characteristic gloss of a photograph.

Boss was staring at someone's portrait.

I only caught a blurry glimpse, but I could swear I saw the narrow shoulders and wavy hair of a lady.

Boss saw me then, for once startled, and he moved at outstanding speed. He straightened his back, shoving the photograph into his breast pocket.

'Feeling anxious?' I asked, instantly regretting my mockery.

Boss looked at me, incensed and grinding the cigarette between his teeth. I had seen that same gesture; the eerie blood-shot eyes, the bare teeth. That was the face he'd shown right after the attack, when I caught him searching his pocket as if fearing he'd lost something – that photograph, surely.

'Not as anxious as you ought to be,' he answered, a clear note of menace in his voice. Instinctively, I moved a few steps from the gunwale.

'Missing your family?' I asked, nodding at his pocket, but he did not reply. Nor did he move. My teeth chattered, no matter how tightly I was wrapped in my coat. Boss, on the other hand, seemed at perfect ease in a much lighter garment.

His stony behaviour only piqued my curiosity beyond good sense.

'Do you even have a family?' I asked again.

'Piss off,' he spat, far tenser than I thought the situation merited. Had I just touched a delicate nerve? I was going to enquire further, but then he cast me a blood-curdling stare while he stretched his thick hands. He seemed ready, truly ready, to throw me overboard.

'You must excuse me,' I said, feigning calmness. 'I am English. We do not handle silence well.'

He simply snorted.

'Former military?' I asked, taking the conversation away from his photograph.

He shrugged and talked with the cigarette between his lips. 'A campaign or two.'

'Pulled out of the army by politicians?' I probed. 'I am sure the pay will be ten times better.'

He took his time to reply. 'The assignments can be ten times worse.'

I nodded. 'I should know about it. If someone had told me last Christmas that this year I'd be hunting so-called witches and attempting to procure a medium for Queen Victoria . . .'

Boss blew out smoke. 'And you seem to have achieved nothing yet. For either task.' The way he smiled at me then was unsettling. 'It may well be down to *me* to take care of you and your idiotic colleague with my own hands. What does it feel like to meet your executioner face to face?'

Again, he opened and closed his fists, as if already preparing for the task.

I could not reply, not only because of his sadistic gesture, but also because he was partly right. We had achieved nothing so far. Nothing. I vowed to talk to Caroline as soon as she woke, and pray that Lady Anne would manage to gather some information. My fate and McGray's were in the hands of those women.

Boss went on smoking in silence, his eyes lost in the sea ahead.

I wondered how much he must be hiding; how much dirty work he might have done for Lord Salisbury; how many secrets – horrible secrets – he must be keeping. And I also wondered how much I might be able to infer . . .

'It must be difficult,' I said. 'Working in the shadows of the PM. Cleaning up after him. Not even being able to tell people your own name.'

Boss ruffled his moustache and said no more. He remained serene, unreadable, as if hovering in a limbo that was untouchable for people like me. No wonder he'd been chosen by the PM. And still . . . my looking at the photograph had definitely thrown him off balance.

The night went a shade darker then. We both looked back and saw that the lighthouse had disappeared behind the horizon.

Boss threw his cigarette to the sea. 'Time to tell the little captain to turn.'

'Are we going east?' I asked as Boss walked way, but he did not even acknowledge my question.

I saw him move away, a dark bale of valuable secrets. He stopped for an instant and I noticed he drew a hand to his coat, to ensure the photograph was still safe in his pocket.

And then he walked on.

17

As expected, that night I also dreamt of guillotines, in manners I prefer not to describe here.

I was only too glad when the steam whistle woke me the following morning, and as soon as I got dressed I looked for Caroline. She was not at the galley, where I found only the towering Harris. The man was polishing a gun, which looked minute in his broad, roughened fingers. For the first time I had a good look at his scalp tattoos; twisted, thorny brambles, knotted like Celtic designs. I could almost have called them beautiful, but the ink was old, the edges blurry as if traced on damp paper. He caught me staring at them, but did not seem to mind.

'Have you seen Miss Ardglass?' I asked him. Harris nodded and made some guttural noises, pointing to the deck.

I went there and found that the morning was surprisingly pleasant. The air was not frosty but crisp, and the sky glowed in a very pale blue. The only clouds were clustered over the port side, towards the prow, blocking the rising sun and only letting through a silver lining. That meant we were travelling down the west coast, along the narrow Sea of the Hebrides, with patches of rocky land on both sides.

Those views were simply striking: an undulating coastline of dark, jagged cliffs, the sharp rocks contrasting with the smooth edges of blindingly white snow. And beyond, blurry and milky in the morning haze, were the outlines of many gentle mounds, all barren and frozen.

It felt as though we were at the edge of the world, hundreds of miles from everything and everyone. No wonder Caroline had decided to take her breakfast outside.

Captain Jones, visibly used to entertaining passengers, had had his boys set a little table and a chair for her, together with a tea set – all heavy pewter, so the wind would not blow the pieces away.

On top of her hood, cloak and thick leather gloves, Caroline was wrapped in a furry blanket made of rabbit skins. Her lip and the graze on her cheek had recovered remarkably quickly, and she sat drinking her tea with elegant composure.

As I approached I noticed a glow in her eyes I had never seen before, her dark brown irises flickering as if they wanted to take in every detail of the landscape. She looked peaceful, even placid, and without her hardened façade her features looked twice as beautiful.

I was tempted to walk away and leave her be, pressing as my questions were, but she felt my presence and turned her head to me. We both flushed.

'Good – good morning, Miss Ardglass,' I said after clearing my throat.

'Good morning, Mr Frey,' she answered, instantly tightening her jaw. Her eyes looked cunning again.

'So Boss decided to take us west,' I said.

'Yes. Captain Jones will take us up the River Clyde to Glasgow. That will confuse the harpies.'

She pronounced the last word with burning rage. I felt so sorry she should be consumed by such murky feelings.

'I had never sailed the Hebrides before,' I said. 'It is stunning landscape.'

She reached for her tea. 'Perhaps you can come back . . . when this is over.'

I laughed, all bitterness. Life beyond the coming Christmas seemed more unreachable than the snowed cliffs on the horizon. She, on the other hand, seemed quite used to that kind of strain.

'How is Mr McGray?' she asked.

'Stupefied with laudanum. Enough to last the rest of the trip.'

'Seasickness? But it is so calm today.'

'His case is acute.'

'How acute?'

'*Acute*. Believe me, only being knocked down with opiates will do.'

She showed a side smile. 'I almost envy him.'

I sighed. 'I do not. At all. I'd never trade my own tribulations for his.'

I wish I had not said that. Caroline frowned, surely reminded of her own misfortunes – far greater than anything I'd ever had to endure.

We stared at the landscape in an uncomfortable silence, both plunged in melancholy, the rocky, icy horizon a very good reflection of our mood. We said nothing, nor even moved, until one of the deck boys brought me a second chair and a pewter mug to share the tea.

I thought I'd better get to the point. This encounter was proving far too awkward.

'Miss Ardglass,' I said, 'you know there are a good deal of questions I must ask you. Where you have been, how you came to know that Miss McGray was in the Orkneys, how much you know about the coven and – gosh, I do not know where to start.'

She frowned. 'I thought Mr McGray would also want to hear this.'

'I'd much rather we spoke without him first. I want to focus on the facts. McGray will only ask you about witchcraft, curses, amulets . . .'

'It may not harm you to learn a thing or two about them,' she said with a sombre tone. 'That is, if you want to outsmart those blasted women.'

She closed her eyes. I wondered if she'd be recalling the terrible events from January, or the death of her dear Bertha, or perhaps something else I did not even know yet.

I spoke soothingly. 'If you ever had a chance to be rid of them, this is it. We . . .'

Caroline raised a hand, bidding silence, her eyes still closed. I wished she stopped refusing my help. There was no indignity in that.

'It is a long story,' she said at last. 'I'd better go to the very start.'

She took a deep breath, rubbed her face and poured herself more tea, as if priming herself for quite a journey.

'It all began last summer. I was in Seville, hiding from them. Spain was the nearest country on the Continent which I'd never visited with my father as a child. France, Germany, Belgium – they all reminded me of him. Those years were the happiest of my life, so it would have been far too painful to walk down the same streets and the same squares without him. One day, an odd message arrived. Somebody had telegrammed me a single word: *Vinegar.*

'I tried to trace the sender, but the telegraphers only managed to tell me it came from somewhere in England. You can imagine how stressed I was. That telegram could not be a random thing. I tried to look for some hidden meaning; an anagram perhaps, but to no avail.

'A few days later a letter arrived. The stamp was from England, but there was no sender's address, and when I opened the envelope the sheet was blank. I knew what it meant; I had already studied a few "witchcraft" books. When I scorched the letter with a candle, the writing began to appear. I'll never forget how scared I was. I was trembling so much I nearly burned the paper.

'The letter claimed to be from *friends*. I came to call them "The Messengers". They told me they knew of my sorrows, that they felt for me, that they too had hated what they called "Marigold's coven". They had wanted out for years, but were too afraid to say so; some of them had had their tongues cut out by the lead witches. They only managed to flee after you and Mr McGray killed the arch-witches, Redfern and Marigold. Now they had gathered in a secret place, like others had done elsewhere; tiny factions, each with their own agenda. The Messengers said they could help me; rid me of the – Ardglass curse. But for that I needed to help them too.'

'*Help them?*' I cried. 'How?'

'They needed something from the Continent. Something they could not obtain by themselves.'

'Did you accept? Did you meet them? Did they—?'

Caroline raised her hand again. 'They never really asked whether I accepted or not. The letter simply ended by telling me I'd receive little parcels; that further messages would be written on the inside of the wrapping paper, also in invisible ink.'

'You used that same paper to send us—'

'Yes, but I will get there in a moment. The parcels *did* arrive, each giving me only a part of the main message, and in disarray and little codes. Not terribly complex, but only understandable if one had all the pieces together.'

'I see. What did they want you to do?'

'They sent me to a small town called Amorbach.'

'Bavaria,' I mumbled, recalling my conversation with Lady Anne. 'What for?'

'They wanted me to steal a book from the abbey.'

'A . . . witchcraft book?'

'I thought so at first. I gathered that those witches had no means to travel there, and even if they did, I doubt they would have been welcome. I remember most witches were unostentatious countrywomen, and that abbey is now at the core of the Leiningen principality. They would have been kicked away the minute they appeared.'

'So you simply went there? Did you not think it was a trap?'

'Oh, I did. But I was also curious. I *had* to know why they needed a book hidden so far away.

'So I headed to Amorbach taking every precaution – Jed and Bertha were always with me and we never travelled at night. Once there, getting into the abbey was very easy; almost enjoyable.

'I simply acted out what I really was: a wealthy young lady travelling with her nanny and a servant, escaping tribulations at home. I pretended to be interested in history and architecture – which I am – and my German is quite fluent, so it was easy to befriend the locals. Very soon there were old *Herren* fighting to give me tours around the abbey, which also ensured I'd never be alone in there. I found the book quite quickly and simply took it. I remember Bertha hid it underneath her coat; the bulge was so obvious, but all eyes were on me. A few days passed and nobody even noticed it had gone missing.'

'What was it?' I asked, on the edge of my seat.

Caroline shrugged. 'It appeared to be nothing; a very old visitors' log, all the pages scribbled on. Something else must have been encoded within.'

'Did you try—?'

'Rest assured I tried *everything*. I examined every single page very carefully; I looked for hidden scratches, I saw the sheets against the light,' she cleared her throat, 'I . . . even looked under the leather binding.

'The only thing I didn't try was scorching the pages to see if there was any invisible ink. I still had to deliver the book, and I didn't want them to think I'd been searching. As I told you, I didn't know how much I could trust them.'

'Very wise. From what you say, I gather you are no longer in possession of the book.'

'No. I was tempted to flee and keep it, so that I could try to find out more.'

'But . . .?'

'After all I've seen them do, I preferred not to. I didn't know what they might do if I didn't oblige, so I gave it to them.'

My heart skipped a beat at that, and I nearly fell off the edge of my chair when I spoke. 'So you *do* know where they are?'

Caroline sighed. 'No, sorry. I should have told you this before. I have never met them.'

I frowned. 'So how did you deliver the book?'

'They must have had someone following me, even if we'd been watching our backs so carefully. One day I came back to my lodgings and the keepers told me I'd received another parcel – hand-delivered by some local boy. It had another message, asking me to return to England. The Messengers said they would find me.'

'And did they?'

'Yes. I stayed in Dover for a week, and a parcel arrived soon enough. They told me to leave the book under my bed and move to different accommodation. I asked Jed – rest in peace – to keep an eye on the place, but he saw nothing.'

I shook my head. 'Wait. This Jed you keep mentioning . . . he was your previous manservant, right? Is he dead too?' Caroline nodded, looking down. 'Gosh, how did it—?'

She covered her eyes with a shaking hand. I instantly cursed my tongue.

'I will get there,' she sighed, clearly postponing that part of the story for as long as she could. 'We waited in Dover for another week or so. I thought my dealings with them were over; I even enjoyed those days. We were already thinking of leaving – when a new parcel arrived.' Caroline shuddered at the memory. 'Just brown paper and jute strings, and yet such a hideous thing to behold. You cannot imagine how I felt. Bertha told me I screamed like an eagle.'

'Indeed, I cannot imagine,' I said. 'What did the – Messengers want from you?'

Caroline bit her lip. 'They . . . they wanted me to watch Queen Victoria.'

'*What?*' This time I nearly knocked the table over. Caroline had to hold the teapot in place. 'Did they tell you about Prince Albert? That the queen wanted them to help her to talk to the dead?'

'No, but that was one of my guesses. Either that, or that the witches did murky jobs for her; some life-lengthening brew or something worse. Whatever it was, the Messengers swore that it would be the last errand they'd ask me to do; that after that I could return to my normal life.' She sneered. 'Or whatever is left of it.'

'So you accepted.'

'I had no choice. And it was not a strenuous task. I simply had to go to Windsor and watch the castle. They told me which house on which street would offer the best view, and even which specific tower to watch. All I had to do was to inform them as soon as I saw green flames.

'The following day they sent me a bird. A magpie. The cage appeared at my hotel with my name on it. The bird was trained to return to them, so I should simply release it the very instant I saw green fires, or – well, kill it if I'd seen nothing by Christmas Day. I would not even need to write a note.'

'And did you see the green beacon?'

'Yes . . . the . . .'

Her eyes misted up. She tried to blink the tears away but did not quite manage. I clumsily looked through my pockets, but found no handkerchief. By then Caroline was wiping her tears with her sleeve.

'The night I saw the flames for the first time was the night we were discovered.'

'Discovered? By whom?'

Even as I asked the question I knew the answer. I recalled Caroline's horrified face back at Kirkwall, when she saw the thugs carrying the cloaked witch away.

I raised my chin. 'You were followed by the same witches who attacked the clinic, were you not?'

'Yes. I saw that damn woman with golden thorns embroidered on her hood. I saw her at the Orkneys and I also saw her at Windsor. Back there I –' Caroline gulped, 'I saw her slit the landlord's throat without even flinching. I . . .'

I gave her a moment, for she seemed quite disturbed, her pupils flickering as if she could not stop seeing the ghastly scene.

'Who are they?' I asked as soon as she seemed less strained. 'From what you tell me, the women who attacked us cannot be the ones who asked you to steal the book.'

'No. In fact the Messengers warned me about a coven they called "The Marigolds"; the women who used to be closest to their dead elders. The most ruthless ones too. I was told that I must flee if I ever saw them.'

'How were you supposed to recognize them? To tell them apart from other witches, I mean.'

'The Messengers said no other coven was after me. If I saw any witch – and as you know, I can very well recognize them by now – I could safely assume they'd be the Marigolds.'

I nodded. 'And . . . they *did* come.'

'Yes. That was the night both Jed and—'

She gulped and said no more, pressing her sleeve against her eyes. I raised a hand, tempted to pat her on the shoulder, but that would have been extremely forward.

'I am very, *very* sorry,' I said after a while. 'I wish I had known. I do apologize if I have been curt, or—'

'You couldn't possibly have known,' she said. 'And nobody's death will ever change how curt you can be.'

We both chuckled. A welcomed relief, before we delved into the murkier waters.

'Excuse me if I don't tell you the details,' she said. 'You only need to know that I managed to get away, release the damn bird and give Bertha a proper burial.'

I nodded, feeling her pain. 'It always helps, does it not? Having a place to mourn one's departed.'

Caroline attempted a smile. 'I read in a witches' book that there is a link between souls and their resting places. You may not believe in any of that, but – right now I choose to do so.'

We remained silent for a moment, hearing only the breeze and the waves breaking against the ship. It almost felt as though we were paying our respects to the dead.

I wished I didn't have to continue the questioning, but I had to.

'And I suppose that was not the end of it,' I said.

Caroline shook her head. 'Not at all. I'd no sooner buried Bertha when I received yet another blasted parcel. Only this one was delivered by Harris in person, and it did contain something crucial other than the wrapping.'

'The tar to produce the green flames?'

'Exactly. A gallon of their best recipe. I cannot believe how intensely it burns. In that note the Messengers told me that Miss McGray was in danger; that I must warn you, and—' Quite unexpectedly, Caroline covered her face with both hands, as if finally overwhelmed by all her burdens. She shook her head again, wiping a renewed wave of tears. 'You know the rest.'

I nodded and gave her time to finish her tea, cold as it was by now.

'Was it then that you met tall, bald Harris?' I asked. 'Is he – one of the witches' men?'

'His father was. And from what he has been able to convey, his mother was a witch. One of them apparently did something that upset the Marigolds and they took revenge on him. Harris must have been only a child when they cut his tongue.' Caroline shivered. 'I do not know what might have become of his parents after the witches mutilated him.'

'I assume he does not know where the witches are,' I said. 'The Marigolds or the Messengers.'

'No. I did ask him, but he told me in notes – his writing is quite rudimentary – that he was sent away for protection; that he has lived up and down the country all his life, never settling anywhere.

'I can only assume that this new coven, the Messengers, recruited him and, given his history, he must be all too happy to help them.'

'That is a sad story,' I mumbled.

'Indeed.'

I sat back, stroking my chin and tying the loose ends in my mind.

'May I ask when that was? The green fire at Windsor, I mean.'

'The third of December,' Caroline said at once. 'I will never forget that date.'

I counted the days in my head. 'From what you say, that must have been the first time Queen Victoria attempted to contact the witches.'

'The first time? Do you mean she did it again? Didn't any of the witches go to her?'

'No.'

Caroline looked puzzled. 'I thought that was the reason the Messengers wanted me to watch. I thought they could not do so themselves because they feared the Marigolds or perhaps other witches would be expecting them; that they feared they'd be attacked . . . like I was.'

'No witch has contacted Queen Victoria,' I repeated, and went on to tell her our entire ordeal, from the PM's dreadful visit. 'Her Majesty,' I concluded, 'knows that we killed the arch-witches. She now wants us dead; McGray and me.'

Caroline shook her head. 'Why would the Messengers or the Marigolds *not* go to the queen? Why go through so much trouble and then do nothing?'

'Excellent question. And that German book you mentioned . . . Everything sounds so . . . disconnected.'

I exhaled, and then remembered the three pieces of brown paper I still carried in my luggage.

'Did you keep their messages?' I asked.

'The wrappings? No . . . well, not all of them. Why?'

'We might, just *might* be able to deduce where those sheets came from. Where they were manufactured. I did something similar on the case of Good Mary—' I stopped myself. I was famous for telling that story over and over like – in McGray's words – a senile grandpa.

'Good Mary Brown?' Caroline asked, her eyes opened wide. 'The black widow who poisoned a dozen husbands after—?'

'Getting life insurances for them,' I completed.

'Yes! I remember reading it in all the papers. Were *you* the one who caught her?'

I could not help straightening my spine, a smug smile forcing itself onto my lips.

'Why – yes. Did you not know?'

Caroline grinned. 'Not at all!' She pressed a hand on the teapot. 'We are going to need a fresh brew. *That* is a story I would very much like to hear.'

DIARY – 1830

Whilst at Ramsgate I formed a liaison with a Young woman – I find in my acts of Connection a deficiency of a wholesome vigour – Thinking that possibly some return of Stricture (if ever there had been one) might be the cause I applied to Dr Courtenay.

[...]

I continued to consult him until the end of February, he orders me to be electrified at Partington, I undergo a course of electricity.

18

We made it to Glasgow well into the night, just as the weather began to turn for the worse.

The busy dockyards, with their jungles of masts and funnels, were lit by the glowing windows of the neighbouring warehouses, where I knew there'd be men, women and children working until the small hours.

We docked with some trouble, given the wind. Then, Captain Jones looked almost nostalgic when he saw us depart. He kissed Caroline's hand with a fatherly gesture as he gave her a card, in case she ever 'required his services again'. Dejected as he claimed to be, his face brightened again upon receiving the last instalment of his pay.

We rushed to St Enoch's train station and secured tickets for the very next service to Edinburgh. That would not depart until very early the following morning, so we stayed at the station's sumptuous hotel.

The expensive lodgings, however, improved my mood only marginally. According to Nine-Nails, the following morning I was grunting at everyone – even the stray dogs – when I boarded the train.

Despite the heavy snow, it was a short trip – a little over two hours – and I used the time to brief McGray on what

Caroline had told me. He took in everything and did not interrupt me at all, but only because he was still somewhat lulled with laudanum. If only I could drug him every time I had something crucial to explain . . .

It was only mid-morning when we made it to Edinburgh, and we found the city buried under three feet of snow. Apparently, we had just missed one mighty blizzard – however, something far worse awaited.

As soon as the train entered the makeshift platforms of Caledonian Station, I saw a cluster of uniformed constables. And as we slowed down, I recognized the auburn hair and aquiline features of Superintendent Trevelyan.

'*Is that the super?*' McGray cried, rushing to press his hand against the window.

'What is he doing here?' I asked, still not believing my eyes.

Boss then came from the adjacent compartment.

'Looks like they're looking for you.'

'It cannot be,' I retorted. 'They are not even supposed to know we—' I saw that Boss lit his cigarette with a conceited smile. McGray jumped on his feet and grabbed him by the collar.

'Did ye tell anyone we were travelling back, ye conniving lump of dung?'

Boss let out a hissing laughter, baring his upper teeth, before he answered.

'Of course. I telegrammed my men last night from the hotel in Glasgow.'

'Och, for piffin's sake! And ye tell us now?'

Boss looked impassive. 'I have to keep Lord Salisbury well informed.'

McGray raised a clenched fist. 'And yer sodding minions went on tattling where my sister is!'

But Boss nearly laughed. 'How could I, you stupid fool? *I* don't know where your madwag sister is right now. Neither do you. And I suggest you save your energy. Something very serious must have happened if my men had to share any information with your sad *super*.'

Caroline stepped in then, looking quite pale.

'Please, tell me those constables have nothing to do with—' She saw Nine-Nails still clenching Boss's collar, and covered her mouth.

McGray pushed Boss against the wall and left the compartment, his breathing sounding very much like the train's engine. Boss and Bob elbowed their way through the other passengers, and Caroline and I took advantage of the path they cleared.

The frosty air made us cough, heavy with the smells of coal and engine grease, as if presaging the news I was about to receive.

The constables made way as soon as they saw us. Everyone looked distressed; for once, even Trevelyan. McGray was already there, and the superintendent had raised a hand, bidding him silence until his eyes met mine.

'Well?' McGray spluttered. 'What is it?'

I could clearly see the tendons on the man's jaw as he answered.

'Please follow me, inspectors. I'm afraid your lodgings are no longer safe.'

19

Before we could even fetch our luggage – or McGray's new horse – we were pushed into Trevelyan's carriage, which took us north, to New Town. We crossed the bleak Queen Street Gardens and then turned right.

The roads there were already muddy, the snow turned into a brown slush, and the carriage skidded dangerously as it turned left. My heart skipped a beat, for I realized we were entering Great King Street, where my own house stood.

At once I gasped.

In the middle of the snow-capped terraces, mine stood out like the charred insides of a chimney, and the windows, surrounded by soot, looked like cannon holes that still spat smoke.

I grabbed the handle and nearly opened the door, even though we were still moving fast, but in my haste I used my injured hand and grunted in pain. I must have looked desperate, for McGray held me by the shoulder.

There was a small crowd gathered around, between officers, neighbours and passers-by, and I recognized the pathetic little fire engine. With its bright red wheels and the shiny brass funnel of its steam-powered pump, it looked more like a child's toy haphazardly dropped in the midst of a battlefield.

McGray did not let go of my shoulder until the carriage had stopped fully, and then he himself opened the door for me. I jumped out, tumbling on the slush, my eyes moving frantically as I took in the scale of the disaster.

The ground floor was still smouldering, albeit weakly. The windows and the door were gone, the threshold still getting a pitiful spurt of water from the firefighters' hose. I looked up. The first – and second-floor windows had also shattered, their frames just as blackened, but there were no more flames there.

My first reaction was to run to the doorsteps.

'*Layton!*' I shouted.

McGray and one of the officers had to restrain me, or I would have sprinted into the still-burning hall. McGray pointed to my right.

'There. He's there.'

No wonder I'd not seen him. Layton was sitting on the kerb, wrapped in a frayed blanket and hugging a cup of steaming tea. Half his hair had burned, a wide section of his scalp now bare and blistered. A woman I recognized as the neighbours' housekeeper was patting him on the back. She cast me a recriminating look when I approached, but I had no mind to care.

'Layton, are you all right?' I said as I flung myself down on my knees.

The poor man was trembling, his eyes staring absently into the brew, and he oozed the strong smell of burned wood. When he raised his chin and looked at me, he managed only a hint of a smile.

'I saved your cufflinks, master,' he whispered, his southern accent as formal as ever. He searched in his breast pocket and handed me a small leather case, peppered with ash flakes. 'Just the gold ones, sir. I had no time to reach for the ivories. I'm sorry.'

A surge of warmth took hold of me, so strong I nearly shed tears. I cleared my throat and squeezed his shoulder with affection, before taking the case with my one good hand.

'What happened?' I asked him, seeing he looked well enough. 'Was it an accident? Did you—?'

I had to stop myself. I knew it could be no accident.

Layton shook his head. 'I told the constables already. I was sorting out the wine cellar, looking for a claret I could have ready for when you arrived. I thought I heard a glass shatter. When I made it to the ground floor, the drawing room was already burning like pits of hell!'

He covered his mouth, that last word a screech. The housekeeper made him drink more tea.

Constable McNair came to us then. His eyes were rimmed with dark circles.

'It happened before sunrise,' he said. 'The paper boy was just doing his round. He says he saw a couple of auld crones – at least he thought they were crones. They looked like beggars. When they walked past the house they threw bricks and jars to the windows. The boy said he'd ne'er seen a house catch fire so quickly.'

'And the crones?' I asked.

'They ran like the wind after throwing the stuff, according to the laddie.'

I stood up slowly, clenching my hands around the cufflinks case.

'I'm so sorry, inspector.'

'Has nobody else been questioned?' I barked. 'The neighbours? The lamplighter? *Somebody else must have seen where they went!*'

Trevelyan came to me.

'We have already queried your neighbours and their servants. People told us they were either asleep or away from their windows. That boy seems to be the only witness.'

The neighbours' housekeeper was casting me an accusing stare. No wonder people would not speak; nobody would want their house to be next. And, with my recent reputation, most of them would be happy to see me go.

'Bloody cowards,' I grumbled.

I saw that the exhausted firefighters were already stepping into the hall, so I strode in right behind them. There were no more flames and I was red with fury, so nobody attempted to stop me.

The hot air, laden with ash, made me cough at once. The nearest man told me something I did not register – perhaps to be careful, as I went to the drawing room.

Everything there was black and grey, flecks of ash fluttering in the air. The structural beams were visible in places, the walls still radiating heat. There was no piece of furniture I could recognize, everything burned to shapeless smoulders scattered all over the floor.

I felt a draught of wind on my head and looked up. The fire had opened a wide hole in the ceiling, through which I could see the blackened walls of my upstairs study. I wanted to go there; see what was left of my dear, cosy haven, but I could not. Half the staircase was gone, and what was left of it was only held by charred splinters.

The sight suddenly felt like a blow on my face: mute witness to some savage hatred, to a repulsive violation to the most intimate aspects of my life. That place, though rented, though not my home for very long, had been *mine*.

A shadow appeared on the floor, and I did not need to turn to recognize McGray's broad shoulders.

'They never did this before,' I murmured. 'Not even when they were at the height of their influence.'

McGray stood by my side, his expression only a little less disgusted than mine.

'This was an act of desperation,' he said. 'Like a fish writhing on the hook. Nae idea what we've done, but they must feel cornered somehow. This is good news, Frey. This means—'

'*Oh, bloody good news!*' I shouted. '*Look at this place!*' and I pointed at the room just as a few chunks of blackened plaster fell from the ceiling.

'Am so sorry, Frey. I ken ye had loads o' yer things—'

'Oh, do go on! Make fun of my burned finery, my merino-wool coats, my tiepin collection . . .'

He frowned. 'I wasnae –'

Right then Caroline walked in, lifting her hem and carefully dodging the heaps of rubble.

'Mr Frey,' she said. 'This is terrible. I—'

'Please, take her away,' I said ominously, turning my back to them.

'We're nae here to mock,' McGray insisted.

'*Get out!*' I roared, and in the empty husk that the house now was, my voice echoed like a gunshot.

I did not turn to see them. The firefighters, surely used to such displays, were the first ones to step out. It took a moment for McGray to follow them and the last I heard was the ruffle of Caroline's skirts.

Through the shattered windows I heard McGray talking to Trevelyan, perhaps explaining my tantrum and asking him to give me a moment alone. His interceding for me only made the fire in my stomach all the more intense.

Brooding, I sat on the debris and my mind went blank.

I must have sat there for at least a couple of hours, playing with the cufflinks case and staring at nothing. At length I was reawakened by fluttering snowflakes. They were coming in from the upper floor, passing through the shattered windows and ceiling. Only then did my own paralysis strike me, and I started to wonder.

Would I have been thus benumbed if a fire like this had happened thirteen months ago – back when I was in London, still enjoying my work; when I was still smitten with my former fiancée; before my dearest uncle died; before I had recurrent nightmares of torches fluttering over water?

None of this, none of the tribulations of the past year, would have happened had I stayed in Oxford or Cambridge. Oxford in particular I had adored, medicine far more exciting than the cheating, treacherous law degree my father and eldest brother had embraced.

I sighed and stood up, if only because my limbs were going numb. I looked out the shattered doorway, and saw the lit windows of the house across the street. There sat a dull, bored man in his sixties, perusing an old book and just about to fall asleep.

I could have been him.

If I'd stayed on in Oxford I might now be a dull, boring professor, stooped over a tedious book, worrying over the cost of coal, the damp on the walls and the sheer stupidity of my upper-class students.

I envied that bored man so very much.

I sighed and looked down, my mind empty again. It was so comfortable not to think, to leave one's mind as blank as a new page. But then I wondered—

Could this be what had happened to McGray's sister? I remembered her frenzied eyes, and how quickly she'd shifted into a blank, empty vessel. Could she have stood back, contemplated the chaos she'd caused – her dead parents, her mutilated brother – and her mind had simply cracked under the strain? That slight, slight possibility of going through the same thing as her, sent a chill all over my body.

Fortunately, at that moment a black carriage halted right before the front steps. The door opened, and to my surprise, it was Joan who alighted.

'Are you all right, master?' she babbled as she ran to me. 'I heard it all! Everyone in town's talking about it! Am so sorry!'

It was not her presence that shocked me, but the fact that she'd come by carriage.

Then I saw Caroline alight too, and things began to make sense.

Despite her uneasy expression she looked refreshed, and was wearing a very elegant overcoat; pure Alaska seal, the upturned collar wrapped tightly around her thin neck.

'I am fine, Joan,' I said, though half lying, 'but – what are you doing here?'

'Am her travelling companion now,' Joan moaned. 'Master Adolphus said it was nae fittin' that she went up and down town by herself.'

'He said it would make me quite conspicuous,' Caroline added, as unhappy as Joan. 'As if people were not already pointing at me down the—'

'They told me you were very upset, master,' Joan interjected as if nobody had been speaking. 'And look at your wrist! My God, you must feel terrible!'

'It is nothing,' I lied again, even if I'd been contemplating madness mere seconds ago.

Caroline stepped forwards.

'Mr Frey, we must take you to a safer place. Your superintendent commanded so.'

'Trevelyan? Why did he not come himself?'

'Master McGray said we should come,' said Joan, already pulling me by my good arm. 'Says you wouldn't resist us. Come on.'

And he'd been right, I thought as she escorted me to the carriage.

A moment later we were riding south fast. I asked where we were going, but they'd been told to keep it quiet.

'They also threw burning stuff through our windows,' Joan was saying. 'But the dogs heard it at once and made a mighty racket. We had time to put out the fire. Only one room caught it.'

'And there were three people at home, instead of one,' Caroline said, 'which made it all easier. Mr McGray was so happy his dogs were fine. And his books. He was also glad his new horse was not yet—'

'Horse!' I cried. 'I forgot about Philippa! What—?'

'She's fine,' said Joan. 'The fire didn't hit your stable. Master Adolphus took her with him while you were brooding. My George will take good care of her. You won't be able to mount for a while.'

I covered my brow, thinking of the mayhem that still lay ahead of us.

We rode past Newington Cemetery, which marked the end of the city, and continued along a wide, white field. The carriage slowed down a mile or so ahead, in front of a cluster of snow-dusted conifers. I saw that the trees surrounded a small plot of farmland, and at its centre stood a group of rather neglected buildings – a small country house, a couple of stables and a few outbuildings dotted around them.

'What is this place?' I asked.

'One o' Lady Glass's properties,' Joan said, pronouncing the nickname without restraint.

'The superintendent said you should all stay here for a while,' Caroline said, not minding at all what her grandmother had been called. 'This place is more difficult to approach without being seen. He said you will be safer here.'

'And Lady Gla— I mean, your grandmother is happy about it?'

Caroline sighed. 'She suggested the place herself. From what Mr Trevelyan was saying before we left, she has news to tell you.'

The carriage stopped then, and I saw that the front door was wide open, Layton and the young Larry dutifully sweeping the snow.

Joan was the first one to alight. 'Don't let that Layton man touch the pantry. I'll start work on your dinner as soon as we come back from the shops.'

'The shops?' I asked.

'Aye. You need new clothes, master. You don't want to wear the same longjohns and underthings every day, do you?'

She was already offering me a hand to help me down, but Caroline cleared her throat.

'Before that, Joan,' she said, rather embarrassed – and not because of the ever so casual mention of my most intimate linens, as I'd soon find out. 'I need a moment with Mr Frey.'

'*Alone!*' Joan squealed.

'Yes, woman, alone!' Caroline snapped as she stretched an arm and shut the door. She even drew the little curtain, and I gulped.

'Sorry, Mr Frey, but there might not be another chance to talk to you. See, before we came to see you I sneaked into my grandmother's house to retrieve some essentials; coats, clothes and so on . . .'

'Sneak? That is your home.'

She smiled with bitterness. 'I shan't stay there. I'll consider myself happy if I never see or speak to that ghastly drunkard again. But I digress. There is . . . there is something I want you to have . . .'

And as she said so she began unbuttoning her coat, and I had a most immoral view of the quilted silk lining. I flushed and gulped, and nearly stopped her, but then I saw that she was simply searching in her inner pockets.

'I was very unfair to you,' she said, producing some small object I did not manage to see. 'You would not be going through any of this chaos were it not for my father. As much as I loved him, he was the one who involved you. And I am so sorry.

'Please, accept this . . .' She put a tiny velvet pouch in my hand, and looked down. 'It is a trifle, and I know this will never compensate for all your troubles, but I could think of nothing else. And also . . . I have treated you quite unfairly ever since my grandmother – offered you my hand, as if I were an unwanted lump of lard.'

I frowned, feeling the pouch. 'Miss Ardglass, this is a ring.'

She blushed intensely. 'I found it in my father's old belongings. I cannot wear it and I have no male relatives to give it to . . . It would have gone to my uncle Alistair, but – you know what happened to him. You were there.'

She said no more, and after a moment looked away. I immediately pictured the death of her pompous uncle, as clearly as if I were witnessing it once more. I felt so sorry for the poor young woman, her only surviving relative a ruthless, alcoholic grandmother whom she despised.

I could think of nothing to say, so I opened the little pouch, only to have something on which to fix my eyes.

It was an exquisite signet ring: smooth gold embracing a wide, flat emerald. The stone had a deep, dark colour, and I could tell it was just the right size for my little finger. I took it from the cushioned box and, from the eroded edges, realized it was a very old piece. There were two tiny letters engraved on the inner face. The first one was clearly an A, surely for Ardglass, and the second, more worn out, appeared to be a D or a B.

'Miss Ardglass, this is obviously a family heirloom. I would not wish—'

'Take it,' she pleaded. 'You'll be lifting a burden from my shoulders.' She appeared to be about to say something else, but then thought twice and opened the door. 'Joan, hop in. We are leaving now.'

I must have been quite perplexed by the unexpected present, for the very next thing I remember is standing on the snowy field, clasping the little ring and my cufflinks case, and seeing how the carriage rode away swiftly.

I only turned to the house when they were out of view, and took a deep breath.

The real work, the real witch hunt, would only begin now.

20

Aiding myself with the only two fingertips not wrapped in bandages, I slid the ring down my left hand's small finger, and stepped into the house.

The first thing I heard was insistent hammering, as if someone were set on bringing the walls down.

The place was damp and quite cold, with the mouldy smell of long-unoccupied dwellings. Old George was lighting the fires, but it would be a while before they began to take the edge off the cold.

'Master Adolphus is over there,' George told me, pointing at the nearest door, which led me to what had been a wide dining room.

Nine-Nails had been busy: there were boxes full of books strewn all over the place, and the long dining table, pushed against a wall, was bursting with correspondence. There were notes, maps and loose sheets, some of them dangerously close to the flame of an oil lamp that did not have a glass chimney. Under the table, his two dogs slept in enviable oblivion.

'Cannae believe I have to stay at the dry cow's house!' he was mumbling through his teeth, his face a few inches from his enormous map of the British Isles. He'd pinned it to the wall with thick nails, and was hammering all his notes and cut-outs in the same fashion.

'After we leave, that wall will be the envy of Swiss cheese.'

He turned to me, visibly surprised, and allowed himself a long sigh of relief.

'Och, thank goodness! I thought ye'd throw a far longer tantrum.'

And to my astonishment he came to me and shook my left hand with earnest.

'Ye rescued that too?' he said, looking at the emerald ring.

'Um . . . a family heirloom,' I said (needless to tell him it was not *my* family's).

'I'm so sorry they got yer house. Really. I ken it won't help but they also tried to—'

'I know, I know,' I said, raising a hand. 'Joan told me.'

'If ye need a place to stay once all this shite's over . . . well . . . Joan'll be more than happy to have ye around.'

I was going to pat him on the back, understanding how guilty he must feel – more than once I'd blamed him for all my misfortunes, but at least this once he'd had nothing to do in the matter. I was going to say so, but I noticed that both our noses were wrinkled at that awkward display of unmanly emotion.

'Let's not think about that right now,' I said promptly, then cleared my throat and went to the map. 'You moved all this quickly.'

'Aye, and I got quite a few letters from my contacts in the witchcraft black market. As I expected, almost all of them are short of supplies.'

'Almost all?' I asked, stepping closer to the map. It was the same map he'd spread at his library, but there were many new pins – or rather rusty nails – scattered throughout England. McGray signalled them.

'These mark the places where people still manage to get hold o' their hallucinogenic cacti and their witch bottles. Like the Ardglass lass said, the witches broke apart into many smaller factions, all working at a much more modest scale.'

'It is an almost uniform belt from Lancaster to Hull,' I said.

'Aye. It narrows down our search.'

I shook my head. 'Not enough . . .'

'Och, thank ye very fucking much for the credit!'

'Sorry, sorry. I meant to say—'

'I ken what ye meant. And yer right. We cannae search all that ground in a week.'

'A week? What day is today?'

'Seventeenth.'

'*What!* It cannot possibly . . .' I began counting with my fingers. 'Oh, damn . . .'

As I said so, Layton brought a tray with a decanter and two tumblers. On a slightly less stressful day I would have been astounded by his efficiency; today I could only reach for the whisky and help myself to a large measure. The burn on my throat indeed gave me sudden clarity.

'What happened to my luggage?' I asked at once, my face stern.

'Och, Percy, ye worried about yer—?'

'I had my notes there! And the pieces of paper sent by Miss Ardglass. And also your sister's—'

I went quiet, staring at the map as my mind whirled. My thoughts flashed so fast that for a moment I could not speak.

'Your luggage was brought along with everyone else's, sir,' said Layton. 'I was just about to smooth out your jacket and shirts.'

'Bring me the little notebook,' I asked him. 'There are two pieces of paper and a small piece of cloth in between the pages. Make sure they are still in it.'

Layton bowed and left. I was going to tell McGray what I had just thought, but the first of a series of interruptions kept me from doing so – Boss came in, bringing an ice-cold draught with him that at once made us tense. It was as if the man had the power to befoul the very air around him.

'Hey, Piff!' Nine-Nails cried. 'My favourite twat!'

Boss was far from amused. His bushy moustache was covered in frost, contrasting with his flushed cheeks. He must have ridden here at full speed.

'I have a message from above,' he grumbled without further ado.

McGray laughed. 'Och, why don't ye say it's from—?'

'I would not finish that sentence if I were you.' He produced a couple of envelopes from his breast pocket. Yes, *that* pocket.

I went to have a look, but—

'*Step back!*' he snapped, pulling the envelopes away from my eyes. He double-checked the addressees, shoved one back into his pocket, and handed me the other. 'You are to burn it as soon as you've read it.'

'Well, we have it now,' I said. 'You can go.'

'I need to see you burn it.'

'Och, for fuck's sake!'

I sighed, seeing no point in arguing. I went to the table, to read closer to the oil lamp and away from Boss's eyes. It took me a while to open the envelope with just one hand, and my effort was poorly rewarded when I unfolded the message.

It was a short, stark and truculent message from Lord Salisbury, telling us off for the mayhem at the Orkneys.

'None o' that was our fault!' McGray squealed, reading over my shoulder.

'Do you think we care whose fault it was?' Boss snarled. 'Everyone in that bloody frozen islet saw that fire. You have no idea how much money is probably passing hands right now so that the London papers don't publish the story.' He scoffed at McGray. 'Not that it would be difficult – who would ever believe such tales from an island of inbred Scotch savages?'

McGray clenched his fists, so I quickly brought the message to the lamp's open flame. As soon as it caught fire I held it up for Boss to see.

'There,' I said. 'You can now—'

'Get yer stinking sorry English arse out o' here,' Nine-Nails blurted out. Boss was going to protest but McGray spoke first. 'Youse are here only to make sure we don't run. What we investigate is none o' yer fuckin' business.'

Boss did not move. Instead, he smiled and leered at the map on the wall, as if making a conscious effort to memorize its contents.

'You are absolutely right. It means nothing to me in which pit you two go to rot. As long as I don't have to drag your dead bodies for too long to take you there—'

'*Get out!*' McGray snapped, and while Boss did oblige, he did so with sluggish movements and an insolent smile on his face.

'Let's get back to work,' I said, seeing that McGray's chest was heaving. I went to the desk and looked through his stack of open letters. One instantly caught my eye. 'Katerina wrote to you?'

Nine-Nails rubbed his face, forcing himself to focus. 'Aye. I also asked her for help before we left.'

'Her handwriting is appalling,' I said. I remembered that McGray's most trusted clairvoyant liked to keep three-inch-long fingernails. I wondered if she'd grown them back and holding a pen was a challenge for her. 'What does she say?'

'She has news, but she wants to tell us in person. She thinks it's nae safe to write down such things.'

'Could she meet us here?'

McGray shook his head. 'Says she's nae coming back to Edinburgh so soon after her trial.'

'Damn! I mean, I cannot blame her, after all she went through, but—'

'But she says she can travel anywhere we ask her to.'

'Good. That should be a priority. As much as I hate to admit it, that woman always knows far more than we expect.'

A thick file caught my attention then. The scribble on the cover read: *Anne Ardglass*.

'Anything useful there?' I asked.

'Mnah. Everything I kent already. But it did surprise me that the auld crone's only seventy.'

'Only?' I echoed.

'Un-bloody-believable, aye? She looks fuckin' ancient.'

I looked at the document that stated her age – not an actual birth certificate, but a conveyancing file from one of the woman's earliest transactions. I arched an eyebrow.

'So . . . She was born the same year as Queen Victoria.'

At once McGray snatched the document. 'What – really?'

'Yes. Her majesty turned seventy this year. Do you not remember? All the blasted papers made a fuss about it.'

'Born the same year . . .' McGray mumbled. 'Both pawky, manipulative bitches and both in dealings with dark magic . . . Very curious.'

'All written in their stars?' I mocked, but McGray simply shook his head.

'Ask her yerself when she comes to deliver her allegedly "important" news. I just hope the auld cow deigns to show up soon.'

We spent the next couple of hours going through his other correspondence and adding more nails to the large map. If anything, the additional points made our task more daunting.

We only stopped our work when we heard two loud female voices arguing at the main entrance. I first recognized Caroline's.

'Stop it!' she was protesting. 'I have told you already; I did not go away to conceal I was with child!'

Joan replied with a seemingly soothing voice. 'There, there, miss. You won't be the last gal to try them toffees before time.'

Caroline burst into the room then, red with impatience. 'Could you make this woman stop?'

McGray and I cleared our throats.

'We've tried, lass.'

'Yes, we have indeed.'

Joan came in, loaded with parcels – my new clothes. 'Oh, but I'm just telling the gal I know how—'

'*Joan*,' I interjected, thinking of the best excuse to get her out of the room, 'could you go to Layton and tell him I am still waiting for the little notebook I asked him to fetch me about three hours ago.'

'All right, master,' she said, hugging the parcels as she cast Caroline a quarrelsome stare. 'But remember what I told you. Not with a bargepole.'

And, once she'd walked out, I turned to Caroline.

'I am so sorry if Joan disrespect—'

'*If!*' Caroline barked, pulling out her leather gloves. 'I have never been called a harlot so many times, in so many different ways, in so little time!' I did not have a chance to apologize more, for she was already looking at the map. 'Are those the places where you think the witches might be hiding?'

'Where people can still get hold of their goods,' McGray explained.

Caroline pulled a grimace. 'I cannot say you have done a terrific job narrowing it down.'

She might as well have jabbed me with a fire poker. '*What?* Did you expect us to figure it all out whilst you rode down New Town shopping for—?'

'Your new longjohns,' she said, silencing me at once.

McGray raised both hands. '*Oi!* Stop it, lassies! Frey, ye ken what she's like. And Miss Ardglass, we only have this information because I've been in touch with witchcraft dealers for years. Show a wee bit o' respect for our job.'

Caroline exhaled, as frustrated as the rest of us.

'You must understand,' she said. 'I am getting desperate.'

'We are too,' I said, still fuming. 'Do I need to remind you we will be dead men in a week?'

Caroline was going to answer back, but she saw my hand then, and that I was wearing the ring. She blushed, and anything she might have been about to say did not come out of her lips. Belligerent as she was, she could not conceal a slight hint of appreciation.

'Percy here told me ye still have the messages the witches sent ye,' McGray said, taking advantage of her unexpected silence.

'I do,' she mumbled. 'I will fetch them.'

She came back a moment later, bringing a tattered tea caddy. Layton came right behind her, looking more apologetic than ever.

'Sir, do, do forgive me! I was going to bring it right away, but then I saw the collars of your shirts, and how that blowsy Lancashire woman—'

'It is all right, Layton,' I said, receiving the notebook. 'You have had a long day.'

Layton bowed low, apologizing again and again as he made his way out. McGray had to close the door on him, before pulling out a chair for Caroline.

We all sat at the table as she opened the little tin and produced pieces of white and brown wrapping paper, all neatly folded.

'I'm afraid I did not keep the entire sheets,' she said, 'only the sections with the messages.'

'A shame,' I had to say, adding our messages to the collection.

'These are the messages I received in Seville,' said Caroline, smoothing out a sheet and a telegram. As she'd told me, the telegram had only one word: vinegar.

Like in England, the telegram had been typed onto a pre-printed form. Caroline had already had someone translate the Spanish gibberish into the Queen's language, and she'd annotated the meaning above the text.

'As you can see, they did not know the specific source of the message. Whether the witches found a way to conceal that, or that piece of information became lost as the message was re-sent and redirected, I do not know.'

She was right. International telegrams often had to be wired to intermediary offices. This might not be an effort to conceal its source, but a genuine fault of the telegraphic network.

'And this is the letter the Messengers sent ye later?' McGray asked, picking up the scorched sheet.

'Yes. If I could not trace the telegram, there was no hope I'd do this one.'

McGray went to one of his boxes, still half full of books, and brought out a thick magnifying glass. We all leaned over the paper and scrutinized the handwriting.

'Not a terribly handsome hand,' I said. 'A little quivering in places. I'd say a young person's, but written in haste.'

McGray and I read the content in fascination. It was a heart-felt note, talking about tyrannical witches, mutilated deserters, and it ended by beseeching Caroline's help.

'*The factions are small and widespread*,' McGray read, and then eyed the map. 'That much we ken.' He turned the sheet and looked at the sections not touched by the fire. He even smelled the paper. 'Nae watermarks,' he said.

'I'm sorry,' said Caroline. 'Had I known back then, I would have scorched it more carefully.'

'Nae yer fault, lass,' McGray said. 'What came next?'

'These.' Caroline unfolded three separate pieces of wrapping paper. They had clearly travelled a long distance, being faded and discoloured on one side.

'They all look different,' I said, picking up one. 'Different thickness and shades of the original colour.'

'Any postage stamp ye could see?' McGray asked.

'No, none of them. They only had the address. I was always told that they'd been hand-delivered by local boys.'

McGray nodded. 'There must have been at least one witch out there doing that. Did the same happen when ye got parcels in Germany?'

'Yes. I had two delivered there. Here they are.'

One of those did have a watermark, quite visible, only partly obscured in the middle by the vinegar writing.

McGray read the Gothic lettering. 'Says *Verp* . . . and then . . . *ngen*.'

'*Verpackungen*,' Caroline said. 'German for Packaging.'

'Nae help,' said McGray. 'What came next?'

'That might be more helpful,' said Caroline, producing the two last messages. 'This one I received in Dover. And the last one . . .' she gulped, for that note must surely bring back tormenting memories, 'I received when I was in Bracknell, not far from Windsor. That is where . . . that is where I took my Bertha to be interred.'

The handwriting – though clearly from the same hand – could not have looked more different; one was fairly straight and composed, while the last one was an almost unintelligible smudge. No wonder – that was the message where they urged Caroline to sail to the Orkneys and set the belfry on fire.

'Did these come through the normal post?' McGray asked.

'No, neither.'

I arched an eyebrow. 'Curious. I did see a little stain in our notes. The ones you sent to us and Dr Clouston. I thought it was a postage stamp.'

'Which one?' McGray asked, and I passed him the sheet.

'Here, on the edge.'

He held it against the lamp's light and looked at it through a magnifying glass. Caroline leaned closer – far closer than I thought proper – to have a look.

'It looks like ink that seeped through another sheet,' McGray said.

'That is what I thought,' I added. 'Two layers of wrapping, this one underneath the one that got the stamp.'

'They probably reused it,' said Caroline. 'They only tore out the section with the stamp and address, and reused the rest.'

'And you in turn sent us pieces torn from the same sheet,' I said.

'Yes. You can imagine how rushed I was; I had no other paper at hand.'

McGray picked our three notes, which, as I recalled, matched perfectly. Then he put them next to Caroline's note. Though those edges were not as clean a fit, the papers' coarse pulp helped, the fibres following a discernible pattern. Very soon we had the four pieces matched together.

The mark I had spotted continued on Caroline's side of the message.

Again, we all leaned over the magnifying glass, staring at the slight curvature of the mark, even holding our breaths as we examined it.

The mark looked like a section of a circle, only with some lines from the centre, and a lobed—

'I know what it is!' I cried, my heart suddenly pounding.

And then we heard a gunshot.

21

'*What the—*'

McGray rose at once, unholstering his gun and striding to the door. He did not even get a chance to open it, for Boss burst in then.

'Damn! She just gave us away!'

And he stepped into the room, his gun in one hand – and a dead raven in the other.

The poor bird was almost burst in half by the shot, its black wings flopping and spilling blood on the old carpet.

'Who?' I cried. 'Joan?'

'No,' Boss snapped, tossing the raven into the nearby bin. 'This old hag . . .'

I jumped to have a look out the window, and saw that a lustrous landau carriage, pulled by three very large horses, had parked by the front entrance. Everyone in Edinburgh knew that carriage very well; it was Lady Anne's.

And when I looked back inside, there she was, her tall, bony figure standing by the doorframe.

Her headdress looked very much like the rubbish bin, both bursting with the black feathers of a dead bird. She gripped her walking cane, but not supporting it on the floor; rather, she grasped it by the middle, her knuckles tight, as if ready to strike someone with it.

Her eyes scanned the room, and when they found Caroline, they half shut in the most spiteful stare.

'You really want everyone to think you are a little trollop!'

Caroline, still poised on her chair, almost seemed amused.

'Are you well, Grandmother?'

Lady Anne stepped closer to her, a tower of black furs and velvet, jerking her cane in the air.

'Alone in a house full of men! Parading yourself in the shops with this vermin's maid – buying *men's* undergarments! Are you his servant as well as his whore?'

Caroline squinted too, in a vicious gesture that nearly equalled her grandmother's.

'That would really upset you, would it not?'

I do not know what sort of poison those words carried, but Lady Anne hurled herself against the girl; an uncontrolled beast ready to tear her apart.

McGray stepped in between them. I thought Lady Anne would clash against him, beat him with the cane, and then they'd embroil in a wild skirmish, but the woman halted, only just managing to stay on her feet. It was as if McGray were a block of red-hot iron she did not dare touch, and the fiery glow in his eyes only enhanced that vision.

'I'll kill ye,' he spat with that throaty, bloodcurdling growl people in Edinburgh had come to fear. 'Put a hand on this lassie and I swear I will. Right here, right now, with my bare hands. That turkey neck o' yers will snap with a wee squeeze.'

Lady Anne ground her teeth, her eyes bloodshot – the only trace of colour in her otherwise ashen face. After the initial shock, she showed a crooked smile.

'All *I* need to do to see you dead is to walk away in silence.'

I covered my brow, unable to look at that malicious grin.

'I should even leave this little vixen to her own devices,' Lady Anne carried on. 'She will never be received in good society ever again. It will take a generation or two to recover our good name.'

'Then leave,' Caroline snapped. 'And may you not break your neck on the front steps.'

Lady Anne chuckled. She looked in the folds of her dress, produced a silver hip flask and helped herself to a good swig.

'I won't do it for you,' Lady Anne said, looking around. She pushed aside the clothes parcels Joan had left on a nearby chair, saw them drop on the floor, and sat down. 'I'll do it for my father and grandfather. I'll do it for myself. All these years struggling with you – with your father's iniquities and insanities . . . All my life's efforts will not be in vain.'

She took another sip and cleared her throat.

'The Ardglass family will outlive those damn witches. *We* shall prevail, not them. Even if that means I have to save the filthy McGrays. I'll have to accept that as . . . collateral damage.'

'Ye done?' McGray asked at once, but Lady Anne did not reply at once.

She had a third sip of what smelled like very expensive brandy.

'Tell your brute to leave.' And she nodded at Boss. The man, as I expected, remained fixed on his spot. He did not even attempt to reply, leaving the arguing to us.

'He will eventually find out anything you might say,' I told Lady Anne. 'His leaving the room will only—'

'He smells,' Lady Anne remarked, hovering the neck of the flask under her nostrils.

Boss smirked, standing his ground as stubbornly as Lady Anne.

I had to force a deep breath and, against all my wishes, intercede for the woman's wishes.

'Pray, do as Lady Anne says,' I asked Boss warily. 'She is our best lead at the moment. Do not make things more difficult.'

Boss took his time, shifting his weight from one foot to the other, each movement making McGray grind his teeth. And then, thankfully, he walked out.

When the door was shut, Lady Anne sighed, eyed the map on the wall with derision, and had a final sip.

'My men in Lancashire,' she said, suddenly shifting to a very business-like tone, 'revisited many of our old sources – spies, villagers, witches' former lovers. I'll spare you the details.'

'What did they find?' I asked her.

'There are at least eight groups at work.'

'Eight!' McGray cried.

'Most of them seem happy to remain hidden and out of trouble, doing small *jobs*, and only for their most trusted clients.'

'Back to their auld ways,' McGray said. 'So who's causing trouble?'

'As far as my men could gather, only two rival bands.'

'The Marigolds and the Messengers,' McGray mumbled.

Lady Anne winced at the mere sound of his voice. 'I do not know about *Messengers*, but the name Marigolds did come to light.'

'And do you know where they are?' I asked.

Lady Anne shook her head. 'I don't have an address book for you, Mr Frey. But I do know the general areas where those eight bands are gathering.' She pointed at the wall with her cane. 'They all fall within those silly little marks you have made.' She put her cane aside and began counting with her fingers. 'Lancaster, Whalley, Grassingdon, Malton . . .'

As she recited the eight names, McGray looked more and more frustrated, surely thinking we did not have time to search each of those places.

Before Lady Anne was done I rushed to the table and leafed through my little notebook, recalling what I'd been thinking before Boss shot the raven.

'York?'

Lady Anne looked up as soon as I said so.

'Yes. Why?'

I could not contain my elation as I pulled out the piece of cloth Pansy had cut out from her own dress. We all realized that she had meant to make a white rose.

22

I placed the cut-out next to the pieces of wrapping paper.

'That looks like a petal,' I said, tapping the faint marks of ink. 'I need to check, but I think only the city of York uses the white rose to frank stamps.'

'That's correct,' said Lady Anne.

McGray came to the table and examined the sheets with the magnifying glass.

'Too many coincidences,' he said. 'These parcels must have come from there.'

Lady Anne stretched her neck. 'Who gave you that white rose?'

'None o' yer fucking business,' McGray snapped. 'We have what we need. Ye can sod off now.'

What a crooked, disturbing smile spread across the woman's face.

'Was it your lunatic sister?'

It was as if she had dropped explosives rather than words. Caroline gasped, my own jaw dropped, and McGray dropped the lens to clench his fists.

He took a tiny, abrupt step forwards, but then halted, his entire body quivering. It was as if a long-caged beast were trying to leap out, and it took every fibre of muscle in his body to keep it contained.

'*Get out!*' he hissed.

Lady Anne did stand up, but clearly because she was as keen to terminate the meeting as any of us.

'Very well. If you do get killed in York, I only hope it is after you've taken care of that damn coven.' She cast me a mocking stare. 'And *if* you return, we may discuss how you intend to pay for the damage you caused to my property.'

'*The damage I—!*'

Caroline had to seize me by the wrist – thankfully the good one – and we watched the horrid woman depart. From the back, with her black feathers and furs, and her slender neck, she indeed looked like a giant vulture.

Once she was gone, Caroline was the first one to speak, but only after we heard the carriage ride away.

'How could she know Miss McGray did this? Do you think she knew we went to the Orkneys? That she found out what the witches have been telling me all this time?'

She covered her mouth, a little too upset to my eyes, though I could not tell why.

I sighed. 'Like she said, it is not a difficult guess. She must have heard that her son, your father, spoke to Miss McGray in January – you know, before he escaped.' I turned to McGray, brandishing the white rose. 'And that of course explains how your sister came to know the witches would flee to York; Lord Joel must have told her all the stops in his witch hunt. That is precisely what the witches fear; hence their hunting Pansy.'

At least my guesswork helped take the edge of McGray's wrath. He took a deep breath as he turned to the map.

'We have a destination now.'

'Still not a very precise one,' I remarked. 'We cannot just travel there, stand by the gates to York Minster and ask passers-by if they are witches.'

'And you can't simply take a train,' Boss said from the threshold – he had clearly been listening to the entire conversation, even when Lady Anne was present. He pointed at the dead raven. 'That old hag must have been watched by the witches. I'm sure it was her carriage that drove them here. They *will* be following you if you travel by ordinary means.'

'And,' I added, 'if whoever is hiding in York realizes we are travelling there, they might flee even before our train gets out of Lothian.'

'Fuck,' McGray let out.

Caroline rose slowly, staring at the map with an arched eyebrow. 'It should not be that difficult to confuse them. Mr McGray, you could send a message to some of your contacts, perhaps in the eight locations my grandmother just mentioned, and tell them you want to meet them.'

'Making sure the witches can intercept those messages,' McGray mumbled. 'Clever plan, lassie. Ye *do* scare me.'

'And then we can travel separately again,' Caroline went on. 'Avoid the main train routes and pretend that our destinations match some of the places you—'

'Wait-wait-wait,' Nine-Nails said. '*We?* Yer nae going anywhere.'

Caroline let out a piercing, '*Ha!* Mr McGray, you just admitted my wits scare you!'

'They do, but we've nae idea what awaits there. Ye better—'

'You should know by now I will not answer to your recommendations.'

McGray nodded. 'Aye, but think about it. Yer life is precisely what those bitches want. Yer the last Ardglass.'

Caroline breathed in, her eyes suddenly sombre. 'I am indeed, whether they kill me or not. I do not intend to have any children.'

I blushed at the candid statement, and even Boss, for once, seemed a little uncomfortable.

McGray looked at her, shaking his head, his blue eyes full of . . . something like compassion.

'That's a pity, lassie. That hourglass figure ought to be carried on.'

Caroline must have been expecting any answer but that, for she flushed intensely, nearly matching the dark red of her velvet dress.

I cleared my throat loudly. 'We'd better start planning our routes. And who you will message. We want to throw the scent away from York, but without it looking like we want to.'

Caroline shook her head, as if thinking she could shed the excess of colour, and cast McGray's trousers a derisive look.

'And you will need new clothes for the trip, do you know that?'

'*What?* Piss off! These are fine.'

'A fine beacon indeed,' said Caroline. 'Do you forget that pretty much all of Scotland knows about the nine-fingered madman with an appalling taste for clothes?' I could have embraced her. 'If you want to be even more conspicuous, I still have some of that tar, so you'll have the green flames to match.'

Boss simply chuckled as he left.

The plan was laid out swiftly.

Caroline, Joan and Harris would travel by stagecoach and ferry to Newcastle, where they'd look for Madame Katerina. The gypsy had been living there since being acquitted by the Scottish courts (it is a long story; suffice to say that the decision caused outrage throughout Edinburgh, forcing her to settle elsewhere). It would be up to Katerina either to hand them any information or to meet us in York and tell us everything she knew in person. I was inclined to believe she'd choose the latter, and that McGray would use the opportunity to resort to her 'inner eye'.

In consideration of my broken wrist (and delicate disposition, as McGray kindly stated), I would travel by stagecoach to Dunbar, accompanied – watched, rather – by Bob and Boss. From there we'd take a comfortable train to Yorkshire, with tickets to Leeds, but we would alight before making it there, either at Harrogate or the even quieter Wetherby, and hire a carriage for the rest of the journey.

McGray would take the longest route of all. First he'd be riding – he could not wait to test his new Carthusian – then he'd follow a random train route across the heart of Lancashire, before turning back east, and then he'd cover the final leg of the journey, again, on horseback.

The entire charade would take almost two full days, which was a hefty price to pay simply to ensure the witches did not flee before our arrival. To add to the tension, we still ignored where exactly in York they might be hiding – or if they were there at all. McGray would pay a surprise visit to the witchcraft dealers he knew were active there, but it was always possible that those swindlers might not be able to offer us any useful information.

I kept dwelling on those thoughts throughout the afternoon – we had also agreed it would be best we all left simultaneously after sunset – and since everyone seemed terribly busy preparing for their respective journeys, I found myself without anything else to do but wait.

First I went to the stables to see Philippa, which very rarely failed to make me relax. Unfortunately, she seemed to feel the tension in the air, and did not welcome my patting – she has always been a temperamental beast, and I was glad she would not be involved in this journey, for she particularly disliked train trips.

All that was left for me to do was to practise my shooting. I had trained to use my left hand in case the other got injured; however, I'd not done it in years, and very soon I discovered that my aim had become appalling.

The two green bottles I'd placed on the farm's northern fence simply stood there, mocking my incompetence as I emptied my gun. When I ran out of bullets I could not even reload the barrel, and I ended up tossing the damn thing into the snow.

As the ice sizzled around the still hot weapon and I did my best to take a deep breath, I heard a mocking caw in the sky.

DIARY – 1831–1834

[1831] From this period I do nothing towards my Recovery, except occasionally electrifying myself until August 1832 when I go to Buxton.

[1833] I suffer much from influenza: on the 1st of July I arrive at Pyrmont where I drink the Waters and take the Warm Bath and the Douche – the stream of which altho under water cuts like a sharp instrument leaving weals upon the flesh . . .

[1834] My Mind was under much anxiety and excitement as I was engaged in the prosecution of the German portion of My Rights – which may have prevented my deriving much benefit from the Pyrmont course of Treatment.

23

McGray looked quite strange, clad in black and dull greys from head to toe. He, Caroline and I stood at the portico in the semi-darkness, lit only by a little oil lamp held by a trembling Joan.

Nine-Nails passed two folded pieces of paper, one to Caroline and the other to me.

'That's where we'll meet,' he whispered. 'Read them and burn them.'

Caroline did so at once, mouthed the words to memorize them, and then held the paper above Joan's flame. I followed suit. When they caught fire, Layton rushed to bring us a tray, where we placed the burning notes. He, George and Larry stood there, in the semi-darkness, looking even more strained than us about to scuttle into the night.

George kissed Joan on the forehead, about to burst into tears, and it was she who had to whisper reassurances into his ear. I gave Layton enough money to find his way to my Gloucestershire estate – his mission was to 'take my cufflinks to safety' – and before I too had some sort of emotional display, I stepped out.

McGray mounted his black horse, almost invisible under the starless sky, and Caroline and Joan boarded their carriage.

I hopped into mine, where Boss and Bob awaited, and before I could utter a word we were all moving – three separate parties, each riding in a different direction, further shrouded by the thick clouds and the roaring wind. Within seconds I lost sight of McGray's horse and Caroline's carriage, thankful for the appalling December weather.

However, I could not sit back and relax. There was no way to tell whether the witches were following us or not. There might be a team of them behind each one of us, or there could be a single group, forced to choose a target out of the three. And judging by my recent luck . . .

Boss and Bob kept their guns at the ready, their faces alert. I did the same, despite my poor aim with my left hand, and thus we travelled for the best part of the next five hours.

Fortunately, we made it to Dunbar in time to take the sleeper train to Yorkshire. Ironically, that was the very same service we could have boarded in Edinburgh, had we not needed to leave in secret.

Boss led the way to a second-class compartment, which we three were supposed to share – according to him, that way we would have a better chance of passing unnoticed. As soon as I saw those one-foot-wide bunk beds, with sheets that stank of the cheapest soap in the world, I told him plainly where he could go, and went straight to secure a first-class compartment all to myself.

The tension had set me on edge, and it did not help my mood to think that the witches might have gone after McGray, who was riding alone, or had decided to intercept Caroline and Joan's carriage. I myself was not any safer; worse even, having to watch my back lest Boss decide to strike me so he might cut his mission short.

I stretched on the fresh, crisp bedding, my mind ridden with those portentous thoughts, the guillotine of my nightmares flashing stubbornly in my mind. I repeated in my head the rendezvous scribbled by McGray – The George Hotel, Coney Street – over and over, fearing I might forget it, as the train cut its way through the pitch-black night. I thought my concerns would keep me wide awake, but I was so tired I fell asleep at once.

It was still dark when I woke up, and for a blissful moment I forgot where I was. The noises and smells of the train slowly crept into my consciousness, and I let out a hearty growl when the entire situation came back to me.

I refreshed, dressed and had my breakfast brought to my compartment, but just as I thought I was enjoying the meal, there was an abrupt knocking. Before I could say a word, the door slammed open, and the voluminous figures of Boss and Bob watched me from the threshold. They shamelessly eyed every corner of the place. I noticed they were not wearing their jackets, and feared they'd taken them off because they were about to beat me to a pulp and needed more freedom of movement.

'As you can see,' I mocked nonetheless, 'I did not jump onto the railway last night.'

Boss ruffled his moustache, which somehow remained as symmetrical as ever. 'Don't do it now. We'll get off soon.' He checked a grubby pocket watch and nodded at Bob. 'Come on, we still have time for some breakfast.'

And they made their way to the dining car without bothering to close my door.

I stood up to do so, exasperated, but just as I touched the handle, the image of Boss checking his breast pocket with inexplicable anxiety came to my head. He was not wearing that jacket right now.

And then a mad, delirious idea entered my mind.

'You cannot do this, Ian,' I whispered to myself, but even as I spoke, I craned my neck to see down both sides of the corridor. The gas lamps were all on, shedding their amber light on the red velvet carpets and the dark wooden panes. The corridor was deserted, and I pictured the PM's men gobbling up platefuls of fried eggs and bacon à la Nine-Nails. *Without their jackets*, a little voice repeated in my mind. I would never have another opportunity like this.

I took a little step ahead, closed my door and then walked stealthily towards the second-class car.

A few yards ahead the train took a sudden turn, and I had to press a hand against another compartment's door. The noise, to my anxious ears, sounded like a slap on someone's face. Before I could move two steps ahead, a very refined old gentleman came out.

'May I help you?' he asked, and I was very much tempted to tell him to sod off.

'My apologies,' I said. 'I lost my balance.'

I bowed and walked on, but the man spoke again.

'That is second class you are going to, young man.'

I ground my teeth before turning back to him, giving what must have looked like a hyena's smile. 'Oh . . . I know, I am only stretching my legs.'

'You can always stretch them at the—'

'*Oh, mind your own business!*' I snapped, and then turned my back and strode away.

I soon made it to the car's door, but the moment I grabbed the handle a young attendant came to me.

'Sir, that is the way to second—'

'*I know!*' I roared, and pulled the door open.

The frosty wind lashed my face, a relentless push as the train rode on. It was not snowing, but the air was so cold I thought it would made my nostrils bleed. Thankfully I only had to endure it for an instant, before stepping into the next car.

There was no carpet there, the varnish of the pinewood panelling flaking in places, and I also sensed the unmistakable smell of the same cheap soap used to clean the CID's headquarters.

I moved swiftly down the corridor, dodging a couple of loud children and a woman lulling her baby to sleep. It did not take me long to reach the thugs' compartment. I recognized it from the night before, more from the scratches and stains on the sliding doors than by the actual number. I tried the handle and, to my utter surprise, found it unlocked.

For a moment I simply stood there, torn by indecision. If I walked inside there'd be no turning back; I'd have to carry out my plan to its very end or . . . well, I'd better not think of the possibilities.

My heart began to pound then. I was already pulling the door to close it again, when a draught of icy wind came from the door to first class.

I gasped, thinking it was Boss coming back, but no, it was just the same attendant who'd just spoken to me, doing his round.

That was all the push I needed. I opened the door, stepped in quickly and closed it behind me, before the young man saw me and asked why I was sneaking into a second-class compartment.

I wrinkled my nose. The cubicle smelled of confined male odours, mixed with a sickening whiff of sweated alcohol. Two of the bunk beds had clearly been slept in, the blankets carelessly strewn aside. The third one, originally intended for me, was untouched, except for one detail: the two men's overcoats and jackets lay there.

I had a quick look around, hoping to find something else, but they never seemed to carry any luggage – no wonder the place smelled like a lion's den. I then went to the clothes, lifting them carefully and doing my best to remember the exact position in which they'd been thrown.

My heart beat faster, pumping into my ears as the engine's noise seemed to grow louder and louder.

The first coat and jacket – from the faded colour and frayed cuffs, I recognized as Bob's – offered nothing out of the ordinary. I found a set of brass keys, a pouch of cheap tobacco and one of those little books with lewd engravings that seem to move when one flips the pages very quickly. There was no money, guns or bullets; Bob must keep those with him at all times. I returned the items to the pockets and put the lot aside.

I moved on to Boss's garments.

His coat was thicker and newer, clearly that of a better-paid man, and it gave off some cheap bay rum cologne. I found the little bottle in one of the breast pockets, but nothing else.

I grabbed his jacket, hoping that it carried more interesting items, or my extremely dangerous excursion would prove useless. My heart skipped a beat as soon as I plunged my hand into the right breast pocket – there I found a small photograph folded in half.

That must be the one I'd seen him staring at on the paddle steamer. I remembered his unease when I caught him, and the haste with which he'd put it away. My pulse quickened further when I saw a little scribble on a corner.

Hilda, 1878.

I gasped when I unfolded it, for it was the faded portrait of a very beautiful woman, dark haired and with pale, piercing eyes.

'So you *do* have a past, Boss,' I whispered, taking in the features of the lady as best I could. There was something arresting in her features; a certain wildness in the way she stared at the camera, the merest hint of a proud smile. I guessed she would have been around thirty, so she'd be around the same age as Boss. Perhaps just a couple of years older.

Right then the steam whistle resonated all along the car. I felt a pang of cold fear as the train slowed down. We were approaching the next stop. I had to move and quickly; I may only have a minute or two before Boss and Bob returned.

My left hand trembling, I folded the photo and put it back, feeling how my own sweat made it stick to my fingers.

Recklessly, instead of walking out at once I looked into the other pockets.

There I found tobacco too, and matches, and a few crumpled sheets of paper. I pulled them out as the train kept slowing down. A trickle of sweat rolled down my temple.

Receipts, wrappings, useless stuff. I grunted, cursing my rashness as the train came to a halt. Boss and Bob must be on their way; perhaps they were already in this very same car and it was too late.

I shoved the papers back into the pocket, and as I did so, I noticed another piece of paper. It had stuck to the inner lining. A telegram. The image of Boss bringing us correspondence flashed in my head. The man had barked at me when I almost saw that second telegram.

'To hell,' I mumbled, pulling it out. If they were to find me there, I might as well make it worth it.

I nearly tore the message when I unfolded it, and then read the single, short line it contained: *Write if they discover d'Esté.*

And the sender was one *Lady Lois Brurs*.

I read it all twice to memorize it, and then the steam whistle sounded again. There was no time. I shoved the telegram back into the pocket, threw the jacket onto the bed without caring where or how it fell, and stormed out of the compartment.

My heart jumped as I saw half a dozen people coming and going, fetching their luggage or buttoning up their coats, ready to alight.

My eyes flickered left and right, but the PM's men were not around. Not yet.

I rushed to the first-class car, but before I made it to the connecting doors a child's voice shouted behind me.

'Sir! Sir!'

I initially ignored the young boy, as I grabbed the door's handle and peered ahead. Even through the two cars' misted-up door windows, I saw the unmistakable shadows of Boss and Bob, towering and broad, in the first-class car. And they walked briskly in my direction.

'You dropped this!' the child insisted, pulling at my jacket.

I turned to tell him to go away, and found the small boy grinning, his stumpy arm stretched out, offering me a small, folded piece of paper.

The name *Hilda* was like a needle into my eyes.

'*Oh, God!*'

I cursed my clumsy left hand. The photograph must have stuck to my sweaty fingers, and then clung to the buttons of my jacket or the flaps of my pockets. Whatever the case, there it was, flaunted in the air like a flag by that little boy.

'It's all right, I saved it for you!' he exclaimed, misunderstanding my shock.

All I could do was grab the damn photo and shove it into my pocket. When I turned, there they were – the PM's men – stepping into the second-class car and standing mere inches from my face.

'What the hell are you up to?' Boss snarled, not bothering to close the car's door, the icy wind and the noise filling the aisle.

Thank goodness his voice and face scared the wits out of the little child, who ran away saying no more.

My hand was still in my pocket, touching the photograph of Boss's – most likely – lost love. I feared if I pulled it out, the photo would stick to my fingers again and fall right before his squinting eyes.

'I thought you two would be ready,' I spluttered, playing indignant. 'But I see you were still stuffing your muzzles.' With my chin I pointed at the egg yolk smeared on the corner of Bob's mouth.

At once I walked past them, jumping precariously from car to car. I only pulled my hand out of my pocket when I was sure they'd not see it. The photograph stayed in place. I turned around to close the door, thinking I'd throw the photo out the nearest window. To my dismay, Boss's hand appeared, holding the door firmly before the latch could click.

'Get our jackets,' he told Bob. 'I'll see that the Inspector alights . . . safely.'

I breathed out, doing my best to disguise my frustration.

Thankfully I had already re-packed my case. I grabbed it, allowed myself one last drink of lukewarm coffee, and then made my way to the frosty platform.

Bob joined us, leaving deep footsteps on the snow. Rather than feeling I'd walked out to the open, it seemed I'd entered a deep cavern. The lights of the modest Wetherby train station were the only ones in sight, and as the train moved away, the glinting railway was all I could see on either side of the platform.

'Quick,' said Boss after Bob tossed him his jacket and coat. 'We need to hire a coach before we hear any bloody ravens.'

I stared at him as he donned the garments. Thankfully he did not check his pockets.

As I followed him into the station – or, rather, the small red brick shed – I tried to lag behind and drop the damn portrait. I could not do it once we'd jumped into a narrow carriage and their eyes were inches from my hands. Bob, to my dismay, never took his eyes off me.

All I could do was move on, praying that Boss did not look at his sweetheart that often.

24

We took a most erratic route, lurking silently across the darkened fields of Yorkshire. We only sped up after the sun rose, so that we did not spend too long on those open fields; mile upon mile of rolling hills, all covered in snow, with only a few bare oaks scattered here and there. Above, the thick clouds billowed and swirled in slow motion, almost like the bubbling surface of a cauldron. They stayed like that throughout the day.

Since we were not to tell anyone our final destination, we stopped at a very small village – Bishopthorpe, I think the signs said – where we would spend the night. We paid the driver, and as soon as the man was out of sight, we looked for a carriage and horse we could buy.

In such a tiny village, there was only *one* someone wanted to sell – a black two-seater, quite narrow, which looked more like an oversized coffin. It came with a horse ready for the knacker's yard, and we also got hold of a map of York, which the keeper of the village's only inn sold us for an eye-watering amount.

There was no chance for me to get rid of Boss's *gal*. We had to share a bedroom at the drab inn (I shan't go into detail, for I am still trying to erase that from my memory), and the following morning we set off without delay. Bob set himself on the driver's seat, so I had to travel in the tiny coach rubbing shoulders with Boss. I did try to pull the photo out of my pocket and toss it out the window, but Boss kept staring at me with suspicious eyes.

It went on like that for hours, so I decided to focus on the map instead. Coney Street ran on the northern side of River Ouse, on the south end of the city; one of the main roads, it seemed. The George Hotel, which covered a substantial plot, was at a prudent distance from the busier train station and York Minster. McGray had chosen wisely.

When I looked up, the city walls could already be seen in the distance – brooding, deterring stone, standing proud on top of the seven-foot-tall promontory that surrounded York. Beyond, looking milky and blurry in the morning haze, rose the ghostly towers of the cathedral, their spires like ominous crowns. I imagined the awe that medieval peasants would have felt at that sight.

'Turn right,' I told Bob when we reached the wall. 'There is a ferry landing there.'

We found it soon enough, the flat boat taking goods and passengers to the other side of the river. Most of them were merchants, their carts loaded with all manner of produce, the drivers yawning and sipping hot brews from steaming tankards. It was almost midday, but with the dull sky and the frosty air, there was an early morning feel to the scene.

Bob paid and we waited in complete silence until the ferry came back. The crossing, in contrast, proved rather tortuous, the noisy little boat swaying in the choppy waters, bringing me unpleasant memories of our ghastly trip to the Orkneys.

Thankfully, after only a few minutes we were dropped on the other side, right in front of York's castle – a rather flamboyant name for the medieval lump of limestone that still acted as the county's gaol.

We rode around its imposing walls, which were covered in soot and then topped with contrasting snow. Beyond, and standing well above the wall's turrets, was the castle's old keep – Clifford's Tower, according to my map. Its ancient walls, round and eroded over the centuries, made me think of a gigantic beehive on top of a snow-covered mount.

We then turned to the left, into the heart of York.

'Go on straight until I tell you,' I commanded Bob.

Coney Street appeared quite wide on the map; one of the city's main avenues. In reality, it was a dingy, pestilent little road, narrower even than the most constricted stretch of the Royal Mile in Edinburgh. Though the road was flagstone, it was covered in so much manure and slush that at points it appeared that we rode on bare soil.

I was glad to see the small sign of the George Hotel to my left, just above a grimy gas lamp that needed to be kept lit despite the hour.

'Here,' I told Bob. He halted right under the lamp's light, and Boss and I jumped off.

The main door was flanked by columns, small and rather vulgar, that supported the two red-brick storeys above. Through the opaque windows I saw old curtains that had been white a long time ago, and even a small section of a ceiling whose plaster was flaking off.

'In there, quick,' said Boss, pushing my suitcase on me, and Bob took the two-seater on, to a narrow ginnel that led to the back of the hotel and, from the smell, to the stables too.

We stepped into the entrance hall – a dark, small place, entirely covered in old wood panelling and threadbare green carpets. Though everything was reasonably clean, the smell of dust and old building prevailed.

A very old man, hunched and with skin so saggy it seemed his skull was a couple of sizes too small for his flesh, came to the counter.

'A room, gentlemen?' he asked without further ado, in deep Yorkshire tones.

'*Two*,' I rushed to answer, still wincing at the discomforts of the previous night (and feeling as if the portrait of Boss's sweetheart burned inside my pocket). He simply sneered as the old man gave us our keys. I had to make a conscious effort not to sprint towards the stairs as soon as I had them in my hand. My face, however, must have betrayed me.

'Stay in the building,' Boss told me. 'We'll wait for the others here, so save the sightseeing for another trip.' And he slightly opened his jacket to pat the grip of his gun.

That gave me reason enough to shove the keys in my pocket, pick up my suitcase and rush upstairs.

A tired cleaner, as thin as a stooping crane, was sweeping my room.

'Would you mind?' I said rather harshly, but unable to keep calm.

'I'll come back later,' she answered lazily, her accent very much reminding me of Joan's – something I must never tell a proud Lancashire woman.

As soon as she was gone I dropped my luggage, locked the door and looked at my claustrophobic room; again, reasonably clean but faded after years and years without major repairs. The narrow window looked over the slushy backyard, where Bob was leaving the cab and horse with a couple of hungry-looking stable boys. I shut the curtains as soon as I saw him, and rushed to light the oil lamp on my minuscule bedside table – quite a feat with just one hand.

As soon as the flame steadied I produced the damn photograph, eager to burn it there and then. I unfolded it and had what I thought would be my last look of that female face.

Again I saw those fetching eyes, most likely pale blue, and that cunning, confident stare. It was a modest portrait, yet the lighting and the pose were quite tasteful.

What could have come of her? Dead? Forced to marry someone else? *Happily* marrying someone else?

I turned it over and read the scribble again – *Hilda, 1878*.

Was that simply the date of the picture, or might it mean something else? Like the year of her demise? Her dress did look old fashioned, but I could not possibly pinpoint the exact year. The paper was crumpled and yellowy, but again, I could not tell if it was five, ten or twenty years old.

And then, as if that little portrait had cast some spell on me, another reckless idea crept into my mind.

I would keep it.

I still had no idea of its significance, but whatever it might be, it would be of much greater value in my hand than as a heap of ashes.

Only I had to hide it. I had no idea what Boss might do if he found out I had been rummaging through his clothes, or if he realized that I had a good inkling as to what might be one of the most painful chapters of his past.

I looked for a suitable hiding place – other than my suitcase or under the bed. As I did so, I thought I must also record what I'd read in the telegram, before I forgot it. I produced my small pencil and scribbled the message on the back of the photograph – *Write if they discover d'Esté*. I also jotted down the name of the mysterious sender . . . *Lady Lois Brurs*.

Even as I wrote it, the truth unscrambled before my eyes.

That sender's name was but a crude anagram of *Lord Salisbury*.

I might have seen it sooner, had I not been so worried about hiding the portrait.

So here it was, right before my eyes! What the Prime Minister, for some reason, feared we – or the witches – might find out!

Could *d'Esté* be another anagram or code? Could it—?

I heard heavy footsteps on the staircase, most likely Bob's, reminding me I should hide the photograph first and contemplate later. If Boss were to realize he'd lost it, it was likely to happen right now, as he took off his coat in the privacy of his own room.

I looked around, squatted and felt the floorboards, but then found a better place. I folded the photograph into four and inserted it into a gap between the skirting board and the wall, just underneath the bedside table.

Then I rose quickly, as if fearing they could see me through the walls, and dropped myself on the bed.

For a long while I waited, expecting to hear Boss growling, hammering my door and demanding I give back what I had taken.

It did not happen.

Still, I had to put that little piece of paper in safer hands. Preferably, hands that could hit back.

I could not wait for Nine-Nails to arrive.

25

I tried to get some rest, but my mind was swarming with qualms. The portrait, the encoded telegram, the fact that McGray and Caroline and Joan might never arrive ... what might happen if we failed to find the York witches, or if they refused to help us, or if they were simply unable to commune with the late Prince Albert and we had to face the full wrath of Queen Victoria?

That last thought made me jump out of bed. I left the room, which suddenly felt suffocating, and after triple-checking that the door was properly locked, I went in search of the smoking room.

It was one storey below, its wide window looking over the road. The opaque, scratched panes further dulled the winter daylight, and the floating specks of dust made me feel as if I were stepping into a foggy marsh. The murky green of the frayed carpets and furniture enhanced the vision.

The only other person around was a chubby middle-aged man who'd fallen asleep clasping his newspaper, so I lounged at leisure.

There was a tall bookcase, as dusty as an Egyptian crypt, full of books with spines so faded I guessed they'd sat there for years.

I looked for something – anything – I might read, each title less appealing than the previous one, until—

I could not repress a gasp. My eyes fell on a tired copy whose gilded title read, *Leaves from the Journal of Our Life in the Highlands.*

I pulled it out and the front cover nearly fell off when I opened it. The title page confirmed what I expected:

QUEEN VICTORIA'S MEMOIR OF THE PRINCE CONSORT

This was the queen's first published book!

It did not surprise me that even this drab hotel kept a copy. The self-indulgent, appallingly written little brick had sold in the thousands, the entire British Empire keen to fish out details of Her Majesty's supposed affair with her Scottish manservant John Brown. Even Lady Anne kept second-hand copies in her properties – bought along with other assorted books by weight, since it was one of those once-famous books nobody had any interest in reading anymore.

The tome was hefty and falling apart, so I had to lay it on the table, where I could leaf through it with just one hand. I was almost certain it would offer me nothing, but at least it would keep my mind busy.

Busy, yet not happy. The oversentimental depictions of the landscapes, the palaces and the people dancing Scottish reels and polkas soon made me yawn. Particularly frustrating was her obsessive naming of every single lord and sir who'd ever lent her a carriage – most of them unknown demi-royals, completely irrelevant to the vast majority of the populace.

And the pipers! Oh, the endless pages she devoted to the bloody, bloody pipers. *They very often played about at breakfast-time, again during the morning at luncheon, and whenever we went out . . .* And she always named them with an uppercase 'P' as though they were citizens of a magical fairy land.

In the end I was grunting with anger. The same capricious hand that had written about the *extreme beauty of Inverary*, the *noble lakes* and the *magnificent timber*, had also signed my death sentence after failing to contact her most trusted sorceresses.

I was about to close the book with a thump, but then found the passage that gossipers like my stepmother would have surely perused over and over. The page looked particularly worn-out in this copy, darker than all the others and nearly falling off the stitching. The name *Brown* was mentioned, followed by a 'footnote' that only left room for three lines of actual text above it. At its core it read:

> *In 1851 he entered our service permanently, and began in that year leading my pony, and advanced step by step by his good conduct and intelligence. His attention, care, and faithfulness cannot be exceeded; and the state of my health, which of late years has been sorely tried and weakened, renders such qualifications most valuable, and, indeed, most needful in a constant attendant upon all occasions. He has since (in December, 1865), most deservedly, been promoted to be an upper servant, and my permanent personal attendant. He has all the independence and elevated feelings peculiar to the Highland race, and is singularly straightforward, simple-minded, kind-hearted, and disinterested; always ready to oblige; and of a discretion rarely to be met with. He is now in his fortieth year.*

No wonder eyebrows had been raised. It reminded me of all the scandals of the Hanovers; the endless lists of mistresses, the many annulled marriages and the endless list of illegitimate children, until at some point none of the princes' offspring was eligible to inherit the crown. Queen Victoria herself, despite her larger-than-life airs, had been conceived at the drop of a hat, from a patched-up marriage only instigated because her more-than-fifty cousins were all barred from inheriting the crown. I wondered if those royals would ever learn.

I read on, looking for more detail, but that was it; one overgrown footnote to her suspected lover. On the following pages, Victoria moved on to describe a torch-lit ball in painful detail and language – *the Highlanders danced pretty nearly alternately*. She even told the number of Pipers, their names and employment histories.

I closed the book, sighing and rubbing my eyes. The chambermaid came in then, bringing me yet another pot of tea – a ghastly brew, but the young woman was so attentive I could not complain.

'You've been on that li'l book all day, sir,' she said, and as she bent down to pick up the cold pot, she winked at me. 'Take it with you. No one will even notice it's gone.'

'Thank you,' I said, 'but it will not be necessary.' I saw her light the lamps, and only then did I realize the passage of time. 'Have no other guests arrived?' I asked her, standing up to peer through the window. The sky had gone pitch-black.

'No, sir. It's been a quiet month. Far too quiet.'

An ominous feeling began to grow in my chest, and it was soon worsened as Boss came into the room, lighting a cigarette.

'Leave us,' he growled at the maid, who curtsied and left quickly. Boss then eyed the room to ensure we were alone – the sleeping old man had gone a while ago – and closed the door behind his back.

He stared at me with squinted eyes, and for a moment I thought he was about to beat me to a pulp.

'Step away from the window,' he said at last, and I went back to where I'd been sitting all the afternoon. Boss remained standing, staring out into the streets. 'Something must have happened on the roads.'

'I know,' I answered. 'Miss Ardglass and her party should be here already.'

'That gypsy woman they went to fetch – is she reliable?'

I chuckled. 'Reliable is not the word I'd choose, but she owes us a lot. And she is unquestionably loyal to Inspector McGray.'

Boss looked doubtful. He had one of those piercing stares that seem to read everybody's mind.

'She will never give us away,' I said earnestly, but Boss only nodded, still unconvinced. He squinted a little more. I thought he was about to say something, but he simply walked away, leaving the door open.

Again I rubbed my eyes. Very soon I would have to contemplate the possibility that the worst had happened; that McGray or Caroline – or both – had been intercepted. What would I do then? How long should I wait? What was that . . .? What was that icy draught that came into the smoking room?

It was as though someone had left a window open, letting in the coldest December air.

The door began to sway, so I went over to close it. Then, before I could lay a finger on the knob, someone pulled it away and I was swiftly dragged into the darkened corridor.

26

A huge hand, thick and gloved, pulled me by the collar, and its pair covered my mouth and eyes before I could even gasp.

I could only growl and jerk as I was dragged into God only knew where, and I could see nothing but stars, with that hand pressing my eyeballs with mighty strength.

I was readying myself to suffer all sorts of torture; to be beaten to a pulp; to be stabbed and thrown into a ditch . . . I heard the sound of doors being pushed open, and felt the air around me grow colder and colder.

The hand on my face slid down to cover just my mouth, but my eyes only met the purest blackness. The other hand loosened its grip around my body, and I heard a creaking door being opened.

That hand impaled me against a cold, damp wall, protruding bricks sticking into my back. As I struggled, I heard the door close, a latch, and then a metallic clink. I was trapped.

A match ignited right before my eyes, and I even felt the heat of the flame as it drew closer to my face. I whimpered and writhed, expecting it to be pressed against my pupils and melt them like beeswax.

A pair of bloodshot, yellowy eyes glinted behind the flame.

I had to blink twice, for a moment unable to believe what I saw. Under the weight of his thick hand, I growled what vaguely sounded like 'Harris!'

The man nodded, and as he did so I saw his scalp, perfectly smooth and covered in seeping tattoos. He saw the recognition on my face. Only then did he let go of my mouth, but quickly pressed a finger against his lips, bidding silence.

I took a few deep breaths, suddenly realizing the ache in my broken wrist. I must have hit something while I struggled. I brought it to my chest and wrapped it with my healthy hand.

'Are they here?' I whispered as low as I could. Harris nodded. 'All of them? Nine-Nails? The women?' He nodded again and then produced a little piece of paper, rolled up like a parchment.

I smoothed it out and read it under the glow of the lighter. McGray's handwriting was unmistakable.

PM's men are a threat. They'll betray us. See us at The Gardener's Arms, Goodramgate Street. Right away. Don't let them follow you.

Rather than shock, I let out a tired moan. As soon as I did so, Harris pulled the note from my hand, crumpled it into a ball and then ate it. Quite literally, he ate it.

'What does he mean?' I asked. 'Am I in danger?' Harris nodded briskly. 'Do we have to leave now?'

Harris nodded again, and at once I thought of the photograph hidden in my room, my gun, Lord Salisbury's money . . .

'Do I have time to get my weapon?' I asked.

Harris looked at me, thoughtful. After a moment he gave me a single nod and then pretended to snap his fingers twice, telling me to make haste. He opened the door an inch, peered out and then let me pass. He pointed at the floor meaning I should join him there.

I slid along the corridor as quickly and silently as I could. Thankfully Harris had dragged me to a broomstick cupboard not far from the servants' stairs. I sprinted to the second floor and soon found the way to my room. Only—

Bob was there, smoking right next to my door, his back against the wall.

He stared at me with wincing eyes.

'What were you doing on *that* side?' he demanded, and with his chin pointed at the broader staircase, a few yards away.

'Looking for the blasted maid, if you must know,' I answered, feigning indignation, and quickly unlocked the door and entered my chamber. I locked it again as noisily as I could, cursing my luck. I could not get out now, with that bloody man standing there.

First things first, I thought, forcing in a deep breath. I pulled the photograph from behind the skirting board, gathered my gun, bullets and the thick wallet still bursting with notes.

For one frustrating moment I debated whether or not I should don my hat and coat. I looked out the window and saw thick snowflakes swirling around the one lamp in the backyard. It would be freezing cold out there. Then again, if I left my room and Bob saw me ready to go out . . .

There was shouting then.

It was a female voice, followed by a very low, yet ominous growl. Bob ran, his heavy steps moving away, and then down the cracking stairs.

There was no time to lose. I put on my coat at once, unlocked the door with my trembling left hand and, without time to reach for my hat, darted towards the backstairs.

As soon as I laid a foot on the first step, I heard the chambermaid's tearful voice. The same woman who'd brought me tea throughout the afternoon.

'I didn't! *I didn't, sir!*' she shouted from the lower floor in clear despair. 'I never even went into your room!'

For a split second I was tempted to move on, but then Boss howled like a wild beast.

'*You lying witch!*'

And his voice was followed by the sound of two mighty blows, fist on flesh, and the poor woman crying in agony.

I ran back to the main staircase, pulling out my gun. Just as I remembered how appalling my aim with my left hand was, I reached the landing, where Boss was shaking the young woman, Bob standing by his side.

The maid's lip was swollen, a thin trickle of blood on her chin, and her hair had burst from her ribbons and flailed in the air as Boss shook her.

'*You took it, you filthy liar!*'

'I didn't! I—!'

'*I took it!*' I hollered. 'I took the photograph!'

All heads turned to me, Bob and the maid quickly, but Boss moved sluggishly, grinding his teeth and exhaling with unabated wrath.

His gaze, fierce, swung back and forth between my face and my gun.

'On the train . . .' he hissed. '*I knew it*, you little swine!'

He threw the maid against the wall. She shrieked and fell on the floor like a bundle of rags, as Boss and Bob took slow, menacing steps in my direction.

'Stop right there!' I shouted, holding the gun firmly, but they only laughed, their heavy feet stomping on the squeaking steps.

I took clumsy steps back, struggling to move upwards while keeping my eyes on them.

'*Stop!*' I shouted again, but they both laughed.

'We saw you practise in Edinburgh,' Boss sneered, and then eyed my coat. 'Are you about to flee? Don't be a fool.

Give me that picture back and I might pretend this never happened.'

I took another step back and nearly tripped.

'Who is she?' I asked, at once wiping the smile off his face. 'Your sweetheart? Did she die in 1878? That's a long mourning.'

As I said so I looked at the maid, indicating with my chin that she should leave. The poor creature crawled on the floor and soon became lost in the hall's shadows.

When I looked back at Boss he was unnervingly close.

'*Stay back!*' I roared, and when they simply laughed and leapt towards me, undeterred, as if about to grab a little child, a burning rage took hold of me.

I shot at the wall, the two men instinctively protecting their faces, and I darted upstairs, shooting twice in their direction without bothering to look.

My legs burned as I made it to the second floor, again running past my room and on to the servants' stairs. A massive shadow came from those narrow steps; Harris, with a gun at the ready and his yellowy eyes alert. He pulled me by the arm into the staircase, just as the sound of frantic steps and voices echoed behind my back.

We descended at full speed, the stairs becoming darker and darker as we went down, until all I could see was the mere outline of Harris's shoulders. Then I heard the crack of metal and wood as he kicked some battered back door, and then the dim moonlight appeared before us. I saw the icy backyard and ran on without pause.

My feet skidded on the slush and I nearly lost my balance, but Harris pulled me by the back of my collar and kept me standing. He effectively dragged me to the stables and kicked the nearest little door open, the old wood snapping like dry biscuit.

I recognized the same measly horse Boss and I had bought that very morning, the poor beast scared and cowering in a corner. Harris jumped on its back, the horse's legs briefly bending under his weight. I was going to protest, but then Harris seized my right arm – yes, the right one – and pulled me upwards.

I squealed in pain, kicking about until I managed to mount and cling to his waist. He spurred the horse without delay and the animal galloped towards the ginnel.

Just as we crossed the backyard, Boss emerged from the backdoor, leaping in my direction with his hands set to grab me.

It did not need too much skill to throw him a kick right at his nose, sending a spurt of blood all over his absurd moustache.

And as Harris took the scrawny horse away, my overcoat flailing in the icy wind, I understood why McGray took so much pleasure in punching people.

27

We rode erratically for just a few minutes, zigzagging across the narrow streets of York.

With the ancient Tudor timber all around us, the overhanging upper storeys and the diamond-paned windows, each stride of the panting horse seemed to be taking us centuries into the past.

Without streetlamps, candles and hearths from within the crammed buildings were all the light we had, and at every corner I expected to see a band of cloaked witches armed with green torches.

Just as I thought so, a large raven cawed. I looked up and saw it fluttering above our heads.

My heart skipped a beat as the bird got lost above the irregular roofs.

How could they have found us? Which of the three parties could have given us away? McGray, Caroline or myself? Could this mean that the York witches had now fled? One more layer of questions to my already baffled head. I remembered McGray's message – *PM's men are a threat. They'll betray us.* What could he mean by that? How could he have found out? Could this be a trap? Could someone have forged McGray's handwriting? Could Harris be leading me to my death?

Just as that thought made me shudder, Harris led the horse into a darkened ginnel, dismounted and then helped me down. He made some apologetic grunt when he saw me clutching my splinted wrist.

'It is fine,' I mumbled, trying to conceal my sudden distrust. 'You – you did what you had to.'

We left the horse there, the poor beast's steaming breath swirling in the air, and continued our way by foot. I did not need to produce the map, for Harris moved with swift steps, turning here and there without a hint of hesitation.

I, on the other hand, kept looking in all directions, fearing to hear the voices of Boss and Bob, or see their tall shadows emerge whenever we turned around a corner. I even watched Harris's every move, fearing that as soon as we reached a dark alley he might produce a dagger and slit my throat. When finally we made it to a curved street marked as Goodramgate (I wondered if McGray had chosen it for ironic effect) my nerves were shattered.

The Gardener's Arms appeared soon enough. The pub's sign, cracked and faded after decades of inclement weather, racketed under the frosty wind.

It turned out to be one of those sixteenth-century buildings, the dark oaken beams curved after hundreds of years supporting the upper floors, the plaster and windows leaning over the road as if about to collapse out of exhaustion.

It also appeared to be the only animated spot around that street, countless moving shadows visible through the steamed-up windows, but the chatter was low and constrained, not the raucous cheer and laughter I always encountered at the Ensign Ewart in Edinburgh.

Harris pushed the door open and the hot, clammy air hit us, heavy with the smells of stale beer, old pickles and confined humanity. It was not the smells, however, that made me cough, but the thick, sickly smoke that floated in the air.

The dubious clientele – all male except for a few unapologetic prostitutes – instantly turned in my direction, all eyes menacing. This was one of those dens where people came to conduct less-than-reputable business.

'*Put t'wood in t'oil!*' cried someone at the bar. I could only blink at the mercilessly bastardized language, until one of the *ladies* came to shut the door behind me. That seemed to pacify the shouting man.

Harris had to place a hand on my shoulder. His half-shut eyes told everyone, 'Don't mess with the dandy, he's with me,' and he led me to a steep staircase, with a banister so sticky I could not suppress a jolt when I touched it. I went up the steps, fearing what I might find there. Thankfully, not darkness or silence.

The first floor was divided into private snugs, separated by wooden panels and smoked glass. The murmur of a dozen conversations could be heard all around us, all in mumbles, all stern. I could only imagine the sort of deals that were being—

'*Ian, my boy!*'

The loud, rasping voice made me jump, just as a plump little figure leapt in my direction. A pair of thick arms locked around me, the grey feathers of a cheap bonnet tickling my nose.

After enduring her effusive greeting, I had my first good look at the woman – Madame Katerina herself.

The middle-aged gypsy was quite changed. Gone were the multicoloured veils and the countless lines of beads and charms she sported at her clairvoyance sessions back in Edinburgh. Tonight she wore a simple grey velvet dress, and her infamously wide bosom, which admittedly attracted half her male clientele, was decently covered. Her fingernails, usually a couple of inches long and curved like an eagle's talons, were now short and polished. At a first glance, nobody would have guessed that only a few months ago she was still the owner of an establishment even grimmer than the present one – half brewery, half divination rooms, where she entertained and swindled the lowest of the Scottish hoi polloi.

The only clue as to her past, particularly her last turbulent months in Edinburgh, was the black satin choker around her neck, which I knew covered the scars left by the gallows.

Despite all those changes, her piercing green eyes remained undimmed, and at that moment were buoyant with anxiety.

'Did they follow you?' she asked Harris before I could say a word. The giant shook his head and Katerina let out a sigh. 'Come in, we don't have much time,' and she dragged me into her dimly lit booth, ensconced in the most secluded corner of the first floor. 'Everyone's here, safe and sound. Well . . . almost.'

The first thing I saw – courtesy of the one lit candle standing right next to it – was a game pie the size of Harris's head, surrounded by pint glasses and tankards. Behind it, his legs stretched almost all across the booth, sat Nine-Nails.

Again I thought he looked strange without his garish tartan trousers. He was lounging back on a bench, moaning, his white shirt stained with dry blood. To his left sat Joan, holding a bowl of warm water, and to his right was Caroline, attempting to press a cloth against his bleeding temple. Clearly, he had arrived only a few minutes before sending me the message.

'*Ouch!* That fucking hurts!'

'Because you keep moving!' Caroline retorted. 'So much for the hard-as-nails inspector . . .'

'What happened?' I asked.

'The bitches found me,' said McGray.

'*They what?*' I yelped. 'And how did you all – Why did you ask me – When did—?'

'We'll explain all,' said Katerina. 'But have some food. I asked them to bring us the good stuff. I'm only sorry they won't have the sort of wine you like.'

Katerina pulled a chair out for me and even wiped it with her sleeve. As she rose, she noticed that Caroline regarded her attentions with disbelieving eyes.

'This young man saved my life,' she told her, patting my left hand and virtually pushing me into the chair. 'Mighty brave and clever, he was. Here, Ian. Look—' and she pulled a little silver locket from underneath her bodice. She opened it excitedly and I saw the tiny photograph of a twelve-year-old boy. Even in the black-and-white portrait the youth's eyes stood out, wide and alert, surely the same bright green as his mother's.

'Isn't he handsome?' she said affectionately. 'I visited him first thing. Well, I still haven't told him I'm his mother . . . Maybe when he's a wee bit older . . . time will tell.' Her eyes were misting up, staring lovingly at the boy's image. She shook her head and put the locket away. 'But eat, my boy!'

She cut me a thick slice of the pie and nearly forced it into my mouth. It was juicy pheasant and pigeon, deliciously spiced with sage and rosemary.

'I got you Yorkshire's best,' she said.

Joan, from afar, looked at Katerina with a clear pang of jealousy.

'That can't be from Yorkshire,' she protested, proudly accentuating her Lancashire inflections. 'Look at all the meat in there!'

I wondered if my eyes looked just as jealous when I saw Caroline tending to McGray's wounds.

'What happened?' I asked him. 'How did you get here? I saw a raven outside. Is it you the witches are following? And why did you ask me to shed the PM's troglodytes? What did you mean they will betray us? How did you *even*—?'

McGray raised both palms. 'Oi, oi, calm down! I'll tell ye— Ouch!' He winced as Caroline bandaged his head, but put on a brave face. 'First things first. Aye, as ye can guess, the soddin' witches found me. They must have spotted me in one o' the trains in Lancashite.'

'Do you mean Lancashire?'

'Nae. The whole idea of going that way was to make them believe we were after their trail over there, and it worked a wee bit too fucking well! They were on me as soon as I stepped off the train in soddin' Burnley.'

'Hey! That's where I'm from!' Joan protested.

McGray did not pay attention.

'Three thugs larger than this one,' he added, nodding at Harris. Then he rolled up his sleeve, to show another thick bandaging. 'They got me with a knife before I could shake 'em off me. The damn peelers at the station did nothing!'

'Bribed by witches?' I asked.

'Maybe, or they just thought the rascals were too much for them to handle. I did manage to throw one o' them to the rails and then ran to the horses' car to get on Inky. I barely had time to mount. Thank goodness it was quite dark and they couldnae follow me.' He had a long swig of ale and flinched at the taste. 'But they did follow my tracks. There were bloody ravens flying over me all that day . . . Yesterday! Damn, it feels it was ages— *Ouch!* What the—?'

'*There!*' Caroline barked, securing the last knot of the bandages. 'I am done, are you happy now?'

'Happier if ye hadnae put yer *gentle* hands on me in the first place. I was sayin', I was arriving in York, just about to cross that bloody medieval gate—'

'Bootham Bar,' Caroline specified. 'They already knew you'd be entering the city that way.'

'Aye,' McGray went on, 'and then those two damned skellums came out o' nowhere with bludgeons thicker than yer waist, Frey.

'They pulled me from the horse –' he pointed at his temple – 'nae the softest landing – and for a second I was convinced they were going to beat me to a bloody mush.' He shuddered and then looked earnestly at Harris. 'Thanks, laddie. I'd be dead if ye hadnae showed up.'

Harris gave a quick nod, as if thanked for lending someone a tuppence.

I looked at Caroline and Katerina. 'How did you know they'd attack him, down to the very instant and spot?'

McGray breathed out, a hand on his brow. 'Ye tell 'im, hen. I'm drained.'

He signalled Katerina, who was striking a match and leisurely lighting up a smoking pipe. I noticed Caroline shifted uncomfortably in her seat.

'The Messengers?' I asked. 'Did they contact you again?'

It was Katerina who replied, but only after puffing some smoke.

'Yes, and we have a good deal to tell you about them. Just as you suspected, the Messengers *are* the York witches.'

28

I was taking a bite of pie when she said this, and crumbs of pastry fell from my open mouth.

'*What?*' I cried. 'How do you know? Is that what you could not tell us by telegraph?'

'No, no,' said Katerina. She breathed out with some impatience. 'I'd better tell you the story in order.

'I knew a thing or two about the surviving witches, and I dug a good deal more after Adolphus contacted me. I originally wanted to tell you that the coven that remained in Lancashire, the one you call *The Marigolds*, is the one you should fear the most.

'They are the ones who've been threatening their old debtors; even cutting a throat here and there to make an example of them. Those are the ones everyone fears the most right now, maybe even your prime minister. They must be the ones he's after; the ones he wants you to find so he can take care of them later.' She looked at Caroline. 'Those are the ones who attacked you and your nanny, my dear. I'm *so* sorry.'

Caroline only nodded once, too drained to say a word.

'Brave gal,' Katerina told her, patting her hand. 'She met me in Newcastle and told me everything you've been through. Of course, I couldn't just leave you to deal with this on your own, so we rushed here immediately. We must have arrived not two hours ago. We came here first to check on my correspondence . . .'

'Your correspondence?' I said.

Katerina nodded. 'This is where I used to get my mail and parcels from the black market. My contacts left them here and my men came to pick them up.' She looked at Nine-Nails. 'Many of the books and specimens in your collection passed through here before reaching you.

'Before we left Newcastle I sent a telegram to my middleman here in York. I asked him to meet us. I was expecting he would have left his reply here, as he usually does . . . but he hadn't.

Caroline's chest swelled. 'Instead we found that there was a little parcel waiting for us. Or rather – for *me*.'

'Is that how you confirmed the Messengers are settled here?' I jumped in.

'Yes,' Caroline said. 'Only the York coven knew that Madame Katerina and I were coming to this – fine establishment. Not even you or Mr McGray were aware we'd stop here. Also, I recognized the parcel at once. It looked just like the ones the witches had sent me before, and this one too had a message written in vinegar.'

'The last clue we needed,' McGray said. 'All the wee parcels came from York.'

'We brought it to this very table and unravelled the message in it with that very candle,' Caroline added. She looked at Katerina. 'Show them, please.'

Katerina, out of old habits, had kept the piece of paper in her bosom, along with her locket. She pulled it out, unfolded it and laid it on the table. I did not dare touch it.

'They warned us of two things. First, that the Marigolds were after Adolphus, so we must send help to the old gateways.'

McGray raised a pint to that.

'And the other warning?' I asked. 'Was that about Lord Salisbury?'

'Yes,' Katerina replied, pointing at the relevant lines. 'They said that the PM's men were bound to betray you and that you should shake them off as soon as possible. Miss Ardglass here knew your meeting point, so we sent the big lad for you right away.'

I looked at the writing. The same hand I'd seen in the messages Caroline had received before. I read the succinct message twice.

'They . . . do not tell us more,' I said. 'Why the PM might betray us or how they came to know that.'

'No,' said Katerina. 'They only stress that every second you remained in their company put your life at greater risk.'

I sat back and pondered for a moment. I remembered Boss's frenzied eyes when he realized I had taken the photograph from his pocket. He'd shown no embarrassment, but pure, unmitigated wrath. Could it be that—?

'Can we trust them?' McGray said then. 'The Messengers. D'youse think they're telling us the truth about bawbag face? I mean, the PM?'

Caroline let out a tired sigh. 'Whenever they've told me I'm in peril they have been truthful.'

But Katerina was shaking her head.

'That doesn't mean these York Messengers are trustworthy. It might only mean they needed you alive and well to do their murky errands in Germany.'

Joan made to say something. Perhaps: *Oh, so you really weren't away to get rid of some trouble!*. I cast her a fulminant stare and for once she remained silent.

When I looked back, Katerina's frown had deepened.

'Now that I think about it,' she said, 'these Messengers might well be the worst ones. My middleman didn't know much about them, only that these York women have made every effort to stay out of trouble while some of the other witches set their claws on each other. They might be saving up their strength until all the other groups – the reckless ones – are wounded beyond salvation. And the fact they sent you all those parcels and asked you to do all those things for them . . . They sound very scheming, very conniving to me.' She lounged back, staring at the ceiling as she smoked. 'Oh yes . . . they might be the most vicious of them all.'

A deep hush fell around the table, the murmurs from the other booths appearing to grow louder. We all looked doubtful.

'What d'ye ken about these York witches?' McGray asked Katerina. 'Ye said ye've done business with them?'

'Yes, a few times, to buy myrrh, sacred candles, mummy ashes, baboon livers . . . You know, Adolphus, my basic supplies.'

''Course,' he said as nonchalantly as possible.

'But you never met these witches in person, I suppose,' I said.

'No, only through my contact.'

'He's the lad that didnae show up?' McGray asked, and Katerina nodded. 'Were ye supposed to meet him here?'

'Oh, no. I gave him a place and time. He was only meant to leave his reply here, either confirming or refusing to see us.' She looked down. 'It's very strange he's not answered. He always, *always* does, even when he can't help me. Usually it's even more crucial to know that he can't help. Like right now.'

Nine-Nails sat back, his eyes suspicious. 'D'ye think the witches might have intercepted the telegrams? Told him to stay away from us or – taken care o' him?'

Katerina puffed at her pipe a few times. She even blew a perfect ring of smoke.

'I really don't know, my boy.'

We all sat there in silence for a while, watching how the smoke hovered in the air, the ring slowly twisting and twirling.

To everyone's surprise, Joan was the one to speak first.

'Those Yorkshire gals do sound iffy, if you ask *me*. When people don't talk straight and show their face, it's always with good reason.'

I arched an eyebrow, unable to contradict her casual wisdom. 'I think the same . . . and yet . . . they are the ones that Pansy – Miss McGray – sent us to meet.'

Katerina raised her chin, concern growing on her face.

'Are you sure that was her message?'

The air seemed to become thicker after those words.

'She could've been warning us,' McGray mumbled. 'Maybe we came to the very place she wanted us to avoid.'

I brought a hand to my brow, my anxieties stirring anew in my chest. For an instant I felt the urge to sprint on my feet and run as far as I could.

'If only there were a way to talk to her right now,' I grumbled. 'If only we could step into her mind and ask her what she—'

McGray's face rose as if pulled with a fishing line. As soon as our eyes met I regretted my words.

'No,' I said. 'You *cannot* be serious.'

Katerina was already smiling. 'Miss Ardglass told me that young Pansy cut out a little rose. Do you have it with you?'

'So that you can use your *inner eye*?' I mocked, but Katerina simply lifted an eyebrow.

'Och, just give her the sodding flower,' McGray snapped. 'What's the point of having a bloody clairvoyant if ye don't use her?' He glanced at Katerina. 'Sorry, hen.'

'Never mind, my boy.'

I exhaled with frustration, rummaging in my pocket. 'Why do I even bother arguing anymore?'

I produced my little notebook, nearly dropping the portrait of Boss's sweetheart.

'What's that?' McGray asked.

'I will tell you in a moment.' I pulled the little cloth flower from in between the pages and laid it on the table.

Everyone stared at it as if it were the most poisonous bloom, Nine-Nails in particular. His jaw was terribly tense, his eyes squinting slightly, like a man who knows he is about to witness a terrible horror but cannot bring himself to look away.

Katerina handed the pipe to Harris, took deep breaths, and then opened and closed her hands as if stretching her muscles.

For a moment, as she brought her arm towards the little piece of fabric, it was as though all the voices in the pub had gone quieter, the smoke around us fouler and denser.

The tip of Katerina's finger hovered less than an inch from the white rose, moving in small circles, yet not descending onto it. As I held my breath, like everyone else did around the table, I thought of two equally charged magnets repelling each other.

And then she touched it.

29

It was as if something stirred the air. Katerina leaned back, drawing in a hissing breath and contorting her face as if stricken by some excruciating pain. And yet, her finger remained pressing down on the white rose, her hand tense.

I'd seen her play that same act plenty of times, but even now, after the woman herself had told me she did lie from time to time, there was a certain edge to her features which I knew could not be faked. A flicker of her eyelids, a tension in her jaw and the tendons in her neck, a quiver in her hand . . . Perhaps she was certain she had powers – Dr Clouston had told me of the astounding powers of delusion – but still, Katerina had the most annoying tendency to be correct in her readings.

She shut her eyes tightly, the way we do when there is a light so bright even our eyelids cannot protect us. She grumbled then, moaned and grunted as her neck writhed, grinding her teeth so hard I feared she'd crush them. I could not repress a shiver; I had only seen her in such a state twice – and the second time she'd been about to hang.

Caroline and Joan were going to reach for her, just as a few curious heads began to peer over the partition's glass. McGray raised both arms, holding the women back, and with a nod commanded Harris to get rid of the onlookers.

I did not see what the giant man did, my eyes fixed on Madame Katerina. And then I recalled the first time I'd seen her thus altered: she had also been touching an item once held by Miss McGray, and the news had not been good.

Katerina took a long breath. The sound, a low, cold hiss, like a seashell pressed against your ear, was eerily familiar. Within a blink I was transported to the Orkneys, to that remote clinic. I was again at Pansy's room, the girl sitting by the window in her snow-white dress, just moments before she cut out the little piece of cloth that lay on the table.

Katerina shook from head to toe, as if stricken by a splash of icy water.

'There's . . .' she panted, 'there's so much . . .' She paused for a while, and only completed her sentence when McGray leaned forwards, ready to shake the words out of her.

'*Sorrow . . .*'

Caroline's lips parted, as did McGray's. His pupils dilated as he tried to speak, but not a sound came from his mouth.

Katerina frowned then, twisting her mouth in apparent confusion, like someone trying to read the tiniest of prints. She was not breathing, but I thought I could still hear that low seashell hiss.

'I see . . . souls, yearning for rest . . .'

McGray leaned forwards, knocking the table with his knees.

'Is Pansy one o' them?'

Katerina gulped.

'She's tired. Exhausted, Adolphus. Of course . . . locked in a little room and surrounded by madness . . . She must be.'

And then she let go of the rose, jumping backwards. She rubbed her fingertip as if she had just pulled it from the fire. Caroline went to her, put a gentle hand on her shoulder and spoke soothingly.

'Are you all right? What did you see?'

Katerina took a long, deep breath, and then stretched out a hand, seeking her smoking pipe. She puffed at it for a moment, her eyes shut. When finally she opened them, her eyes were all confusion.

'She wanted you here,' she muttered, slowly raising her gaze to meet McGray's. 'This is where you should be.'

But McGray had other troubles in mind.

'Ye said she wanted to rest . . .'

His words lingered. Nobody else could think of anything to say, not while Katerina looked at him with such concern.

'Something is about to shift, my boy . . . I'm *so* sorry.'

McGray sat back and rubbed his chin, his eyes welling up with tears. A gloomy sort of resignation began to settle on his face like a dark shroud.

I remembered the blood-curdling image of Pansy moving like a white vulture, the snip-snip of the scissors, the ghastly instant when I thought she was cutting her own flesh. Until then I had never even contemplated that the girl's despair might turn on herself.

Katerina cleared her throat.

'But now you know you're after the right coven. Your sister knew these are the ones who can help you.'

Caroline looked down, as gloomy as Nine-Nails.

'My father must have told her everything,' she whispered, going back to her bench. 'Maybe she always knew about the connection between the witches and Prince Albert. Maybe she spent all these months expecting this mayhem to begin . . .'

I nodded. That would explain the steady decline in Pansy's health. And McGray seemed to be thinking the same. A wave of exhaustion had swept over him, his eyes half lost, listening to Caroline as if her words were a dull dream.

Quite selfishly, I could only think that this was not the time to mourn, with enemies on all sides.

I nearly said something of the kind, but Katerina gently squeezed my arm, bidding composure, and with her other hand she reached McGray's four-fingered one.

'I'm *so* sorry, Adolphus,' she said in the most motherly tone, 'but you will have to deal with this later.' She gulped. 'If you even want to be alive to see her again.'

Her eyes were beseeching, the candlelight flickering on them.

McGray, still looking down, tensed his jaw as his frown deepened. He reached for the cloth rose, which looked minute in his fingers, and stared significantly at it.

Another wave of feeling began to take hold of him, a mixture of anger and . . . something else I could not quite read. Determination, perhaps. The cut-out began to tremble in his hand, so he shoved it in his breast pocket – out of sight and out of mind. Maybe this was not so bad; the situation forcing him to postpone those thoughts.

'So,' he said, a slight quiver in his voice. He cleared his throat. 'At least we have some clarity now.'

'Do we?' I asked.

'Aye. Did ye nae hear? Pansy sent us to the right coven, in which case we need to make every effort to meet Katerina's man.'

'No,' I protested. '*No!*' I repeated as soon as I caught Katerina about to say something. 'Let us not rush. As far as I know, we might be walking straight into a trap.'

'A trap?' Nine-Nails cried. 'Katerina just said that we're at the right place.'

I raised my voice. 'Allow me to summarize things from the very start.' And I did not wait for them to agree. 'Nine-Nails, you killed the Queen's most cherished witches—'

'Hey!'

'*After* you did so, their surviving sisters broke into different factions – covens.'

'Aye.'

'As far as we can tell, only two of those factions concern us. The Marigolds, who *presumably* are the ones who decided to blackmail their old clients, including the Prime Minister . . .' McGray nodded. 'And the Messengers, whom we now know to be settled here in York.

'They coerced Miss Ardglass to carry out two tasks for them.' I looked at her. 'Correct me if I get anything wrong, Miss. One of those tasks – stealing the German book – is downright puzzling and I will not even attempt to figure out its meaning right now. The other – watching Queen Victoria – initially made some sense.'

'Yes,' Caroline said. 'As I told you before, I assumed the covens would be competing to be the first ones to reach her and gain her favour. The Queen's support would give them a decisive advantage over all the other witches.'

'Indeed,' I said with a nod. 'Now, I understand why the Queen would want us dead . . .'

'Because everybody kens she's a fickle, revengeful, suet-gobbling auld coo.' Needless to state who said that.

'Crude, but more accurate than I could have conveyed,' I added. 'And the Prime Minister asking us to find them for him also makes sense, especially if he felt threatened by them. Besides our personal connections to the witches' case, few people in Britain are more versed in quackery than you two.' I nodded at Nine-Nails and Katerina, who smiled as if I'd paid them the highest compliment. 'Up until then, all the developments seemed to make sense. Now, however, both sides' actions have become illogical. The PM's alleged betrayal . . . and the witches failing to contact Queen Victoria.'

Katerina cleared her throat, a knowing expression in her eyes. 'I think I can explain that last one.'

'Please do, ma'am,' I said.

Katerina drew in air. 'The senior witches, Redfern and Marigold, must have been the ones who talked to Prince Albert. The only ones who knew how. And now they're both dead.'

'I also thought that might be the issue,' McGray said, 'but it didnae make sense to me. It's just contacting a dead man. Ye cannae call it *advanced*. People do séances all the time.'

'I can think of two reasons,' said Katerina. 'Maybe they never really talked to Prince Albert. Maybe they just spied on the Queen for decades, so they could answer all her questions about her dead husband. Only the most senior witches, the now dead ones, would have known that. They would have kept all that knowledge to themselves, only passing it on when one of them died.'

I leaned forwards. 'Of course! That must be what—'

'*Or*,' Katerina interrupted, 'something much more sinister.'

'Sinister?' McGray echoed. Katerina lowered her chin, the light projecting dark shadows around her eyes.

'Sometimes,' she mumbled, 'the dead don't want to be contacted. Sometimes they yearn to be left alone and move on. Something tells me that's Prince Albert's case. He's been mourned for almost thirty years, Adolphus. Thirty! That's far too long not just for the living, but for a spirit too. It might be his own wife's grief that won't let him rest, and the witches might have used that.'

'Used that?' Caroline asked – to my astonishment, quite interested in the topic. 'What do you mean? Could they have jinxed him?'

Katerina munched at her pipe, looking at Caroline with a hint of an approving smile. 'Probably. They could have anchored his soul; entrapped him somewhere in between worlds, where they can summon him at will. Those are very powerful, very dangerous arts.'

Then she noticed the unabashed derision in my eyes.

'What?' she demanded.

'You have not changed at all,' was my most diplomatic answer.

McGray, unsurprisingly, was staring at her without an ounce of disbelief.

'I hear ye, hen. That would be the sort of jinx only the arch-witches would've been able to keep under control.'

'It's like they have him in a cage,' Katerina explained, seeing my incomprehension. 'Anyone could easily open it, but then the soul would simply fly away, maybe even causing harm. Only the ones who anchored him would be able to talk to him and then safely put him back in his cage. Even I couldn't contact him through that sort of curse.'

Caroline sat back, nodding as if the entire business now made perfect sense. Joan's face too seemed to have been enlightened with a transcendental truth.

'Oh, for goodness' sake,' I said. 'How can you all—?'

'So,' McGray interrupted, 'it would really help us to figure out if those witches truly invoked Prince Albert.'

'*Of course they did not!*' I cried.

'Och, how can ye be so sure?'

'*Because it is all nonsense!*'

And as I yelped so I banged both hands on the table, for an instant forgetting my broken bone. The pain made me see stars, and all I could do was reach for one of the ale tankards. Not the best idea.

'My gosh, this is ghastly!' I said just as the landlord came to clear the empty glasses. 'Oh, do excuse me. Did you not know that?'

He simply left, glaring at me and grumbling unintelligibly between his teeth.

'Even if yer right,' McGray conceded once the man was gone, 'and the witches just humoured the auld coo, it took them proper knowledge to do so. We cannae, in three days, gather enough information about that sodding German bitch to put up a convincing act.' He let out a low moan. 'Finding the York witches still seems our best chance to keep our heads on our necks.' His face suddenly seemed illuminated. 'We could try to find out why they've nae contacted Queen Lard. If they can summon sodding Albert in some way, they might even want to help us. We could take them to the Queen ourselves! That would be our only hope, if it turns out that the damn PM really wants us dead too.'

'Thank you for mentioning that,' I said. 'As I told you before, that feels very illogical to me. Why would the PM turn against us right before we found the witches for him?'

McGray drew the last message closer to himself and reread it in silence. 'It sounds more like he was planning to betray us as soon as we found the witches.' He looked sideways. 'Maybe he wanted to present them to the Queen himself? Get all the credit? He did say he needed her to influence his rivals in Parliament.'

'That is one possibility,' I said.

'Also,' McGray added, his tone darker, 'there's the chance that . . . he never intended to help us. Maybe he just wanted us to lead him to the witches and then strike us all at the same time. We're dead; the witches givin' him trouble are dead; the Queen's just as happy. All with just one clean blow.'

The candle's flame flickered, as if someone had just tried to blow it out, and I felt a chill.

I remembered the way Boss stretched his hands at the steam ship; the way he looked at me as he admitted he could not wait to 'take care of us'. I preferred not to mention it, for I still had another theory.

'Or . . . the witches here, the Messengers, realized we were about to find them, and decided to turn us against the PM. Divide and conquer.'

It made sense. So much so, that even the superstitious McGray buried his face in his hands, groaning in frustration. He downed his pint and winced, the drink too vile even to his rustic palate.

'Who the fuck can we trust, then?' he grunted.

I shook my head. 'Right now . . . Nobody. Something tells me that we have been moved on the board like bloody pawns by every single player in the game, and we cannot even tell what for!'

Nobody spoke after that and, for an annoyingly long time, Harris's loud munching was the only sound at our table. Caroline sighed, staring at the dark ceiling as if praying for clarity. Katerina drummed her nails on the table and Joan simply looked down.

McGray, at last, sat up.

'I have to trust Pansy,' he said, casting a firm gaze at Katerina. 'If ye say she led us here—'

'Oh, for goodness' sake,' I blurted out, but McGray did not seem to notice.

'This middleman – what's his name?' he asked Katerina.

'He only asks me to call him Geoff,' she told him.

'And ye said ye gave him a place and time to meet us?'

'Yes. Tonight at eleven.'

'Where?'

'At the field by the Minster's Chapter House.'

'*What?*' I cried. 'That is one of the most conspicuous—'

'It's an open space,' McGray interjected. 'From there it's easy to see if anyone's coming – friend or foe.' He looked back at Katerina.

'How reliable is he?'

'No saint,' she admitted.

McGray stroked his stubble, and I had to chuckle.

'You cannot possibly be entertaining the possibility of attending that meeting. At best, you will find no one and only expose yourself to the Marigolds or Salisbury's men. At worst, this is a filthy trap and a pack of witches will be waiting to ambush you.'

'Och, shut it, Frey! These York bitches might be the only ones who can explain all this mess. And if that sod Geoff shows up he could lead us straight to them.' He turned to Katerina. 'Does he deal with them in person?'

'Yes,' Katerina said. 'He told me so.'

McGray raised his eyebrows as he looked at me. 'See?'

'See what? I still think—'

'Shut it. It's happening. And don't worry, I wasnae going to bring ye along. Yer more useless than ever with that wrist!'

Caroline jumped in. 'I would not say so.' I nearly thanked her for her vote of confidence, but then she spoke on. 'He and I could mount guard, Mr McGray. Watch over you.'

'What?' McGray and I protested at the same time.

'If you are to wait for that man on the fields around the minster, Mr Frey and I could watch from the Great Tower.'

McGray arched an eyebrow.

'Perfect vantage point,' he said. 'Youse could take a lantern and give us a sign if things look iffy. We'd have plenty o' time to get away. Yer brilliant, lass!'

I let out a growl. 'This could be terribly dangerous! You cannot seriously expect this young woman and I to sneak into that cathedral in the middle of the night.' I had to bite my lip not to add *unchaperoned*.

'Harris and Mr McGray are the best fitted to attend that meeting,' Caroline said, 'for obvious reasons. And unless you expect Joan or Madame Katerina to be the ones to help me, you will have to—'

'I *can* do it.' I jumped in before my manhood was questioned any further. 'That is not my concern. It is *you* I do not want to put at risk. You have been through enough!'

There was a slight, very slight flush on her face, but she shook it away at once.

'You might need someone to shoot for you,' she said, eyeing my broken wrist. This time, even the mute Harris nodded.

I breathed out. 'Assuming that I'll agree – how are we supposed to break into York Minster in the middle of the night?'

Katerina let out a *pff* as if I'd just asked how to pour milk into my tea. She stood up and went to the landlord, who was cleaning one of the nearby booths – or, most likely, hunting for gossip he could sell later.

The man stooped solicitously, so that Katerina could whisper into his ear. He shook his head after a while, whispered back, and I heard Katerina say, 'I know, I know.' After what felt like a never-ending discourse, she came back to her seat.

'His men can arrange to let people into the minster,' she said, albeit with a tense voice, and shifting uncomfortably on the bench.

'But?' McGray asked.

Katerina sighed and then pointed a finger at me. 'Do *not* insult his ales again. His dense brother brews them.'

Not twenty minutes later, the landlord came back and called Katerina. Again they whispered in the shadows, before the man disappeared down the creaking stairs. Katerina came back to us, bringing a rough sketch of the minster and its surroundings.

'You two will go to the north side of the cathedral,' she whispered, looking at Caroline and me. She smoothed the paper on the table and pointed at that spot. 'There is a tiny servants' door on the corner where the north transept joins the nave. It's so narrow the columns conceal it almost from every angle.'

'Will it not be locked?' Caroline asked.

'It usually is,' Katerina answered, 'but there will be someone waiting for you. He'll let you in and take you to the Great Tower. You're to pay him on the spot.'

'How much?' I asked.

'Fifteen pounds.'

'*Fifteen bloody pounds to go inside a damn cathedral?*'

'Och, shut it,' said Nine-Nails. 'It's the sodding PM's money.'

'Fifteen,' I repeated nonetheless, shaking my head.

'And you two,' Katerina told Nine-Nails and Harris, 'should leave now, so you aren't all seen leaving at the same time. Wander around through these alleys on the east side,' she made a vague gesture over that section of the improvised map. 'That will give Caroline and Ian time to position themselves.'

'And we can also shake off anyone who might try to follow us,' McGray added. He looked at me and Caroline. 'Any questions?' We shook our heads. 'Alrighty. Here we go.'

McGray and Harris then stood up resolutely, and put on heavy overcoats and hats to conceal their faces. McGray checked that their guns were fully loaded, pocketed extra ammunition, and just before they stepped out of the booth, Katerina put a little dagger in his hand.

'Just in case, my boy,' she whispered, almost choking, and then she patted McGray's stubbly cheek. He seemed about to say something, taking in a long breath, but then simply nodded and left. As soon as they disappeared down the stairs, the entire pub felt a little gloomier.

Joan and Madame Katerina were the next ones to go. They'd wait for us in the safety of the pub's 'good chambers' – as the landlord called them.

Caroline and I waited in silence. I cradled a greasy tumbler in my hand, sipping a gin so ghastly I feared it would render me blind before we even made it to the streets. If only I'd had time to bring the little flask Layton had put in my luggage . . .

I saw Caroline fidgeting with the furry trims of her leather gloves, all of a sudden looking awfully small and vulnerable. I wanted to say something – anything to ease the wait – but all the words I could think of sounded silly in my head.

Caroline looked up and met my gaze, and even though she said nothing, for a moment her cunning eyes glowed with a flicker of compassion. She felt as sorry for me as I did for her.

I took another sip, shuddering from the foul, sharp taste.

'Oh, enough,' I said, slamming the glass on the table. 'I'd rather meet painful death than take another swig of that.'

Caroline sighed and stood up. She wrapped herself in her hooded cloak and donned her gloves. I'd also left my bowler hat at the George Hotel, so I had to make do with a horrid old thing Harris had found in the pub's sticky cloakrooms.

'Can I have the gun?' Caroline asked and, quite begrudgingly, I handed it to her. I'd be armed just with a heavy lantern brought by the landlord. And even that was not supposed to be lit until we reached the cathedral.

We went downstairs and, just as when I'd arrived, all eyes followed us as we were led to the door. I walked briskly, thinking it would be a relief to step out, but I was wrong.

The door shut behind us, and suddenly all the noise and the warmth from the pub were gone. Caroline and I stood alone amidst the icy, silent darkness. The wind lashed us with snowflakes, and the scant light from the nearby windows projected long shadows all around us.

Caroline instinctively came closer to me, clasping my right arm, her brown eyes alert and wide open.

And thus we walked into the shadowy, meandering streets of York.

30

Our feet went deep into the fresh snow, the gentle crush of our steps the only sound around.

We meandered through those dingy, medieval streets, with the overhanging upper storeys looming over our heads.

By now most windows had gone dark. The only lights came from the murkier public houses, which entertained the worst of the worst, but even those had sunk into a tired, drunken stupor.

'I am glad the streets are deserted,' I whispered. 'Nobody out at this hour can be up to any good.'

'Like us,' she said after a painful gulp.

Thankfully, it would not be a long stroll. We approached the minster from the west, carefully avoiding the eastern alleys McGray and Harris were to take.

I realized that we were only a street away from the gates of Bootham Bar; the very spot where McGray had been attacked not two hours ago. I thought I'd better not mention that.

Little Blake Street, as narrow and dark as the others, came to an abrupt end, and York Minster suddenly appeared before us – a mass of stone so vast that only a small fragment could be seen in between the buildings.

We walked into the esplanade, but we still could not see the cathedral in its entirety. A faint glow of candles came from within its countless stained-glass windows, but most of the building remained shrouded in the night.

After a moment of silent admiration I quickened my pace, since we'd just left the safety of the crammed streets. We'd never be more vulnerable if anyone, witch or otherwise, were to strike us.

The very moment I thought of it, the caw of a raven cut the air, clean and sharp like a knife. I could not see it, but I heard the flapping of its wings as the bird flew away.

We rushed north, walking past the imposing main gates. In the darkness I could not see the oak or the wrought-iron hinges and bolts; only the vague shape of the thick stone arches that framed them, and the empty niches once occupied by statues of saints.

We turned right, staying as close to the walls as possible. My eyes went along the thick, square columns lined up ahead of us. I could only see their edges, turned tawny by the candlelight from within. No sign of a door.

'Can you see it?' Caroline asked. I could hear the tension in her voice.

'No,' I admitted, though I did see the point where the north wing merged with the main nave in a right angle. The north transept, with its narrow windows ending in pointed arches, was faintly lit as well; however, that corner, the very spot we were heading to, was as black as a mourning veil.

Caroline pulled at my arm, quickening her steps. I did so too, eager to reach the meeting point.

We stood in front of that corner and for a fearful moment I thought there was nothing there. Then, as my eyes grew more accustomed to that deeper darkness, I saw a stony shape emerge from in between the columns and buttresses. It was half an archway, connected to the wall of the nave, and a rusty oil lamp hung just above it, unlit.

As we approached, we saw three narrow stone steps, so tightly cornered by the cathedral walls that the snow had not reached them at all.

The door itself, very narrow and made of very dark wood, only became visible when I took the lead and climbed the low steps.

I had to leave the lantern on the floor, consciously keeping my injured hand away from view, and with my left I rapped gently on the battered wood.

And we waited.

I held my breath, staring ahead, and I wondered how long it would be safe to stay there. My pulse quickened with every passing second, Caroline's hand tightening around my arm.

Then there came a clinking sound, and that of a key and a latch.

A crack of dim light appeared right before me, almost blinding in the middle of that murky night, and the little door opened with a soft creak, as if pulled by a ghost.

I rushed inside, pulling Caroline with me, and the door closed behind us with a sharp creak, magnified by the acoustics of the nave.

Instantly I sensed that mixture of incense and damp, stagnated air, so characteristic of churches, and then, so close he made my heart jump, I saw the man who'd opened the door.

He looked like a mummified body; pale, wrinkly and bony, his jutting cheekbones his most prominent feature. Wearing the black clothes and cap of a sexton, and with his long, twisted nose, he reminded me of an eerie *medico della peste* – even more so by the odour of incense and oil that his clothes gave off.

'D'you have the money?' he said at once with a rasping voice, his little eyes flickering from Caroline to me. His set of keys dangled from the door's keyhole, his hand still grasping it. That man was ready to throw us out if we did not comply.

Caroline took the lamp from my left hand, so I was free to pull the money from my breast pocket. The sexton examined the notes with distrustful eyes, and as he folded them and inserted them into his cuff, his sour countenance shifted.

'This way,' he said, his crooked smile revealing he only had two front teeth.

We followed him towards the great tower, our steps echoing across the cathedral.

Even on that grim night, neither Caroline nor I could ignore the impressive nave and vaulted ceilings, the sobering arches meeting so high they even looked blurred through the floating incense. There was something in those stones that inspired reverence, as if they had soaked voices and humours along the centuries, and now imbued the air with their collected impressions.

I looked around at the ancient stones. There were green men spewing vines; contorted faces, some demonic, protruding from the supports of every arch; gargoyles with sharp teeth and fools with gruesome noses. How was one supposed to meet religious enlightenment in a place bedecked with the most disturbing monsters imaginable?

Caroline must have been having similar thoughts, for I saw her condensing breath swirling in quicker intervals. And no wonder. The cathedral was almost as cold as the streets.

We walked below the dome of the great tower, and when I looked up I felt a strange vertigo. Those colossal columns ascended so high that the tower's walls vanished beyond the reach of candlelight, like a perfectly square chasm that rose into solid blackness.

I looked to my left, to the chancel and organ. From there, a line of dead monarchs sculpted in dark stone, all bearing gilded crowns, looked down at us with stern faces. For an instant I had the foolish fear they'd spring to life, jump down their ornate columns and strike us with their sceptres.

When I looked ahead, Caroline and the sexton were already at the opposite transept, some twenty yards away. The man was lighting Caroline's lantern with a taper. When I joined them, he led us to the very corner of that wing, to a door as narrow as the one through which we'd entered.

'You go up this way,' he said, 'until you reach a landing. From there you—'

'Will you not come with us?' Caroline protested. 'It wasn't tuppence we paid you.'

'I can still throw you out,' the sexton said, his hands clenching the thick set of keys. 'Or we can call the archbishop, if you prefer.'

Caroline gasped at the man's insolence, but there was not much we could do.

'We shall be fine,' I whispered to her.

'Ignore the side doors at the landing,' the sexton resumed, 'and go to the end of a long corridor to the next flight of steps. You'll have to cross the transept roof through the outside. You'll see the only door. From there it's all the way up. I left the trapdoor open for you.'

He unlocked the door, and when he pulled it to, a draught of icy, damp air rushed into the nave.

Caroline, still indignant, turned and stepped quickly into the spiral stairs. I followed her, but caught one last glance of the sexton as he shut the door.

'Good luck,' he said, showing his two yellow teeth in an odd grin I did not like at all.

I went after Caroline, ascending through that constricted spiral, so narrow I pictured McGray's shoulders rubbing on both sides. There was no banister, so I had to press my left hand against the cold stone, and to the right I had to use my elbow.

Very soon I was panting. Caroline, however, was having an even worse time than me; she had to deal with her long skirts and cloak, as well as balancing the lantern in one hand while carrying the gun with the other.

'We can watch from the tower!' I mimicked, all sarcasm, and then in McGray's accent, 'Occhhhh aye, what a wondrous idea!'

'Is that meant – to be Scottish?' she said between troubled breaths. And we'd not even made it to the first landing.

When we reached it we both had to stop and breathe. Caroline handed me the lantern and then mopped the sweat from her forehead with her sleeve.

Still panting, I raised the light to inspect the space. Like the sexton had said, there was a long, vaulted corridor ahead of us, and two little wooden doors, each barely a foot and a half wide. They had no locks, just rusty latches on oak so battered I thought it might crumble in my hands.

As instructed, we ignored them and went to the end of the passage. There was another door there, beside the next flight of steps. Through the latch hole, eroded after decades of use, came a chilling draught. Caroline opened it, for my one good hand held the lamp. She snatched it and again took the lead.

'I can hold the lamp for you,' I said as I followed up the steps. 'You are already holding the weapon.'

'I can do it myself, thank you very much.'

I grunted, now feeling the sweat dripping down my temples. 'Yes, I know you are perfectly able. Offering help does not mean I think you are a clumsy invalid.'

'Indeed, Mr Frey,' she said, again struggling for breath. 'The one closer to invalidity right now is you.'

'Why, you silly little brat,' I muttered, and we soldiered on.

The constant spinning of the stairs made me queasy, and the saltpetre stench of the stone did not help. Eventually we made it to the next landing, where I had to support my hand on the wall to catch my breath.

There were two doors. The one to our left was the source of the draught, the wind whistling through the latch hole and the cracks in the tired wood. The one to our right, instead of wind, let in a very faint glow.

'This must be the top corner of the south transept and the rose window,' I said, but Caroline did not pay attention.

She opened the door that led to the transept's roof, the wind hitting us like an icy, merciless hand, and we made our tortuous way fully exposed to the elements.

I sheltered my face from the wind, holding my hat in place. I could barely see anything to either side, Caroline's lantern a tiny spec of light amidst the immensity of the cathedral.

To my right was the tin gable of the transept, covered in snow. The nave ran to my left, with its pointy windows and flying buttresses. Ahead of us, tall and sturdy like a black monolith, rose the Great Tower.

There was a wrought-iron handrail, but grasping it did not mitigate the stabs of vertigo every time the wind hit us with renewed strength. Our feet skidded on the snow-covered pass, each step a conscious effort, until Caroline finally made it to the base of the tower and pulled the iron latch.

The wind slammed the door open, and I saw her rush into the little landing. I stepped in and had to make a mighty effort to pull the door and close it.

We both panted for a moment, before moving on.

That would be the longest flight of steps, spiralling on and on to an unthinkable height. We passed another draughty door, which must lead to the central roof of the nave, but the steps continued. Just as I thought my entire life had been nothing but that tortuous ascent, we reached a narrow window cut into the three-foot-thick wall.

Caroline sat there to catch her breath, her hands trembling when she placed the lantern on the steps.

I stopped by her side, wiping the sweat from my face with my sleeve.

'This – would be – the perfect trap,' I said between breaths. I shuddered at the thought of being marooned there in complete darkness, with countless steps in either direction. The crooked, eerie smile of the sexton came to mind, and I instantly picked up the lantern. The sooner we made it to an open space, the better.

We ascended the last steps without talking, and I welcomed the growing cold and the whirling air. Snowflakes began to flutter around me, until we made it, at last, to the top of the tower.

The trapdoor was indeed open, the final steps already dusted in white. I jumped out, my legs burning and too tired to make any triumphal remark. The roof was covered in snow, deep and untouched until our arrival, and at that height the wind blew mercilessly and unchallenged. At once it blew my hat away.

I turned back to the trapdoor, left the light on the snow and offered Caroline a hand. She took it gladly, even if her face suggested otherwise.

'So here we are,' she said, raising her voice under the blustering wind.

We went to the north side of the tower, Caroline produced a pair of tiny opera glasses and we both peered down.

The entire city of York spread before us, only a few windows lit. I squinted to make out the ancient Tudor buildings, cramped against each other along the narrow streets. Crooked and subsided, they made me think of lines of old, bony men, who only managed to remain standing by supporting their shoulders on those of their neighbours.

Further away I saw sections of the city wall, lit either by windows or the few lamp posts around the medieval gateways.

Beyond those eroded stones there was nothing but smooth blackness, as if that wall marked the very end of the world.

The air clutched at my chest, cold and oppressive, as if a terrible storm were about to break. Madame Katerina would have told me I also had *the eye*.

'Here they come,' Caroline said, pointing at the minster fields, slightly to our right.

I saw the tin roof of the chapter house, round and pointy like a witch's hat, and connected to the nave by an L-shaped passage. Just to its left, in the middle of the flat terrain, I recognized a tiny black spot.

'McGray?' I asked her.

'Harris,' she said, passing me the binoculars.

They were so minute, and my left hand so clumsy, I nearly dropped them into the void – I pretended not to see Caroline's look of recrimination. Then I struggled to find the right spot, for once magnified, everything seemed a black blur.

'*There!*' Caroline grunted, pulling my hand to the exact spot. Her blind precision impressed me, but I'd never have admitted it.

'Who would have said one day you'd actually benefit from all those evenings fishing for gossip at the operas . . .' I mumbled.

I saw it was indeed Harris, his bulky shoulders unmistakable. But even through the lenses he was merely a silhouette, barely lit by the glare of the minster's candles.

'Where is McGray?' I asked. 'Have you seen him?'

'No, only Harris. Can you still spot him without the glasses?'

I tried and shook my head. 'I cannot, I am afraid.'

'I can. I'll keep watch on him. You keep the glasses and look around for trouble. And for Mr McGray.'

'One and the same,' I mumbled. I did not like to be ordered around like that, but this was not the time to protest about such trifles. I simply snorted and obliged, panning slowly from left to right.

We watched in silence for a few minutes, the wind battering us all the time, my ears so cold I imagined them snapping off in frozen splinters.

'Someone else is coming,' I said, pointing at the chapter house. I was going to pass the lenses to Caroline, but—

'I see it,' she said, raising a palm. 'Is that Mr McGray?'

I looked through the glasses again and, despite the darkness and the distance, I recognized his confident stride. A tiny light ignited about him.

'Is he smoking?' I cried, the spark like a beacon in the middle of the night.

'He might be trying to help us locate them,' Caroline said. 'Or—'

She gasped. I looked at her and saw her staring a little above McGray.

'What?' I asked, and immediately pointed the binoculars in that direction. My heart jumped as I saw three dark figures approach from the north-east fields. Two were tall and bulky; one small and slender, swathed in a billowing cloak.

'*Witches!*' I snapped. Caroline instantly reached for the lantern and held it high up, waving it from side to side.

Two beams of white light, bullseye lanterns, appeared just then, from the western side of the cathedral. Their glow cut through the darkness like long swords, and we heard indistinct shouting.

'God!' Caroline panted. A ball of fire had ignited on the northern side, from where the three figures came. It was golden at first, but then it turned green, and like the two beams of light, it too darted towards McGray and Harris.

Their two shadows looked clearer now, running towards the chapter house, but they had nowhere to go; they were cornered from all sides.

'They need help,' I spluttered, stepping back, but even as I said so I pictured the endless flights of steps, the long corridors and the passage across the roof. We might as well be in Scotland.

'I won't just stay here and watch them die!' Caroline cried. She spun round and ran to the trapdoor, but froze midway and let out a gasp.

I followed her gaze and saw that the hatch, a minute ago as dark as a wolf's muzzle, now glowed from within.

We heard the echo of a gunshot coming from the ground, and then a second, and then more shouting in the fields.

Caroline took a step ahead, desperate to do something. I dropped the binoculars and stopped her.

We watched the light grow brighter, and then came a sound that made us quiver – low, laboured breaths that reminded me of a snorting bull. A moment later a shadow projected itself against the curved walls, climbing the steps slowly, and as huge as its heavy breathing had promised.

Caroline pointed the gun, her finger tense on the trigger. Then we saw the shadow jerk like a vulture bent over a carcass. I felt my heart pounding. And then . . .

Why the light? I thought with a chill. *Why not simply catch us off guard in the dark, or—?*

Just then something flew upwards; a dark green bottle, corked and sealed with wax. It fell back onto the snow, rolled in our direction, and a nasty wave of prickles ran throughout my body as I understood.

I hurled myself towards Caroline, my arms stretched, and before I could even scream, the entire world burst into fire.

31

We both fell on the deep snow, the searing heat seeping through my clothes. The blinding green light blasted my eyelids and I growled in pain, feeling myself on fire.

Caroline's hands pushed me up and forced me to roll on the snow. I heard a sizzle, like red-hot iron being plunged in water. I smelled my burning clothes, and then heard Caroline's desperate wails as she patted me down.

I forced my eyes open, the emerald fire swirling on the very snow. Dark specks of the witches' oily tar were dotted all over the tower's roof, each feeding a green flame.

The folds of my coat had been splattered too, and were on fire like the hems of my trousers. Caroline was trying to smother them with little success. I rolled desperately from side to side, and as I did so I caught a glimpse of the trapdoor. There I saw a pair of thick hands digging their nails into the snow, like an enormous, dead beast rising from its grave. I roared in a frenzied mixture of wrath and pain. '*Shoot him!*'

Caroline whimpered, kicking the snow as she desperately looked for the gun. I crawled away from the greater fire, struggling to put down the flames on my own clothes, while I saw that gargantuan man emerge from the staircase. His face looked disturbingly familiar; he was a witches' man. I had seen his face months ago, in Lancashire.

He must have recognized me too, for he grinned malevolently as he approached me with stomping steps. I will never forget his crooked, yellow teeth as I saw him come closer.

'*Shoot him!*' I shouted again, seeing Caroline from the corner of my eye, still groping about for the gun. The man reached us then.

With his bare hand, the giant grabbed my leg, even if my trousers were still burning, and he pulled me away. I shouted and writhed as he dragged me across the roof, passing over patches of fire and hot tar, and then he lifted me like a ragdoll and pushed me onto the balustrade.

My limbs tingled with vertigo as I saw the immense abyss before me. The snowed fields and roofs, now reflecting the green glow of the fire, were ready to shatter my body as I crashed onto them. The giant laughed.

I clasped the carved stone with both hands, not even feeling the pain in my broken wrist; all I felt was the unyielding push of those thick hands. Suddenly my limbs began to prickle, and my mind projected a fleeting image of golden torches above a quiet loch.

Then I heard another gunshot in the fields.

The giant let out a deafening howl and I saw him fall backwards, his frame a black silhouette against the green fire. For an instant he pulled me with him, but then his grip loosened and I slid back into the void.

I shrieked, my fingers sliding on the wet stone. I gripped the balustrade so tightly I saw stars, and then something clenched my left wrist.

Caroline grunted, pulling with all her might, her dishevelled hair flailing in the wind. I kicked about until I managed to hook my leg on top of the banister. I used my right hand too, the pain searing, and propelled myself forwards as I howled in pain.

Again we fell on the snow, my body rolling until I hit the thug's trembling belly. The man was juddering at intervals, like a freshly beheaded chicken. I preferred not to look, and when I turned away I found Caroline's panicked face just inches from mine.

She was on her knees, as pale as a ghost and her eyes misted with tears. She gulped before she could say anything.

'I thought you'd die,' she panted. 'You – you were slipping from my fingers.'

I could not answer, forcing in troubled breaths and feeling as if my entire body floated in the air. I managed a fleeting smile, but then saw something flicker behind Caroline's shoulder.

My eyes must have said it all, for she turned and we both saw the glow of another light coming from the trapdoor. And we heard a female screech.

Then something shifted in me.

My heart pounded, my ears buzzed and my broken wrist throbbed painfully. And all that pain brought a wave of rage that set in my chest like fire itself. I wanted those women dead; all of them, and their brainless thugs too.

I looked for the gun, my frenzied breath steaming up before my face. Caroline had dropped it right next to her skirts. I stood up and rushed to it, almost picking it up with my right hand. I seized it with my left and turned to the trapdoor, where the shadow of a cloaked figure could already be seen.

I strode there, my breath hissing, my clumsy hand tense around the gun, and I faced the hooded witch, her cloak spread around her like the wings of a bat. I did not see her face, for at once she threw a vial at me. Instinctively I protected my face with my right forearm, shooting blindly at the stairwell.

We heard another sizzle, my nose and eyes burned, and I felt heat seep into my arm. My coat, the bandages and the splint were dissolving into black char right before my eyes. Caroline shrieked and ran in my direction. Panting, she ripped off my sleeve and what was left of the wooden splint, and dropped them. We saw them disintegrate on the snow, where Caroline threw her leather gloves, the tips also being corroded into ashes. No wonder people once thought that was black magic.

We both coughed uncontrollably at the acrid fumes, but I would not stand still.

I ran down the staircase, where the glow of a candle quickly faded away. I ran breathless and recklessly, supporting myself on the cold wall with my right elbow, each step an unnerving leap of faith into the darkness.

Caroline ran behind me, and from the shadows I guessed she'd brought the lantern with her.

'We need to get out of here!' she cried. 'This is the perfect trap, you said it yourself.'

We passed the window we'd seen before, where she'd stopped to breathe.

'They're running away,' I said. 'They must have used up all their—'

And then we heard a cacophony of cackles, multiplied as their echoes swirled upwards. The light from below began to turn brighter, and we heard a horde of swift footsteps.

'They're coming back!' Caroline cried, just as my heart jumped.

'Come!' I said, running down even faster than before.

'*Are you mad?* They're coming from—'

'*Follow me, dammit!*' I howled, quickening my pace, spiralling directly towards the pack of witches. I saw the shadows of hooded heads fleeting on the curved walls, and hands jerking in the air like the wings of vultures. Their voices, clear and crisp, sent bolts of fear to my chest. Caroline let out a long, terrified moan, and then the narrow wooden door appeared before us.

I kicked it open, the ancient oak at once coming out of its hinges, and I sprinted out of the tower. The wind hit me on the face as I saw the long roof of the central nave in front of me.

Caroline stepped out just as the shadows of three witches appeared. I saw the glint of their vials, raised in the air by surprisingly young hands, ready to throw their acids at our faces.

Caroline roared, raised the lantern and tossed it at them. We turned our backs immediately, not waiting to see what happened; we simply heard a choir of shrieks as we darted across the roof, towards the twin belfries.

Amidst the darkness Caroline took the lead, grasping the iron handrail and pulling my right arm. I turned back briefly and saw the dying green flames atop the great tower, and below, coming from the slim door, burning candles and a mass of black shadows rushing to catch us.

I shot blindly at them and ran on. I thought of shooting a second time, but then we reached the battered door to the south belfry. My bullets would be more useful if they cornered us in there.

Caroline pulled the latch, let me in first and then locked it behind her.

That was a frantic run: in complete darkness, feeling my way down that spiralling passage, the uneven steps making our descent frustratingly slow. We heard the door above our heads crack, and then the mocking cackles of the witches.

'They're here!' Caroline spluttered, grabbing my shoulder. The shape of the walls began to clear, the glow of the witches' lights approaching, and I quickened my pace to the point of recklessness.

We made it to a small landing. We could keep going down, or go through a flat corridor. I chose the latter, and we ran as fast as our legs allowed. Very soon we reached a dead end.

I heard Caroline punch the wall in frustration, and realized I had no idea where we were.

The cackles came louder.

Just as I cursed our luck, we both felt a cold draught. To our left there must be another door, but without light we'd not seen it. Caroline groped and as soon as she found the latch she opened the door and we sprinted back onto the roofs.

I only realized where we were after we'd run some ten yards. That was the passage along the south aisle's roof, the flying buttresses arching over our heads and to our left, like gigantic pergolas. The great tower rose before us, as did the familiar south transept, with its spiky pinnacles and over-hanging gargoyles.

'*They're going back!*' someone yelled from above, and I saw a lonely little light in the middle of the nave's central roof, on the same passage we'd only just crossed.

I shot in that direction, raging, and would have shot again had Caroline not pulled my arm.

We heard the witches' voices behind us, but neither of us dared look back. We made it to the pointy tower at the end of the passage, where we found another ramshackle door. Caroline opened it and we found yet another flight of bloody steps.

'Blast!' I panted as we ran down, again groping our way to find the steps. It turned out to be a very short flight.

'It ends here,' Caroline said with some relief, and the stairs opened up to a long corridor.

As we ran across I tried to picture the shape of the cathedral. At the end of that corridor we'd find the last flight of steps, the same one we'd climbed first, and then the heavenly ground.

Caroline flung the door open, but she only managed to descend a couple of steps before we saw the glow of candles appear before us.

'*They're coming this way!*' a woman shrilled from below, and my heart leapt.

Caroline halted and I crashed against her. It was a miracle we did not stumble and roll down the steps. The echoes of female cackles became louder, merely a few yards below us.

'Where do we—?'

'*Up!*' I yelled.

We ran to the adjacent corridor, which we both recognized at once, and then climbed up again.

I grunted, my heart pounding and my knees burning. The stairs spiralled on and on, and as our tired steps slowed down, the witches' shrieks and cackles came louder and clearer.

For a horrid moment I thought we were doomed. They seemed to be everywhere, even in the fields around us, and we could not keep running up and down the minster for ever. It was only a matter of time before they caught us.

Caroline had to pull me when we reached the landing. She opened the door that led to the transept roof, the same one we had crossed before reaching the tower. As the icy wind hit us again, Caroline let out a scream. I panted too, for on the other side, from the base of the tower, came the fleeting lights of two witches. The same ones I'd just seen on the nave's roof. There were now witches both behind and right in front of us.

It was my turn to pull Caroline, for the poor creature was paralysed, and I kicked the adjacent door. I only remembered where it led once we had stepped in – we were now inside the cathedral, and ahead of us was a narrow balcony. To the right it was overlooked by the imposing rose window, the stained glass radiating from its centre like fine petals. To the left, beyond a stone balustrade, there was nothing but a precipice, some forty feet deep and all the way down to the nave's main floor. I grasped the cold banister and looked down at the marble flagstones. The candles there were like tiny glow-worms. I looked around in despair, but there were no more stairs or passages or doors.

We'd run a perfect loop. And now we were trapped.

32

Caroline ran as far as she could go, all the way to the wall, and she punched it with both hands.

She then ran back to the banister, next to me, and grasped the cold stone as she looked down. Her jolts were those of a freshly netted bird.

'No,' she mumbled darkly. 'This is not how it ends . . . This—'

The door opened with a slam, which echoed all across the cathedral. We startled and saw three witches emerge from the shadows. They were all swathed in black cloaks, carrying small lanterns whose glow did not manage to penetrate their heavy hoods.

I pulled Caroline away from the banister and planted myself in front of her, pointing the gun at the incoming witches. I must have had one or two bullets left, and only three women blocked our way. We might still have a chance, but only if I did not fail a single shot – with my clumsy left hand. I gulped. I had to let them come closer.

As they approached they all searched in the folds of their clothes. I saw the glint of little vials; yellow and green glass, surely containing the most horrendous substances. I pictured them throwing their acids at us, cackling as they saw our faces melt like wax, before their thugs joined them to throw us over the banister. My heart went cold with fear and suddenly I found myself shouting. *'Which one of you shall I kill first?'*

I kept the gun pointed at them, feigning as much courage as I could, but they immediately noticed my trembling arm.

They all cackled, their strident voices filling the minster like the squawk of their ravens, their hoods jolting eerily in the dark. Very soon I understood why.

A towering thug, also wrapped in a hood, came behind them. The man was so large he had to stoop and jerk to pass through the tiny threshold. I cursed my luck as the witches moved aside for him, forming a tight, impenetrable barrier.

And from behind the man emerged yet another figure. A woman, also cloaked, but quite tall, and whose frame I recognized at once, even before the surrounding candles lit the golden threads that trimmed her hood.

I felt how Caroline shivered against my back, and remembered her story about that witch; how she'd seen her slit a man's throat without the slightest hesitation, right before her men had shot Jed and old Bertha.

'Stop right there!' I howled, tearing my throat, as they took slow steps forwards.

Together they formed a tight, impenetrable wall, enclosing us very slowly, as if savouring the panic on our faces. Surrounded by the incense mist and lit by dim candles, they were like a vision from the netherworld; the grim reaper flanked by her lesser demons.

They did halt, but only because the arch-witch raised a gloved hand. She produced a little silver flask, had a sip and then passed it on to her sisters. Some narcotic for courage, I could tell from the opiate smell; something to send them into a killing frenzy. As they drank, their bodies shivered like crows shedding water from their plumage. Even the giant had a swig.

'Drop it,' the arch-witch commanded, pointing at the gun with her pale chin; the one feature of her face the hood let me see. Her voice, though deep, was not that of an old woman. I noticed that all their shoulders were squared, their spines straight. The crones were dead; it was the younger generation we were fighting.

I stood firm, my arm not flickering an inch, but my eyes must have betrayed me.

'Drop it *now*,' she repeated, taking a longer step ahead. I tried to make out more of her face, but she was careful to pull down her embroidered hood. 'Shoot any of us and you will shriek like a child at the things we'll do to her.'

Caroline gripped my arm more tightly, nearly digging her nails into my skin, but not out of fear. She was incensed – I could hear it in her breath.

My own stomach had gone ablaze at the witch's complacent tone.

'So it is *you* first, madam,' I said, my voice so poisonous I did not recognize myself.

I was expecting her to cackle but, to my surprise, the woman faltered. I stretched my arm, moving the gun to make it clear I pointed directly at her concealed face.

'Too scared to give your life for your weird sisters?' I sneered with more bravado than good sense. 'Mrs Marigold would be *so* disappointed.'

There was a moment of deep, blood-curdling silence. I saw the vials again, in gloved hands ready to throw them. Maybe they too doubted their aim, hoping they could come closer before they attacked.

I felt a bead of sweat rolling down my spine. My arm began to ache from the tension.

Shoot the giant first, I thought, but then something moved in the shadows.

As if I'd summoned him, there came a second man, as tall and brawny as the first one, moving stealthily in the semidarkness. And behind him, as silent as spectres, I recognized the frames of three other women who stayed close to the exit, surely to block our escape – as if that were needed.

Not looking back, the arch-witch raised her vial for us to see. 'Give us what we want and we might – *might* spare you.'

'*Go to hell!*' Caroline shouted, making the women laugh, their cackles an eerie concert bouncing throughout the nave. The arch-witch laughed, and then I caught a glimpse of her moist tongue, stained most likely from drinking her rousing brews. Amidst the shadows, the woman smacked her lips in a repulsive manner.

'Give us what we want, dear,' she repeated, this time in a silky tone far more disturbing than her shouting.

'What they want?' I muttered, but Caroline did not answer.

Something shifted in the background then. It was the second thug pulling down his hood. I saw a bald scalp, and under the light reflected by the rose window, a set of old, blurred tattoos.

Harris.

The man looked almost relaxed, chewing a piece of straw.

My chest swelled, but he pressed a finger to his lips, commanding silence. Still munching the straw, he approached the thug in front of him with short, furtive steps. Neither he nor the three witches right before us looked back.

The arch-witch took a tiny step forward, shaking the vial. 'Have you seen what this can do to your pretty skin, my dear? Have you ever *felt* it?'

Again, Caroline said nothing. We were both thinking of the poor orderly, his neck ruined forever, and also my wooden plinth turning into sizzling char, as if burnt by an invisible flame.

The witch chuckled. 'Spare yourself from this. All you have to do is answer our *one* question.'

Caroline remained stubbornly silent. I wanted to see her face, but I did not dare. I kept my eyes fixed on Harris, following his stealthy moves and readying myself to pull the trigger as soon as hell broke loose. What I heard next, however, nearly made me drop the gun.

The arch-witch raised her voice. 'What was in the German book?'

I gasped, not believing my ears. 'The German book!' I muttered, unable to repress myself.

So the Marigolds knew about it too! But how? *Why?* Caroline had found nothing of consequence in it; she had told me so herself. I remembered the moment vividly, as the steam ship took us along the icy Scottish waters. Her eyes had been truthful.

Unless . . .

I noticed she had gone perfectly still, even holding her breath. I could still feel her hand gripping my right arm, and even her thumping heartbeats through her fingertips.

The arch-witch let out a triumphant cackle, reading her reaction.

'So you *do* know what we want, dear!' and again she smacked her lips, as if savouring her next meal.

Caroline laughed then, so eerily she made me shudder. Her voice came out as a throaty, spiteful growl, which grew louder as she spoke.

'Your lot turned my father insane and reduced him to a mindless wreck for *years*. You forced me into hiding. My poor Bertha, the most loving creature I've known in the world, bled to death in my arms because of *you*! And now you want my help? *You all damn dogs can rot in hell!*'

There were mocking giggles, whilst Caroline panted with uncontrollable rage.

'I'll rather burn and melt to oblivion than help your filthy nest,' she hissed. 'But don't expect me to go down without trying to rip your bloody eyes out.'

Harris also laughed, pressing the straw between his teeth with very convincing glee. Almost too convincing. My heart jumped then, as I glanced at his old tattoos.

That was the exact same design embroidered on the arch-witch's hood.

Could he—?

As if reading my thoughts, Harris looked straight into my eyes, still laughing, and then he spat sideways. I saw his piece of straw arch in the air as it fluttered into the nave.

'If you won't speak,' the arch-witch snapped, 'we won't waste more time. We have other means to find things out. And even if you speak after we've started with you –' a nasty chuckle, 'we will *not* stop.'

She and her surrounding sisters lifted the vials in the air. One struck a match, holding a bottle of tar, and another one raised a very thin, very sharp dagger. Their raised arms suddenly looked like the fingers of one single claw about to tear us apart.

I aimed at the arch-witch, right at her heart, but then, the very instant Harris's straw must have touched the floor, the entire cathedral shook.

An explosion, was my first thought, the thunderous noise reverberating through stone, flesh and bone. Everyone startled, and a couple of vials fell to the floor and exploded in nasty vapours.

It was the organ, booming in a strident, deafening chord like a roaring monster.

Harris moved like the wind, punching the other man at the kidneys before pushing him onto the balustrade. I recoiled, the acid fumes already burning my nostrils, and had a fleeting view of the three witches looking around in confusion.

It was but a split second. Caroline was the first one to react, letting out a furious shriek and throwing herself towards the witch to the left, who'd just dropped her vial. The witch to the right leapt after Caroline and I shot at her without time to aim properly. The woman howled in pain as the witches by the door darted forwards and they all intertwined in a blurry skirmish of cloaks and hoods.

I saw no more, for the arch-witch pounced on me, shrieking like an eagle. She threw her vial at me, which I barely dodged, and then charged against me with her entire body, trying to reach for my gun with one hand, the other one swiping at my face with unnatural fury. As we struggled I heard the screams and grunts of the other women, the mighty punches exchanged by Harris and the thug, and the never-ending chord that surrounded us all.

The witch grasped my injured wrist. I screamed and in the searing pain kicked the woman with all my might. I saw her sprawl away like a shapeless bundle of black material, her embroidered hood falling from her head as she rolled on the flagstones.

When she stopped skidding, and still on all fours, the woman looked up at me.

My heart stopped, for at once I recognized her face.

'*Hilda!*' I shouted, unable to contain the word. For an instant, even with the fierce fight taking place behind us, she froze, casting me a flabbergasted look.

I only had a split second to look at her, but there was no doubt – there was the same face from the picture: the pale eyes and the dark curls, now only streaked by a few silver strands. The organ's chords seemed to grow louder and more screeching as she glared at me.

Simultaneously, I raised my gun and she produced a dagger, seemingly out of nowhere, but neither one of us would be able to attack the other.

One of the other cloaked women, the late arrivals, struck Hilda from the side, and right then I received a mighty blow on my ribs.

I fell on my side, watching how the towering thug rushed in my direction, his body a swelling shadow. Harris intercepted him and they resumed their fight, pulling each other towards the stone banister.

'Are you all right?' Caroline asked. She'd flung herself onto her knees next to me, ghostly pale but apparently unscathed.

'What happened to the—?'

A nasty, pained howl interrupted me. I looked at the door and saw that one of the women had sunk to her knees, covering her face, her hood wafting smoke. I could no longer tell who was who. Just as another two witches bent down to aid her, I caught one last glimpse of Hilda's embroidered hood, the pattern hanging on her back and then scuttling away through the narrow threshold.

Caroline helped me stand. I then raised my gun and pointed at the kneeling women, but Caroline held my hand.

'They helped me!' she said.

I struggled to catch my breath. 'They did?' and then I turned to them. To me, all the unadorned cloaks still looked the same.

'Are you the Messengers?' I asked them.

The injured woman crouched, whimpering and keeping both hands against her face. The other two patted her back gently, and then rose to their feet. I still could not see their faces, and they said nothing. I did not like that silence at all.

I turned to Harris, to my dismay, the very moment he gave the other thug one final push, and the man's enormous body plummeted onto the minster's floor. The splatting noise he made when he hit the flagstones almost made me gag. I also heard female screams come from the nave, and frantic footsteps – surely Hilda and her witches running away.

Only then did the strident organ chords end. However, their dark echoes hung in the air like a persistent fog. Harris simply rubbed his hands, catching his breath as casually as if he'd just changed the wheels of a carriage.

Far from relaxed, I turned to the two silent witches and pointed the gun at them. I was not sure I still had bullets. If I did, it could not be more than one.

'Are you the Messengers?' I repeated, this time raising my voice.

Again there was no reply. I turned to Harris, keeping the gun up.

'Who are they? Are these the York coven?'

He grunted, moving his hand to indicate I should lower the gun. I did not. Instead I turned to Caroline. She was staring at the hooded witches with growing distrust.

That instant of distraction was enough for Harris to come to me and, with a sudden movement, he grabbed my left arm and yanked it up.

'*What are you—?*'

I tried to pull away, but his grip was unrelenting. Caroline came to my aid, battering Harris with all her might, her fists laughably small next to the thug's body. As we jerked I had fleeting visions of the two women, seemingly still, but every time I looked they appeared a little closer.

Like he'd done once before, Harris squeezed until I thought my bones were going to snap. I still refused to let go, gagging in pain, but I could not keep my grip and the giant had no trouble pulling the gun from my hand.

He threw it over the banister and held me in a firm lock, so that I faced the witches. They had both produced little knives, the thin blades catching the candlelight.

'*Get away!*' I shouted to Caroline.

She ran to the end of the balcony, desperately looking for any means to escape.

Harris kept his hold on me, turning his back to her, and I saw Caroline no more. I only heard her scream; a long, shrill screech that chilled my blood. Then she sounded muffled, as if gagged, and a moment later, all of a sudden, she went silent.

All the while I growled, jerked and kicked about, until the witches appeared again, one coming from each side.

I heard frantic steps coming from the staircase. I looked there and saw a shadow lurking under the threshold. The sexton.

'I'm sorry, sir. They came before you.' But there was not an ounce of shame in his damned face. 'And witches always pay well.'

I could not shout any of the curses that burned in my head, for then one of the witches held my temples firmly. I struggled, but could not escape Harris's unyielding grip. I felt the woman's bony hands tightly wrapped in cold leather. They gave off a pungent chemical stench.

The other woman covered my face with a damp rag, the smell unbearable. I tried to hold my breath but to no avail; that nasty substance made its way through my nostrils and into my lungs, and the last thing I saw was the twinkle of a silver blade.

DIARY – 1844

I am very sorry to say that instead of giving to Dr Granville's vigorous Prescription in regard to the use of the Bath Waters any trial, on my arrival at Bath I sent for the Physician who stood highest in Reputation there, Dr Barlow [. . .]

My course was interrupted by the necessity of my coming to London on the Business of my Claim to succeed to the English Peerages of my Father – I returned to Bath – found Dr Barlow in a dying state . . .

33

The world swayed very, very gently. It was like lying in a little boat, my back on mullioned cushions, dozing as the soft breeze rocked me to and fro. Gradually, that heavenly zephyr went colder and damper, until it became painful to take in breaths. The air around me was so humid my splintered wrist began to ache, and I remembered the moment the witches' giant had snapped my bones. My back *was* cushioned, but it also burned, and I remembered the green fire. And then a general ache – legs, back, knees and head – began to spread. I thought I heard myself groan, but could not be sure it had been me. In any case, I did not want to know, I did not want to feel, and it was not difficult to drift into blissful unconsciousness once again.

I cannot remember how many times I came and went, unwilling to open my eyes and forcing myself back to sleep, but each time it took a little longer. Each time the air felt a little damper and each time my wounds pained a little more, until they would not let me rest.

Even then, when I gave up sleeping, I kept my eyes shut, listening to a slow dripping that seemed to come from far away. The sound was crisp and sweet, and it echoed around me, as if bouncing within the walls of a – cathedral . . .

I yelped, sitting up and opening my eyes without thinking.

I only held myself for a second, for I'd used my right hand to propel myself upwards. At once I felt a stabbing pain and I fell on my back again, holding my broken wrist. Someone had put it back in a splint.

Then I noticed a golden glow right above my head. It was a little oil lamp, hanging from a low, vaulted ceiling. As I blinked, the outlines of red and ochre brick began to take shape, humid and stained with saltpetre.

Was I inside a crypt?

A low voice came from nearby. 'He's up.'

A child's voice.

I sat up again, every inch of my torso aching. And there she was, standing right by my feet – a young girl, about five years old, wrapped in a very thick coat. Her wide blue eyes, strangely familiar, were framed by dark curls. She stared at me with equal measures of fear and curiosity, her hands fidgeting with a piece of red ribbon.

'He – hello?' I mumbled, attempting a smile, and then looked over the girl's shoulder.

I must indeed be inside a crypt, which opened up into a larger vault. Only a small section was visible from where I lay, but I recognized some odd columns, or rather stacks of flat stones, dotted all over a gritty floor. They reminded me of the twisted towers of books in McGray's office, only placed in an almost perfect grid. Before I could even wonder what they were, a long shadow projected itself on them, dancing on the ancient brick. A woman.

I saw she was thin and slightly stooped, swathed in a ragged shawl, her auburn hair tied up in a careless manner. And she brought a little steaming bowl. My pulse quickened.

Her face still in shadows, she leaned and whispered into the girl's ear. I only made out her name – Daisy. I arched an eyebrow, for it sounded familiar.

The girl nodded, cast me a last look and then ran out of sight. In turn, the woman came into the crypt, speaking with surprisingly pleasant, well-modulated enunciation.

'You'll have to excuse the rough handling. We had to make sure the others thought you were dead.'

The words did not really sink in, for instantly I recognized that voice. I gasped and recoiled, just as her face came into the light of the hanging lamp.

'*You!*' I cried, staring at that still young face. She had never been handsome, but her rodent-like features were unmistakable.

She smirked. 'Do you even remember my name – Mr Frey?'

A torrent of memories came to me.

'Miss Oakley,' I spat. 'How could I ever forget the likes of you?'

Indeed I could not. She was the witch we had chased all the way from Edinburgh to Lancashire. She had, at one point, looked after Caroline's father in the asylum. And she had fled the Marigolds' almighty coven no matter the cost.

'Are you one of – one of the Messengers?'

'If by that you mean the witches who contacted the Ardglass girl, yes.'

'Miss Ardglass . . .' I mumbled. 'What did you do to her? And McGray! Where are we? *What—*'

'There, there. Lie down. They're all fine. Here, drink up.'

She knelt down by the bundle of rags and blankets that were my bed, and offered me the steaming drink. It gave off a pleasant herbal scent, but I still saw the clay bowl with suspicion.

'The last time you offered me a hot brew,' I said, 'I ended up in a Lancaster hospital – after nearly spewing my spleen out.'

Miss Oakley twisted her mouth. She took a long swig herself and gulped it down. Only then did I take it, but only with short, cautious slurps.

As I felt the reassuring warmth seep into my hand, the very ground trembled in a rhythmic vibration. The brick walls, the vaulted ceiling, even the brew rippled.

'What's happening?' I asked.

An altogether different voice answered, 'We're under the bloody train station.'

Though I shall henceforth deny it, I cannot describe how happy and relieved I was to hear McGray's Dundee accent.

He emerged from the shadows, looking terribly haggard, unkempt and scruffy – so unscathed.

'I heard the dandy scream,' he told Oakley. 'He all right?'

'Yes, but he'll be better after he drinks his brew,' she answered, with the tone of an aggravated nurse.

McGray nodded. 'Aye. Drink up and we'll explain all.'

'Drink up?' I squealed. 'Do you not remember this woman once tried to—?'

'"Course I remember! I had to carry yer vomited sorry frame after ye fainted like a drunken debutante. Believe me, I wouldnae let ye drink if there was the slightest chance I'd have to witness that again.'

I sighed and gulped down the hot drink. To my annoyance, the herbal brew was delicious and comforting; a tad bitter, but scented with mint and sweetened with plenty of honey. I cleared my throat, my mind a little sharper.

'How did you end up here?' I asked Nine-Nails. 'Did they catch you as well?'

He looked at Oakley with half-shut eyes. 'Aye, very similar to what happened to ye and the Ardglass lass.' I leaned forwards. 'She's all right. You'll see her in a moment.

'Harris and I saw yer signal from the top o' the belfry. The PM's bastards came from one side and these bitches from the other.'

'We saved you!' Oakley barked. 'One of my sisters got her face scarred for life! And don't forget that you had enemies all around you. Our Lancashire sisters must have heard that you were looking for someone to let you into the minster, so they swarmed there like locusts. They bribed the sexton to let them in and get you, but the man was so stupid he thought all we witches were on the same side. My sisters simply walked in to save you and he did not even look twice.' She allowed herself a smirk. 'What a shock it was for them when we attacked them from behind. In fact, we had a worse time dealing with the Prime Minister's agents.'

Nine-Nails let out an explosive laugh.

'Even they couldnae foresee what was coming. We fought them, these witches fought them, and ye should've seen the damn look on their faces when they saw the green fire on top o' the minster. And as soon as they ran, these bastards turned against me.'

'Hey!' Oakley protested.

'Och, sorry! Are ye offended? It was *ye* who almost suffocated me with that damn chloroform after Harris pinned me down.'

'Did Harris know you'd be attacking us?' I asked.

'No,' Oakley said. 'He hadn't even met us in person until last night. I shouted one of the lines in our messages to him. He recognized us and did what we asked.'

I frowned. 'Just like that? Is he that loyal to you?'

Oakley looked proud. 'He is. Some of my sisters have been in touch with him all his life, sending him money and keeping him from peril. His parents – well, I will spare you the things old Marigold did to his parents.' She had to force in a deep breath.

'So what happened to Bob and Boss?' I asked, but McGray shook his head.

'They fled. Quite soon in fact. As soon as they thought these bitch—'

'*If you call us that one more time!*'

McGray snorted. 'As soon as they thought these *dainty flowers* were goin' to kill us, they ran away.'

'Thinking they'd do the job for them?'

'That is part of the things we need to tell you,' said Oakley. 'As well as why we made them think we wanted to kill you. However, they're clever. They might find that you are alive very soon. We have a precious window of opportunity, so we must act fast.'

'A window for what?' I asked.

'We'll explain. Right now, if you feel fit enough. The coven has already gathered.'

'Here?' I asked.

'Indeed.'

'Pray, how long have we been here?' I asked.

'It's almost noon,' said Oakley. 'So the sooner you join us, the better.'

'Can ye walk?' McGray asked, offering me a hand.

'Of course I can bloody walk! I am not lame.' I knew I looked and sounded like a stubborn grandfather, struggling to stand up with just one hand, every single bone in my body cracking as I did so, but I still refused to take his hand.

Not too keen on spending more time lying in what felt like a catacomb, I was happy to follow them. The main cavity was vibrating again, the muffled sound of engines' wheels more discernible, now that I knew what they were.

I pressed a hand against my pained temple as we walked in between the grid of columns. I stared at them and the arched ceiling.

'What is this place?' I asked.

'An old Roman bath house,' Oakley said. 'These stacks supported the heated floors. That vault you were in must have been a furnace to produce steam.'

I was going to ask how she knew all those things, but then I remembered that she was a witch. Those women were always ten steps ahead of everyone.

Something metallic clinked under my feet. I stopped and picked up a tiny, rusty old coin, stamped with the head of a full-lipped man.

'Och, stop pickin' up trinkets!' McGray protested.

'These *trinkets* must be more than a thousand years old. Does nothing impress you?'

'I'll have time to be impressed when the entire sodding government doesnae want me dead.'

I put the little coin in my breast pocket and walked on.

Oakley climbed a short flight of steps that led to a very low threshold. We then entered a smaller vault, perfectly round, like the minster's chapter house. Its walls were decorated with multicoloured tiles, each piece the size of a fingernail, depicting the most precious and intricate Roman motifs – a fisherman pulling bursting nets from the sea, dancing young women with bunches of grapes in their hands, men bathing in scandalously scant clothing, a man being strangled by bright green snakes . . .

All was lit by a small fire at the core of the room, five feet below the stones on which I stood. Most of the space was occupied by what must have been a bathing pool, seven or eight yards wide, rimmed by red glazed bricks, some of which still glimmered under the light as if brand new.

There, seated around the crackling fire like the knights of King Arthur, the witches parleyed.

34

McGray and I followed Oakley into the dry pool, treading on the same steps the ancient Romans would have used to plunge into the hot waters. As we descended I had a good view of that eerie gathering.

There were at least a dozen women, from teenage girls to a couple of old, hunched crones, all dressed in black, the flames casting sharp, dancing shadows on their faces. They were passing round a bowl with a steaming beverage, each taking a sip and then mumbling some unintelligible invocation. It sounded like some Celtic language, but I could not be sure.

There were only three of their brawny helpers, Harris one of them. He sat a little apart from the group, his sweaty scalp shining before the fire, and he looked rather tense. So did the witches around him, who would only have met him that day and, like me, were intimidated by his size and looks. I felt somewhat thankful – after all, he *had* fought the Marigolds to defend us – but I also preferred to keep my distance, especially thinking of how effortlessly he'd thrown a man to his death.

Little Daisy was the only one who did not seem to fear him. The girl stood on one of his knees, quite entertained following the fuzzy outlines of the man's tattoos with her little fingers. She turned to look at me, as inquisitive as before.

No wonder her face had looked familiar. She was the daughter of the poor nurse whom Lord Joel, Caroline's father, had poisoned before escaping Edinburgh's asylum. I would never forget the sight of that young woman lying in bed, struggling to breathe as the strychnine slowly took her life. That little child had the same wide blue eyes and the same dark hair.

Caroline, quite understandably, sat on the other side of the circle, as far from the child as possible, her eyes buoyant with conflicting emotions. Her father had murdered that little girl's mother, yes, but that young witch had played the part of a nurse for years, pretending to look after Lord Joel, when in reality her job was to ensure that the man never came back to sanity. If she were still alive, she'd surely be a Marigold, and Caroline knew that.

I could already tell she would never forgive these women. She might move on, and the violence of that hatred might recede to some extent, but it would remain rooted deep in her heart for the rest of her life.

In return, most of the women around the fire cast her resentful looks, all well aware of the story.

I thought Miss Oakley held the most hostile stare, but then I met the piercing blue eyes of a sour middle-aged woman, her arms crossed with indescribable contempt. And she had good reason – she was Mrs Greenwood, the mother of the murdered nurse. She was holding the hand of a woman whose face was entirely covered in bandages, leaving only narrow slits for her eyes, mouth and nostrils. She was the witch I'd seen fall to her knees at the minster, her face wafting vapours. I felt a shudder.

Mrs Greenwood glared at me then, but the very instant our eyes met, someone took hold of my right arm.

I started when I saw that aged face, the skin as pale as that of something that dwells underground, every inch wrinkled like ancient bark. Her mouth was half open, with a set of blackened teeth bent in all directions, and she had a crooked nose, perhaps broken many years ago. Above it, a pair of eyes stared at me, so sunken and surrounded by folds of skin I could barely see the spark of their pupils. Still, I recognized them at once.

'Nettle?'

The old woman grunted, unable to speak, for the elder witches had cut her tongue decades ago. And they had also forced her to live as a hermit in the middle of the Lancashire wilderness, where McGray and I had had the good fortune to meet her.

She examined my splint and bandages, and then looked up. Her small, veiny eyes were full of expression.

'Did you do this?' I asked, aware that the woman was a seasoned healer.

Nettle gave a nod and a growl. Miss Oakley came closer.

'She did her best, but you've taken quite a battering on that bone and didn't let it rest. You may never be able to move your hand as before.'

'Why is it always me?' I moaned, while Nettle led me to a seat by the fire. McGray sat next to me.

'Would ye prefer this?' he asked, showing me his nine-fingered hand.

I could not answer, for Caroline came to sit between us, almost begging for protection from the surrounding witches. I could not blame her.

Looking around, I saw an empty seat on top of a thick slab, placing it a little higher than all the others. Nettle took it, and I had a chance to look at her with more attention.

I remembered her wearing rags, which she used indiscriminately to wrap herself and to mop the floors. Now she sported a plain black dress, clean and almost regal in comparison, and a thick shawl of the same colour. She was the arch-witch now; the eldest and wisest in that circle of survivors, all eyes fixed on her with deference. And Miss Oakley, who sat to her right, was her voice.

'Again, we are terribly sorry we had to bring you like this,' she said after Nettle gave a short nod. 'As I told you all, we needed all the other factions to believe you were dead.'

'The Marigolds too?' Nine-Nails asked, and Miss Oakley nodded. 'Feisty bunch?'

Nettle winced and moaned.

'Vicious,' said Oakley. 'The worst of the worst from the former days. While we treasured the ancient wisdom, they hoarded the muscle, the money – and they're trying to keep the influence too.' Nettle poked her elbow, nodding at Caroline. Oakley tensed her lips, looking at her with renewed bitterness. 'They were the ones who shot your maid. Not us.'

She pronounced those words with visible effort, almost choking on them.

Caroline looked livid.

'Is that supposed to be an apology?' she spat. 'Bertha would not be dead if you had not sent me out to do your dirty work on the Continent!'

Oakley bared her teeth. 'You have no idea what dirty work is! *What your family did to us—!*'

Nettle seized her by the wrist, shaking her head very gently. On our side, McGray was the one to pacify Caroline, patting her on the shoulder.

'We'd better move on,' McGray said. 'Youse obviously brought us here 'cause youse think we can help each other. Am I right?'

Nettle nodded, and Nine-Nails looked straight into her eyes.

'Can *ye* commune with Prince Albert?'

It was as if the question had stirred the fire, the logs crackling and the flames twirling, and I felt a sudden pang of hope. If anyone in the land could help us, it must be Nettle.

Nevertheless, my hope was short-lived. Oakley twisted her mouth.

'We . . . we don't know yet if that will be possible.'

Caroline leaned forwards. 'That's why nobody has contacted the Queen, is it not? Nobody knows how to summon him.'

'Indeed,' said Oakley. 'Most of that knowledge has been lost. That was one of the many secrets only the two most senior witches, Marigold and Redfern, had access to. It was an ancient tradition to share the most precious knowledge between them, in case one of them died. It had never happened that both leaders perished on the same night. We lost so much, and I don't mean just all the potions and remedies; the cats stopped obeying us as soon as they died, and every day more and more of our ravens fly away, never to come back. The Lancashire sisters only have a handful left, and we've had to use magpies, but what we can get out of them is very limited.

'Even some of the remedies we thought we knew so well don't seem to work the way they used to, and we can't tell why. Our sisterhood will never be the same.'

All the women looked down and a sombre silence fell upon the vault.

I felt a wave of guilt, and McGray's face told me he thought the same. We had inadvertently cut the head of something far more complex and deeper than we could have imagined.

'We *do* want to help the Queen,' Oakley went on. 'We need her sympathy. That will protect us from the Marigolds and from people like Lord Salisbury. We must learn how to commune with Prince Albert again.'

I chuckled. 'The late Marigold and Redfern did not *really* talk to him, did they?'

Nettle hummed and swayed her head from left to right.

'We don't know for sure,' Oakley said for her. 'Like I just told you, all that knowledge was lost.'

'D'ye think they trapped his soul?' McGray jumped in.

'That is a possibility.' Oakley answered, and then looked at me. 'And it's also possible that they simply deceived the Queen all those years. None of us here knows for certain.'

McGray shook his head. 'Those two auld hags must have made provisions in case they both snuffed it. Surely! I cannae see two witches as cunning as them letting all that wisdom die with them.'

Oakley let out a sigh.

'They did make provisions. Only . . . it is not straightforward.'

'What d'ye mean?' McGray asked.

Oakley tensed her lips, but Nettle gave her a nod, encouraging her to talk. 'One elder witch was told, long ago, *not* the knowledge itself, but – where it had been hidden.'

We all turned to old Nettle, who interlaced her hands and gave us the most tired gaze.

'Ye ken where the spells are!' McGray gasped.

Nettle did not nod or shake her head, she simply stared at the fire. The reflections danced in her eyes, as if her very pupils were shifting shape. I shuddered, and then the old woman raised her hand, two fingers pointing up.

Oakley again sighed, rather vexed, clearly reluctant to reveal what came next.

'There are two sources,' she said. 'One was that German book.'

Caroline looked up, so fast her neck could have snapped. All eyes were on her again, all angrier, all more menacing.

'However,' Oakley said, her voice darker, 'Miss Ardglass – you betrayed us.'

35

Caroline's jaw dropped. Suddenly she seemed afraid. Guilty, even.

And Oakley was smiling with mockery.

'You know what I'm talking about, don't you?'

One of the older women leaned sideways, picked up a cloth bag and pulled out the thick book. It was bound in bright red leather, with a gilded spine and elaborate gold corners.

Caroline recognized it at once, and she went a shade paler.

'Is that the book you stole from Amorbach?' I asked her. She only nodded, her mouth dry, and I had to speak for her. 'But that is only a logbook. Miss Ardglass saw it; there is nothing but visitors' names in it.'

'There was something else,' Oakley said. 'She took it. Show them.'

The old witch brought us the book. She offered it to Caroline, who refused to take it, so I received it for her and placed it on my lap. The woman opened it at the back cover, and I saw that the leather had been ripped off. I lifted it carefully and looked at the bare sheet of wood at the core. Someone had cut a hole in it; a perfect oval.

Nettle pointed insistently at the book.

'There was something nestled in that gap,' Oakley said, 'and there's new glue on that leather. Miss Ardglass, you opened up the cover and then pasted it back together.' Her voice became grim. 'What was in there?'

I cast a quick look around, studying the witches' faces. They were all at the edges of their seats, like ancient Romans at the coliseum, holding their breaths before the lions killed the last Christian.

Caroline's lips parted, quivering. Something of a whimper came out, but then—

'D'ye mean youse don't ken either?'

McGray's high-pitched question took everyone by surprise, even me. The witches began murmuring, a few gasped, and I only stopped looking at them because the book slid down my legs and fell onto the ancient tiles.

As I picked it up, it opened naturally near the end, on a page that had clearly been read and reread. And a name had been underlined with soft pencil.

When I read it my heart skipped a beat.

'God . . .' I mumbled. I was going to say something, but then one of the women, Mrs Greenwood, shouted something malicious, and I thought better. I closed the book again, hoping nobody had seen my reaction. I must tell McGray as soon as we were alone.

'Of course we didn't know,' Oakley came back. 'That was precisely the point of getting it.'

Nine-Nails was not convinced. 'And why would an auld witch in Lancashire choose to hide her knowledge somewhere in soddin' Bavaria?'

The eyes were turning more and more hostile. I saw women shift in their seats, and I feared they might produce little vials of acid – or set Harris against us.

'It's all right,' Caroline said, resting a hand on McGray's arm – I winced at that. 'I did take something.'

'What was it?' Oakley repeated.

Caroline took a deep breath, shut her eyes as if about to jump off a cliff, and then spoke. 'It was a miniature.'

Her voice echoed for a moment, everyone around utterly confused.

'A miniature?' I asked. 'Do you mean – a miniature portrait?'

Caroline nodded. 'Yes. Watercolour on ivory. Very beautiful.'

Oakley and Nettle exchanged puzzled looks. The older witch twitched her face and made a few fine movements with her fingers, noticeable only if one looked carefully. They must all carry some meaning, for Oakley turned to Caroline and spoke resolutely.

'A portrait of whom?'

Caroline bit her lip. 'I – I don't know. It didn't have a name.'

'She's lying!' Mrs Greenwood said at once, provoking an uproar.

Nettle banged her palms on the arms of her seat. She did not need to growl; there was instant silence. She looked at Caroline, her expressive eyes requesting the truth.

'It had no name, I swear,' she insisted.

'Anyone ye recognized?' McGray asked.

Caroline shook her head. For a moment she looked as confused as everyone else. 'No, it – it was the portrait of a very young boy; four or five years old. Curly hair, light brown, with very pretty blue eyes.'

Nettle moved a single finger and Oakley spoke.

'Can you tell us anything else?'

Caroline nodded, though frowning. 'There was a date on the back, but it made no sense to me. It was – 1799.'

'1799?' McGray echoed.

'I found it really odd too,' Caroline said. 'The logbook was for visitors in 1818 and 1819.'

At that, McGray arched an eyebrow, his eyes opening just a smidgen wider, but he was quick to compose himself. I knew him too well to ask. Not yet, at least.

'Nothing else?' Oakley insisted.

'No,' Caroline said. 'And that is the truth. I swear.'

But there was a slight flicker in her eyes. From that short distance I could tell she was concealing something. In the dim light, that flicker went unnoticed by almost everyone else.

'Why did you take it?' Mrs Greenwood demanded in the distance.

Caroline glared at her, her chest now heaving, and I knew she would not hold back.

'*I did not trust you!*' she spat. 'Any of you! You could not expect blind loyalty from someone you contacted through anonymous notes, could you?' The witches, agitated, were all whispering to each other, but Caroline raised her voice. 'I still don't trust you – not fully. Forgive me if I thought I might need some leverage for the future.'

Nettle raised her hands, appeasing the coven.

'Where is it now?' Oakley asked.

Caroline took a deep breath and, at least to me, it took her just a second too long to answer.

'I took it to Edinburgh. It's hidden in my grandmother's house. It's quite safe there.'

As Caroline made all sorts of reassurances, I held my breath, quite sure she was lying – one more question I must save for later. I exhaled slowly, hoping that my own expressions did not betray her.

'Mr Frey—'

Oakley's sudden address made me jump.

'Y-yes?'

'You also seem to know something you haven't told us.'

My heart skipped a beat. I clenched the book, handing it to the old witch so that I did not have to meet Oakley's gaze.

'What do you mean?'

When I looked back, both she and Nettle were casting me piercing stares.

'Our sisters,' said Oakley, 'heard you call that witch by name.'

My lips parted, mostly out of relief, but they took it for guilt.

'At the minster,' Oakley remarked. 'You called her Hilda. These sisters heard you.'

Three of the younger women, whose figures I recognized from those dreadful minutes, were nodding.

I sighed, pretending to be defeated. 'I . . . yes, I did.'

McGray turned to me, perplexed.

'How did you know that?' Oakley asked before he could speak.

'I did not have time to tell you this at the pub,' I told McGray, and then looked back at the witches. 'I saw her photograph merely a few hours earlier. One of the PM's men had it in his pocket.'

'How did ye see it?' McGray asked.

I cleared my throat. 'I – well . . . I looked through his stuff on the train, when he was not looking.'

Nine-Nails whistled. 'Who would've said ye had it in ye?'

'I gathered she was Boss's – the man's lost sweetheart. He nearly shot me when he realized I'd—' I was going to say 'taken it', but thought better, 'when he realized I'd seen it.'

Like before, I felt as if the photograph, still in my breast pocket, had caught fire. I rushed to speak on. 'Why is that woman so relevant?'

Oakley hesitated.

'Shall I tell them?' she whispered to Nettle, and the old witch simply let out an apathetic groan. '*What does it matter?*' she seemed to intimate.

Oakley did not look too convinced, but she spoke nonetheless. 'She is . . . Lord Salisbury's half-sister.'

McGray nearly fell from the seat. 'Fuck, yer joking!'

Oakley sighed with impatience. 'And her mother was one of our own.'

I felt as if my jaw had dropped all the way to the floor. Caroline, on the other hand, simply laughed through her teeth. This was the sort of ballroom gossip she would have been listening to her entire life.

'Daughter of the second marquis,' I said, my eyebrow rising. 'Was that, shall I say – *arranged*?'

Oakley smirked. 'The royal families are not the only ones who produce heirs at their convenience. Ill-timed offspring was the sort of stratagems Marigold and her predecessor loved to carry out. And Hilda was their masterstroke.

'They chose the second marquis after very careful consideration. He was already very well positioned in the House of Lords, and promised to go even higher. The intervention was very well timed too.'

McGray chuckled at her calling it 'intervention'.

Oakley went on. 'The marquis's first wife, mother of our current prime minister, had died a few years earlier. It wasn't difficult to ensnare him and very soon our sister was with child – Mrs Marigold, very much like the arch-witch before her, knew of a special brew to augment fertility.'

I blushed slightly.

'And then youse blackmailed the PM's dad?' McGray asked.

'Indeed,' Oakley replied. 'And as I said, the time was perfect. The second marquis had been knighted recently and was looking to marry again – an earl's daughter, as far as I recall, to help him climb higher in parliament.' Nettle nodded. 'If it had transpired he'd just fathered a child with a woman who practised witchcraft . . .'

McGray was smiling wryly. 'What did youse ask from him?'

'Among other things,' said Oakley, 'the second marquis ensured that one of our spies became Queen Victoria's lead bagpiper in Balmoral.'

I nearly cricked my neck when I looked up, the dreadfully dull pages of Queen Victoria's memoirs instantly acquiring new meaning. Oakley gave me an inquisitive look, and I had to think fast.

'That – that was genius,' I said. 'Pipers are around all the time; at social gatherings, under the Queen's window waking her up every morning . . . Even better than a scullery or chamber maid.'

'Indeed.' Oakley nodded. 'He wasn't the only piper Marigold employed – we had them all over Scotland – but the man in Balmoral was certainly the best asset. If Marigold and Redfern swindled the Queen into believing they communed with Albert, they would have used information gathered by him.' She shook her head. 'Unfortunately, the man became greedy and tried to blackmail them. They took care of him at once.'

The two older witches showed slight smiles, seemingly approving. Nettle was not so amused.

'So,' McGray said then, 'this lass Hilda is the dirt the PM wants to keep quiet?'

'He must have given the photo to his men to show them who they were after,' I added, and Nettle nodded, the creases around her eyes deepening.

'She had the gall to blackmail Lord Salisbury herself,' said Oakley. 'Repeatedly! She is the reason he is hunting us; she is the reason he kept his men watching you, so that you could lead them to us.'

I leaned back a few inches. Boss and Bob had had full access to our work from the very start. They had stared freely at the map where McGray had marked all the possible witches' hubs.

Nettle's eyes had darkened. She stared at me with a sadness and exhaustion I cannot describe.

'And now we brought them to you,' I mumbled.

'Indeed,' said Oakley. 'And that is why we urged you to shake those men off. They would have disposed of you as soon as they found us. And then they would have killed us all, regardless of which coven we belonged to. Lord Salisbury used you. He *never* intended to help you.'

There was a moment of tense silence, some witches looking down, others resentful.

McGray, to my surprise, cackled. 'We should've seen through that! A politician's word! A soddin' Englishman's too!'

And then, echoing in the vault, we heard the eerie cry of a toddler. A young woman came through one of the many dilapidated archways, carrying a restless child – I could see it was a girl. She handed her to Oakley, who kissed her on the forehead and tried to lull her back into sleep.

'We are prepared to run,' she mumbled. 'Start again some-where else, like we did before. However, we still have a chance to be rid of these threats forever. And that's why we need you.'

She embraced her little girl closer to her chest.

'You can save us,' she said. 'And if we play the cards well, we can still save *you*.'

36

'Och, sod off! We've been told those porkies before!'

Caroline again held McGray's arm. Was she looking for excuses to do so?

'Pray, let them speak,' she said. 'You can swear at them later.'

Oakley cleared her throat. Asking for our help was clearly very difficult for her.

'As I told you a moment ago, there is another source of lost knowledge.' The second she paused to breathe felt like an eternity to me. 'It is an ancient herbarium. It holds the last key to contact Prince Albert.'

'Did you not just say you thought it was all lies?' I protested.

'That book will confirm it,' Oakley said, raising her voice. 'That is the book we know Marigold and Redfern consulted right before they first summoned the prince's spirit. And they went back to it a couple of times.'

Nettle let out a troubled growl. She had probably had that information from the arch-witches themselves – before they mutilated and banished her.

'Where's that book?' McGray asked.

'That's why we need your help,' Oakley answered. 'It's kept in one of the Oxford libraries.'

McGray turned to me at once. 'Ye studied there for a while!'

All the other witches were also staring at me. They had clearly done their homework.

'Indeed,' I said. 'I studied medicine there, but it was only for some eleven months, and over ten years ago.'

'Which is still better than no knowledge at all,' said Oakley.

I let out a resigned breath. 'Which library?'

Nettle drew a circle in the air and then cupped her hands. Oakley frowned, a little confused.

'It's very close to a domed building. A rotunda, it seems.'

'That will be the Bodleian Library,' I said, and Nettle nodded vehemently. For the first time in days I smiled. 'Well, that makes things easy. We can simply bribe the chief librarian or the deans. If we pulled the right strings, they'd grant us full access to—'

Nettle was already shaking her head. She even unsettled the toddler.

'Nobody, *nobody* must know we are looking for this,' Oakley said. 'That is imperative. Neither Lord Salisbury nor the Marigolds.' She eyed old Nettle, who this time shook her head. 'I cannot tell you in detail, only that if they find out we sent you there, chances are they will immediately figure out how to contact Prince Albert. They must not even know which book you took.'

I arched an eyebrow. 'The librarian is bound to notice a book went missing.'

'We'll give you an old herbarium of ours to leave in its place,' Oakley said. 'It might be months, if not years, before someone realizes it's a fake. Your intrusion, even if noticed, hopefully will be forgotten by then.'

Caroline frowned. 'I understand why you don't want the other covens to know this, but – why should you conceal it from Lord Salisbury, when he'd be your easiest way in?'

McGray was nodding. 'The bastard doesnae need us anymore.' He looked at me with frightening concern. 'He already has all the information he wanted. From now on he can go hunting witches on his own.'

I breathed out as I buried my face in my left hand. I felt so, so tired. And Caroline and McGray looked equally wasted.

'We are in each other's hands,' Oakley said. 'Neither side has a choice, unless you want to spend the rest of your lives hiding and fearing your own shadow.' She looked lovingly at her toddler, her eyes pooling tears. 'And I can tell you . . . some days you feel it is a hell not worth living, and you think that if it were only you –' she gulped, 'you'd just let them strike you and get done with it.'

Nine-Nails, Caroline and I exchanged looks. Exhausted as we felt, there was still rage in our eyes. That same rage I'd felt at the top of the minster tower. We would not let them win. We would soldier on and chop the gorgon's head.

One of the witches passed me the bowl of hot brew. I received it and took a long swig of the bitter concoction, resigning myself to one more disastrous spree.

This, I feared, would be the last one.

37

The magpie, which we were meant to release as soon as our job was done, stared curiously at everything from its little cage. It had to spread its wings from time to time to keep itself balanced, for we rode along some of the direst, darkest roads of old York. Caroline's pale chin and the magpie's white plumage were the only discernible shapes.

'Is this the same bird they gave you last time?' I asked her.

'I think so,' she said, the cage resting on her knees, her face almost entirely covered by her black French hood. McGray, seated in front of us, looked at it intently. Tucked underneath his seat was the herbarium we were supposed to leave at the library, and somewhere in its pages a little riddle meant to tell us the title of the ancient witchcraft book, so that I could search for it in the library's catalogue. Oakley and Nettle, it seemed, had taken care of everything.

They'd even had a battered, nondescript carriage ready for us, pulled by an equally forgettable horse; dark enough to blend into the night, but not the shimmering jet of McGray's 'Inky'.

That horse, along with Katerina and Joan, were meant to join us somewhere outside the city. Oakley had sent them word to leave quietly. They would pick up Caroline and travel with her to Edinburgh, where she'd fetch the miniature portrait and hand it to Nettle's witches. That mysterious little item was clearly crucial to them.

Very soon we passed the city walls, leaving behind even the dimmest lights, and I do not know how Harris managed to keep us on the road.

As if not content with the deep darkness, I heard Nine-Nails pull down the windows' shutters. A moment later he struck a match, its sparking flame filling the tiny space with golden light. I felt as though we were crouching inside a little burrow in the ground.

McGray lit a cigarette, which then became the only source of light, and then looked at Caroline with quizzical eyes. He spoke in the softest possible whisper.

'Ye lied to them, lass.'

She raised her chin. 'Why, of course I did!'

'So did *you*,' I told McGray.

He snorted. 'Och, so did ye! *Three bloody times, Percy*, I saw ye!'

'Three?' Caroline echoed. 'Which one did I miss?'

'First do tell us,' I said, 'where did you keep the portrait? It is not in Edinburgh, for sure.'

I saw a hint of a blush on her face.

'Ye have it with ye?' McGray asked, leaning forwards, as if fearing Harris might hear him through the carriage wall.

Caroline grunted and pushed the birdcage into McGray's hands.

'Look away,' she commanded. 'Both of you.'

I did so, mostly to conceal my own flush. I heard the ruffle of her skirts, and nearly began whistling 'Phyllis Is My Only Joy' out of sheer tension. From the corner of my eye I saw McGray attempting, most libidinously, to have a peek of Caroline's ankles. I threw him a discreet kick.

'Done,' she said at last.

McGray struck another match, struggling for space now that he had the cage, and held it close to the white handkerchief Caroline was unwrapping.

'Is this your last secret, Miss Ardglass?' I asked, but she simply sneered and turned over the last fold of fabric.

There, nestled in lace like the most precious relic, lay the little oval portrait.

It was just over two inches wide, the ivory so thin it was translucent like bone china. McGray and I leaned closer to inspect it.

Like Caroline had said, it depicted a young boy of curly hair and wide blue eyes. His cheeks were rosy, his jaw soft and his lips a delicate speck of pink, but it was the watercolour technique that impressed me the most. That tiny object was an exquisite piece of art, with brushstrokes as fine as hairs; thousands of them melding together to produce the gentlest transitions from light to shadow. Contrasting with these were the crisp folds on the boy's collar, and his eyes looked so crystalline, the white sparks on the pupils so expertly placed, that I almost expected them to reflect the glow from McGray's match. Only very proud and wealthy parents could have commissioned something of the kind.

'Looks like an upper-class brat,' McGray said. Indeed, the boy stood at ease, with his arms crossed in an almost pugilistic stance. His clean, direct gaze was confident too, with his left eyebrow raised, the other almost straight.

'More illegitimate offspring?' I asked.

'He could be,' said Caroline, 'but look at the date.'

She flipped it and we saw the fine writing that followed the lower edge.

RA Cosway, 1799.

'The name o' the laddie?' McGray asked.

'No,' Caroline answered. 'Names and dedications are usually written at the centre, not the edge. This is the signature of the artist.'

'That is no German name,' I said. 'This was either painted in England, then taken to Germany, or the painter travelled all the way there for the commission. He . . .'

I stopped, squinting and looking closer.

'What?' McGray asked, as he struck a new match.

'I don't know,' I mumbled. 'He seems somehow – familiar.'

'How can he?' Caroline asked. 'If the date is correct, he is dead by now, surely.'

'That, or he'd be nearly a hundred,' McGray added. 'Even older than fat Vic.'

'I thought he might be Prince Albert,' said Caroline. 'He was German, after all. But then someone told me he was the same age as the Queen. A few months younger, even.'

'And what does this have to do with communing with him?' I asked. McGray snuffed out the match, and the last spark in his eyes told me he already had a theory.

'D'ye remember how Katerina needs a token? Something with a person's *imprint*?'

'Indeed,' I said. Sadly, I was far too familiar with the gypsy's divination techniques. 'Are you going to tell me this is the object the witches would have used during their séances?'

'It could well be. It could even be their link to his spirit; the object they've been using to anchor him. For that they'd need something the late Albert loved very much in life.'

Caroline's eyes opened wider. 'Could this boy, perhaps . . . be his father?'

'I'd need to check the history books,' I said, 'but if this was painted in 1799, this child would have been the right age to father him.'

I saw that Nine-Nails was squinting.

'Lass, ye said that the logbook covered 1819?'

'Yes. I should remember. That is also the year my—'

'Yer grandmother was born,' McGray completed, remembering the documents given to us by Superintendent Trevelyan.

Nine-Nails stroked his stubble for a long while, looking as if he were about to speak but the hypothesis could not take full shape in his mind.

I spoke first. 'If that was the year Prince Albert was born, this could have arrived in Germany precisely then; sent as a present for the mother – or for the newborn.'

'One of those "gestures" the royal families are so fond of,' said Caroline. 'Perhaps to remark how very much alike father and son looked as children.'

'He does resemble Prince Albert a little,' I said. 'That small chin . . . the Hanoverian chin.'

McGray let out a long, groaning sigh. Confusion itself must sound like that.

'If this was the token for the séances,' he asked himself, 'why send it all the way back to Bavaria? They would have needed it. Why hide it in that auld book and—' He turned to me all of a sudden. 'Percy, what did ye see in that visitors' log? I saw ye about to wet yerself when it nearly fell off yer lap.'

I sighed. 'Oh, long story . . .'

'Then ye'd better shorten it.'

'There was a name circled there. A name I know.'

'Whose? How?'

'When I was going through Boss's pockets I also found a telegram.'

'Did ye take it?'

'No,' I said, 'but I did take Hilda's photo and transcribed the message there. That accounts for two of my – can you call them lies? I simply did not tell them I had this with me.'

I produced the photograph. 'Here. I transcribed it.'

McGray struck another match, the better to see, and he and Caroline needed but a second to read the one-line message – *Write if they discover d'Esté*.

'Who the hell's Lady Louis Brurs?' McGray asked, pointing at the sender's name.

I could not suppress a slightly smug tone. 'That is an anagram for *Lord Salisbury*. It may have been luck, but I realized it very quickly.'

'And I assume d'Esté is the name you saw in the logbook,' Caroline said.

'Indeed. That cannot be a coincidence. Also, the witches never mentioned it, even though it is clear that they were looking for it in the book.'

Caroline shook her head. 'Perhaps it was a code? Something to signal there was something else hidden in the text?'

McGray still looked quizzical. 'Is d'Esté an anagram for anything?'

I quickly jumbled the letters in my head. 'I doubt it. I can only think of . . . *steed*.'

Nine-Nails squinted again, as if striving to see a speck of dust that fluttered further and further away.

In the end he shook his head. 'I'll mull over this. Frey, what was yer third lie?'

'Again, not really a lie,' I said. 'Oakley told us about the Queen's bagpipers. Victoria says plenty about them in her published memoirs. I was reading a copy at the hotel, while I waited for you. And I do mean *plenty*; not only how proficient or handsome they were, but also their careers, their families, their previous and subsequent employers . . .'

Caroline shifted in her seat. 'Did anything suggest which ones might have been the witches' spies?'

'I do not remember. I was barely paying attention to the fine detail.'

'Where's the book?' McGray asked.

'I left it at the hotel. It is not the kind of literature I'd clutch to my bosom.'

'It should be easy to find another copy,' Caroline said. 'Every second-hand bookshop will have one.'

'Would it be worth it to find out more?' I wondered.

McGray nodded gently, his mind clearly at work. 'Maybe . . . Or it might muddle things even more.' He shook his head, perhaps putting to one side whichever thoughts he was having. 'If only we had more time . . . Nae, right now we should focus on the task at hand; dwell on these things later.'

'Wait, wait,' I said, raising my hand. 'You also concealed something from the witches. What was it?'

He handed the cage back to Caroline. 'So nothing about all this mess of names and dates makes youse wary?'

Caroline and I exchanged mystified looks.

'What are you talking about?' I asked, but McGray only shrugged. 'Might be nothing. I might tell youse later.'

'Might tell us!' I cried. 'What do you bloody—?'

I could not finish the sentence, for the carriage halted then.

McGray pulled up the shutters, and my heart leapt when Harris's face appeared almost pressed against the other side of the glass.

I let out a long breath, not even attempting to conceal my relief. So did Caroline. Our nerves were shattered by then.

'Are they here?' McGray asked.

Harris only raised his large hand and made a sign, asking McGray and I to come out. He then walked back to the front of the carriage, out of our view. We heard female voices, and there was a slight sign of relief in McGray's eyes.

He was going to open the door, but stopped just as his hand touched the handle.

'Put that away,' he told Caroline, pointing at the miniature, which still lay on the seat next to her, poorly wrapped in the handkerchief. 'And Frey, give her that picture.'

'Wha—what?'

'It'll be safer in her . . . her . . .' For once he blushed too. 'Wherever she's been hiding things.'

I could only assent and hand her the photograph. McGray then jumped off and I followed him closely, my feet sinking into the deep snow. Caroline, busy hiding the portraits, would take a moment to join us.

The night was so dark, the road cutting through woodland so thick, I could only just make out the shapes that stood ahead: a wide stagecoach, the horse so black I could only see the glint of his eyes, and two short, plump females coming to meet us.

The only light around was McGray's cigarette, but it was enough to show how pale and worried Katerina and Joan really were.

'You're fine!' Katerina let out, rushing to grasp McGray's hands. 'Thank goodness! Everyone in York is talking about a green fire at the minster. And that the sexton found people trying to – well, he said *steal*.'

'They said they found two dead men,' Joan added, on the verge of tears. 'One on top of the tower with a shot in his head, and the other splattered all over the main floor. And then you didn't come back . . . *We feared the worst!*'

McGray squeezed Joan's shoulder. 'There, there, hen. Ye see we're all right.'

And while Joan sobbed, Katerina looked bitter. 'And that sexton even said he stopped the robbers all by himself. They might as well give him a medal! And I thought my contacts were trustworthy! I'm *so* sorry, my boys. I nearly sent you to your deaths!'

I sighed. 'It's a waste of time to point fingers now. Things may even have turned for the better.'

'What is that business with Miss Ardglass?' Katerina asked, lowering her voice and eyeing the carriage. 'We were only told to take her straight north, back to Edinburgh. And they even sent us that scrawny driver to watch over us.'

She said it loud enough so that the man, atop the driver's seat, could hear her clearly. The man did not even flinch.

'The Ardglass lass will explain it all,' McGray said. 'But do make sure she makes it to Edinburgh. She is so fuckin' stubborn.'

Caroline joined us in time to hear that, but she rather seemed to take it as a compliment.

'Dear girl,' Katerina said, 'the coven asked me to tell you, word for word, that – *they want the little boy*. Whatever that means. And that if you try to deceive them again, you will only cause your own death – and the death of these two.'

Caroline looked at McGray, and spoke only after choosing her words very carefully. 'Should I tell them where it is? That way I might join you for this new task.'

I was going to say something, but right then, brought by an abrupt draught of cold wind, we heard a raven caw.

'*Och, damn youse!*' McGray howled to the skies, and the rest of us looked up in fear. Even the tall, muscly Harris.

The magpie's cage was still in the carriage, but the bird flapped its wings so violently we all heard it.

'Nae,' McGray told Caroline. 'Ye go with them and – show them.'

'Go with them?' she echoed.

'Aye.'

'No,' she said stubbornly. 'You two will need all the help you can get.'

'Lass . . .'

'Mr McGray, do you think your chances are any better aided only by the flimsy, limply, crippled Mr Frey?'

'*Hey!*

Nine-Nails rubbed his face with exasperation.

'That's a very fair point, lass, but if ye think I'll allow ye to—'

'*Allow me!* Who do you think you are? You have absolutely no authority over—'

At that point McGray lifted her by the waist, carried her on his shoulder like a jute sack and pushed her into Katerina's stagecoach.

'Aye, I'm playing the brute-force card, deal with it.'

Caroline grumbled incessantly, invisible to the rest of us now that she was in the carriage. McGray let out a loud *shush* and we heard them exchange angered whispers. He told me later what they'd said, and I quote verbatim:

'I still don't trust these Nettle bitches. Do ye?'

'Of course I don't!'

'Good. So we need someone to keep an eye on them; someone who can warn us if they're up to anything funny. Ye still have that portrait. That's all the leverage we have left. And leverage is what we need right now. Ye said so yerself.'

'But—'

'That wee portrait will save our lives. I can feel it in my gut!'

I would only come to understand that a little later. Caroline too. At that moment, however, she only agreed to go because we heard the raven a second time. And McGray rushed out before she changed her mind.

He gave a last few pats to the enviably calm Inky, and came back to us.

'Ready. She'll go with youse,' he told Katerina and Joan. The latter had a shameless smirk on her face.

'"T'was about time someone put that gal in her—'

'Joan, you should make haste,' I interrupted. 'We all have to go now.'

She looked up, and within a few blinks her face shifted into unexpected sorrow.

Now I wish I'd let her speak on, to tell us something puerile and keep the harsh reality out of our minds for another minute or two. From then on, we might not have any more chances to smile.

'Be careful, sir,' Joan told me gravely, squeezing my arm as her eyes welled up.

Katerina held a similar expression, holding McGray's nine-fingered hand between hers. It was as though we were bidding farewell to our respective surrogate mothers, and I did not like at all the ominous finality that the moment had suddenly acquired.

Joan clung to McGray in a clenching embrace, while Katerina came to me to shake my hand.

She gasped then, looking down. I realized her index finger lay right on the signet ring Caroline had so recently given me. Katerina tenderly caressed the emerald, just with the very tip of her finger. Then she looked at me, her eyes misty, yet glowing with a most unexpected hint of . . . I can only call it joy. And then she smiled.

'You . . . you have been mighty brave,' she whispered, and then blinked her tears away, slightly embarrassed – something I had never seen in her. 'You all have. But the winds will shift soon.'

I had no idea what all that meant, and she gave me no time to ask.

'Godspeed, my boys,' she told us both, letting go of my hands and stepping backwards towards her stagecoach. 'Godspeed!'

She and Joan rushed into the coach, and I caught one last glance of Caroline, looking down and in deep thought.

As their stagecoach faded in the darkness, I had a haunting presentiment; that those women were heading into an even grimmer quest than ours.

38

Harris drove almost all night, keeping to woodlands and narrow country roads. With the Marigolds and perhaps also the PM's men after us, catching trains was an impossibility, so the journey would be long. At least that would give McGray plenty of time to study the witches' instructions – they'd written them in a manner that only someone truly versed in witchcraft might understand. I also had a chance to ponder our options once we arrived in Oxford.

Other than a two-hour pause to give the horse some rest, we only stopped the following night, at a dreary little inn in the middle of the road.

As we alighted I saw that the skies had cleared. The waning moon, barely a sliver that would vanish completely the next night, was just enough to see that all the fields around were covered in a smooth, white blanket. We wrapped up in our coats and strode briskly into the inn.

The place was packed with travellers, many of them Oxford staff and academics with accents from all over the British Isles, so we managed to blend into the crowd. Even the magpie and its cage did not draw too much attention; eccentric zoologists are a rather abundant breed.

McGray, Harris and I sat at a secluded table, far from the crackling fire, around which most of the customers clustered.

After the innkeeper brought our meal, and once we were sure no one looked in our direction, McGray pulled out the witches' message. He unfolded it on the table and I saw that most of it was penned in a compact, nearly illegible hand. I leaned forward to read, but he shook his head.

'Don't bother. It took me all day.' He lowered his voice. 'The book they want is called –' he paused for dramatic effect – '*The Red Book of Hergest.*'

I blinked a couple of times. '*The Red Book of* what?'

'Hergest!' he repeated, all condescension.

'Am I supposed to have heard of that?'

McGray snorted. 'It's an ancient book o' Welsh remedies! I thought ye might've heard of it in yer almighty sodding Oxford. Don't they teach youse the history of medicine?'

'Medicine indeed, not quackery.'

'That *is* history! Ye never heard of the physicians of Myddfai?'

'Were they of consequence?'

'*Conse—!* They were a dynasty of Welsh healers that lasted over five hundred years. They were so well respected even the bloody lofty English nobles looked for their aid.'

'You must be talking about the Middle Ages.'

'Aye. If my memory doesnae fail me, the last man in the dynasty lived in the fourteenth century. He was the one who collected all his family's knowledge; five centuries of wisdom.'

'And that wisdom included how to talk to the dead?'

'Perhaps. The Myddfais most likely kent a thing or two about – well, magic.'

I nodded. 'It makes sense. Back then medicine and magic were treated as one and the same thing.'

'And that would explain why the witches want this to be a secret. The Myddfai manuscript was copied several times down the centuries. There must be several other copies scattered all around the country. Even the book they gave us is a copy.'

He patted his chest, for he'd concealed the book underneath his bulky overcoat.

'A copy? Then why—?'

'An incomplete copy, that is.' He poked the message. 'Here they say that the complete work is exactly three hundred and sixty-two pages. This one is too, but I leafed through it; they padded it up with pages from other books – Welsh poetry and whatnot – to make it look just as thick. This is also supposed to be the exact same size and colour.' He pulled down his lapel, just enough to show the edge of the dark red leather cover, convincingly worn and flaky. 'It seems they have been planning this for a while.'

Again, I looked at Harris, who now was downing a three-pint tankard in one gulp. I wondered whether his oblivion was genuine, or simply a very well-rehearsed façade.

'If it is a fourteenth-century manuscript,' I said, 'it will be kept in the Old Reading Room – Humfrey's Library, as they call it.'

I produced my little notebook and began tracing a basic diagram of the building; a quadrangle around a central court-yard, its west face connected to a T-shaped wing.

'This west wing is the Humfrey's Library,' I said. 'The catalogues and indexes are kept here,' I drew a little square at the very entrance to the Humfrey's wing, 'exactly in front of the librarian's desk. Now that we have the book's title, it will be easy to find its exact location in the register.'

McGray nodded in approval. 'Ye remember it all very well, Percy.'

'Yes, I spent endless hours studying there. I am only hoping things have not changed much in the past decade.'

'And how d'ye think we might get in?'

I needed a long swig of claret to answer that.

'Erm . . . we might have to – improvise.'

It was McGray's turn to blink in incomprehension. 'What?'

I cleared my throat. 'We will not be able to use the front entrance – besides the exposed location, it is solid oak with bolts and locks the size of Harris's feet.'

'What's the other option?' McGray urged.

'We might go in through the south gallery. There is a side entrance, a ginnel, for carts to bring and take books, furniture and so on.' I added a dotted line there. 'The gate is only wrought iron with a chain.'

'Are ye planning to gnaw on it?'

'No, but while we were travelling I remembered this case I worked on a few years a—'

'Good Mary soddin' Brown?'

'Oh, do shut up! No. A burgled jewellers' on Regent Street. The robbers cut a random link of the back door's chain, walked in, helped themselves, and when they left they bent the cut link back into shape. The owner only called us because there were several missing pieces. It was *I* who deduced how they'd broken in.' I looked at Harris. 'I thought we might as well make use of the brute force available.'

He nodded proudly.

'We'll need a good bolt cutter for that,' McGray said. 'Easy enough to get hold of. That'll take us into the courtyard. Then what?'

I sighed. 'That is when we will have to improvise. There are several doors there, but I know they are all locked at night. And they are all bolted oak, except for the one that leads to the Humfrey's wing.'

'What's that made of?'

I snorted. 'Iron sheet. It is meant to protect the oldest manuscripts in case of a fire.'

'Och, for goodness' sake!' McGray sat back, covering his face. 'Nae wonder the witches kept their most important spells there.'

'There might be a window we could use,' I said, staring at my own diagram, 'or a passage, or even the old heating pipework. But as I said, we will have to look for that once we are there. I did a good deal of exploring as a student, but never looking for a clandestine way in.'

McGray snorted. 'I expected better from ye.'

'We should have plenty of time to work things out,' I said. 'It is December, so the library will close at three o'clock.'

'*Three?*'

'Yes. No lights of any kind are allowed. No candles or oil lamps or—'

'No lights in a sodding library?'

'There are thousands upon thousands of highly combustible books there, wooden beams and floors that have had hundreds of years to dry. Someone once calculated that the entire place can burn to cinders in less than a half-hour.'

'Wait, Percy, we *are* bringing candles, are we nae?'

'Oh, of course.'

McGray leaned forwards slowly, reaching for his drink and casting me a dubious look.

'In that case *I'll* hold them,' he said. 'Ye've butterfingers even on yer right hand.'

I could not retort, for then there was a racket of voices coming from the front door. Five young undergraduates, all upper-class Oxonians, all visibly warmed by brandy, were herding in, their tired servants dragging a mountain of cases and trunks. Their raucous laughter interrupted the ghost story an old man was telling by the fire, their shoes splattered mud and slush all around them, and the massive greyhound they brought with them, as arrogant as its owners, made a beeline to the best spot by the fire.

The inn-keeper rushed to attend them, even though they'd already taken a table where they soon began to throw bread buns at each other.

'Were ye like those imps?' McGray asked me, wrinkling his nose as if someone had plunged his face into a cesspit.

I shook my head, refusing to believe I had ever looked that boyish. I then realized one thing—

'We need new clothes,' I mumbled.

'What?' McGray asked.

'We look far too conspicuous for Oxford,' I said, eyeing Harris's tattooed head. 'Even if we will be there only at night. We should think of—'

My voice was completely obscured by a deafening burst of laughter. When we turned we saw a young manservant lying on the floor, on top of a pile of suitcases. One of the Oxford boys had stuck out a leg to make him trip, and now the brat in the white suit was throwing chunks of bread at the poor chap.

McGray was squinting with malevolence.

'Aye,' he told me. 'We need to *blend in*.'

The inn-keeper and the young aggravated servant (who turned out to be his son) were not difficult to bribe. They let us raid the students' chests, and McGray and I helped ourselves to all the clean clothes we needed. The inn-keeper also sold us a mighty bolt cutter his son fetched from the stables (I could only wonder what they used it for . . .).

The following morning, after I'd had a good night's sleep and a shave, we were ready to go.

McGray, in a dark grey suit that miraculously fitted his broad shoulders, looked almost decent. *Almost.*

He noticed my assessing look as we walked back to the carriage.

'What?' he asked.

'Even without the stubble and the tartan you look too rough for Oxford. If people ask, you will have to pass as my valet.'

'*Och, nae!*'

'And your accent – gosh! You'd better not speak at all. We can always say you are mute or mentally challenged.'

McGray opened his mouth to protest, but—

'Dammit, I hate it when yer right.' He then saw Harris, who was checking the horse's straps. He made me stop. 'What about Goliath over there?'

I stared at the man as he installed himself on the driver's seat – huge, rugged, with ghastly manners *and* a real mute himself. I could get away claiming I had one mute servant, but *two* . . .

'There is no way to disguise *that*,' I said. 'He can drop us a mile or so from the library and join us separately.'

McGray twisted his mouth as he whispered.

'I'd rather keep him in sight. After the way he turned against us in York . . .'

'I know,' I mumbled, 'but we will have to trust him now. We have no choice.'

I said so as I realized just how powerless we really were, about to embark on yet another manic expedition imposed on us. I shook my head and jumped into the carriage, a growing tension settling in my chest. The magpie, jumping from one side of its cage to the other, seemed to share my anxiety.

We'd arrive in Oxford that very evening, well after the sun had set. This, one of the shortest days of the season, happened to coincide with a new moon and a clouded sky.

I preferred not to mention it, lest McGray tell me they were all bad omens.

DIARY – 1846

January 22nd. I place myself under the Treatment of Dr Seymour M.D. of No 13 Charles St Berkeley Square – He visits me, he reads this book – He expresses it as his Opinion that no organic Evil exists – that there is no reason that he can see why I should not be made well – further he says that he has known worse Cases than mine . . .

June 13th. Dr Seymour determines to make an external Application all along the Back-bone and on the lumbar Region: He prescribes the following Ointment

R   Iodidi Hydrageri 3i
Adipis preparatae 3i

I make use of this, and after a few applications it occasions a very unpleasant sensation of Itching and Irritation of the Skin where it had been rubbed on.

July 3rd. It is nine days since the unguent was rubbed upon my Back – and the VERY DISTRESSING SENSATIONS – the consequences continue unmitigated.

Ramsgate – September 22nd. Soon after breakfast I am seized with great Distress about the Bladder – Yesterday I had been obliged to take one of Dr Seymour's Soothing Drafts to stave off the Effects of the Cantharides . . .

39

The city appeared like a small cluster of golden lights against a black background, the echoes of the many church bells brought by the wind.

Harris took the carriage south-west, circumventing the city along the River Thames. As I'd told him, he halted at the edge of Christ Church Meadow, a vast park of grassland that at the moment looked as dark as the entrance to a cave. The perfect spot to step into the city without being seen.

Nine-Nails bent down to pick up the bolt cutter and stuck it under his belt, the tool pressed against his back.

'I thought Harris was going to use that,' I whispered.

'Let's bring it,' he said. 'Just in case he has any – mishaps.'

He checked that both our guns were fully loaded, passed me one, and then felt his breast pocket, where he carried more bullets. I sheathed my gun, hoping I would not need to use it.

The magpie had gone to sleep, and it was not disturbed even when McGray lifted the cage to pick the book from underneath.

'We should not encounter anyone,' I said, pocketing the three candles and the box of matches we'd taken from the inn, 'but if we do, just remember—'

'Aye, aye, I'm a witless mute.'

At that I took one last, deep breath, and then opened the door.

We stepped down and I went to Harris. 'Drive north and turn left on Pembroke Street. Keep on until you see a church. There is a small graveyard in the back, quite secluded; nobody will see the carriage if you leave it by the south fence. The time it will take you to drive the carriage there, and then walk, should be about the same it will take us to get to the library through this route. If we have not arrived yet, there is an unlit alley, Brasenose Lane. You can wait for us there.'

He gave a brief nod, his little eyes somewhat absent, and I could not tell for sure he'd fully understood my indications. I stepped back to re-join McGray. He nodded at Harris and we turned on our heels, walking silently into the darkened park.

And so the deed began.

I wrapped myself more tightly in my overcoat, feeling the cold of the night seeping through my garments. We could not see the snow, but our feet plunged at least five inches into it, and after a few steps all my toes were numb.

Looking ahead I recognized a line of gaslights in the distance, about two hundred yards away, following the grey walls of Merton College. Its old, eroded stones made me think of a smaller version of York's city walls. Rising behind it were the very old college buildings, only a handful of their narrow windows lit from within, but enough to let us see the slanting roofs and tall chimneys.

'This stretch is called Dead Man's Walk,' I whispered when we were nearly there. 'Most appropriate.'

'There's a wee gate there,' said McGray, pointing to the corner of the wall to our left. I followed him and saw that it was flimsy wrought iron with a heavy chain. We could see the college's darkened gardens beyond. They were deserted.

'We should walk around the grounds,' I whispered, but McGray was already pulling out the bolt cutter. '*McGray, no, we'd better—*'

We heard a noise then. It sounded like soft steps, muffled in the snow. And the ruffle of clothes. We looked around, striving to see, but the fields were shrouded in complete darkness, as if we stood at the edge of a black abyss.

'Sod it,' McGray said. He pushed the heavy book into my hand and then cut the chain with one swift, clean movement.

I managed to catch the links in the air before they made too much of a rattle. McGray took the chain from me and laid it carefully on the ground, before opening the gate.

We crossed the gardens in a few long strides. A line of bare trees flanked the footpath, their branches like a thick cobweb looming over our heads, and from higher above came the gleam of a couple of lit windows. I felt my pulse rising, like McGray must have too, for we did not dare say a word until we made it to the other side of the path. Another iron fence awaited us there.

The cutter still in his hand, McGray clipped this chain without a flinch. This gate screeched loudly when he pushed it, the noise deafening in the deep silence.

I could not help looking back, peering into the leafless gardens, and I thought I saw a shapeless shadow move around. McGray pulled me by the arm and we rushed into the street.

We took the first turn, if only to move away from view as soon as possible. I realized we had, quite fortuitously, walked into Magpie Lane. There were gas lamps hanging on both sides of the narrow streets, shedding plenty of light on us. I pushed my hat, hoping it would conceal the best part of my face if I looked down.

'What was that?' I whispered, pressing the book against my chest. I looked back as I spoke, and exhaled when I saw there was no one behind us.

'Nae idea. I thought ye'd seen.'

'No, I only – put that away!'

Only then McGray realized he still had the cutter in his hands. He hid it immediately.

'This way is much shorter than what I had planned,' I said. 'We will make it to the library long before Harris.'

'Let's just wait where ye told him. I don't want to parade all over the damned place.'

We made it to the end of the lane in a couple of minutes, stepping directly into the broad high street.

Despite all my years away, I instantly recognized every building. The bookshops, the Old Bank buildings, and the tall, narrow Gothic windows of St Mary's Church. The stained glass was lit from within, and from the nave came the faint echoes of a boys' choir rehearsing Christmas carols.

That was the only sound around. The usually bustling high street looked like a ghost town; no carriages, no pedestrians, no businesses open.

'Ahead?' McGray asked, and as soon as I nodded he quickened his pace. I followed suit. Deserted as it may be, this was the most exposed point in our route.

I even held my breath as we crossed, feeling like a gazelle swimming in a crocodile-infested river. I counted my steps, looking in all directions; looking for ravens in the darkened sky, looking for witches crouching in every shadow projected by the streetlights. I had to remind myself that the library was but a few yards away, on the square right behind St Mary's Church.

I put my first foot on the kerb, the stained glass so close I could make out the faces of the saints. And then, just as I let out a relieved breath, the sweet notes sung by the boys were interrupted by the caw of a raven.

We both froze. I held my breath and saw McGray's condense before his face. The bird squawked again and I peered around, looking for it, but McGray pulled me by the arm, so suddenly I nearly dropped the book.

'How could they find us?' he growled as we walked into the square. The round dome of Radcliffe's Camera, its creamy stone walls lit by the lamps all around the quadrangle, had never looked so much like a mausoleum.

'Could it not have been just any raven?' I mumbled, hopefully.

'Let's nae bet on that. Where's the alley?'

'Here,' I said as I turned left and then right, walking briskly around the camera. Behind it we saw appear the tall, solid walls of the Bodleian Library, crowned with spiky stone pinnacles, like carved lances pointing to the sky. The side gate, cut into the thick walls, was on this side of the square, its iron bars guarding the deeper darkness beyond. As ever, no light came from the medieval windows, their stone tracery looking like gaol bars.

We rushed to the alley and crouched against the old walls of the library's south gardens. To my dismay, the opposite walls, the Gothic King's Hall College, were all dotted with hanging gas lamps. And the patches of snow clumped at the edges of the building seemed to glow in mockery.

'Ye said there'd be nae lights!' McGray snapped.

'I have not been here for nearly ten years!'

McGray covered his brow. 'So much for yer *expert* advice.'

I ignored him and looked in all directions. As expected, there was no sign of Harris.

'And now we just wait,' I said, exasperated.

McGray lit a cigarette and I had to snatch it from him, so nervous I barely managed to hold the book under my right forearm. After a few smokes I realized how suspicious we must look; two men in hats and long coats, standing in a desolate alley, on one of the quietest evenings of the year.

My heart skipped a beat when we heard muttering voices. I did not dare peer into the square, where the sound came from, but very soon two long shadows, projected by the college's lamps, appeared on the flagstones before us. Two people, walking side by side.

I started when they appeared around the corner, but I was not the most scared of all.

The man was clearly a middle-aged professor, a little tipsy, walking arm in arm with a very young, bespectacled woman, perhaps one of the new librarians.

They halted, their faces as pale as the snow around them. They did not move until McGray tossed his cigarette and snapped.

'Och, go away!'

And so they did, like scaredy-cats scuttling the way they'd come.

'You were not supposed to talk!' I hissed.

McGray smiled roguishly. 'Those two won't speak.'

We waited again, every second a torture. My mind wandered, the most fatalistic images rushing into my head. Harris dead, Harris lost . . . Harris heading our way with a pack of witches at his back . . .

'He's taking too long,' McGray mumbled, lighting a second cigarette.

'Indeed,' I said after a while.

I cannot tell for how long we waited. It could not have been more than five minutes, but it felt like hours, my heartbeats racing in my chest.

'Sod it,' McGray said, 'I'll cut it myself.'

'What if Harris comes and doesn't—?'

'Ye wait here. If he's nae arrived by the time I make ye a signal, just join me. We cannae stand here any longer.'

Begrudgingly, I assented and saw him stride briskly towards the library. His dark coat became a jerking shadow against the barred gate, and the clink of the chain, though faint, sounded piercing in my worried ears.

I looked alternatively at McGray and the alley. Along the latter I saw the old walls narrowing in the distance, and growing darker as the lamps became sparser. I thought I saw something move . . .

Then there was a metallic rattle and I heard McGray swear. I looked back at him and made out his projecting elbow as he struggled with the chains. He was grunting from the effort. I felt tempted to go and tell him to be quieter, but then I heard the flap of wings.

I looked up, at the nearest lamp, and saw how a large raven perched itself on top. The dastardly bird looked down, its feathers shimmering over the gaslight, its beady eyes fixed on me.

I turned back to the alley, squinting, and then saw something appear. A spot at first, darker than the street shadows, moving rapidly. I recognized the shape of narrow shoulders. It was a cloaked figure swathed in black, tall but slender. A woman.

At once I ran to the library, the raven cawing behind me. I felt a cold prickle on my back, as if the creeping fingers of that hooded shadow were already upon me.

McGray nearly elbowed me, using his entire body as lever. 'Hurry, *hurry*,' I told him.

'They're here?'

He did not need me to answer, for the raven squawked again. McGray focussed on the gate again, his temples beaded with perspiration. I looked down at the chain and saw the reason for his troubles – the links were as thick as his thumbs, the padlock wider than his fist.

I saw him squeeze the cutter again and again with all his might, the veins popping out of his hands and temples. I made no attempt to intervene – even without a broken wrist I would have been useless. All I could do was stand there and wait, watching how the cutter bit into the steel at an infuriatingly slow pace.

'How far were they?' he grunted.

'I – I don't know. Fifty yards last time I saw. Maybe less.'

I looked back, my eyes fixed on the entry to the alley, the raven still perched proudly on the lamp.

Then came a metallic clink and McGray exhaled in relief.

I did not even catch a glimpse of the cut link. McGray had already pulled the chain, opening the gate just enough to squeeze through the gap. I dashed in right behind him, pushed the iron bars back, and as I turned I saw a shadow emerge from the alley's corner. A black hem, waving in the wind.

At once I pulled McGray away from the gate and we rushed across the ginnel and into the library's inner courtyard. I saw the ends of the chain dangling like a pendulum, the link blatantly cut, but we had no time to do anything about it. We hid right next to the passage's threshold, our backs pressed against the cold wall. Before us, out of reach of the streetlights and without moon or stars, the courtyard was draped in absolute darkness. I could only make out the outline of the Gothic pinnacles that crowned the building, catching the dim light from the street-lamps. Above them there was nothing but an evenly black sky.

We waited, straining to hear. There were soft steps coming from the street, and then the faint flapping of wings. Could a raven see us even in that deep darkness? Most likely.

I heard the ruffle of McGray's clothes as he drew out his gun. I put the book down and did the same, my heart pounding. If it was a witch I'd just seen, she'd certainly know we were there.

We waited on, but nothing happened. We heard no more steps, no wings or squeaks, and nobody touched the dangling chain.

A sound came then, startling us. The chime of bells, all over the city, marking the half-hour.

McGray took the chance to whisper, 'What now?'

I did not answer, but simply walked by the wall, groping the limestone and looking for a door. The first one was just a few steps away: bolted oak, locked. I felt the broad latch, the steel ice-cold, the keyhole the size of my thumb, and I remembered the rings of heavy keys that the librarian always carried. The cutter would be useless here. I walked on, hearing McGray's soft steps right behind me, and reached the tower at the courtyard's corner. There was another door there, also locked.

I looked around, trying to imagine the courtyard. There'd be two doors on each corner, but it was foolish to hope one might be unlocked. I wanted to groan.

Then, slowly at first, something began to creep up my foot. A diffuse, unexpected warmth, like the hesitant touch of a hand that emerged from under the ground.

I sprinted, barely managing to contain a squeal. I heard McGray rush in my direction, stepping on something metallic, and I felt the warmth again, now on both feet.

And then I understood – it had been a draught of balmy air, and it had come from an iron grate on the ground. Underneath that panel ran the pipes of the Bodleian's laughably useless underfloor heating.

I squatted, hovering my hand a few inches from the ground. There it was, the warm air blowing gently upwards. I touched the grid, looking for its edge. The steel was wet, still melting all the snow around it. This was an exhaust vent, designed to cool down the water and ensure the very flammable floors did not overheat when the library was closed.

McGray touched it too, and we both found the thick bolts that kept the panel nailed to the ground.

'Can we?' he whispered.

I shut my eyes, trying to recall my student days, when everyone, students and professors alike, moaned about the merciless cold. I remembered the wide grates that ran all along the floors, and how we always fought over the lecterns closest to them. The pipes ran along stone ditches, so that they were never in direct contact with the wooden floorboards. They might be just wide enough so we could squeeze through. And the boiler never burned at night – what we were feeling was the residual heat from the day – so the pipes would not be blistering hot.

'Maybe,' I said.

McGray did not wait a second and began working on the bolts. He snapped the first one, and the noise of the pin skidding on the ground was terribly loud. He was more careful with the other three, while I kept watch on the corner of the ginnel, expecting those cloaked silhouettes to emerge at any moment. For the time being, all remained still.

I knew I'd seen those women. I was sure. And they must have seen *me* and the broken chain. Why were they not coming for us?

I had no time to wonder much more. McGray pushed me, for I was still standing on the grate, and he lugged it aside. My eyes now more accustomed to the dark, I made out the edges of a two-foot-wide culvert, through which ran a set of twin lead pipes.

McGray plunged a leg inside. 'Dammit, this is fuckin' wee . . .'

'Can you get—?' I began, but by then Nine-Nails had dived into the ditch, face first, barely managing to squeeze in his broad shoulders as he lurched and snorted. After much struggle I saw his boots disappear in the direction of the nearest wing of the library.

I shoved the book under my coat, pressed snuggly between the clothes and my chest. Then, after one last resigned breath, I forced myself down.

That indeed was the lowest, most humiliating moment of my life.

I crawled in the clumsiest and most graceless manner, squashed in between the still-warm pipes and the icy, wet stone, the channel covered in unidentified grime built up over countless years. I could see nothing at all, and the only sounds I could hear were the irate grunts of McGray, who was having a much worse time than me. I heard him drag himself forwards, his clothes rubbing tightly against the ditch. The sound made me think of someone trying to push a cork all the way into a wine bottle. He had a far less elegant allegory:

'This is what constipation must look like . . .'

I ploughed on, at least happy that the clothes I was wearing were not my own – but then I remembered that my favourite suits had all burned to ashes in Edinburgh, and a wave of despair took hold of me. I halted for a moment, my broken wrist aching from the cold and the damp. I tried to force in a calming breath, but each attempt was painful, with my lungs compressed in that tiny space. I rested my forehead against the warm pipe; the last trace of physical comfort in a world that had turned against me.

'There's a grate,' McGray said then, a faint trace of hope in his voice. He was much further ahead than I expected. 'D'ye have the cutter?'

I growled. 'No. I barely got myself into—'

'Och, fuck it!' he snapped, jolting like a living sardine trapped in a tin. 'I cannae even move my arm in here!' And then he banged the iron grate with all his might. He crawled further ahead so that he could kick it, and he did so again and again with unmitigated fury. The pipes vibrated and the deafening blows travelled all long the channel.

'McGray!' I protested, but then the grate gave in, and I heard it propel upwards and then fall again. The racket was terrible, perhaps reaching the furthest corners of the building.

The echoes still lingered when McGray jumped up, letting out a liberated exhalation. I crawled on, the ditch now faintly lit by a weak golden light. I saw McGray's nine-fingered hand appear, and he pulled me upwards so that I could sit on the edge of the ditch.

Suddenly I could breathe again, and my eyes could see the weak glimmer of the streetlights through the library's wide windows.

I put the book aside and allowed myself a long, exhausted sigh.

We were finally in.

40

'Now all of Oxford knows we are here!' I moaned, reaching for the matches and candles in my pocket.

'Och, I'm *so* sorry!' McGray exclaimed, rubbing his grazed hands and elbows. His coat was torn at the shoulders and his trousers at the knees. 'Did I spoil yer fuckin' *brilliant* idea to get in?' He looked around. 'D'ye at least ken where the hell we are?'

As he said so I lit the first candle, the wax very soon dripping onto the ancient floor. I saw two stained-glass windows, one on each end of the wing, and the intricately carved arches, the creamy stone meeting above us in a vaulted Gothic ceiling. There were no books or shelves. The wide corridor, in fact, looked more like an excessively decorated church. I knew at once where we were.

'This is the Proscholium,' I said.

'And where are the books?'

'On the first floor. The stairs should be over there.'

I signalled the north side of the wing, where the stained-glass window let in some light from the streetlamps. McGray picked up another candle and lit it from my flame. He pulled me upwards, grabbed the book from the floor and we headed there, the flames of our candles quivering with our brisk steps.

We saw a heavy oaken door appear to our left.

'Where does that go?' McGray asked.

'Directly to the street,' I said, and McGray grunted. That was one of the many locked entrances we could not use.

Opposite that gate, to our left, was the darkened arch that led to the stairs. We turned that way, and just as we did so, mingled with the sound of my steps, there came the muffled echo of clinking metal.

McGray and I halted at once. The noise, erratic, came from behind us. From the floor. My pulse raised.

We waited in silence, and I saw McGray's breath condense above the gleam of his candle.

'Are they coming?' I mumbled.

McGray frowned as we listened. The rattle faded slowly, but the silence that followed was even more unnerving.

'We'd better hurry,' Nine-Nails muttered, and on we went.

The steps were low, the staircase wide – nothing like the suffocating passages in York Minster, and we made it to the first floor in no time.

We stepped off the stairs and I raised my light very carefully, fearing that with each movement I might drop the taper or shed a spark and set the entire place on fire. Slowly, the full scale of the library became apparent.

We saw the fifteen-feet-tall, double-decker bookcases running from end to end of the wing, all crammed with books. Rows of slim oaken columns supported the balconies that allowed access to the highest shelves, each equipped with a wheeled ladder. The air, though cold, held the musky, almost cinnamon scents of leather and old paper. Above us, the ornate ceiling, heavy with medieval plinths and gilded carvings, glinted feebly over the candlelight.

'This is called the Arts End,' I said. 'We used to come here and mock the chaps doing Divinity Studies.'

I turned and raised the candle towards a pointed stone arch, right in the middle of the wing. It led to a wide, darkened corridor.

'That is Humfrey's Library,' I said, and then pointed to the arch itself. 'The catalogue should be there.'

It turned out to be exactly where I remembered, right next to the arch and opposite the librarian's desk. It was nothing but a neat bookcase with tomes visibly newer than all the others around it. I rushed there and shed light over the books' spines. McGray joined me, bringing more light.

'Hergest, you said?' I asked him.

'Aye, *The Red Book of Hergest*.'

I soon found the relevant tome of the catalogue. McGray had to pull it out for me – my one good hand holding the candle. He took it to the librarian's desk, along with our fake book, and opened it.

'Ye search,' he said, taking the taper from me.

'Let's hope it's recorded correctly,' I sighed, turning the pages swiftly. 'These things are famous for going out of date very quickly.'

'Don't they use a card system?' McGray asked.

'Only for printed books. The ancient manuscripts are listed in these catalogues. An old tradition.'

I ran my finger down the endless index, noticing how Nine-Nails kept a worried eye on the entrance to the staircase.

'Here,' I said, my heart jumping as I spotted the title. '*Hergest, Red Book of*, MS III. Gosh, that is a really old code.'

I instantly walked past the arch, into the Humfrey's wing. As we approached, our candles cast long shadows over the endless rows of ancient books, their spines faded, some even crumbling. Those bookcases were shorter, with lecterns attached to them, flanking both sides of the long space. Above them, in between the ornate beams, hung gloomy oil portraits. Those sallow, cracked Elizabethan faces seemed to follow our open flames with contemptuous eyes.

The manuscripts' codes were noted on paper slips on the side of each bookcase. As I expected, our book seemed to be at the very end of the corridor. I walked faster.

We heard another metallic sound, and again we halted.

The sound seemed to come from within the walls, and when I realized it my pulse quickened.

'Are they crawling in the damn pipework?' McGray mumbled.

'I – I cannot see how,' I said. 'They'd need to climb the vertical pipes, and those—'

'I'll fetch the damn thing,' McGray interrupted, and then eyed my wrist. 'Ye go and watch the exit.'

I saw him walk towards the end of the library, lighting the code slips. I went the other way and stood under the wing's arch. Between the light from the church-like windows and that of my taper, I had a fair view of the staircase. I also saw the pitch-black trenches that ran along the floor, the heating pipes underneath. I fixed my eyes on them, feeling the weight of the gun in my breast pocket – less than useful if my one good hand was taken by a little candle.

I tried to draw the weapon out without dropping the light. I nearly did so, as two sounds, both metallic, came to my ears, one right after the other.

One was the renewed echo from the underfloor piping. The other, to my astonishment, came from where McGray worked.

'Oh fuck!' he cried.

I peered into the darkness, seeing only the outer glow of his taper behind the bookcases.

'What is it?' I asked, looking back at the grating.

'*It's chained!*'

'What?'

'The soddin' book's chained!'

A cold prickle ran across my chest. I did not want to move, fearing who might come from the stairs or from under the floors, but then the noise of chains from McGray's side became a deafening rattle.

I grunted and ran to him. I found that he had pulled a book from the shelves; a thick, old tome that now lay on the lectern. I recognized the red leather binding that gave it its name, and also the thick, black chain, which McGray now pulled frantically.

'Oh yes,' I whispered. 'I'd forgotten that. It is to avoid theft.'

Nine-Nails bared his teeth to let out a shrill. '*Och, is it?* What part o' yer sodding Oxfordian brain thought I hadnae realized that?'

He covered his face with both hands and sank onto the nearest chair, which moved backwards with a rumbling sound. When that faded, the silence was absolute – on both sides of the library. I strived to hear, my eyes fixed on the archway. There was nobody there. Not yet.

I bent down to examine the book. One end of the chain had a thick iron clasp, fixed to the back cover. The other end, a cumbersome ring, was threaded onto an iron rod that spanned the entire bookcase. I ran my finger along the cool metal, to which all the books on the shelf were chained, and saw the four heavy padlocks that kept the bar affixed to the book rack.

I snorted. 'We'd need to unlock all four padlocks, dismount the rod, unthread all the other chains and then put everything back in place.'

When I looked up McGray was peering over my shoulder, also waiting for someone to come after us.

'D'ye think it's safe to go back through that ditch and fetch the cutter?'

I gulped. 'All the way back? I would not think so. We have no idea who or what is lurking in there. You do not want to be trapped in a trench and stumble across a witch with a vial of acid.'

McGray rubbed his face, at once panicked and exasperated, but then he squinted.

'The librarian must have the keys to this,' he said.

I laughed. 'Indeed, but I doubt he leaves them here at night.'

'Still, we have to try. Ye better go and look at the auld sod's desk.' There was a strange shrill in his voice. 'While yer at it, I'll see if there's anything else I can do here.'

I knew too well I'd find nothing, but still I made my way back to the Arts End.

The air felt colder, even denser now. I peered in the shadows, listening carefully as I approached the desk.

There was a pewter pencil holder, where I stuck the candle, pushing aside the very flammable loan registry, and then pulled at the drawers. They all had keyholes, most of them unlocked, and for good reason: they only contained useless trinkets – bent nibs, empty inkpots, receipts from a decade ago . . . I even pricked my finger with the rusty needles of a cheap sewing kit. Only the last two drawers I tried, both at the top of the desk, were locked. That looked promising.

'McGray,' I whispered, 'do you think you might pick a small lock?'

No answer.

'McGray?' I said, raising my voice just a little. I picked up the candle and shed light onto the corridor, but there was no trace of him or the glimmer of his taper.

The next few seconds stretched to an unthinkable length. I took a hesitant step, and then I heard a dull thud, followed by what must be a chair falling backwards.

At once I picked the makeshift candleholder and ran to him, dripping hot wax all over the floors. I shed light on the lectern, and the first thing I saw was McGray's taper, smoke still ebbing from the snuffed wicker, then the knocked chair. McGray was standing in front of it, a rectangle of red leather in his hands.

I gasped.

'*What have you—?*'

I could say no more. Nine-Nails had ripped the entire book from its covers, and now the stack of yellowy vellum lay on the reading stand like a nude corpse, its threads sticking out like torn ligaments.

He looked at me with the guilty eyes of a young boy who has just eaten the entire apple pie.

'I thought I'd spare ye seeing the butchery.'

McGray snatched my candle, and while I stared at the mess, he went to the desk and fetched the witches' fake book. He left the pencil holder with the candle on the lectern and began pulling that book apart too.

'It'll work even better,' he said as he worked his destructive way. 'We'll leave these pages in the auld covers. It'll take yer stuck-up Oxfordian sods even longer to notice that—'

'*How could you do this?* This book is a relic! It was already ancient when Henry VIII chose his first trollop!'

'The book or our lives,' he said. 'I cannae save 'em all.'

He picked up the old covers, still attached to the chain, and inserted the fake pages. They fit like a glove.

'We need to stick them together somehow,' he said.

'*Do we?*' I squealed, but Nine-Nails did not even notice my sarcasm.

'Aye. Arabic gum, needle n' thread, *anything.*'

I took a deep breath, forcing myself to accept there was no turning back.

'There is a little sewing box in the desk,' I told him. 'Bottom-left drawer.'

This time he lit his candle again and left me the other. 'Good. See if ye can stitch with one hand.'

'*You* will be doing that,' I snapped, but he had already gone.

Clumsily, I picked up the ancient covers, which turned out to be much heavier than I expected.

I looked at the point where the front cover was attached to the spine. The now torn leather had covered a thick flap of oak. That wood had not seen light in half a millennium, until the fateful night when a hare-brained Scot made his way into—

Something caught the light. Something almost white compared to the dark wood and leather. There was paper sandwiched in between them. I brought the candle closer and looked at the ripped stitches more carefully. Those threads, though visibly worn, did not look five centuries old.

I held up the cover, separating the leather from the wood as if opening an envelope. I did not even notice the pain on my wrist when I used those fingers to pull out a thin bundle of neatly folded cotton paper.

Before I unfolded it, before I even paid attention to the smudges of ink, I thought of Caroline Ardglass. I recalled the poor creature facing the York coven, confessing how she'd taken the boy's miniature out of the old German book, and how it had been hidden within the covers. Ancient books, now it seemed, were the witches' preferred hiding places.

McGray was already coming back, with a bobbin that looked ludicrously small in his hands.

'Alrighty, I've never even darned a damn sock, but we'll see how— What the hell is that?'

'I think – this is the very reason old Nettle wanted this book,' I said as I raised the sheets. They looked quite old, but not even close to the age of the book in which they'd been concealed.

McGray put aside the thread, dragged a chair and tried to reach for the papers.

'Back off!' I snapped. 'I have seen what your hands can do.'

Very carefully, I unfolded the sheets on the lectern, and we both leaned over them. The first page was packed with neat, tight handwriting, the calligraphy very elaborate and old-fashioned.

Nothing, absolutely nothing, could have prepared me for what I was about to read.

London, 9 July 1818

Dear Madam,

Thank you for sending us the portrait of d'Esté as a young boy. We realize your bagpiper must have gone through a great ordeal to get hold of it.

The d'Esté bastard is undoubtedly ideal for the deed. The chin, the lips, even the eyebrows — all George III.

I cannot stress enough how crucial it is that d'Esté himself recalls nothing of the nocturne feats. Augustus already holds enough grip upon his father, and we will not show as much patience to his whims as the old Sussex. I trust this shan't be a problem for ladies of your skill; I would abhor having to silence the young man permanently.

My dear Victoire is conscious of her part and has religiously drunk the draughts prescribed by your Lancashire sisters. Her countenance and spirits improve day by day.

We shall, however, require additional tonic. Send it to the previous point, but do not dispatch anything before the day after the morrow, when our nuptials shall be taking place.

We will be departing to Amorbach shortly afterwards, as planned. I shall communicate the precise date as soon as it is confirmed. The deed, ideally, should be carried out whilst we are on the roads. However, we have invited the young man to join us in Bavaria, should any eventuality occur. Make him ready.

Do not fail us again.

P. Edward Augustus,

Duke of Kent and Strathearn

PS. I have honoured my pledge and signed and dated this missive. Do NOT interpret that as weakness, Madam. Should you or any of your sisters disclose any part of our agreement, however small, you shall all pay tenfold. As you know, we have the agents and the means.

41

McGray and I stared at the document for a good while, open-mouthed.

I felt my heart beating fast, and only took my eyes from the letter when wax from my candle began to drip all over the lectern. I straightened the taper while McGray brought the other sheets up.

Those looked equally old, but the text on them had been written with vinegar, the scorched lettering barely visible after seven decades. I had to squint to make out the titles. One read: *For deep slumber*, and then listed a variety of ingredients. I only made out the line *poppy seeds bruised in wine*.

The last sheet, penned in a twisted hand that made me shiver, said: *For strong seed*.

McGray's eyes flickered from one document to the next, buoyant with excitement. It was a while before he managed to speak.

'I can sort of guess who these people are,' he mumbled, pointing at the names on the first letter, 'but confirm them to me.'

He pushed the sheet closer to me.

'P. Edward . . .' I read, my mouth dry, '*and* Duke of Kent . . . that can only be the late Prince Edward. And that makes this

Victoire – whom he was about to marry – *Princess* Victoire of Saxe-Coburg-Saalfeld . . .' I gulped. 'Queen Victoria's mother . . .'

McGray gasped. 'Taking witch draughts.'

'Oh, Lord! This means—'

'That wee brat in the painting . . . He was the Queen's *dad*. The Queen's dad – was a bastard!'

That last word resonated across the library. My first reaction was disbelief.

'What date was on the portrait?' I said. 'Do you remember?'

'Aye, 1799. So the lad would have been in his, say, mid-twenties when they wrote this letter. Perfect age to use him as – well, *steed.*'

I nodded, so many ideas reeling in my head I felt giddy. 'Prince Edward lived in sin with some famous French trollop for nearly thirty years. Everybody knew it. In all that time they had no issue. Yet –' I looked at the dates, 'it says here he married Princess Victoire in July 1818. For Queen Victoria to be born in April the following year . . .' I looked down, counting the months – 'she must have been conceived within *weeks* of Prince Edward's marriage.'

'Thirty barren years,' McGray mumbled, 'and then he claimed he impregnated his new wifey in a few weeks?'

'Yes. It did raise eyebrows back then, but all the rumours were quashed when the girl turned out to be the spitting image of George III.'

McGray shook his head. 'So they turned to some bastard from within the family to ensure the baby looked the part?'

'No wonder I thought he looked a little like Prince Albert,' I said. 'He and Victoria were first cousins . . . He had the Hanoverian chin.'

'What a horde of inbred freaks!'

'And that is why the witches needed the logbook! Not only had they hidden the portrait there . . .'

'Where its mere presence would be suspicious if someone ever found it . . .'

'Yes, but it also proved that this Augustus d'Esté was in Amorbach at around the time Queen Victoria was conceived.'

McGray nodded, looking back at the first letter.

'Says here – Sussex.'

I repeated the word, drawing the royal family tree in my mind. 'That has to be – the Duke of Sussex . . .' I shut my eyes, stretching my memory to all the royal gossip my stepmother was so fond of. 'His name was – *Augustus* Frederick. Dead long ago. And I remember there was some scandal around him . . . I think his marriage was annulled by George III. That must have been after he fathered the boy in the portrait. That would have rendered him illegitimate.'

'But still family,' McGray mumbled. 'Still young and fit for – well, *this*.'

'If Augustus d'Esté was an illegitimate child . . .' I said, 'and as it says here, he was Victoria's true father – she was *never* a rightful heir . . .'

I sat back, covering my mouth as the full extent of the finding crept into my mind.

'She really is naething but a fat bastard!' Nine-Nails cried.

'And now they call her the grandmother of Europe!' I added. 'She has married her children into all the major royal houses, from the Hapsburgs to the Romanovs. They'd all be tainted with illegitimacy!'

Even the cynical Nine-Nails could not fail to be shocked.

'Crafty crones . . .' he whispered. 'When they said they were influential, they were nae joking. With this they can hold all those inbred bastards by the balls!'

Now it all made sense; all the persecution and all the violence. For the covens this evidence was worth every death and more.

McGray held the documents with almost religious reverence.

'And now they're in *our* hands. Think of – of all we can do if we keep hold of this!'

I took a deep breath. 'Are you suggesting we use this to blackmail the Queen of Britain?'

'Don't tell me now ye'll get all scrupulous and—'

'The most powerful sovereign in human history? Who now—'

'Are ye done—'

'Who now rules over most of the known world? Over an empire on which the sun never sets? Are you suggesting we can blackmail *her*?' My voice echoed throughout the library.

'That's right, aye.'

My hands, for the first time in years, were trembling with genuine excitement. 'That is – *bloody brilliant*! If the Queen herself could not touch us, neither could the PM . . . But we need to think of the mechanics very carefully. We cannot just knock at the gates of Buckingham Palace saying—'

'*Excuse us, may we please have a chat with the fat bastard to tell her she's a bastard?*'

'Precisely. And we must ensure there is no way they can touch us. We could act just as the witches—'

A loud metallic rattle interrupted me then, bringing me back to the here and now.

We were still in the Bodleian Library, with no escape route other than a narrow ditch in the ground, and the very possibility of murderous witches and their men waiting for us to come out.

McGray at once drew out his gun and we listened. The sound came and went. It was indeed a rattle, at times frantic, at times less so. At one point it sounded as if it were right underneath our feet, and it instantly faded away.

I looked down, but there was no heating on this wing's floor.

'Did that sound . . .' I said, 'like a bird trapped in the pipework?'

McGray was still listening, his eyes half shut. 'Maybe. I don't think they'll come here. They'll rather wait till we come out and strike then. They ken how we entered.'

'That ditch is the only way out,' I mumbled.

I blew inside my cheeks, looking at the documents with frustration – all that knowledge, all that proof . . . all utterly useless if we could not leave that frosty building.

McGray put his gun on the lectern, deep in thought. After a moment he reached for the sewing box.

'I'll get started with this. My mother always said her needle craft helped her think.' He threaded the needle and began his clumsy work. What an odd sight; Nine-Nails McGray, sitting by a candle, surrounded by ancient books and doing needlework. He noticed my gaze. 'Och, don't just sit there! See if ye can find another way to get out!'

I stood up, slowly looking around, those ornate beams and elaborate windows oppressive like never before. A golden gaol.

Then, as I walked past the endless lines of bookcases, the candle quivering in front of me, I realized something.

I did not have to remember. All the knowledge in the land was there, within arm's length.

I rushed to the catalogue case, but this time I looked into the lines of little drawers where the cards were filed. I balanced the pewter holder on top of the cabinet and began searching, flicking card after card until I found a compendium of the library's refurbishments. That book must contain detailed blueprints. I pulled out the card, but then had to hold it with my teeth so that I could retrieve the candle – my right hand was now quivering with aches.

As I turned, I saw the double-decker bookcases before me and rushed to the nearest wooden staircase. The book I needed was on the upper level.

I climbed the swirling steps, but then, as they turned towards the north window, I noticed a peculiar light coming through the old stained glass. The glows, diffuse, came and went erratically, as if those grimy windows were gigantic eyelids.

Something was wrong.

I climbed onto the mezzanine, which led to that end of the wing, and walked quickly towards the window.

The glass closer to me was less sooty, giving me a fair, only slightly blurred view of the street below. Amidst the streetlights I saw a gathering of black cloaks, billowing in the wind, each figure holding a candle.

I gulped, seeing how they paced, their movements restless. Quite a few figures stuck out; tall, broad-shouldered men flanking their mistresses. Then another figure joined them, also carrying a candle, but smaller and fidgety, and running towards the corner tower.

The figure disappeared, and then the others followed it. I remembered the door we'd seen just opposite the staircase, the one that led directly to the street.

They were coming in.

42

'*Oh God . . .*' I groaned, the book card fluttering from my lips.

I could not contain the tension anymore. I ran across the balcony and nearly rolled down the stairs as I made my clumsy way back. In my haste the candle went out, but McGray's was just a few steps ahead. He was leaning over the librarian's desk and scribbling on a small piece of paper.

'They're coming in!' I spluttered.

'What?'

'They are coming in! Someone is *letting* them in.'

He dropped the pencil, his face losing all colour as he looked at the north window. Just in time to see the last glows disappear.

'Shite . . .'

We heard what sounded like a multitude of steps on the ground floor, along with murmuring voices. They were not being discreet. They knew we had nowhere to run.

'Any way out?' McGray asked.

I could only shake my head. 'I've not even looked at—'

Nine-Nails seized my arm and pulled me to the Manuscripts' Wing. 'We have to hide.'

'Hide? How are we going to—?'

He jumped onto the nearest lectern, the wood cracking under his weight, and shed light over the top of the bookcase.

'Will have to do.'

He offered me a hand and I clambered clumsily, supporting my feet on the bookshelves and trampling on ancient bibles.

The footsteps became louder. I even heard a couple of female voices, and then, as clear as if they were inches from my ears, the frenetic flapping of wings.

McGray pushed me with all his might, so hard I landed on the dusty top of the bookcase and then rolled towards the other side. I growled as I clung to the very edge, and I heard McGray sprint above my head, jumping from this bookcase to the next. The wood cracked so loudly I thought the entire case would crash. His candle went off, its last rays on the red book tucked under his coat, and then I saw no more. I only heard the wood cracking as McGray shifted position, but then there was total silence.

Very carefully I rolled on my chest, the bookcase underneath also cracking with each movement. I tried to reach for my gun, but then the sound of wings dashed through the stone arch. I looked up and saw the blasted raven fluttering in between the old beams, describing ample circles all across the ceiling, until it perched itself at the centre of the nearest joist, right above my head. Was it marking my position?

I lay flat on the dusty surface, decades of cobwebs and dead vermin right under my chin, each breath tickling my nose and throat.

Then the footsteps flooded the library, the glimmer of candles spreading along Humfrey's wing. I could not tell for sure, but it sounded like a dozen men and women.

From where I lay I could see nothing, only that someone pointed a beam of light directly at the perched raven.

None of them spoke, but the tension in the room was palpable, like a silent beast slithering a mere couple of feet below my chest. I heard a soft, hissing breath, from someone struggling to keep quiet, and again I felt a prickle of fear.

These people were smart. They *knew* we were there. Not in any other wing or corridor. They knew we were right *there*. What were they waiting for? Were they positioning themselves? Surrounding us so that they could strike us in one swift blow? I imagined them surrounding our bookcases, slowly stretching their hands in our direction, like the ghastly tentacles of a sea monster.

My heart thumped against the wood, resounding like a drum in my head.

I looked right, but only made out the outline of McGray's back. He too lay flat on his chest, his gun at the ready. And he had something in his hand. I half shut my eyes, striving to see what it was, and recalled the little vial of acid McGray had picked up after the Orkneys attack.

And then something moved to my left.

I felt it rather than heard it, like an invisible spider crawling on that side of my body, and I could not repress a gasp when a set of thick fingers emerged from the edge of the bookcase.

Then everything happened at once.

McGray roared. I heard him throw the vial, heard the shatter of glass, and a ghastly sizzle as a man howled in pain on my right. Just as that happened, the thick hand to my left slammed the top of the bookcase, so close to my eyes I saw the dirt on the man's nails.

A second hand emerged, hurling itself towards my face. I ducked away, desperately looking for my gun, just as another pair of hands appeared near my legs.

I heard McGray shoot and sprint but I had not time to look. I jumped to my feet as the hands stretched to catch me. The raven squawked, the joist level with my chest, and right then the nearest hand clasped around my ankle.

I jumped up, clung to the oak beam, making a hook with my right arm, and then shot without aiming. The man's grip loosened and he fell backwards, crashing on the floor with a mighty thud. Not two feet beyond, a second man jumped on top of the bookcase, the entire structure creaking under his weight.

Without thinking I clambered onto the beam and crawled away. The raven spread its wings and I saw its black beak darting straight towards my eyes. I swung my arm, hitting the blasted bird with the butt of my gun, the impulse nearly throwing me off the joist. I saw it fall like a dead fly, right next to the broad man who was writhing on the floor, his clothes oozing acid vapours. On the other side of the bookcase, the man I'd just shot was pressing his blood-stained shoulder.

I heard the man behind me, his thumping steps almost crushing the old wood, and I crawled swiftly towards the centre of the library, away from the bookcases. I dragged myself on my knees, a hand and a pained elbow, panting as I felt surges of vertigo and watched the mayhem below.

Six or seven witches shrieked like eagles, running towards McGray. Amidst their flashing cloaks, a lanky man, blatantly a library clerk, was pulling at his hair.

'*No!* Not the books!' he shouted.

McGray was throwing them at the witches, the chains rattling in the air as the volumes rained on the cloaked women. I saw candles rolling on the floor, vials being flung at Nine-Nails as he jumped erratically from case to case, and a couple of witches climbing up the shelves like spiders.

I could see no more, for right then the entire beam shook beneath me, and a split second later a bullet hit the edge of the carved wood, just inches from my elbow.

I looked manically in all directions. The shot had come from the entrance, where a cloaked woman held a lantern and a gun. I recognized Hilda's embroidered hood, but had no time to react. Behind me, the giant thug was climbing onto the beam.

Hilda shot again, and I could swear I felt the heat of the bullet right next to my ear. I shot back at her, missed, and the shaking of the old beam made me lose my balance.

I hugged the joist, grunting and refusing to let go of the gun. I could hear the man approaching; I could feel the repulsive moisture of his breath, rank with some nasty brew. And I also saw Hilda raise her lantern and her gun. She had a clear shot. And I could not move.

The detonation glowed amidst the shadowy room, expanding slowly as if time itself had stretched, and then the beam gave in.

It cracked once and then the entire support plummeted to the floor.

Everything blurred before my eyes. I even thought I saw the gleaming bullet fly above my head as my body rolled uncontrollably along the falling wood.

I hit the man's enormous body and we rolled together onto the floor. I kept spinning further on, until my back crashed against the foot of a lectern and I hollered in pain. With the impact I dropped the gun and saw it skid away, all my limbs numb.

There were gunshots, I heard McGray and the women shouting, the clerk whimpering. And then, behind stars, I saw many hands coming to me from all directions, grabbing my arms and legs and neck, and dragging me to the centre of the library.

I heard the metallic shrill of two knives, their blades being sharpened against each other in perfect rhythm. I saw the blades hovering right above me, ready to rip me apart. I writhed, growled and shouted like I'd never done before, but those hands would not let me go, pinning me against the floor like a pig for slaughter.

The blades caught the glint of a candle. I saw them draw towards my face but I refused to shut my eyes. I thought I could already feel them plunging into my flesh, but then there came three gunshots in quick succession.

A body fell on top of me, someone pulled it away. There were more shrieks, and then I heard McGray's booming voice.

'Let him go or this burns!'

There were a couple of cackles, then a gasp, and then a woman squealed, *'Stop!'*

Hilda's voice resounded very close to me, repeating that word. The pack of witches froze around me, just as Hilda herself pressed the flat of a blade against my neck. I went still too; a mere glitch and the icy steel would slice my throat.

Only then, when an absolute hush followed, had I a clearer view of what happened.

McGray was standing in the middle of the library, the book pressed under the arm with which he pointed his gun at the pack of witches. He had picked one of the candles and held the flame dangerously close to the vellum pages, so much so that the edges were already turning black.

Even then, held by a horde of savages about to disembowel me, a part of my mind could not help feel fear for those pages. Inside those covers, between the leather and the wood, were the letters and the spells. The evidence of Queen Victoria's true origins. Our only viable chance of getting rid of her threat.

The silence dragged on, but it was suddenly broken by the burst of a loud, maddened cackle. Hilda pressed the knife a little harder on my neck, and I could not contain a soft whimper.

'Give us that!' she commanded, her voice roaring like a bouncing bullet.

'Let us go,' Nine-Nails retorted, his voice unnervingly calm.

Hilda pulled me by the hair, tilting my head sideways to hold the thin blade a mere inch from my eye. I could not take my gaze from the needle-like knife, firm and ready to stab.

'You burn that, he dies!' she spat. 'And then *you*.'

I forced myself to look at her – enraged, weathered, with lines under her eyes that spoke of a lifetime of hardship. Those pupils, streaked with veins and bulging like a serpent's, flickered with wrath as she glared at McGray.

'I burn this,' he said, taking careful steps in our direction, '*ye* die. And all yer dogs die with ye. Yer brother will see to that.'

McGray pushed the flame onto the book, golden lines of fire appearing on the edges of the vellum. The witches gasped, and I whimpered again as Hilda made to stab my eye. The tip of the blade, sharp like a needle, was now so close to me my eyelashes brushed it when I blinked.

I gulped, every muscle in my head tense, breathing in short, panicked bursts. I forced myself to remain as still as possible, lest my trembles accidentally plunge my eye into the knife.

For how long would they play that game? Would McGray let them have my eye? Would Hilda simply tear my face piece by piece, while McGray singed page after page? Would it all end with McGray setting the damn book on fire and the witches slicing me apart?

'Give them that,' I hissed.

Cautiously, as if feeling new ground, McGray pulled the candle from the book, but it must have been just a quarter of an inch. And he waited for Hilda's reaction.

After the longest, most tortuous second, she also pulled the knife away from my eye. An equally short distance.

I have never heard such a deep silence. I even heard my own blood throbbing in my temples.

McGray spoke first. 'What pages d'youse need?'

Hilda frowned. 'What?'

'What *pages* d'youse need?'

'You do want to die, don't you?' Hilda hissed.

McGray must have read something in her expression, for he smirked. It took him what I felt was an unnecessary length of time to speak again.

'Youse have nae idea what's in here!'

Hilda did not answer, dumbfounded, but then she let out a drilling howl, her fingers grasped my hair with all her strength, and she pulled my head backwards as the glinting knife plummeted into my eyes.

There was a spurt of blood and I whined, thinking it was mine, but then Hilda's body fell on me, the woman moaning in pain while the air filled with gunshots and screaming.

I felt the knife pull back and all of a sudden only a pair of hands remained clasping my arm. I stirred and tried to crawl away from that young witch, until a thick fist landed right on her jaw and the woman flew backwards. A nose covered in bulging bandages entered my field of vision – Boss, aiming his gun and throwing fists at the shrieking witches and their men.

Bob and another four men I'd never seen ran past me, shooting and clashing against the witches and their thugs.

'Stay there or you die!' Boss barked at me, but he did not manage another step forwards. '*What the—!*'

He ducked and fell on his side, just as a shot detonated frighteningly close. It was McGray, swinging his gun left and right, and striding towards me as he held the book up high. The leather flaps burned like a torch.

'Move!' he shouted at me, and I scrambled up with the clumsiness of a toddler.

'*What are you doing?*' Boss shouted, glaring at the burning book, but then Hilda, her shoulder dripping blood, tried to sprint over him and in our direction. Boss held her by the ankle, the woman fell forwards, and they rolled about in a savage skirmish.

I did not have time to see much of that, for McGray ran like the wind along the library, the ablaze pages glowing amidst the endless lines of flammable books and shelves.

'*Put that out!*' I shouted, my still-numb legs struggling to follow his pace.

He only stopped when we reached the staircase. There he bashed the book against the archway, trying to smother the flames and throwing lit cinders all around.

'You'll set the entire bloody place on fire!' I shouted, the echoes of the fighting behind my back.

'D'ye think I care right now?'

The flames barely out, McGray pushed the book into my chest. I held it, hot as it was, while he passed an arm over my shoulders and helped me run down the steps.

'*They're fleeing!*' some witch yelped, and I heard a bullet hit the wall as we ran with renewed strength.

'How did they find us?' I babbled as we made our way down.

'Boss or the Marigolds?' McGray added, but then we reached the ground-floor gate, the one through which I'd seen the witches come in. It was still open, a fidgety young man mounting guard. McGray pointed his gun at him and the chap crouched against the wall, whimpering.

Just as we set foot on the street, we heard shouting and thumping steps behind us.

'To the carriage,' McGray spluttered, waiting for my directions.

I'd barely nodded to our left when he pulled me and we ran desperately towards the Sheldonian Theatre.

'We don't even know if Harris will be there,' I panted. 'Or the carriage. He might be the one who betrayed us!'

'Nae other option.' He eyed the book. 'And don't ye dare drop that!'

'*Don't I—!* You were the one who set it on bloody fire!'

McGray could not retort. Right then we turned north and ran into Broad Street, which, to his dismay, was indeed broad and very well-lit throughout.

'Fuck it, Frey! This the best ye could do?'

'We couldn't go back to the bloody square through which they— *Left here!*'

'Course left here!' he snapped, for we turned into an equally wide road, streetlamps dotted on both sides.

We darted ahead with all our strength, my legs finally reawakening. In my mind there was nothing but that broad street, those slippery flagstones under my feet, my burning knees and my frenzied breaths.

In the distance, rising above the mismatch of Tudor, medieval and Victorian buildings, was the belfry of Christ Church College. It was barely a shade lighter than the pitch-black sky, and it looked so far away I growled.

'There,' I panted, pointing at it with my broken wrist.

We raced on, staring at the tower, seeing it approach at an impossibly slow pace.

Then we made it to a crossroad; a space as wide as a small town's square and open in all four directions. We were back in High Street, and though we crossed it in swift strides—

'*There they are!*' someone screamed from my left. I had a quick glance before we passed the corner, and saw a black cloak running past the nearby All Saints' Church.

'Dammit!' McGray grumbled.

I did not dare look again, focussing once more on the tower. It looked tantalizingly close now, above the sober Gothic buildings that flanked the street.

I veered to the right, towards a clump of yews that grew almost exactly in front of the vast tower. Their thick, evergreen canopies blocked all the light from the lamp posts. There was the small graveyard, looking exactly as I remembered it.

McGray did not need instructions. He turned right, and there, parked at the very corner, next to the rows of ancient tombstones and covered in shadows, we found our tattered carriage.

The first thing I noticed was the smashed wheel, its splinters spread all across the street. The carriage would be useless now.

And then I saw something far more harrowing – a dark lump on the ground, at the very edge of the graveyard and visible only because the snow there had not yet turned into slush.

Harris's body.

McGray leaned over him, stretching out a cautious hand. I walked closer and saw the man's face, his old tattoos speckled with snow, his eyes wide open but his stare blank. There was a fine streak of scarlet all across his throat.

'The poor lad . . .' McGray mumbled.

I said nothing, far more stricken by that sight than I thought I might be. What a sad life that man had lived, not even a slight redemption at the end. And still, all we could do for him was close his eyelids.

McGray jumped upwards and opened the carriage door. The tired horse started when it felt the movement.

'What are you doing?' I hissed, my eyes fixed on the lit road. 'We have to go now!'

I heard the flapping of wings, but it was only McGray, emerging with the magpie in his hand.

'Hold it,' he said, sticking the unlucky bird under my arm, legs up. 'If ye let it go—!'

He shoved his gun under his belt and rummaged in his pockets. At once he produced a tiny piece of paper – the one I'd seen him scribbling before the witches broke in – and then the very bobbin he'd used to stitch the old books.

'We need to tell Oakley and Nettle we have these documents,' he whispered as he tied the note to the bird's leg. Once it was secured he took the magpie and threw it up into the air. 'While Caroline still has the wee portrait.'

I watched how its black and white plumage fluttered along the street, glowing above the streetlights before it became lost in the night.

'What if Hilda or her witches intercept it?' I mumbled. 'How much about the Queen did you tell them in that—?'

I said no more. A sudden draught brought the sounds I feared the most. Frantic footsteps. Shouting. And then gunshots.

This was far from over.

43

I turned to McGray at once, clutching the book under my arm.

He was already busy untying the horse from the carriage, dropping the straps and grasping the reins.

'Hope ye can ride without a saddle,' he babbled, already hauling me onto the horse like a sack of flour. I barely had time to prop myself up before McGray mounted behind me. Then the first running shadows appeared on the main street; a mixture of cloaked women and Salisbury's men, fighting each other as they made their stumbling way towards us.

McGray shot a warning bullet in their direction as I shoved the book under my right arm. Then he spurred the horse, made it turn so fast I feared the animal's legs would tangle and break, and we galloped southwards, away from the wide road and the tearing screams.

The street funnelled into a narrow passage, flanked by Gothic windows and stone arches. McGray turned alternatively right and left, and I clung to the horse's neck as best I could with one hand, my legs tight around its flanks. The icy wind made my eyes water, and with every turn I felt myself slide from the horse's bare back.

'Where are you going?' I shouted.

'I don't care! *Away!*'

The horse entered a wider street right then, just as we heard three quick shots behind us.

'Damn!' Nine-Nails shouted, spurring the horse and taking the first turn. I tried to look back but McGray blocked my view. He shot back twice.

'Who's following?' I asked. 'Witches? Boss?'

'Nae sodding difference! They all want us dead!'

I heard galloping behind us, those strides heavier, faster and stronger than those of our pitiful horse, and then another gunshot.

McGray turned back to shoot, he did so once, but then I only heard the frantic click of the trigger.

'Shit!' he shouted, out of ammunition and unable to recharge it mid-gallop.

All he could do was steer the horse left and right, zigzagging violently along the street as the bullets kept coming.

With each jerk I felt my legs slide from side to side, my entire body tilting as I clung on precariously. I grunted, knees and arms burning from the effort, and I felt the book sliding down my arm.

'Don't do that!' I shouted, pressing the book against the horse's neck, but with each stride it slid a little further down.

If I don't they kill me!

The shooting stopped – I could only guess our pursuer was out of bullets too – but there was no respite. I heard two cackles behind us, one male and the other female, those eerie voices becoming louder and louder as they caught up on us.

I felt the bursts of hot breath from the horse, the poor beast exhausted. McGray spurred it, shouting desperately, but we did not move any faster.

I looked ahead and saw, a hundred or so yards away, the stone balustrade of Folly Bridge. The city ended there; those were the last lamp posts in sight. Beyond them, the safety of the moonless night awaited. We had but to cover that distance.

Only the horse jolted then, the animal neighing wildly as McGray let out curses. The book slid from my grip again, most of it now dangling below my arm. I growled and clutched it harder against the horse's thumping body. My arm and elbow burned, my broken wrist throbbing with pain.

'What was—?'

Then I understood. Someone had hit the horse's rump. A large, muscly shire horse, at least a foot taller than our mount, flanked us from the right, galloping parallel to us towards the bridge. I only saw the bulky shadow of its rider, and behind him the billowing folds of Hilda's embroidered cloak.

McGray steered the horse away just as the man threw a blow at his head. McGray only ducked it partially, half the fist still catching his temple. Even I could feel his entire body shaking from the punch.

The percheron charged at us again, hitting us with unthinkable strength and throwing our horse to the left.

Again I gripped the book, my arm now numb, as I looked ahead. The bridge was so close I could hear the waters of the Thames gushing below. I thought I could even smell them.

But our horse was also slowing down, neighing and whimpering, its troubled breaths wafting up before us. And then the percheron approached.

The thug thrust another fist in McGray's direction. He managed to duck it this time, but as he did so the shire horse positioned itself a little ahead of us, and Hilda stretched her arm towards the book.

'*Damn you!*' I snarled as she seized the bottom corner.

I pressed the book harder to my side, feeling her determined pull. I cursed my broken bones and my legs sliding from the horse's back. I cursed that damn woman who jerked and hauled, so close to me now I saw her smacking her lips with that repulsive, stained tongue, and I also sensed the nasty smell of her *magic* narcotics. No wonder the wound on her shoulder did not seem to bother her.

There were gunshots behind us, just as we entered the bridge, and I heard a booming shout behind our backs.

'*Stop!*'

It was Boss, his voice mixed with the sound of many galloping hooves.

'*Oh, damn you all to hell!*' I howled as I fought to keep the book. I heard Hilda cackle, and I roared like an animal as the last inch of the book slipped inexorably from my grip.

Another shot.

It sounded so deafening I thought it had hit me in the head. At once our horse plunged down, its snout hitting the muddy road as the poor beast let out a piercing, agonizing whine.

In an instant I lost the book and rolled onto the ground, clashing and thumping against McGray as we went.

My body was so shattered I could not resist any more, and I rolled freely on the trampled snow until I ran out of momentum.

I lay across the bridge, facing upwards, into a black sky suddenly decked with dancing, blurry stars. My head tilted limply to one side, and I caught a last sight of the witches' percheron, galloping away at staggering speed as the bullets chased it. Another two horses went after them, and very soon they all vanished into the night.

Dazed and breathless, all I could do was lie on the icy stone as I heard hooves halt a few yards away. I also heard rasping voices, McGray's included, but I could not make out what they said or what was happening.

Three men, all of them holding guns, surrounded me. Boss was at the centre, grinning.

Again I saw the bulky bandaging around his nose. I remembered the victorious kick I'd thrust him as Harris and I had fled from him in York.

'I have this to thank you for, Mr Frey,' he said, tapping the white bandage. 'Shall we – level the field?'

He raised his foot and I saw it hover right above my face. I saw the grimy sole of his boot and pictured him trampling on my skull.

I could not contain a gasp and the man roared in laughter.

'Nah, you look lame enough already.' He nodded at his two men. 'Take him.'

They lifted me, my body lax as if made of rags, and then a third man came from behind to blindfold me.

The last thing I saw was Boss's mocking grin, and his voice dropped an octave when he spoke again.

'Don't spoil him yet, chaps. Her Majesty will be very much amused.'

DIARY – 1848

Monthly Abstract. Ramsgate

Wednesday – January 12

I walk this day in my room (thanks be) one hour and 18 minutes.

[August, dates illegible]

Alas, alas, I only walk in my room

[. . .]

Alas, I only walk in my room for 6 min. [last entry]

44

What a strange trip that was.

They hauled me most unceremoniously into a rickety cart, someone pressing a gun on my temple the entire time. I sat there for hours, striving to hear McGray's voice, but to no avail. I began fearing he'd put up too much of a fight.

With the constant racket of the wheels, my eyes covered, and every single bone in my body aching, I soon fell asleep. I dreamt time and time again of the Queen's guillotine, the shiny blade descending ever faster, yet somehow never touching my neck, as if only designed to prolong my agony.

I only woke when the cart stopped and someone, perhaps a village doctor, jumped in to reapply the splint around my wrist. I mumbled a thank-you, and they put a large chunk of bread in my hand. I devoured it, stale as it was, and then they offered me a tankard of watered-down ale. After the unrefined meal the cart resumed, and again I lost track of time. At one point I saw some daylight through the blindfold, but it gave me no inkling as to the hour.

It must have been dark already when we stopped again, and I heard the roar of a steam engine. They made me board a train, and from the movements I guessed they made me sit in a small private compartment. Again, someone sat next to me the entire time, a gun held firmly on my temple. And again I fell asleep.

This time I did not even wake when the train stopped. The guard had to stir me, and then they led me to another carriage.

'Where is my colleague?' I asked as they steered me off the train. Nobody answered. I sniffed the very cold air, and I thought I recognized a whiff of sea.

They put me in yet another carriage, but this time the trip was quite short. They led me down some damp steps. I heard the turn of a key, and after they pushed me a few steps forwards, someone finally took the rag from my eyes. I blinked several times, feeling the fresh air against my skin again, and looked around.

I was in an underground cellar, the old stone walls dotted with stains of saltpetre, the air rank and stagnated. There was a narrow bed, like the ones I'd seen in gaols, but the sheets were pristine, and there was a change of clothes neatly folded on them. Next to the bed stood a ewer and basin, with soap, towels and warm water. And closer to me, a cushioned chair and a little table, on which a lonely candle lit a rather generous dinner – bread, fresh fruits, sweetmeats and cheese, alongside a carafe of claret and a jug of water.

'Last supper?' I mumbled, turning on my heels, but the man who'd brought me was already closing the door and locking it. I could not even see his face.

I sighed and, with the stoicism of a prisoner on death row, I groomed myself, sat at the table and poured some claret. At least the food was decent.

I could fill pages and pages with the thoughts I entertained on that sleepless night; all the fear, all the doubts. I thought of the things that could have gone differently; I thought of all the chances I'd had to flee and had wasted; I thought of the things that, in hindsight, I would have never done. And every train of thought ended with 'So what? Nothing can be helped now . . .'

In the morning – or at least I thought it was morning – I heard the key in the lock. The door opened and two men came in, one holding a sconce with candles and a blindfold.

The other man, armed, was Bob, casting me an accusatory look. No wonder – his head was bandaged and there were red specks of blistered skin on the right-hand side of his face – splatters of acid, most likely from his scuffle with the witches. I felt somewhat lucky.

'This chap will blindfold you,' Bob said without a trace of feeling. 'Be good and we won't have to spoil you.'

I found it slightly odd that it was him and not Boss who came for me, but I preferred not to ask. If it indeed carried any meaning, it could only be bad news.

'Good morning to you too, gentlemen,' I said instead, as the younger man tied the rag over my eyes. 'May I ask where you are taking me?'

'None of your business,' Bob snapped.

'Indeed. How silly of me.'

They led me up the stone steps, and then into the frosty air. As we rode another carriage, I smelled the cool, salty air, and heard the almost peaceful sound of seagulls all around.

After some time the carriage halted, and I heard the wheels of a second one. The grumbles and shakes I heard were unmistakable – they were bringing Nine-Nails, most likely tied, gagged and manacled.

They made me alight, and after a short walk I heard my own footsteps on a slanting board, the wood creaking, and the gentle crash of waves many feet below. Were they guiding me onto a ship, or walking me down a board to throw me into the cold sea?

'Watch the step,' a young man told me, holding me a little more tightly as I felt my way down. I was setting foot onto a deck. A fisherman's ship, surely, from the smell.

Again I heard McGray's muffled snorts.

'My colleague suffers acute seasickness,' I said, raising my head. 'You want to give him some laudanum.' Nobody replied, and I sneered. 'You *will* want to.'

I was taken to a cabin that stank of old crab, and pushed onto a hard wooden bench. After what felt like a never-ending wait, the ship began to move. At last I had a small inkling as to where they were taking us.

My suspicions were confirmed about an hour later, when I heard Boss's voice as he pulled me by the arm.

'Come on, Mr Frey. Time to meet Her Majesty.'

He led me back to the deck, the air only slightly less cold than before. I felt the warmth of the sun on my skin, and some golden rays passed through the blindfold.

To my surprise, Boss removed it then. I even faltered, suddenly confronted by the vast view of the choppy sea ahead of me.

The waves clashed against the prow of the small, rusty ship, white foam under a dull sky. The grey clouds, dotted uniformly as far as the eye could see, were only slightly tinted gold by the weak rays of the setting sun.

Less than a mile away, tall and imposing, were the Needles of the Isle of Wight.

More than needles they made me think of teeth – pyramids of jagged, white stone, hit relentlessly by the waters. The sea birds glided around them, accentuating their monumental size. Behind their glowing outlines sat the island itself, its cliffs sharp as if freshly splintered by a giant knife.

There was an onslaught of frosty wind, and just as I shivered, somebody passed me a thick overcoat. I wrapped myself tightly in the heavy garment, and the lapels, trimmed with black fur, gave me instant warmth.

'Don't think we're soft,' Boss said behind me. 'Lord Salisbury told me you must look presentable.'

I smirked. I liked a world in which even the most loathed conscripts had to be properly attired when facing their monarch.

'Lord Salisbury,' I mumbled to myself, looking at Boss's surprisingly neat clothes. So *there* he had been: informing the Prime Minister that he and his men had caught us. And of course he'd chosen to do so in person; to get all the praise face to face and make the most of his victory. His triumphant grin was all I needed to picture the scene.

'Ironic, is it not?' he said, stepping a little closer to me. 'We were also at sea when I told you I could not wait to take care of you and your colleague. Do you remember?'

I winced at his foul breath, but did not bother coming up with a witty reply. The man did not deserve my efforts.

Instead, I looked around. There were four armed men, all in black winter coats, distributed on the deck. Still I saw no trace of McGray, so I had to face the island alone.

My honest composure surprised me. There I was, standing at the prow of this steam ship, escorted at gunpoint to meet the Queen – most likely to be executed afterwards. It did not feel real. None of it did. I was like a distant witness to someone else's fate, and the white, majestic coastline only emphasized that impression.

The ship made its way around the northern side of the island, the English coast always visible to our left – grey, misty and foreboding. I saw the entrance to the isle's main port; a gash in the land, a couple of ships coming and going, their funnels leaving trails of dark smoke.

We did not turn there, but continued east and then south, hugging the landmass as the very short day came to a close. The shadows of the island were already very long on the sea.

We made it to what I thought must be a sandy beach, that evening entirely covered in snow. Towards its northern end there were two piers. One was long and narrow, the other one shorter but much wider, its dark posts trimmed with bright caps of snow. The ship headed to the latter, and as we approached I saw a cluster of black figures already waiting for us.

One of them, plump and shorter than the rest, was clearly Lord Salisbury.

The ship docked there, and as the sailors tied the lines and placed the ramp, the Prime Minister and I held the most peculiar exchange of stares.

I stood a good foot above him, at least for one brief moment looking down on his bushy beard. He was biting a thick cigar, his teeth half bare. His bulbous nose had turned red from the cold, and the bags under his eyes had never look so puffy. I must have looked far worse.

'Get off,' Boss commanded me as soon as the gangway was in place, and I did so in as dignified a manner as I could.

'Lord Salisbury,' I said with a brief nod. The man glared at me, his eyes bulging and his teeth crushing the tobacco.

'Don't you *Lord Salisbury* me, you treacherous little leech!' he hissed through his clenched, yellow canines. 'I offered to save your pathetic life and you rascals betrayed me! I should have killed you both at the very start.'

I had no energy left to feel indignant. I simply gave a half-smile.

'Your sister sends her regards.'

The man went every shade of red, unable to utter a word. Then we heard his men struggle behind us.

They were bringing McGray down the gangway, still mana-cled, gagged and blindfolded. He stumbled from side to side, moaning, and when they released him from all the ties, he instantly ran to the edge of the pier, clutching the nearest post to let out an imperious spurt of sick.

He was still panting when Boss approached him. The man handed him a rag to clean his face, and pressed the barrel of his gun on McGray's temple.

'What a pathetic sight,' he murmured.

After a moment, once his greenish face was cleaner, Bob and another man shoved McGray closer to me, and they escorted us towards the beach.

I had a closer look at Nine-Nails. His cheekbone was grazed, his wrists scuffed from the manacles, and he walked with a slight limp. His hair was a mess, but that was nothing new, and he had not changed clothes, proudly sporting his same overcoat, creased, stained and torn in places.

When he looked at me he wrinkled his nose. 'Och, look at ye, all prim n' pretty.'

'You could have accepted their clothes,' I whispered.

'They can *fuck* themselves,' he barked, the swearing travelling along the beach like the echo of a bullet.

We walked along the snow-covered sand, the beach ending abruptly to give way to a dense pine forest.

Three young scullery maids, in their thick winter uniforms, were giggling and running about, but they stopped and formed a line when they saw us pass. They all carried wide baskets, where they'd been collecting red hawthorn berries and clippings of evergreens, clearly to make wreaths. I realized that the day was Christmas Eve.

We made it to the second, narrower pier, where the forestry opened up into a neatly landscaped clearing. Perfectly round, surrounded by dense, almost solid greenery, the small field reminded me of the witches' coven in the catacombs of York.

Instead of a fire, however, the centre was taken by a wide tent, like a maharaja's. Its thick canvas, dyed bright red and trimmed with golden tassels, was nailed firmly to the ground, and I saw three smoking stovepipes sticking through the canopy.

The tent rested on two layers of rush matting, also used to carpet a wide pathway that led to a nearby carriage. A couple of young boys ran around, their sole task to scare away the seagulls and vermin, for the tent gave off the sickly sweet smell of suet pudding.

A very slim valet, barely skin and bone, stood shivering a few yards from the door curtains.

'Prime Minister,' he said with a deep bow. 'Her Majesty is expecting you.'

He eyed McGray and me with a hint of compassion. Then he called the boys, who helped him draw and tie the curtains, as if opening up a theatre's stage.

As they did so, Boss whispered into McGray's ear, holding his gun less than an inch from his eyes.

'Give me a reason to blow your brains out, Nine-Nails. I *beg* you . . .'

There came an instant waft of hot, heavily-scented air, as if they'd opened a window into the exotic east. Inside the tent, the rush matting was further covered with a thick Persian rug. At the centre, in front of the stoves, sat a heavy mahogany desk. Also covered in exotic cloths, the desk was crammed with books, document boxes, quills, framed portraits, a steaming tea service and a silver tray piled with sweet treats.

And there, ensconced in cluttered opulence, we found Queen Victoria herself.

45

Wrapped in layer upon layer of black furs and taffeta, she looked like a perfectly round bundle, her sallow face almost as white as her strands of sparse hair, neatly arranged so that they covered any bald spots. Her head was trimmed not with a crown, but with the most elaborate plait of black velvet, decked with silk flowers and finished off with white fluffy feathers. Wide pearls hung from her ears, her lobes pulled down by the weight. Then again, everything in that face had given way to gravity a long time ago – the heavy bags under her bulging eyes, the skin on her neck. But most noticeable were her plump cheeks, hanging heavy all the way from her cheekbones, pulling her entire face downwards in a tired grimace. Her right hand rested on the desk, holding a dipping pen, and I saw that four lines of pearls, tight around her fat wrist, held a miniature of Prince Albert, painted on ivory and guarded by glass.

She winced momentarily at the cold draught, but would not look at us. She gazed sideways, at the tall, hefty man who stood next to her. His skin was the colour of cinnamon, his cheeks plump and very smooth, but framed by a curly, jet-black beard. He wore an elaborate turban, white and gold, and despite the sultry air inside the tent, he'd wrapped himself in a heavy sort of tunic, thick and as richly embroidered as the Persian rug beneath his feet.

He held a small book in his left hand, his chest perked up proudly as he recited slowly with a deep, exotic voice. With each syllable he made a nod and a swirling stroke with his right hand. And with each syllable the Queen nodded too, her eyes following his, captivated, without blinking, as if entranced by a snake charmer.

We were about to interrupt the Queen's Hindustani lessons, and she would not like it.

The wispy valet went to her, his steps measured and well calculated. Lord Salisbury stepped in with the same care, as the man whispered softly into Her Majesty's ear. Victoria tilted her head, her pearl pendants swinging slightly.

McGray took a step closer to me, and he whispered too. 'Fuck, she's fat.'

'*McGray!*'

'I mean, ye hear stories, but ye never really think she'll be quite so—'

'Shut up. *Shut up!* I beg you.'

Sadly, I knew what he meant. The Queen's was not a healthy plumpness. That woman had clearly eaten her sorrows away for decades, with no one to stop her or even suggest that her actions might be harmful in the slightest.

Victoria raised her hand and the dark man, her Munshi, instantly went silent, though eyeing us with clear contempt. She listened as her eyes went to Lord Salisbury, and then, with an unexpected flicker, to McGray and me.

I felt a shiver when our sights crossed, and at once I recognized the same pale blue I'd seen in the child's portrait. Even the shape of the brows, one curved and the other almost straight. I only looked into them for a split second, for then I remembered one is not to stare at the Queen, and I instinctively bowed my head as low as I could. McGray's head had to be pushed down by Boss.

Lord Salisbury spoke then with a tone so soft, so deferential, I would not have recognized him.

'Your Majesty, forgive my intrusion, but the task has been accomplished. These are – *the men*.'

I did not dare look up, my legs suddenly trembling. I heard Victoria shift in her seat, with the ruffle of countless layers of fabric.

'Why do you look at me like that, Salisbury?' she said. Her voice was slow and rasping, but with a rich quality to it; clearly trained to make itself heard across wide rooms. 'Are you expecting a medal?'

'Ma'am, I—'

'I thought you were better than this. I commanded you to fetch these men the Lord knows how long ago. I was still at Windsor!'

Very carefully I looked up, without lifting my head. Salisbury had removed his hat, and I saw how profusely his scalp and temples sweated.

'There were certain developments, Your Majesty.'

'Developments?' she mocked.

'Indeed, Your Majesty. If you would not mind – it would be better to discuss the matter privately, given that—'

'Nonsense. Abdul and Walter can hear whatever you say.'

The Munshi gave Lord Salisbury the proudest, most self-assured sneer, holding his little book against his swollen chest.

The Prime Minister looked incensed, but all he could do was gulp and speak on.

'These men inadvertently led me to . . . the coven.'

It was as if the word had sent a chill around the tent, the fires unable to fight it.

Victoria shifted again, the chair now cracking under her weight. 'What?'

Salisbury at once regained some of his confidence.

'There are remnants of the old coven, Your Majesty. Spread all across the country. I have already deployed men. If you gave me but a little time I am sure I can trace them and bring you the appropriate woman for—'

'I don't want them anymore.'

Silence.

The words had come so unexpectedly, so casually, it took us all a moment to realize their actual meaning. The fire crackled in the stoves and the waves washed on the beach.

Lord Salisbury himself let out a pant before he could speak.

'I . . . I – I . . . I beg your par—?'

'*I don't want them anymore!*' Victoria howled, so violently I feared her voice alone would bring the tent down. '*Are you deaf?*'

My curiosity was stronger than my good sense, so I looked up. Victoria had slammed both hands on the desk, her blue eyes bulging like wide marbles, her chest heaving.

Between her and me, the Prime Minister clenched his hat.

'Your Majesty, pray excuse me, but I . . . I do – wonder . . . as to such a radical change of heart?'

Sluggishly, Victoria leaned back, her unblinking eyes fixed on Salisbury.

'That is the reason I wanted Abdul to be present,' she said. 'He has made me see the foolishness of my actions. I have been –' she caressed the ivory portrait on her wrist – 'I have been seduced by heresy. Those women were the voice of the Devil! They ensnared me and put my very soul at risk of damnation.'

McGray drew in a sharp breath, surely to let out something much worse than an *Och*, but he had the sense to contain himself. After that the silence was deep, as we all struggled to take the words in.

Was this a sudden whim? Was the Queen toying with us and teasing the PM? How could she possibly be serious?

I saw my befuddled frown reflected in the silver teapot, and then Salisbury's hands tremble with an anger he could only just contain. His little eyes flickered madly as he glared at the Queen's man.

'If I may, my queen?' the Munshi interjected, every syllable carefully modulated.

I had never seen eyes so dark in my life, his lashes so thick and black, and for a moment I thought he had applied mascara.

The Queen nodded and Lord Salisbury could not repress an enraged snort.

The man walked leisurely, theatrically, around the desk, speaking slowly and condescendingly, as if imparting a lesson to a group of children.

'The Devil promises the same gifts as does – the Lord, as you would call Him. But the dead, sadly, are dead. We will not see them again until the end of eternity. That is the promise of the Lord. *Any* other voices we might hear whispering at night, ghosts and – apparitions? – those are the work of the Devil. He whispers in our ears all the time. And he is crafty. He knows how to use our deepest desires, however rightful and pure they may be, to find ways to lead us to him – to hell.'

Lord Salisbury looked as red as the canvas behind him. 'Your Majesty,' he grumbled, 'this man is no Christian! Whatever twisted teachings—'

'*I was the twisted one!*' Victoria shouted. '*I! Appointed as Defender of the Faith by the Lord himself!* I have read and reread the Bible. Abdul is right. He's made me see the truth. I *will* see Albert again, and my children too. But it will be in heaven, not through mediums who are at best charlatans, and at worst devil worshippers. Old King James was right to burn and hang them all!'

So everything I'd read about her was true, I thought. Her whims, her inconsistency, her unexpected fits of rage. The past days had been a living hell for us all, while this monstrous woman spent her Christmas holiday in her private lands, picnicking in the snow all wrapped in pearls and furs, only to tell us she had simply changed her mind.

Lord Salisbury threw me a quick glance, and for the first time we looked at each other with a dash of mutual understanding.

'What – what shall I do with these men, Your Majesty?' he said after a sigh.

Victoria let out a vexed breath, the air flapping her lips. She sat back, made some gesture with her hand and the valet brought the tray of treats nearer to her. In seconds she gobbled three heaped spoonfuls of suet pudding. She ate anxiously, chewing and smacking her lips almost as loudly as McGray himself, greasy lumps rolling down her marten fur collar. I felt sickened and, though I did not look directly at her, I could feel her probing stare.

'They committed murder, did they not?' she said, a nasty chunk of suet stuck to the corner of her mouth. 'They killed those women, wicked as they might have been . . .'

McGray was going to retort, but Boss pressed the gun firmly against the back of his neck.

'Indeed, your Majesty,' said Lord Salisbury. 'And they know – far too much, I'm afraid.'

I clenched my fists at that. Of course we knew too much. Too much about *him*. Too much about the Queen as well . . . alas, all the evidence had been snatched from my hands.

'What are your names?' she spat suddenly.

For a moment I could not answer, stunned at her addressing us directly. Lord Salisbury began to speak, but Victoria barked.

'They can speak for themselves, can they not?'

Salisbury nodded, bowed and took a timid step back.

'Your names!' Victoria snapped, and I cleared my throat. Never, in all my life, had I enunciated so carefully.

'Ian – Ian Frey, Your Majesty.'

She let out a humph. 'And you?'

McGray shifted his weight from leg to leg, and the instant it took him to reply was a gruelling torture. I feared he'd tell her to sod off, or something worse, and the PM's men would shoot us at once.

'Adolphus McGray,' he said at last. 'But abody calls me Nine-Nails.'

Again there was silence, deep and tense.

Cautiously, I looked up. Victoria was staring at Nine-Nails, but there was a new spark in her eyes, intense and shamelessly lascivious. The Queen clearly had a soft spot for brawny, slightly wild men. The spark, sadly, was very short-lived.

'Try them for murder, then,' she concluded. 'Make sure they are found guilty and dispose of them discreetly.'

She could not have sounded more casual had she asked her valet to throw the pudding away.

'Death sentence, Your Majesty?' Lord Salisbury asked with a sickly mellow tone, the question solely intended to rub salt on our wounds.

'Of course, you fool!' Victoria spluttered. 'You have done that sort of thing before.' She leaned towards the tray. 'Now take them away.' And as she gobbled again she began humming a very off-key rendering of 'I'm Called Little Buttercup'.

I shut my eyes as a horrible chill began to spread across my body.

So thus the Queen had passed our death sentence – in between mouthfuls of pudding and humming cheap theatre songs.

I tried to breathe, but the air seemed to clog in my throat. All my limbs had gone numb, and suddenly I saw stars all over my shut lids. I was about to faint.

'Take them away,' Victoria commanded. '*Now!* I cannot bear the sight of a grown man shaking.'

Somebody grasped my arm and pulled me backwards, and only then I realized it was me the Queen had referred to.

I took a couple of stumbling steps, but then someone spoke. My blood had rushed to my head, and in my dizziness I had to guess the meaning of the words.

'May I speak, ma'am?'

My heart skipped a beat. It had been McGray's voice! Was he about to call Queen Victoria a *fat bastard* to her face?

When I looked, however, I saw him bowing low, struggling to keep his ground as Boss and another man tried to take him away. His careful balance astounded me; resisting the guards' pulls yet keeping himself from growling or hurling himself ahead.

Victoria stared straight into his eyes, the Munshi extending an arm in front of her, as if to protect her. The old woman smacked her lips as she took a stumpy hand to her bosom. Was she in fact *relishing* the tension?

She smirked and waited until the last possible instant, when a third guard came to take McGray out, to speak.

'The Queen gives you a minute.'

I shall never forget the speed with which Lord Salisbury turned his head. All the other attendants turned to her too, open-mouthed. And amidst those puzzled faces, the Munshi's stuck out. The man was not shocked, but angered. Could it be that he felt threatened? Could he perhaps recognize a certain glow in the Queen's eyes? One he'd seen right before he became her favourite?

She certainly looked flushed, and if the tent had not been open to the December evening, I bet she'd be fanning herself.

I wondered if McGray's Scottish voice had anything to do with it. Perhaps he reminded her of the late John Brown?

I caught all those impressions within a blink, for McGray did not wait to deliver a very well-calculated blow, though in the kindest possible tone.

'We learned about yer father, ma'am,' he said, and then went to the jugular. '*Augustus.*'

The impact was instant.

Victoria swung her hand violently, knocking the tray of treats from the valet's hands. Silver, scones and chunks of pudding spread all over the floor, the rattle freezing everyone around. Her eyes popped out, opened so wide I thought they, too, would fall off and roll on the intricate rug. Her jaw dropped, her teeth caked with suet, and when she exhaled, her steaming breath looked like that of a dragon.

'Everybody out,' she hissed. Her commanding voice had suddenly acquired an eerie, childish quality. The valet recognized the tone immediately and stepped out in quick, stumbling strides.

The Munshi did not move.

'You too,' said Victoria, waving a dismissive hand at him, and the man's face became almost as ashen as mine.

'But – my Queen—'

'*Now!*' Victoria roared, '*Or I'll ship you back to the dung hole you came from!*'

And as she shouted she picked up a framed portrait of one of her daughters and threw it at the man's face. The Munshi even whimpered when he scuttled away.

As I saw him leave I became aware of the duller light. The sun had already set, the pier right in front of the tent nothing but a thin black line cutting the indigo waters.

Only Lord Salisbury remained, along with Boss, who kept his gun ever pressed on McGray's neck. Nobody touched *me*. I must have looked so pale and stricken nobody considered me a threat to the Queen.

'Shut that!' she snarled at the PM, pointing at the curtains and, reduced to the duties of a manservant, Lord Salisbury obliged.

The curtains drawn, Victoria stirred in her creaking seat, her gaze going from side to side as she clasped the arms of the chair. Her bulging eyes finally settled on McGray's.

'My father's name was Edward,' she spluttered.

I was expecting McGray to cackle or swear, but he did not even sneer. He spoke with utmost respect.

'Yer Majesty is far too clever to believe that.'

I was expecting the Queen to shout at him to speak properly, but she knew her Scottish inflections very well.

'The Queen does not *believe*, young man,' she hissed. 'That is the truth.'

However, her lower lip, pushed out in an angered pout, had a slight quiver.

'We,' McGray signalled me, 'accidentally came across evidence that says otherwise. The name Augustus d'Esté—'

Victoria banged both fists on the desk, an animalistic growl coming from her mouth, together with half-chewed pudding crumbs. So she knew. I wondered for how long; how she'd found out.

'Is this true?' she demanded, appealing to Lord Salisbury.

The man's beard stood on end. 'They – they have no evidence, Your Majesty. My men saw to that.'

Boss nodded, and McGray, for the first time in this audience, allowed himself some laughter.

'Saw to that?' he repeated, looking at Lord Salisbury. 'Youse saw nothing. Tell Her Majesty how yer rats let the witches take—'

'*Silence!*' Victoria shouted, and then turned to Salisbury. 'The witches took what?'

The man gulped, and it was McGray who had to speak for him.

'Letters, Yer Majesty. From the late Prince Edward to the coven. They couldnae be more damning.'

Victoria sat back, her bosom heaving and one of her bulging eyes twitching.

'If any such correspondence had ever existed,' she murmured with a hint of a crazed giggle, 'I am sure my mother and father would have dealt with it. *They would have dealt with everything and everyone involved!*'

Again, McGray could have laughed, but he did not.

'That's precisely what the witches feared, so they kept the most crucial letter, signed by the auld Duke, as a guarantee to their safety. And they hid it within the covers of an auld book in the Oxford libraries. Nae place safer to keep a wee piece o' paper.'

Victoria's frown deepened, her gaze growing more sombre as the truth began so settle in.

'They have nothing!' Boss snapped. When the Queen glared at him he cleared his throat and spoke with more deference. 'Excuse me, Your Majesty, but I must tell you – they have nothing.'

'Explain yourself,' Victoria demanded.

Boss's curled-up moustache was shaking with emotion. 'I saw them drop that book. My men and I were chasing them. This lame imp dropped it.'

The Queen stared at my broken wrist and a grin began to appear on her face, but then McGray spoke.

'He didnae drop it. The witches took it.' He eyed Lord Salisbury. '*His* half-sister did.'

It was as if an invisible string pulled the Queen's face towards the PM. Even the stickiest crumbs of suet flew from her mouth like projectiles. She stared at him for a moment, her eyes flickering as if they swam on boiling water.

'So it is true!' she hissed, her voice like poison, and I was only glad she was not looking at me. 'Those whores *did* ensnare the old marquis!'

It was Lord Salisbury's turn to stumble. He withdrew one more step, his back now touching the red canvas. Suddenly he looked like a cornered kitten.

'I heard rumours,' Victoria mumbled, her mouth dry, 'but I always refused to believe—' She seemed to choke then, spreading her arms on the chair. '*And your men let your bastard sister take those letters?*'

Her bloodcurdling stare now fell on Boss. The man swallowed painfully and his gun began to shake.

'Damn fools . . .' Victoria whispered, her face moving slowly from left to right, her eyes jumping from one face to the next. 'You are all but a handful of useless, idiotic – *fools!*'

She clenched her fingers around the armrests until her hands trembled and the wood creaked.

'Your Majesty?'

I looked up, for McGray had spoken so softly I could not believe it had been him. I noticed a slight tilt on the corner of his mouth.

'They don't have them,' he said.

Victoria's entire face contorted; her frown deepened, her nose wrinkled and she raised her upper lip as if smelling something foul.

'*What?*'

McGray raised his chin. 'They don't have those letters, Your Majesty. Those are nae the witches I meant.'

Boss stammered. 'But – but I saw—'

Salisbury raised a hand to silence him, and then approached Nine-Nails with short steps. 'Explain yourself.'

McGray's eyes were glowing now. 'I kent the witches had us cornered inside the library, so I hid those papers while my colleague here looked for a way out.'

Salisbury frowned in a manner very similar to the Queen's. 'You did what?'

'I hid them. It was pretty much certain they'd catch us, so I thought I should at least keep those papers safe.'

I could not contain myself. 'Why did you not tell me?'

McGray chuckled. ''Cause yer a *terrible* liar, Frey. Would ye have defended that damn book quite so savagely had ye kent there was nothing in it?'

I shook my head. 'Well, I do not know, but . . . where did you—?'

'That was the most brilliant part,' McGray said with a frank smile. 'I just put them in another book! A needle in a bloody haystack!'

Both Victoria and Salisbury shook, as if his shoes and her chair had suddenly burst into flames.

'*You must retrieve them!*' the Queen cried, her fat index pointing at Salisbury, and the PM sprinted to the exit.

'Yes, Your Majesty. I shall telegram at once—'

'Hey-hey-hey!' Nine-Nails protested. 'Hold yer horses, auld man. They won't be there anymore.'

Salisbury already held the edge of the curtain. He did not let it go as he turned his head back to McGray. 'Huh?'

I looked sideways, and then gasped. 'The magpie!' I whispered. 'You sent a message with the magpie!'

McGray nodded. 'Aye, to Oakley and Nettle. I told ye! Telling the catalogue number o' the book I chose. This idiot here must have seen us release the bird.' He nodded at Boss, whose perfectly curled moustache seemed to have gone askew.

'Did you?' the Queen pressed.

The man was so tense he did not even notice he'd lowered the gun.

'He – he did release some bird before we caught up with them, Your Majesty.'

If they looked pale, they went ashen after McGray's next sentences.

'It's been almost two full days since that happened.' He eyed the PM. 'A *long* time to waste, bringing us all the way here. The other coven' – he purposely avoided naming them as *the York coven* – 'will have seized those papers by now.'

Salisbury darted to McGray and grabbed him by the lapels.

'You will take us to those papers! *You will*, or I will personally rip out each and every one of the nineteen bloody nails you have left!'

McGray winced, for the PM had spat a couple of times on his face.

'Nae, we won't.' He looked at Victoria. 'Youse will let us go, and we will ensure that those papers never see the light.'

Victoria tilted her head backwards, as if someone had pushed it against the back of the chair. Her mouth hardly moved when she spoke, her face almost completely frozen with disbelief.

'You are blackmailing the Queen . . .'

'Nae only *the* Queen,' McGray added, and then quoted my words. 'Half the royal houses of Europe would be tainted. From the Hapsburgs to the Romanovs—'

'This is treason,' Victoria interjected, opening and closing her hands, her voice a throttled pant.

McGray squinted one eye. 'Is it *really* treason if yer nae the rightful monarch?'

'Treason!' she repeated, gathering air and shouting ever louder. 'Treason! *Treason!*'

And she brushed off half the documents from the desk, splattering ink all over the bright red tent.

'This'll be a scandal that will make John Brown look like a walk in the parks of Bawd-shire.'

The Queen again seemed to struggle for breath. I went to McGray and whispered, '*Do not milk it anymore, for the love of God!*'

I could tell he still had a few shrewd remarks up his sleeve and no wish to hold them back, but he would not have the chance.

Right then we heard the distant echo of a steam whistle. It did not sound like that of the ship that had brought us. It was deeper – and yet familiar.

We heard men barking orders outside, and frantic steps coming our way.

Salisbury pulled the curtain so forcefully some of the stitches tore.

'*What the Devil?*' he shouted as a pale guard came forwards.

'A ship, sir,' the man panted. 'It's coming to dock.'

He pointed to the beach and the pier. Behind them, the long shadow loomed on the indigo waters. The deck was dotted with the fire of torches.

Their flames were bright blue, as if trying to emulate the tones of the twilight.

I had to blink, not believing my eyes. I recognized the tall brass funnel and the spotless, deep green of the hull.

'Captain Jones's ship,' I muttered, but no one paid attention.

There were men running to and fro at the beach, preparing their weapons as the steamer positioned itself by the narrow pier.

'*Bring men!*' Salisbury shouted. '*Shoot those blasted whores! Don't you let them—*'

'*No, you halfwits!*' Victoria's voice resounded over the mayhem, all necks turning to her, even those already at the beach. Her eyes were bloodshot, her face like a red balloon about to burst. '*The fires are blue!* Are you blind too? *Blue!* They come to parlay!'

I winced at that – the Queen of the British Empire so well versed in witchcraft codes.

'Help me!' she yelped, pushing herself upwards with the pitiful strength of her plump arms. She became a grotesque mass of black materials, jerking, shuddering and whimpering. '*Help me up, you damn fools!*'

The valet rushed in, bringing her an ebony cane, and behind him came the two young boys and even one of the maids we'd seen before.

Between them all, they helped Victoria up, her shudders not helping, and when she was finally on her feet the Munshi came in, bringing a heavy cloak which he wrapped around the royal shoulders.

Victoria walked around the desk with great difficulty. She was not much taller on her feet, the feathers of her headdress only just reaching McGray's chest. Still, we all bowed as she walked past us, Lord Salisbury deeper than everyone else.

The Queen planted herself but a few yards from the tent, panting after walking but a dozen steps, and she waited as we all watched the ship dock.

The twilight was swiftly giving way to the night, and in the gathering darkness it was just the blue torches we saw move. They lined up and advanced slowly along the pier, seemingly floating above the water.

A small group of torches remained at the end of the pier – perhaps so that they could flee if things went awry? Again I had to blink, for there was one familiar figure at the centre of that cluster.

I recognized Caroline's hourglass figure, her face brightly lit by the blue flames around her. She, however, did not carry a torch. Instead, she held a restless magpie, her gloved hands firm around the bird's wings.

The rest of the women advanced with cautious steps, the Queen's guards keeping their aims on them. I saw some of those arms tremble, a man dripping sweat from the tip of his nose.

The witches, cloaked as ever, did not seem to be carrying any sort of weapon or vial. They would not be so reckless as to attack the Queen directly – or so I hoped. I did not want to be caught in the middle of that battle.

As if sharing my thoughts, McGray took a discreet step closer to me, perhaps readying himself to haul me and sprint away if needed.

At last the witches came close enough for us to recognize them. I'd seen the three front women around the fire in York. One of them was Mrs Greenwood, holding her torch high. And in the middle, her hands gloved and clenched tightly, came the sour face of Jane Oakley. Old Nettle, I noticed, had not come, her wisdom too valuable to be put at risk.

Oakley reached the rush matting just as the first snowflakes began to fall, fluttering bright around the torches' blue glow. The instant she set foot on the coir, the young witch dropped to one knee, her cloak spreading around her, and she bowed her head low.

Victoria, standing less than a yard from her, looked visibly pleased.

Oakley clearly knew the royal protocols, for she did not speak until addressed by the monarch.

'Rise, woman,' Victoria told her, but Oakley remained on her knee, lifting only her face.

'Your Majesty,' she said.

So this must be how it had happened every year for the past two decades, I thought. Witches coming from the coast, meeting the Queen on this secluded beach and performing their séances in the safety of a tent just like this.

Only tonight the Queen did not seem so welcoming.

'You are all heretics,' she spat, her face wrinkled with disgust. 'Do you know that? You are disgusting creatures, crawling underground like vermin.'

Oakley said nothing. She simply held the Queen's stare.

Victoria sneered. 'I understand these men led you to –' she stopped then, eyeing all the people around – 'led you to certain letters.'

Oakley nodded. 'They did, Your Majesty. We had someone seize those papers immediately.' She cast us a quick look. 'It was easy to get in, with all the workers that were fetched to repair the library's ceiling.' She then looked back at the Queen, her tone reassuring. 'The documents are safe now, Your Majesty.'

We all looked at Victoria, waiting for her reaction. The woman had shut her eyes, her shoulders dropping as she exhaled with relief. However, when she opened them again, her gaze was sterner than ever.

'You will surrender those papers. At once.'

Oakley made another respectful bow. 'We shall not, Your Majesty.'

She had not even raised her voice, but it was precisely her calmness that caught everyone's attention. Victoria could not have looked more muddled.

'*What did you just say?*' she stuttered. With her furs and feathers lifted by the wind, she reminded me of a spiky hedgehog.

Oakley shifted neither her expression nor her tone. She did not even blink.

'They are safe, Your Majesty. We will keep them so. But we shall not surrender them.'

'You will not—?' Victoria began, but then choked again. She trembled from sheer fury and the Munshi had to hold her.

Victoria's chest swelled as she gathered air, and then her voice snapped like a gunshot.

'*You will hand them to me!* And you will agree to it now! Don't you see my men around you?'

As she said so she jerked her cane, using it to signal the guards.

Boss let out a low, menacing chuckle, and I saw him raise his gun as if to prove the Queen's point.

'There are no safer hands than ours,' Oakley insisted, still eerily calm. 'Do you see that magpie, Your Majesty?'

She raised a hand and pointed at the pier, where Caroline stood. She still held the bird, albeit with a terrified look on her face. The two witches next to her had drawn out broad knives, the steel blades reflecting the blue fires. And they held them so that they only just touched the feathers on the bird's breast.

'We are to send that bird to our matron,' Oakley said. 'When she sees it she will know that we are safe. That she can trust you.'

'*Trust me?*' Victoria squealed.

'Indeed. If our matron does not receive the bird, she will see that all those letters and documents become public.'

Victoria was choking, slowly sliding from the arms of the Munshi. Her valet had to run and bring her the chair, and he set it just in time to support the royal buttocks.

'Not only the letter from the late Duke of Kent,' Oakley went on, impassively. 'We also have portraits, visitors' logbooks, Sir Augustus's journal, the accounts from bagpipers who gathered information from the royal palaces – and their names will all match those which Your Majesty herself mentions in her published memoirs.'

Victoria gagged, some ghastly, repulsive sound coming from the depths of her throat. The valet produced a little hunter's flask and offered her some spirit, but Victoria knocked it off with a savage slap. She tossed her cane forwards, missing Oakley by a couple of inches.

'You will all die! *I will see to that!*'

Oakley turned to Lord Salisbury, as if the Queen were a mad inmate and the PM her executor.

'You will leave us be, my lord. You will let us all go right now or the magpie dies and all the secrets become public.' She squinted rather malevolently. '*All* the secrets, sir.'

In the distance, one of the witches pushed the knife closer to the bird, the tip now lost in the plumage. I could tell how nervous Caroline was, fearing that her trembling accidentally pushed the magpie to its death.

On our side, the Queen was shaking and kicking about, until she fell from the chair. Her shouting made my hair prickle against my scalp.

Oakley's voice turned assuaging. 'Those letters will be destroyed after your death, Your Majesty. You have my word. Your descendants will be safe, but ours shall be too. Children should not have to pay for the sins of their parents.'

Victoria shouted and choked, the valet and the Munshi moaning around her, begging her to take their hands so that they could pull her up. The witches had, quite literally, brought her to her knees.

Lord Salisbury turned to us, his face livid, wishing that he too could drop on the floor and kick about like a youngster. He barely managed to speak.

'Go.'

I blinked, my jaw dropping slowly. McGray did not find words either. We had both expected the debate to carry on for much longer.

Boss was the first one to retort.

'Sir, you cannot let them—'

'*Now!*' the PM growled, which coincided with a high-pitched squeal from the Queen. The shrill sound was like a physical push, and McGray and I strode swiftly out of the tent, towards the pier.

We walked past Oakley as she stood up.

'As I said, there cannot be safer hands than ours to—'

'*Be gone!*' Victoria howled, still on all fours. '*Before I kill you all myself!*'

I shall never forget my panting breaths or the way my heart pounded as we crossed the creaking pier. With every step I expected the Queen to change her mind, or the PM to tell his men to shoot us all, or Boss or the Munshi to lose their nerve and charge madly against us.

None of that happened.

We strode next to Caroline. The poor young woman, though still tense, was on the brink of tears, her dark eyes overjoyed when she saw us pass.

McGray and I jumped onto the deck and found Captain Jones and his boys hiding behind the gunwale, all holding a gun in each hand.

Once more, the sway of the boat made me feel that none of it was real. How had we possibly escaped?

Just as I thought so, Oakley and Mrs Greenwood joined us, and Captain Jones ran to untie the ship.

Very soon the steamer was moving, albeit slowly, and we saw how Victoria's guards began to light lanterns around her tent. Her tearing screams travelled all along the snowy beach, reaching the very depths of the sea, and for a brief moment I felt sorry for her.

Then my broken bones ached from the cold and the damp.

I owed that to her. My entire life had almost been completely shattered because of that woman's selfish interests.

McGray and I stood in silence, unable to take our eyes from the island as the ship gathered speed. We caught a last glimpse of her waving arms, hitting everything and everyone in their trajectory. A seventy-year-old child on her knees, throwing a tantrum and hitting even those who tried to help her stand.

A moment later, once we sailed at a good distance, Oakley nodded at Caroline, and she let the magpie go.

Everyone, both on the ship and on the island, watched those black wings fly away, until they became lost in the thick winter night.

And then, at last, I managed to breathe.

Royal Family Tree

Sketched by Detective Inspector A. McGray.

Found in documents confiscated from the *Commission for the Elucidation of Unsolved Cases Presumably Related to the Odd and Ghostly*, Edinburgh.

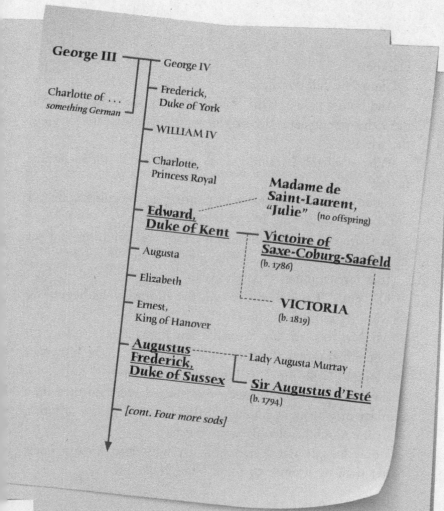

George III

Charlotte of . . . something German

George IV

Frederick, Duke of York

WILLIAM IV

Charlotte, Princess Royal

Edward, Duke of Kent

Madame de Saint-Laurent, "Julie" (no offspring)

Victoire of Saxe-Coburg-Saafeld (b. 1786)

Augusta

Elizabeth

VICTORIA (b. 1819)

Ernest, King of Hanover

Augustus Frederick, Duke of Sussex

Lady Augusta Murray

Sir Augustus d'Esté (b. 1794)

[cont. Four more sods]

EPILOGUE

5 January 1890, Gloucestershire

Darkness.

Complete, full darkness.

And then a golden strip of light, cutting the void as Layton drew the curtains and the bright white fields appeared beyond the window.

'Wha— what?' I mumbled, so groggy I did not recognize myself.

'Good morning, sir,' he said, pouring my morning coffee. 'I am sorry to wake you, but you have a visitor.'

'A visitor?' I asked, rubbing my eyes and grunting as I sat up. 'Who on earth calls at this ungodly hour?'

'It is forty minutes past noon, sir.'

'Oh, gosh!' I snatched the cup, the strong aroma beginning to work its miracle. 'Who is it?'

'Mr McGray, sir. He arrived a few hours ago.'

I breathed out with irritation. I could not make him wait any longer. 'Tell him I will join him in a mo—'

'Typical!' the man himself remonstrated as he stormed in, a tumbler of whisky in his hand. 'Bloody Lord Percy, ordering everyone around from his satin sheets!'

I only let out a resigned sigh. By now even Layton knew better than to attempt to force Nine-Nails out.

'Shall I bring you breakfast – or lunch, sir?' he asked me.

'Breakfast,' I answered. 'One needs some discipline in life . . .'

He left with a bow and McGray installed himself in the armchair by the hearth. I took a few sips of coffee in silence, and McGray had the decency to wait, swirling his own drink.

'What brings you all this way?' I asked.

'I sent ye a letter and three telegrams. We were worried ye hadnae survived the decade!'

'Oh?' I said. 'I am so sorry. The post is mighty slow in these regions,' and as I said so, I discreetly covered the messages on my bedside table with my cup and saucer.

'I was worried,' he admitted. 'That lass Caroline too.'

I smirked. They were bound to be. After all, I'd abandoned our sorry party as soon as Captain Jones docked at Leith Harbour. Thankfully it had been in the morning, for I managed to catch the first service to England.

'I know,' I said. 'I am sorry, but it seemed the best time to leave. I do not have any lodgings – or even any clothes left in Edinburgh.'

McGray smiled. 'That bitch Lady Glass is still moaning ye owe her. Joan says the servants heard she'll sue.'

'She will not,' I said bitterly. 'If she knows what is best for her.'

Nine-Nails chuckled. 'Her granddaughter will be happy to remind her!'

'Speaking of Miss Ardglass,' I said, 'how come she joined the witches going to the Isle of Wight?' I had spent the entire trip back sleeping, too drained to enquire as to how things had turned the way they did. 'Oakley and Nettle would have known very well where to find the Queen, but Miss Ardglass bringing Captain Jones . . .'

McGray lounged in his armchair. 'I'd better tell ye in proper order.

'It all started while the lasses were travelling back to Edinburgh. Caroline showed the miniature to Katerina almost as soon as we parted.'

'Oh, do let me guess – she used her inner eye!'

'Mock her as much as ye want, but aye. She said the wee thing *stank* of witchcraft. But she could also tell it was nae amulet or token. She felt it wasnae connected to Prince Albert at all, but very much to Victoria, and – why ye grinning like that?'

'Do not mind me. Go on.'

McGray shook his head. 'They arrived in Edinburgh – remember, Caroline told the witches that was where she'd hidden the wee portrait. As soon as they arrived, a wee bit before the witches reached them, the lass began investigating. It took them just a couple of hours at the newspapers' archive to piece everything together.'

'A couple of hours?' I asked. 'How?'

'They had the name d'Esté from the PM's telegram. That name turned out to be extremely rare and connected to a lot of royal gossip.'

'Tell me.'

'The name died out long ago and it was only resumed at the beginning of this century. It was given to the laddie in the watercolour, Augustus. The chap indeed was the illegitimate son o' the auld Duke of Sussex.' McGray winced. 'Well – *sort* of illegitimate.'

'What do you mean?'

'I've had more time to look into it. Sussex secretly married one Lady Augusta Murray. They tied the knot in Rome, and then again in London. As yer surely aware, the highest royals need permission from the sodding parliament to marry.'

'Indeed, when your descendants are potential candidates to the throne. That is to ensure that such marriages do not diminish the status of the royal—'

'Aye-aye, all that shite. The House o' Lords declared that marriage null and void. Augustus had already been born, so that instantly rendered him and his wee sister illegitimate. It was a huge scandal back then. Pages and pages of gossip in every newspaper.'

I arched an eyebrow, drawing the royal family tree in my mind. 'So, if our Augustus was the son of the Duke of Sussex . . .' My jaw dropped.

'Indeedy,' McGray said. 'If that marriage had nae been annulled, Augustus himself would have become king.'

'Dear, oh dear!'

'And I also found many articles about the "mysterious" trip to Germany Vicky's parents took right after they married. They travelled all the way there only to come back a few months later, so that their bet on the throne could be born on British soil.

'Many people, later on, gossiped that Victoria's real father had been her mother's comptroller, one – what was his name?'

'Sir John Conroy.'

'Aye, that's the twat. O' course, all that gossip ended when Vic turned out to be the spittin' image of Mad King George.'

'She was still his great-granddaughter,' I said. 'And from the portrait we saw, Augustus must have looked a good deal like him too.'

'Right. His looks and his age made him perfect for the scheme of the Duke of Kent; ye ken, Vicky's impotent *father*.'

'Indeed.'

'I found an auld article that mentions very briefly how Augustus d'Esté travelled to Bavaria. Just on the crucial dates when Victoria was conceived.'

I nodded. 'And Oakley did mention a – journal?'

'Aye. They told Caroline that their spying bagpipers managed to get hold of the poor sod's diary. Augustus had a really depressing life – a pitiful career in the army, nae wife or children . . . he tried to claim his dukedom but failed . . . and then he died of some mysterious debilitating disease. Nae physician was able to diagnose him and the man spent his entire life subjecting himself to every treatment imaginable. Thermal springs, ointments, electricity . . .' McGray shivered.

'The old witches silenced him, I suppose?'

'Most, *most* likely. Apparently, he mentions names of famous physicians he consulted. Most o' them, Katerina reckons, were at some point witches' clients. Those who were nae died mysteriously after Augustus contacted them.'

'Poor man,' I muttered.

'I wouldnae say so. He was a troublemaker, as was his mother, always trying to regain power and influence. Imagine if they'd ever discovered the truth!'

I recalled fragments of that ominous letter penned by Victoria's alleged father: *I cannot stress enough how crucial it is that d'Esté himself recalls nothing of the nocturne feats . . . I would abhor having to silence the young man permanently.*

And then I wondered if the old duke might have been silenced too. He had died when Victoria was only months old. Perhaps he'd threatened the witches not long after his heir was born.

I shook my head. Any such speculations were now pointless.

'So Caroline learned all that, inferred what we'd just found at the Oxford library, and then she surrendered the boy's portrait to the witches?' I asked.

'Aye. Nettle read my message and she immediately sent Oakley to Edinburgh.'

I raised a hand. 'Before you continue, I must tell you . . . Sending that message with the magpie was bloody brilliant.'

McGray stared at me in silence. Very slowly, he arched a suspicious brow. 'But?'

'No buts. That was, hands down, a brilliant move! I owe you my life.'

He still watched me with mistrust. This might be the first uncompromised compliment he'd had from me.

'What happened then?' I asked, before the mood became too ladylike. 'After Oakley joined Caroline in Edinburgh, I mean.'

'As ye well said, the witches kent where to find Victoria. They'd been meeting her there on Christmas Eve for the past twenty years. It was the best moment to lay down the terms for their silence. The fact that it saved us was . . .'

'Purely coincidental?'

'Something like that, but mostly thanks to Caroline. The quickest way from Edinburgh to the Isle of Wight was by sea. Caroline went straight to Cap'n Jones and he was pleased to help her. He's a wee bit in love with the lass.'

'I cannot blame him,' I said, and as soon as I realized what I'd just given away, I blushed intensely. I hid as much of my face as I could behind my cup of coffee.

'So, to be fair,' McGray added, 'we really owe our lives to *her*.'

I laughed softly. 'That accounts for that miserable look of yours.'

'Saved by a bloody Ardglass, Frey!' he snapped. 'My auld man must be turning in his grave.'

'At least we are rid of them,' I sighed, reaching for my cup, but McGray snorted.

I raised an eyebrow. 'We . . . we are, are we not?'

McGray sighed. 'Nae too sure. I mean, I seriously doubt Salisbury and fat Vic will ever bother us. They have far too much to lose. I'd still keep away from London, if I were ye.'

'Oh, indeed.' I studied his face for a moment. 'You still seem rather worried, though.'

Nine-Nails nodded. 'That witch Hilda is still alive,' he said. 'I doubt her half-brother will simply forgive and forget. He's already looking for her and her coven.'

'How do you know that?'

McGray cleared his throat before gulping down the rest of his drink. 'Those bastards raided our office.'

I looked up, spilling some coffee myself. '*What?* Salisbury's men?'

'Aye. I went in one morning and found the place empty. Trevelyan told me they came in the small hours and took everything. My auld books, my specimens . . . the lot is gone.'

I could not bring myself to shut my mouth. 'Were they looking for any evidence you might still have on—' I refused to say *Her Majesty*, 'Victoria?'

'Clearly. Or on that Salisbury pustule.'

'Did they raid your home as well?'

'Nah. They showed up the day after, but by then I'd sent all my stuff to my dad's auld farmhouse near Dundee.' He looked down, staring at the slush on his boots, and I felt for him.

No matter how ludicrous and disturbing his collection of odd and ghostly paraphernalia had been, it had taken him years to gather.

'The place looks bloody bare now,' he said. 'I'd forgotten how big the "Spooky Bothy" really was.'

He looked at his tumbler, as if judging whether or not those last drops were worth raising his hand.

'I assume yer nae coming back?' he asked, keeping his gaze down.

I sighed, but for a good while said nothing. The answer already hung in the air.

'It feels wrong, does it not?' I mumbled after a while. 'That it should all come to such an unceremonious end?'

McGray, to my surprise, chuckled. 'I wouldnae call it that. Even on my bloody deathbed I'll be chuckling at the memory o' that sad bitch's tantrum!'

We laughed earnestly, and McGray squeezed the last dregs of spirit from his glass. He stared at the rolling grounds, the perfectly smooth, white fields dotted with gnarly, leafless oaks.

'I said it before – nice patch o' land ye have here.'

I nodded. 'A nice patch indeed.'

Acre upon acre of hunting grounds, a large country house, a few guest cottages . . . all for a single man, all requiring maintenance. I was not sure what I'd do with them – or with my life – after that. I was only certain I would not decide it that day. I would not even think about it before my right hand had healed completely. A couple of doctors had seen me already, neither giving me better advice than Nettle and Oakley. The rest had worked marvels, but I could already tell that my wrist would ache every winter for the rest of my life.

I looked at the stump of McGray's finger, and felt mildly lucky.

I sighed. 'Go now and let me dress. I will show you the parklands. You can go back to your Auld Reekie tomorrow.'

'Alrighty. In the meantime I'll dispatch a telegram for Joan. She's worried sick for ye.'

'Is she?'

'Aye. She gave me some scones to bring ye, but – well, when ye see her just tell her they were scrumptious.'

He left before I could answer.

I was going to get dressed right then, but my coffee was still hot, and I decided Nine-Nails could wait a few more minutes. I sat in bed, leisurely sipping the last of the brew as I rejoiced in the white view. Until—

Something moved.

I thought it had been just my imagination, but then it moved again.

A small black silhouette, perched on the naked branches of the nearest oak.

It had wings.

The asylum had returned to relative normality now that Dr Clouston was back.

He had remained in the outskirts of Aberdeen for a couple of weeks, even well after Inspector McGray had returned from his mysterious ordeal. One day the haughty nurse Jennings had shown up in Edinburgh, demanding news. She had said very little – in fact, she'd only stayed for an hour or so, before returning to the doctor to tell him things seemed safe. Dr Clouston had returned a couple of days later, bringing along a few patients from his Orkneys' clinic. To everyone's surprise, Miss McGray was amongst them.

And then odd things began to occur.

The first of them – that midnight caller.

'We don't usually allow visitors this late,' said Cassandra Smith, protecting the flame of her candle. 'But Doctor Clouston said we could make this one exception for you.'

The cloaked, hooded figure nodded in acknowledgement, following her closely.

Their steps echoed along the shadowy corridor, mingling with the muffled moans of the neighbouring inmates.

'I appreciate it,' said the visitor. 'I am sorry I had to keep you up this late.'

'Don't you worry,' said the head nurse, despite her tired eyes and her aching back. 'I happen to – understand.'

She strove to see the reaction under the hood, but the visitor's face had turned away, the cloak concealing every gesture.

They made it to the last door in the corridor, and the head nurse turned the key as quietly as possible.

'You keep it locked?' the visitor asked in shock.

'For the girl's own safety, yes,' Cassandra replied, a little flushed.

Regardless of the hour, they found Pansy by the window. As ever, she was staring at the snowed gardens, dimly lit by the asylum's lamp posts.

The visitor took the candle from Cassandra's hand, then walked rather hesitantly towards the girl.

Indistinct shouting came from the corridor just then. Cassandra thought she'd ignore it, but she could not. In her line of work, a second's distraction could cost an inmate's life. Or an orderly's.

'I need to check on that,' she said. 'Would you . . . mind?'

The visitor, delineated against the gleam of the candle, did not even turn.

'Of course. I will be fine.'

Cassandra left then, and the visitor stepped closer to Pansy's little table, producing a small box tied in pink ribbons.

'I brought you whisky fudge. I hear it is your favourite.'

As expected, the girl did not react.

The visitor placed the pretty box on the table, the gloved hands trembling.

An icy draught came from the window, open less than an inch.

'I'll get that for you . . .'

The visitor struggled to pull the window down, but it finally closed with a loud thump.

The visitor stepped back, seeing a very faint shift on Pansy's face. A small sign of gratitude?

Cassandra Smith came back then, more flushed than before.

'I am so sorry . . . Doctor Harland says you can't be here.'

'What?'

'I told him that Doctor Clouston had given you leave, but he's asking questions, and—'

'Don't worry, Miss Smith. The last thing I want is to get you in trouble. It *is* late, after all.'

'I'm so sorry,' Cassandra insisted. 'You came all this way . . .'

The visitor only sighed while the head nurse picked up the candle. The room already felt warmer.

'I will be back,' the visitor said, leaning down to kiss Pansy's temple. Their eyes, though of entirely different shapes, had the exact same tone of brown.

Soft and tenderly, Caroline Ardglass whispered.

'Sleep well, dear sister.'

Historical Note

Separating fiction from fact:

All the entries from Sir Augustus d'Esté's journal are real (so don't blame me for his dreadful punctuation and syntax!).

Also real are all the quotes from Queen Victoria's memoirs (which truly are as dull a read as Frey proclaims). And while I described as accurately as possible all the convoluted circumstances that led to her birth, there is no evidence at all to suggest Augustus and she were father and daughter.

It is remarkable, however, how very much alike they looked. The miniature I mention is real[1] and it bears an uncanny resemblance to the four-year-old Victoria as painted by Stephen Poyntz Denning in 1823. The shapes of their eyebrows and lips are extraordinarily similar, and these can be spotted in other portraits of Victoria as she grew up – the one painted by George Hayter in 1833 is my favourite example.

---

[1] At the time of publication, the miniature is a permanent exhibit at the V&A museum. Catalogue no. P.7-1941. It was donated to the museum by Mrs Emma Joseph in 1941, after the death of her husband, S.S Joseph, who was an avid collector of miniature portraits. In the catalogues it is often referenced that S. S. Joseph acquired his pieces *from an unrecorded source*.

Victoria's legitimacy was indeed questioned during her lifetime. The thirty-year-long, albeit childless affair between her father and Madame de Saint-Laurent was common knowledge. Understandably, the Duke of Kent producing an heir to the crown at the snap of a finger raised many an eyebrow.

Potts and Potts mention in their book – *Queen Victoria's Gene* – that 'if Victoire, keen to produce a child who might well be heir to the British throne, had suspected her husband's fertility, she might well have tried to improve her chances with another man'. Their rushed trip to Germany right after their wedding, when they should have been 'at work', only to return to England so that the heir could be born there, also appeared illogical.

As Frey remarks towards the end of this book, Vicky's resemblance to George III really was what silenced the gossip. Consequently, her father, if not Edward Duke of Kent, must necessarily have been related to the old king, and since Victoria had more than fifty illegitimate cousins, there was an ample pool of choices.

It was jolly good fun to dig into the royal family tree looking for a candidate suitable in age, resemblance and circumstances, and Sir Augustus provided all I needed and more.

He is well known amongst medical circles for being the first recorded case of multiple sclerosis. His journal has been studied in depth for this reason, and the symptoms he exhibits are all in fact tell-tale manifestations of the condition. In my fictional world, however, his disease would have been induced by the witches.

Prerogative of the historical fiction writer.